D0101112

GAIA TWIST

Prologue

Sunday, July 24, 2816

Community Room, Childcare Center B-35-4, Capital City, Earth

Someone jumped on a balloon and there was a loud pop followed by gales of five-year-old laughter. 35 Laurel looked around the room, pushed a dark strand of hair back from her forehead, and felt herself smiling. It was Jonah's birthday party and there were little boys and girls everywhere, playing, laughing, and making a truly epic mess. She and her friend 34 Risa would be cleaning up later, but for now it was just pure fun, like a party is supposed to be. Laurel's carefully planned activities had all worked pretty well, she was over her hostess jitters, no one was hurt or sick, and there was Jonah, ruddy and beaming, clambering to the top of the pillow pile she had set up, king of the mountain. Risa caught Laurel's eye from across the room and gave her a happy wink. Things were going nicely. What more could a mother want?

Naturally, the moment of appreciation was fleeting. Little Sindra spilled juice on her white party dress, and as Laurel went dashing off for a towel, Mika started crying for some reason, but little inevitabilities didn't matter. Everyone was happy and having a good time.

Anyway, it was time for the cake. Laurel had designed it herself and, as a splurge, had Conforty Confections up on Level 40 create it. They had a high-end 3D food printer and Laurel was proud of how it had come out. There were 10 globes representing the Hundred Worlds, arranged in a giant letter J for Jonah. Each globe was artfully frosted with different colors, and their swirling atmospheres all formed the number 5 for his age. No doubt the inventive beauty of it was lost on the gaggle of kids, who were more interested in the sugar, but Laurel thought any adult witnesses, now or in the future, might appreciate it even so. She made sure to give herself a nice, clear view for her brainbox to capture for posterity.

Both children and adults enforced upon themselves the traditional rule that there was no eating your cake until everyone was served, which some children found more difficult to master than others. But Laurel and Risa teamed up and served as fast as possible, and after a minute or two Laurel's work of art had been reduced to 24 gobs of chocolate on paper plates poised in front of 24 eager five-year-old faces. Jonah got to lead the chant, "Three, . . . two, . . . one, . . . eat!" and they all dug in.

The reaction was not what Laurel expected. Almost as one, the glowing little seraphic faces suddenly looked stunned. The expressions went slack, and some children seemed to be having trouble swallowing.

Laurel looked at Jonah and his eyelids started fluttering. He dropped his fork and his arm flopped down limp at his side.

There was a sudden, terrible quiet in the room.

Laurel ran over to her son. "Jonah? Jonah? What's wrong, sweetie?" Slowly, the small boy turned his head to look up at his mother. His eyes cried out, but he made no sound. His head flopped to one side and his torso started convulsing. Gurgling sounds choked up out of his throat. Desperately, Laurel hugged his little body to her chest and cradled his head in one hand. His legs twitched, he coughed once, and then he stopped moving. His body collapsed out of his chair and onto the ground. All around him, little five-year-old bodies were doing the same.

They were all dead.

1

Thursday, July 28

Southwest Saskatchewan

There was one small opening in the night sky where a few bright stars shone through low and gloomy clouds. Along the darkened ground, a lone coyote trotted doggedly westward. He was moving at hunting speed, though there was no prey in sight. He was running away from death.

The coyote was far beyond his home territory by now, separated from what was left of his pack and all alone. He had learned, from watching his friends die, to avoid eating the carrion that was all around him. It was poison. He needed to find meat that was fresh. As a wild animal does even when under duress, he picked his way along quickly and smoothly, following a network of drainage ditches that pierced vast fields of soybeans.

He was running out of time. He had gone without sustenance for far too many days, and he was weak. His normally fluid motions were showing signs of impairment, and his emaciated muscles could not last much longer. The bare ground hurt his feet, and he was breathing too fast. But still he pressed on.

There came the slightest scent on the night air. Prey! The coyote paused and lifted his snout for a better scent.

There it was, more certain now, coming from the southwest, somehow separating itself from the ubiquitous stench of the dead animals around him.

It was a bird. The particular flavor of the scent was not familiar, but the coyote didn't care. It would be food. He adjusted course and hurried forward with all the stealth and speed he could muster.

Twenty minutes later, his nostrils were exploding with the intoxicating aroma of what could only be an entire flock of birds. He crested a small rise and looked out on a new land full of sweet smells, and good air, and live prey. The delicious fever of the hunt rose in his veins.

But when he spied his quarry, he faltered, because where the birds should have been there was a wire fence. Inside the fence were those structures Men made for their unfathomable purposes. Fences and structures meant humans, and humans meant danger.

So be it. There were birds in there, he could smell them plain as day. Flesh. Meat. And the coyote needed, wanted, was desperate to eat. His tongue lapped out in an involuntary lick of his lips, anticipating. Humans be damned.

After a long look around, he slung himself low to the ground and crept closer to the fence. The wire mesh was too tight to squeeze through. He trotted quickly around its perimeter, sniffing and searching for an entrance or a hole. Nothing. The overpowering aroma of the birds was driving him to distraction. There were no low places he could jump over, either. He needed to eat.

So he began to dig.

■ ■ ■

Inside the house, 22 Galen Sjøfred sat alone in his favorite old easy chair, reading one last chapter in his book by the dim light of a single glow lamp. It was late and he should have turned in an hour ago, but Tolstoy had him caught up in another world.

A sudden squawk from the henhouse pierced Galen's bubble and he was jolted back to the present. The chickens were going crazy, screeching and crying in alarm. Galen sighed, stood up, and strolled over to the pegs on the wall where his shotgun hung, cleaned and ready for action. He tossed a handful of cartridges into his pants pocket and shuffled out the back door, automatically triggering on an outside light as he went.

■ ■ ■

When the birds detected his digging and began screaming their wild danger calls, the coyote paused his furious effort for only a fraction of a second. He couldn't stop now. He was almost under the fence. He could even see two of the birds in the structure, looking large and delicious. They were panicked, but trapped somehow and unable to flee. He would have them soon. His tired front legs flew at the dry soil, raking and scrabbling as fast as he could, and his hole grew deeper. He arched his back down and pushed forward, making a tunnel that reached under the fence, and he started up again on the other side.

The birds were raucous, but still they didn't leave. Just a few more crusty pawfuls of dirt and he could feel an opening on the far side. He crunched his already-bare ribcage down as thin as it would go and squeezed himself headfirst under the fence, ignoring the sharp wires tearing painfully along the skin of his back. His snout felt the air. He struggled his front paws outward, and then with a triumphant heave he pulled himself all the way through. He was in. Looking up at the lowest-roosting bird, he felt a familiar surge of bloodlust coursing through him, thirsty for a kill. He opened his jaws and lunged.

And then with the very short and very loud blast of a shotgun, he was dead.

∎ ∎ ∎

"Damn coyotes," mumbled Galen. "That's the third one this month. They must be getting desperate."

2

Friday, July 29

Headquarters of the Organic Resources Administration, Capital City, Earth

Capital City, the unimaginatively named seat of government for all of Earth, rose magnificently above the beaches of eastern North America in a densely-packed forest of gleaming, 100-story towers interconnected and intertwined like a scaffold for holding up the sky, hosting tens of millions of people as they worked, played, and buzzed about their lives. And in the penthouse of the third-tallest building in town, perched 180 stories above the ground like an eagle's nest above a jungle, were the offices of the Earth Authority's Minister of Organic Resources, 96 Skervin Hough.

The rank of 96, used as a title like "Mr." and "Dr." from historical times, meant he was very nearly at the top of the official social hierarchy, which was where, he was quite certain, he belonged. He carried an air of ascendancy in his square shoulders, thick neck, strong chin, fierce eyes, and confidently dark Mediterranean coloring. Like all people of his level, there were no wrinkles, no asymmetries, no blemishes. Imperfections were for the lower classes.

Skervin had visitors—two 70-ranks, sitting deferentially on the other side of his desk in chairs that had been placed slightly off-center so as not to block his view. They were from the Citizen Welfare administration, and they had been making an impassioned plea for Skervin's organization, known as ORGA for short, to improve its forestry practices in China.

Skervin had heard enough. "Listen, 71 Terza, that was a really terrific presentation."

Terza tried to interrupt. "Well I wasn't quite finished, but the real takeaway is—"

"I know, I know. I got it. Don't keep selling past the sale," said Skervin with a fatherly smile. "I mean, you were really prepared for this, weren't you? And I can see why! I mean, if there were a way for ORGA's tree sprayers to adjust their deployment parameters there in the Yangtze Basin, it would make a tremendous difference for you. This is terribly important, isn't it? I'm so glad you brought it to us."

Terza dared to allow herself a satisfied smile.

"Maggi!" Skervin called out in no particular direction, still smiling at Terza. His assistant, 61 Maggi, appeared a moment later, emerging gracefully from a distant corner of the office.

"Yes, 96," said Maggi, standing ready to serve.

"Listen, 71 Terza and 79 Joffrey have brought this urgent topic to our attention. Can you get their proposal over to 51 Schwenker at the Ag Performance Lab right away so he can get started on it? Tell him I want a complete assessment."

Terza nodded positively and said, "Thank you, 96."

"My pleasure, my pleasure of course. I'm just so glad you two are doing such a good job on this. Great job on the pitch, Terza. Good luck now."

Skervin stood to signal the end of the meeting, stepping back from his desk to reveal the rest of his sturdy build and a finely-tailored suit made of expensive natural fibers. He was 67 years old but he considered that only a technicality, because in all other ways his body looked and acted 15 or 20 years younger. This was life at the top.

. . .

The visitors said their *thank-you*s and Maggi escorted them across Skervin's vast office and out to the plush waiting area. As the door closed behind them, Terza let out a shiver and Joffrey exhaled, about to start comparing notes. But at just that moment, a tall, energetic-looking woman called out to them from a neighboring office and walked over to say hello.

"79 Joffrey," she smiled. "How are you?" Her tone was pleasant, but there was a slight sharpness in her glinting green eyes.

"91 Ettica Sim! Nice to see you. And do you know my colleague 71 Terza Liu? Terza, 91 Ettica is, uh, well—" He turned to Ettica. "Would you say you are second-in-command at ORGA?"

"Something like that." Ettica was 42 years old and unusually tall, and she walked with an athletic bounce in her step that came from hard workouts in the gym every day, evidence of the self-discipline and relentless ambition that defined her. Whether that ambition was for her own, personal success or that of the greater good was a question of conscience that she wrestled with in many a quiet moment. She adopted a supportive tone. "So, how'd it go in there?"

Joffrey hesitated. Terza smiled and looked like she might be about to answer, but Joffrey shushed her with a look. Ettica gave a knowing nod and put her hand on Joffrey's shoulder, steering them all back toward her office. "You'll have better luck next time. Let's talk about it."

Terza gave a little laugh and looked confused. "Better luck! How can we do better than that? He just said yes!"

Joffrey made a small, resigned shake of his head and frowned. "Humph," he mumbled.

Ettica ushered her two guests into seats on the luxurious sofa in her office and produced some fine cognac in crystal goblets, smiling maternally as they sipped.

"Mm, this is good," murmured Terza inadequately. A long pause followed.

Finally, Joffrey broke the silence. "Who is 51 Schwenker?"

With barely a thought, Ettica ewaved the question to her brainbox, the artificially intelligent computer software running in the peppercorn-sized eardot that she and everyone else wore in their ear canals. It gave her the answer via brainwaves and Ettica replied matter-of-factly to Joffrey. "Someone at the Ag Performance Lab here in ORGA. A report writer, it seems."

"Well that's good, right?" asked Terza hopefully. "We'll need documentation to move forward . . . ?" She let her sentence dwindle as she saw Joffrey's shaking head.

"Schwenker's a bureaucrat, then, isn't he?" sighed Joffrey. "He's going to write a report to cover Skervin's ass and it's going to get buried. We'll never see it again."

Terza was still trying to be optimistic. "But Skervin seemed to know Schwenker personally . . . ?"

Ettica answered. "96 Skervin remembers the name of everyone he has ever met, no brainbox required. You don't get to be a 96 without some pretty magnificent skills. Though I suppose," she added with a flash of her green eyes, as if not able to help herself, "I remember everyone, too."

"But how can he *not* do this?" Terza insisted. "We're talking about adding an average of two or three months to the life of every person who lives in the city of Chongqing! And all it takes is a 2.7% adjustment in ORGA's forest spraying footprint, which Skervin can authorize with the stroke of his pen!"

Ettica took a moment to answer. "What's in it for him?"

"Preserving the health of 17 million people?"

"No, you're thinking about it wrong. Those 17 million people aren't *him*. What's in it for the Minister of Organic Resources?"

"I don't believe this!" cried out the flabbergasted Terza. "A bribe?!"

"No, not like that. Not what's in it for Minister of Organic Resources the *person*. What's in it for Minister of Organic Resources the *position*?"

Terza was still stunned. "I can't even begin to imagine . . ."

"Well there's your problem," observed Ettica calmly. "You need to imagine." She looked over at Joffrey, who was shaking his head in resignation.

"What she means," Joffrey explained to Terza, "is that Skervin's looking for some quid pro quo: something that benefits ORGA in return for something that benefits us at Citizen Welfare." Joffrey turned back to Ettica. "I'm honestly disappointed he'd take that kind of a position on an obviously humanitarian issue like this one. But in retrospect I guess we should have believed all the rumors we've heard about the man. Well, we'll work on it."

Joffrey stood to leave, followed by Terza. "Thank you," he said to Ettica. But just at the door he turned back to her. "Why are you telling us this?"

Ettica shrugged and smoothed her burgundy dress. "Maybe he wants me to," she said enigmatically, with that glint in her eye again. "Or maybe I actually care."

■   ■   ■

A few minutes later 61 Maggi was back in Skervin's office, listening attentively as he reeled off a long list of instructions for her on a dozen or more tasks. She was small, trim, and carefully dressed, a picture of decorum and—what Skervin appreciated most about her—efficiency. Her brainbox was of course recording, but she paid attention now to make sure she understood it all. When Skervin was alone with Maggi he dispensed with social graces and unleashed his vigorous intellect, letting it run fast and agilely across the huge array of concerns that faced one of the 10 or 12 most powerful people on Earth.

"Get a review with those antediluvian operations people for the North Pacific kelp. Their numbers are down 4.2% and I damn well want to know why . . . Set up a dinner with Mineral Resources. I haven't seen 95 Landiger for 19 days . . . Launch Phase 2 of the Harvester 317 model upgrade program . . ." His list went rapidly on.

ORGA, the Earth Authority's Organic Resources Administration, was Skervin's dominion. He had been in charge of it for nearly 18 years now, and no one dared challenge his reign. In the view of Earth Authority, the central and only government of Earth in 2816, everything that *grew* was an organic resource to be managed: crops in the fields, forests, livestock, fish, kelp. Agricultural algae. Petri dish meat. And most of all, the primary food source for all people on Earth: soybeans. Skervin would even have claimed artificial human organs if he could, but he could never quite win that argument against the annoyingly reasonable 93 Perka Yang over at Citwel, the Citizen Welfare administration, which looked after the medical, economic, and educational needs of people. So, she got artificial organs. Skervin still had plenty. Because Citwel notwithstanding, under Skervin's control was an immense, worldwide enterprise dedicated to organic resource production. All the food on the planet was produced by Skervin's farms and ranches. All the wood used for any purpose, including his magnificent desk, came from his plantations. All the organic components of nonfood items like textiles, industrial solvents, and structural materials were his. To this day, even after 18 years in his position, the sheer immensity of his power and reach moved him. It was a gigantic responsibility and he was brilliant at it. It gave him a deep, satisfying, and visceral satisfaction. And yes, why not say it? Pride.

Running it through with Maggi, Skervin reached the last topic on his mental checklist. His machine gun pace slowed and he felt a tiny knot begin to form in his gut. His brow furrowed ever so slightly.

The dead kids.

The reports he had received about the incident last weekend were disturbing. The first report came from Citwel because it was medical, but it was obviously food poisoning, which was going to make it ORGA's problem. Luckily, the Authority Police hadn't divulged it too widely before an alert ORGA staffer picked it up and called in the ORGA propaganda department. The parents were all debriefed and sworn to secrecy on pain of arrest; the restaurant was shut down; all related electronic communications and records were censored or blocked; other inquisitive agencies like Commerce and Infrastructure were misled and distracted. In short, it was contained.

Problem was, Skervin's people had been working on it all week and they couldn't figure out how the food poisoning had happened. That meant it could happen again, and it would have to be contained again, and the risk of scandal went up. That was not acceptable. Skervin wanted answers.

"The food poisoning," he said tersely to Maggi. "We're going out to the Nutritional Products Lab and see what's taking so long. Set it up."

"Cover story?" asked Maggi, matching her boss's condensed form of speech. She knew as well as Skervin did that the secret of the embarrassing incident must never leak.

Skervin hardly needed a millisecond to sort through a dozen possibilities before choosing: "Publicity. Make it look like we're angling for more research funding this year. We're touring our labs, touting their brilliance. We'll call it a 'fact-finding' trip and everyone will figure we're bragging. If I mention it to 93 Cashington tonight over drinks he'll probably copy us over in Infrastructure, and pretty soon everyone will be doing publicity tours. It'll be fine."

God I'm good, he thought.

Galen's Farmhouse, Southwest Saskatchewan

22 Galen was up and about at dawn, thinking over the coyote he shot the night before. He shuffled around the kitchen in dusty farm clothes, cooking himself a couple of coop-fresh eggs to perk up the rest of his food fabricator-made breakfast. (Fab food always had the right taste and the right texture, but it had no soul.) He was still in good shape for age 60, but his looks had weathered over the years. His longish blond hair was now fading toward white, and his skin was tanned and wrinkled from years outdoors, though his blue eyes were still bright and clear. The kitchen windows looked out on lush rows of soybeans that stretched out in every direction across the plains.

In unguarded moments, his heart still ached for his beloved wife Joanna and little daughter Lillian, lost long ago. But, he told himself, he was a quiet man who had no trouble being his own company. He had his books, as many acquaintances as one could want just a viewscreen away, and, though they were far away on another world, a family that loved him.

The family meant more to him than he wanted to admit. It was his mother, his two sisters, and their families, all of whom lived together in a cozy house by a lake on the far-away planet of New Gaia. Maybe he should have moved back there after Joanna and Lillian died; it was home, after all. But back when it happened he just couldn't face them, couldn't face anyone, and now ... well, now here he was in Saskatchewan. He sent them recorded messages every week and they faithfully did the same, trading news and thoughts and wishes across the light-years, just as letter-writers from the nineteenth century had done across the Atlantic Ocean a millennium ago.

Over the years there had developed a special kinship between Galen and his niece, Kessa. She was in her early twenties now; about the age his own daughter would have been. Kessa had started sending him personal messages when she was just eight years old, a little after her father—Galen's brother-in-law—had died. Kessa was a free spirit, an independent thinker like he was, a lover of nature and of beauty. When Kessa was younger, Galen would tell her whimsical stories of princesses and magic, and she would ask him all her questions of the world. She grew up fast, as all children do, but Galen couldn't help but admire how her wonderful spirit grew even faster and stronger than the rest of her. Kessa was the one who had started the helpful practice, obvious in retrospect, of recording herself watching Galen's messages and sending her reactions back along with a new message of her own. As the years flipped quickly by, she surprised him again and again with prodigious intelligence and rapidly deepening wisdom of life until now, though he had four decades on her in chronology, he often felt he had as much to learn from her as she from him. They read books together, they talked philosophy. They even laughed, on three-day transmission delays, at each other's jokes.

Sure enough, that morning there came a familiar ping from the comm system and he smiled. It was a planet capsule—a p-cap—from Kessa. He laid aside his breakfast and sat happily down in front of his largest screen.

Kessa had recorded the message three-and-a-half days ago from her home on New Gaia, 423 light-years away, and it had been shipped here as physical cargo on a faster-than-light ship. That people on distant planets could carry on conversations like this was thanks to the Alçubierre Drive, that miracle of modern technology suggested almost apologetically by Miguel Alçubierre centuries ago, discarded, and then rediscovered and improved centuries later. It allowed a spaceship to make the trip from New Gaia to Earth in just a few days, or more than 50,000 times as fast as light itself could travel. The speed itself was stunning, but what made Alçubierre technology truly transformational was that it overcame the pesky problems that physicists just a few centuries earlier were convinced made faster-than-light travel impractical. The trip took 68 hours from the perspective of Earth and New Gaia, it took 68 hours from the perspective of the people on board, and no one got stretched, squished, old, or anything similarly untoward. There were reasons for it, but Galen didn't really care. From his perspective, it simply worked.

And here was Kessa in her message, bright as life, blonde hair and blue eyes like his smiling back at him from the big screen. Usually

Kessa was full of tidbits from around the homestead—the squash plants were getting visible bumps now, Mom had been invited to give another talk—and her own theories and insights about the world. "I was looking at the cobwebs in the grass this morning. Isn't it amazing how they suddenly appear when the dew forms? We probably wouldn't even notice them otherwise. How many other things are like that? A lot, I bet."

But today when Galen turned an extra camera on himself and listened to Kessa's dispatch, all he heard was girlish joy. "Less than a week! Marta and I are heading to Earth to visit you in less than a week!" (Kessa's "week" was a subjective term. The Hundred Worlds all used Earth's calendar when referencing dates across planets, though their own local calendars ran on different cycles and translation was often required. Luckily for Galen's technologically-boggled mind, New Gaia's cycle was close to Earth's, and most of the time the days matched.) "Marta's practically packed and everything. I'm not, of course. But I will be! I can't wait to see you in person! Did you know I'm 23 years old and I have never given you a hug? I will, a week from my Thursday. Peace be! I love you!"

Galen couldn't help but smile. When it was his turn to record his own message, he said, "Not sure you'll get this return message in time, but if you do, have a safe trip!" Also, he reported, "There was another coyote trying to get into the chickens last night. That's the third one this month. It's curious. I'll try to figure out what's going on before you arrive." As he said it aloud now to Kessa, it felt like more of a promise. He decided he better hurry up and get started.

■ ■ ■

In theory, tracking down the coyote mystery should have been easy. Galen was, after all, the Authority's designated field monitor for Southwest Saskatchewan. The vast plains were all but uninhabited these days, with soybean fields reaching as far as the eye could see, tended by huge robotic machines that moved stoically back and forth across the great expanses. The agribots were faceless farmers-in-a-box that treated every acre like every other, churning out endless oceans of soybeans for transport to the processing plants, where it was transformed into an enriched, gelatinized vegetable protein paste called Nutribase and piped by tube to every kitchen, to be transformed by refrigerator-size food fabricators—nicknamed "fabs"—into familiar dishes that looked and tasted every bit like the real, original thing. Well, except for the soul.

Food production on Earth was a factory operation to end all factory operations, perfected and mechanized through centuries of development, implemented by robots and managed by algorithms and a few human controllers who directed operations by remote control. In the minds of many, field monitors like Galen were decoration at best, a kind of useless nod to the antiquated idea that robots needed human supervision. Actually, Field Monitor 22 Galen wouldn't have argued too hard with that point of view, but he didn't mind. At least no one bothered him out here, and he did his job humbly and dutifully, monitoring his sector, taking the occasional authorized trip in an aircar to check out trouble spots, and making his daily rounds of the agribot pens to cast a human eye on the great machines.

He might have even argued that chasing down the coyote mystery was practically part of his job. But then again, the Authority didn't like people asking questions. Galen had spent the last 20 years building himself a life free of conflict, and he had no wish to attract undue attention from anyone. He resolved that he would conduct his self-assigned investigation quietly and with caution.

His first theory was disease or infection. Rabies maybe. He went back to the makeshift burial pit he had scraped out in the middle of the night and uncovered the most recent dead coyote. He put on sterile gloves and used a syringe to pull a blood sample, which he walked inside to his med analyzer machine. The machine's analysis was negative: poor nutrition and stress, but no rabies or other fatal disease.

Galen looked at the coyote's body. It had flopped like a dishrag as he picked it up with his shovel. It was far lighter than he expected; the poor thing was emaciated. Starving, probably. The other two had been the same way.

Coyotes were like any other wild animal, he thought. Life was hard and not always successful. Prey animals could get eaten. Predators could starve.

Couldn't they?

∎ ∎ ∎

It was just as well Galen kept dutifully to his rounds, for he himself was being monitored from a centralized control rooms in a city somewhere, the eardot in his ear canal glowing as a little white blip on a huge map on someone else's bank of monitors. That was nothing special; on Earth in 2816, the Authority tracked everyone, all the time. It wasn't a concern; it wasn't a cause; it wasn't even a question.

Though, as events transpired, from some people's perspective, maybe it should have been.

3

Monday, August 1

ORGA Nutritional Products Laboratories, Atlanta, Earth

The flying flotilla of Minister of Organic Resources 96 Skervin Hough swooped down on the ORGA's Nutritional Products Laboratories in Atlanta first thing Monday morning. Skervin posed and smiled dutifully for the requisite greetings and public ceremonial folderol in the sweltering heat at the landing pad, careful to show off his politician's smile and splendid gray ORGA-wool suit, but the moment Maggi gave him the nod he broke loose and strode purposefully indoors, eager to get to the real business of his trip. His second-in-command, 91 Ettica Sim, was with him as usual, as were a half-dozen lower-ranking staff.

The entourage was greeted by 78 Kapcheck Wills, the NutPro lab's affable director. Unlike almost everyone else there, Kapcheck seemed undaunted by the intimidating presence of the minister. His tangled, sandy hair and casual clothes contrasted strongly with Skervin's formal attire, and Kapcheck strolled along by Skervin's side on long, loose legs that seemed in no hurry. He chatted easily, smoothly following the minister's lead toward any place or topic of conversation as if it were the most natural thing in the world.

Urged ahead by Skervin, the party marched rapidly through long, glassed-lined corridors that bordered machine-filled, highly automated laboratories carrying out the most advanced food-science research on Earth for the most important product on Earth, Nutribase, the food that everyone lived on. Kapcheck would have liked to play the tour guide, but Skervin pressed quickly forward until the party arrived in a windowless executive conference room containing no laboratory equipment at all.

"Is this room secure?" asked Ettica as they settled into chairs around a conference table dominated by a huge screen on the far wall. Ettica sat up straighter than the others, green eyes darting around the room to inspect.

"Yup," nodded Kapcheck easily, moving to the front of the room as the screen turned itself on.

"All recordings off," ordered Ettica, tapping her ear twice in a universally recognized gesture. She seemed to be speaking to any hidden devices in the room as well as Skervin's own staff, who obediently ewaved the appropriate command to their brainboxes.

96 Skervin ignored everyone else and focused his strong-browed gaze straight at 78 Kapcheck. "Status report," he demanded.

"You mean the food poisoning, of course. I'm sure you've been getting our reports this week—"

"I have but I don't like them. I want to hear it in person."

Kapcheck ran a hand across his tangled hair and, easily as ever, began. "We know it was a toxin. The symptoms were similar to botulism—the facial paralysis, the trouble swallowing, the weakness of the muscles in the arms and legs. But botulism takes hours or days to show symptoms, whereas this one caused death within minutes. The autopsy scans showed massive cerebral trauma and neural damage. It was as if someone electrocuted the brains. And what really has us stumped is that the toxicology tests are all coming back negative."

"What do you mean?"

"It doesn't appear to be any poisonous substance we know about. It's an anomaly. We're calling it Toxin-X for now."

"That's cryptic. Have you isolated it? Do you know its chemical structure and its mechanism of action?"

Kapcheck shrugged. "No, no, and no. It's very strange. So far, we haven't even been able to isolate it. It must have been present in incredibly minute amounts, because Citwel couldn't find any foreign substances in any of the victims' tissues, and we can't find anything unusual in the uneaten food."

Skervin glared at Kapcheck with his dark eyes. "That can't be. You have to look harder."

Skervin was a powerful and angry presence, and Kapcheck's offhand demeanor was rapidly transforming into defensive tension. "I, uh, I agree. We're continuing to work."

"Work faster! It's been over a week. You need to figure this thing out."

"Well, really, a week is not that long for a completely unknown agent. I mean there's just the logistics of setting up—"

"Don't give me that, Kapcheck. You need to deliver some answers!"

Kapcheck was normally a confident man and he was secure in his own world of agricultural engineering, but Skervin's world of politics and Skervin himself had a way of unmooring him. "Yes, in good time, but—"

"Answers, Kapcheck!"

"Yes, 96," said Kapcheck weakly.

Ettica stepped into the charged pause that followed, speaking in her naturally pleasant voice. "Why don't you tell us about prevention, Kapcheck? We don't want this happening again. What went wrong with the food preparation?"

Kapcheck frowned. "We don't think it was food preparation. We actually think it's something in the raw Nutribase."

"How do you know?"

"For one thing, we did a complete forensic analysis at the restaurant and also at the childcare center where the party was held, and they turned up empty for all typical causes of food poisoning, like improper heating, contaminated equipment, anaerobic storage, and so on. But the really convincing evidence is our rats."

"Rats?" asked Skervin, reasserting himself.

"Yeah, we have an ongoing experiment where we feed rats on samples of Nutribase from the factories. It gives us a baseline for other experiments, and it doubles as a quality control measure."

"If the rats get sick, you know the sample is toxic?"

"Right."

"So why didn't the rats detect something earlier?"

"Not sure, but probably because there was nothing wrong with the samples of Nutribase we happened to be getting in the lab. We didn't see any problems until today. But this morning, I'm happy to report—that is, I guess I'm happy to report—we actually did. Some of the rats died."

"They did? And you're certain it was the same thing? Toxin-X?"

"We can't absolutely prove it was the same thing, but it was all the right symptoms. The rats just seized up and collapsed. It was actually rather brutal to watch. Do you want a demonstration?"

"No, I get it," said Skervin. "That is good news. It means you can at least detect the toxin, even if you don't know exactly what it is. Do the Nutribase production plants in the field have their own rats, doing the same thing?"

"Uh, no. They're not set up for animal research—"

"That's not research, Kapcheck! That's just production quality control! For God's sake, get some rats out in those production plants. Fast! And get me some answers on what this Toxin-X thing is."

Skervin made motions toward Ettica as if to leave, so Kapcheck screwed up his nerve to add a final point. "There is one more thing you should know."

Skervin glared again. "Which is?"

"The childcare center may not have been the only occurrence of Toxin-X poisoning."

"What?"

"There may have been other cases of poisoning with this same toxin in the past. They were smaller, so we didn't notice. We wrote them off as botulism, probably, or even as death from other causes altogether, not even considering food poisoning."

"I guess I shouldn't be surprised. How many?"

"We can't be sure, but the metadata analysis we've run so far is predicting almost 100 other previously unidentified Toxin-X cases."

"Hmm."

Kapcheck was relieved that this new topic seemed safe, and he began to warm to the subject. "What's really fascinating is when they happened. Look at this." He touched a control and brought up a bar chart on the glowscreen. "These are the dates across the bottom axis, and the height of the bars is the number of cases."

Ettica said, "There are big gaps between your bars."

"Correct. That's because the incidents all come in bursts. We get a bunch of cases one day, then nothing for a few days, then another burst."

"I see that," Ettica said, "but over time the bursts are getting closer together."

Kapcheck was looking pleased that his chart was telling its story so well. "Right! They're coming more often. And also, the bars are getting taller each time. More incidents, more often! Kind of a nice little puzzle, wouldn't you say?"

Skervin's thick neck muscles tightened and he pounded a heavy fist down on the table. "Puzzle!! Kapcheck, this is not a nice little puzzle! This is people dying from eating ORGA's food, goddamn it! Do you know how bad this is going to look if you don't stop it? We can't contain this information forever. You have to crush this thing!"

Kapcheck was shocked out of his academic line of thought. "Of course, of course! I know it. I know we do. It's just, well . . ." He looked away, uncomfortable.

"Well what?"

Kapcheck finally gathered himself to turn back and look Skervin in the eye. "Frankly, we're stymied. We've given this thing everything we have, and we're coming up empty. We're kind of over our heads on this. We . . ." Kapcheck looked at Skervin as bravely as he could. "We need help."

"Goddamn it, Kapcheck, figure it out!" Skervin exploded. "Kapcheck, you listen to me. This is not acceptable, you understand? Look at your chart. It's an exponential growth path that's going to reach ten thousand cases within a month." Kapcheck was momentarily impressed at Skervin's ability to do that math in his head, but Skervin wasn't pausing. "This has gone far enough! I am spending billions on this lab. You are in charge. Don't tell you me need help. You solve it, you fix it, and you do it *now*, got it?"

Kapcheck struggled to keep his chin up. "96, if we could consult with some other groups. There are some outstanding toxicology experts in the interstellar scientific community who might—"

"Out of the question. No. You will not. First of all, off-worlders have no business here. They don't know about us. All they do is bring in disease and dissention. We wouldn't even let them in here if I had my way. And second, if word about this thing ever gets off planet, the whole galaxy is going to know. That means everyone on Earth is going to know, too, and then what happens? Panic. Everyone begins to suspect our planet's food supply is poisoned. There's food hoarding. There are riots in the streets, Kapcheck!"

Skervin's tone and presence were so overpowering, Kapcheck looked as if he had just been shot. He collapsed into a chair as Ettica gathered up the entourage and Skervin stormed the door. "I want full reports every day from here on out!" he yelled without looking back.

■ ■ ■

Skervin was still wrestling to master his emotions as he, Maggi, and Ettica settled into the luxurious cocoon of his air limousine and his flotilla lifted away from the NutPro lab. An image of the ineffectual 78 Kapcheck, standing up there saying "nice little puzzle," still burned in Skervin's mind. He shouldn't have lost his temper. He knew better than to let frustrations rattle him like this. He was a 96 for God's sake, way better than his animal instincts. What was wrong with him?

He took a purposeful breath, pursed his lips, and forced himself to think it through. 100 cases of food poisoning, so what? Things happen. He was blowing this out of proportion. There was plenty of room for things to get worse before it was a real concern. It was a problem that the lab wasn't getting a handle on the nature of "Toxin-X;" of course it was, but why was it bothering him so much?

As soon as he asked himself the question, he knew the answer: No one had said it yet, but this was the start of an epidemic. He knew it was; he could feel it. That exponential growth Kapcheck was showing him was a map of the future, and the Toxin-X crisis was about to get much, much worse. Skervin was starting his response early and strongly, which was smart. Yes, he told himself, very smart.

Ettica, ever practical, interrupted his thoughts, asking about information security. "You're right about the risk of news leaks, Skervin. Should I schedule a new report from 68 Tappet?"

"Yes. Better bring him in in person. He better be getting farther than Kapcheck is."

■　■　■

Two hours later, Skervin was back in his office in Capital City and 68 Tappet Holson, Skervin's head of covert security operations, was being briskly escorted in by Ettica for a briefing.

68 Tappet had that air of a policeman about him: the kind of bearing and presence that permeates through any particulars of dress or speech, which in his case were conservative and unremarkable. He had a pale, thin face and limp, dark hair. He was below average in height and not strong or athletic, but he stood up straight, moved deliberately, spoke carefully, and maintained a formal bearing at all times. His goal in this life was to do his duty, and he had spent his entire career in law enforcement of all kinds, ranging from foot patrols when he was young, to detective work as he progressed through a successful career, and now to "special assignments" for the Earth Authority Minister of Organic Resources. What his superiors

always liked about him, and what he in fact liked about himself, was that he was never troubled by doubts. When given an assignment by an appropriate authority, his entire goal was to carry it out. Thoughts of "why" or "is this right" never crossed his mind; never disturbed him. Law and order were maintained by a system, and his duty was to that system. This philosophy gave Tappet clear guidance for all that he did, and though the performance of his duty was often full of challenges, he lived life with a clear and untroubled conscience.

Skervin got right to the point as Ettica and Tappet appeared. "What's our status on Toxin-X information security, Tappet?"

Tappet responded in kind, all business: "Counting the additions from the NutPro lab you authorized two hours ago, there are now 207 people with authorized first-tier access, spread across 17 groups and departments within Organic Resources and three in Citwel. Second-tier access . . ." He went on for another minute, reeling off statistics, before concluding, "The numbers of authorized people and systems now involved are expanding the risk perimeter to—well, exceptionally high levels, as I'm sure you're aware."

Skervin maintained a steady and silent glare. Of course he was aware the risks were high.

Ettica asked, "Are you getting cooperation from 93 Perka at Citwel?" Skervin flinched at the mention of his despised chief rival.

Tappet's body language suggested some doubts, but aloud he said, "No problems to report at this time. Citwel is following the same containment protocols ORGA is."

Ettica turned to Skervin and tipped her head in a helpful gesture. "I'll pay Perka a visit and make sure they don't forget. Our crisis, our rules."

"Good," nodded Skervin. He was only too happy to let Ettica deal with 93 Perka.

"In terms of active containment procedures . . ." 68 Tappet went on with his report for several minutes. He detailed everything he, and more generally the secretive organization he had recently organized, was doing to keep Toxin-X a secret from as many people as possible.

When he was finished, Ettica spoke up. "What about incidental inferences? You know, unwitting discoveries. People who figure out the secret more-or-less accidentally. Like, I don't know, a guy in ORGA Fisheries pulling a report on recent toxicology studies at the NutPro lab, or a Citwel doctor who gets a botulism case and starts doing research on her own."

"Too many possibilities," Tappet observed. "No way we can prevent every single accidental discovery."

Skervin said, "Where are the highest risks? Let's put extra effort on those. Other ORGA departments? Medical people? Travelers? Aerial imagery? Farming?"

"Farming shouldn't be an issue, should it?" Tappet said. "It's all automated."

Skervin nodded. "Mostly. But we do have a few people out there in the fields somewhere. Field monitors, we call them. Better have a look at them, too."

Galen's Farmhouse

Galen's working theory about starving coyotes still didn't feel right. He decided to try asking around. He still didn't want to attract attention, but he couldn't help trying the simplest inquiries to the net, blandly seeking any reports or news on coyote problems from anywhere else. Nothing.

He tried asking around. "Have you noticed any problems with coyotes lately?" he asked his fellow field monitor in Southern Alberta on the comm.

"Like what?" she said.

"I don't know. Anything strange. I've had three of them in my chickens in the last month. They look . . . you know, hungry. Starving, maybe."

"Nothing strange about that. They're coyotes."

"I know, but they seem particularly desperate. They practically walked right into my gun."

"Get over it, Galen. That's what coyotes do."

He tried comming the field monitor in northern Montana instead, but he was no help, either. Galen let it rest.

Lake Peace, Planet of New Gaia

The icy water of Lake Peace slid over Kessa's body as she swam naked before dawn. She found the cold exhilarating, and she luxuriated in the invigorating sensation of silky water flowing over every pore as she glided along. It was still dark, and except for her gentle ripples, all was hushed and deeply still. She swam softly, kicking gently and dipping her arms gracefully in and out of the water lest her splashes disturb the delicate quiet that preceded the day.

Kessa reached the tree-lined shore and clambered out onto a large rock where her towel waited, dabbed quickly dry, and then, because she couldn't bear to leave the scene just yet, she suppressed a shiver and spread her towel back down on the rock to sit for a few moments more.

This was the planet New Gaia, and it was Kessa's home. Lake Peace, a shimmering gem just a few clicks around, nestled between low hills within a vast, green forest burgeoning with life. Kessa's senses—always extraordinary and now heightened even further by the frigid swim—danced across a spectrum of perceptions. The early morning air was brisk and fresh, tinged with the scent of forest and the gentle texture that comes near fresh water. Early morning light was painting every surface with the fleeting grace of those perfect, magical morning colors that last only a moment and can never be captured by mortals. There on her rock, hardly moving, entranced, Kessa felt herself at one with a miraculous world.

"Kessa!" came her sister's distant call from the house a hundred meters away. "Kessa? Where *are* you? Kessa! It's breakfast time!"

Kessa felt herself dragged out from the reverie and a little shiver ran through her body as the sharp-angled everyday world materialized around her. She must have been lost in her unintentional meditation for some time. Collecting herself, she stood up, gathered the towel around her, and headed comfortably back to the house, making nimble little leaps now and then to save her bare feet from sharp objects along the forest path. At 23 years old she was certainly an adult, but as she danced along there was still a bit of child showing through in her sprightly step and careless air.

A hundred feet from the house, the trees cleared and a rough lawn appeared, equal parts grass, moss, and small flowers. Like most buildings on New Gaia, the house appeared to grow naturally out of the ground and the forest, half-hidden by vines, half-buried by moss, and blending in the way a branch blends into a tree. Kessa floated in toward breakfast, drawn like a honeybee to a flower by the delicious aromas and cheerful sounds of familiar voices. She entered the kitchen to find a table full of family crowded into chairs around a well-provisioned table and chatting amicably. Cheerful faces turned and acknowledged her as she came in.

"Kessa!" smiled her mother. "Did you get a nice swim?"

"It was wonderful."

"Well I'm glad. But now you can't wear a towel to breakfast. Go put on some clothes."

Kessa reluctantly agreed and soon reappeared in standard New Gaian garb: a simple shirt and pants, both made from three or four layers of thin, flowing fabric tied easily and loosely about the waist. It was dyed in a rainbow of colors that played together as she moved and different depths of material showed through. She had paid no attention to her hair, which was still wet and tangled. Soon enough it would dry and straighten itself out a little, leaving her with messy, soft, shoulder-length blonde tresses that danced just like her clothes. She squeezed around the backs of chairs and settled into her usual place at the far corner amidst three generations of family.

"I saved you some pancakes," said Marta, walking back from the kitchen with a covered plate and passing it down the table in Kessa's direction. Marta was blonde and naturally pretty like her sister Kessa, with the same sky-blue eyes and pale skin, but she was a little shorter than her tall sister, more fully shaped, and neater, with a visage that suggested sobriety and concern—both for others and for herself. Marta's hair, as usual, was combed and pulled back in a careful ponytail.

"Thanks!" said Kessa.

"They might be a bit cold by now."

"Well they look delicious. Who made them?"

"Mom did."

"Thanks, Mom. Mm, is that a bit of purberry mixed in? Great idea."

Kessa's mother Lana smiled. "It is! No one else noticed. Do you like it?"

"Yummy," replied Kessa around a satisfyingly sweet mouthful.

By now everyone was watching her eat so Kessa changed the subject. "So, what's everyone doing today?"

"Packing!" exclaimed Marta. "You and I are leaving for Earth tomorrow!" Kessa felt a shudder of excitement.

"We're all so excited for you," smiled Lana with genuine feeling. "But meanwhile the rest of us have a lot to do, don't we?"

"Anders and me are going to help Dad," Nils piped up. He was Kessa's 12-year-old cousin, sitting across the table next to her burly Uncle Kjell.

"'That's 'Anders and *I*,'" corrected Uncle Kjell. "Clearing out the drainage channels around the house. They always need it this time of year. And we'll learn some hydrology while we're at it."

"Sounds good?" offered Kessa a little hesitantly, giving her 14-year-old cousin Anders a questioning glance. Anders rolled his eyes just a bit, but aloud he said a polite "Yeah."

"At least it's more helpful than traipsing off to another planet," grumbled Kjell.

Kessa paid no attention, but Marta was wounded. "Uncle Kjell, this is an important trip! We're going to be learning a lot of new things. It's going to be good for everyone—"

"Of course it is, Marta," interrupted Aunt Mia soothingly. She gave her husband Kjell a reproachful elbow and he grumbled but went quiet. Marta struggled to recover her composure. It was a small exchange but she already felt shaken. She was always sensitive about shirking any responsibility, and Kjell had an unintentional way of making her feel inadequate.

But Kessa cheerfully ignored the whole dialogue. This was her family, and she loved them all. She never allowed herself to compare

Uncle Kjell to her fading memories of her father, who had died years ago. "What are you up to today, Aunt Mia?" she asked.

"Community duty," Aunt Mia reported. "I'm off to the Aspen North hyperloop station. We have a maintenance crew going." There were approving nods all around. Citizens of New Gaia all served community duty a few days each month, taking care of work that on other planets might be done by paid government employees or contractors.

"Well I'm staying home," Grandmother said. "The garden needs all the attention it can get at this time of year. Maybe I'll pick some more string beans. They just keep coming."

"Which is a good thing!" agreed Kessa's mother. "Let me know if you need help. And you too, girls. Let me know if there is anything else you need for the journey." She gave a little sigh that sounded both frustrated and determined. "I'm going to try to get some time in my lab after I take care of a few little things around here." Lana, a fair-haired, strong-boned woman in her late fifties with intelligent blue eyes and a well-crinkled smile, moved about so gracefully it was easy to overlook the clumsiness of her imperfect prosthetic left foot and the cane she sometimes used. Yes, there were fancier things modern medicine could have done for a missing appendage, but she had been born that way and it was part of who she was.

"Any scientific breakthroughs expected today, Mom?" Kessa asked her playfully.

Lana shook her head good-naturedly. "Not this week, I'm afraid. Not until I figure out why my samples keep getting contaminated . . ." she trailed off. Lana was always humble about her professional work, especially around her family, but in fact she was one of the Hundred Worlds' greatest experts on phytochemistry, the chemistry of plants. From her unassuming lab upstairs, she did original research and led interplanetary teams that were constantly advancing humanity's understanding of how plants used chemical arsenals in their struggle to survive against their enemies: other plants, bacteria, viruses, animals, and humans.

Lana knew her work mattered, but at that moment she had no idea just how crucial it would soon become.

Kessa turned to her six-year-old cousin Beatrix, who was politely but expectantly waiting her turn. "And how about you, Beatrix?"

"I am taking lessons from *you!*"

"Right you *are!*" said Kessa, possibly covering a look of embarrassed surprise.

"And what are you learning about today?" prompted Aunt Mia, looking at Beatrix.

"I don't know. Ask Kessa."

"Yes, well . . ." said Kessa with a slight hesitation. She was, as usual, unprepared. But before any looks of alarm could start creeping across anyone's face, she changed tacks: "Today, Beatrix, you and I are going to learn about . . . mushrooms! We're going to go out on a mushroom hunt and see how many we can find. All different shapes, and colors, and textures, and lovely smells. And we'll talk about which ones are safe to eat and which ones are—she scrunched up her nose at Beatrix—*poisonous.*"

"Ooh, that sounds good," Beatrix chirped.

In case any of the adults were still skeptical, Kessa spun out a few more details about the biology and ecology they'd be learning as well, all valid educationally.

Marta, always the big sister, whose own specialty was government and law, looked as if she might still think Kessa's lesson plan was just a fun hike in the woods while everyone else was working. But here on the eve of their great adventure together, Marta was feeling particularly close to Kessa, and she kept any objections to herself.

■　■　■

After dinner that night, Lana left the boys to finish cleaning up and went to find Marta and Kessa. "May I talk with you, girls? Let's go upstairs. It's quieter in my bedroom." She led the way to her room, which was out of the way at the end of the upstairs hall. It was usually her sanctuary in a crowded, busy household, and it wasn't often the girls were invited in. Lana sat in a chair and beckoned her daughters to perch close to her on the bed. She reached out in a welcoming way, took both their hands, and gave them a motherly smile that worked the crinkles around her affectionate eyes.

"What is it, Mom?"

"I'm so happy and excited for your trip tomorrow. I know it will be a wonderful adventure for you both, and I know you will take care of each other and keep yourselves safe. And I'm so glad you will be seeing Galen! He is a wonderful man."

"He is," smiled Kessa. "I can't wait to see him in person."

Lana tightened her grip on their hands. Her fingers were strong. "Now, I don't want you to be alarmed, but there is something I want you to know before you go. My brother, your uncle, Galen . . . well, you know the culture on Earth is very different from ours. There are so many people there, and well, the way they govern . . ."

"You mean the Authority," Marta prompted.

"Yes, the Authority. It's very strict there. Very regimented. There are so many rules."

"We know that, Mom. We'll be careful."

"Yes, but there is more than that. Galen . . . Galen doesn't do well with authority. He never has. Why he ever emigrated there in the first place is . . . well, it was for love, but that is a story for another day. Anyhow he's there now, and he's been there a long time. And girls—" Lana paused and looked first Marta, then Kessa in the eye. "Galen had some trouble there, years ago. Something terrible happened, and he, well he sort of dropped out of their society. That's why he lives out in the middle of Saskatchewan now . . ." And then carefully, sadly, Lana told her daughters about her brother's painful past.

Galen's Story

Galen preferred to remember his wife Joanna laughing, with a big white-toothed smile, and her head tilted back, and her soft brown hair tossing across her shoulders.

Yes, that was Joanna. Not the screaming one during the air taxi crash, reaching out helplessly toward poor Lillian as her little body fell away from the car, crying "Mommy," dropping into the tangled depths of the city 40 stories below. Not the broken and bloody Joanna dying on a stretcher as they tried to take her away; the one giving him one last, painful look of pleading—for Lillian's life, and for her own, and for his. But only her last plea was answered.

He preferred not to remember the anguish. He preferred to blot out the guilt as best he could. But like blood that had soaked into the soil, it was always there, just below the surface, welling up and seeping inexorably between his toes whenever he stepped too hard.

Because it was his fault, wasn't it? In a way? In a terrible, unthinking, stupid, stupid way? If only he had thought. If only he had realized the consequences.

It had been 20 years ago. He had been a 68 then. A rising executive, full of talent and promise. One of ORGA's budding stars, it seemed. His life at work was project status reports, and personal calls, and 15-minute briefings that usually went well. It was a world of politics, too, but Galen's style of cultivating allies and avoiding fights made him many friends and he did extremely well.

And then he'd come home and there was lovely young Joanna wrapping him up for a sweet-smelling kiss, and precious little Lillian toddling over with her arms held high, begging to be swept up in his arms and swung around, all gurgles and laughs.

It was the Import/Export Committee that did it: the '96 Policy Update. How boring that sounded, in retrospect, though it was so engrossing at the time. The committee chair, 83 Skervin Hough, had big ambitions. Everyone said he was headed for the minister job, and this was going to be his signature achievement. Earth was in danger, he argued, from alien invaders. People, plants, and animals streaming in from all over the Hundred Worlds were putting Earth's entire ecosystem at risk. ORGA's awesome responsibility of managing all organic resources of the planet carried with it the responsibility to guard and protect. Border controls must be redoubled. Visitors must be searched. Organic imports should be banned outright. Outside views and advice and influences of any kind must be viewed with greatest suspicion. Skervin had a catchy slogan for his views, too: Our World Our Way.

83 Skervin's isolationism was not universally popular, and in the end it came to a vote of the Import/Export Committee. Committee member 68 Galen, always one to avoid a fight, found himself, somehow—how stupid of him!—as the sole remaining swing vote. He agonized about it for days. He looked for ways out. He had long talks with Joanna. And eventually, his principles won out. Our World Our Way was bad for Earth and bad for the rest of the Hundred Worlds, and he resolved to vote against it.

Thinking he was being diplomatic, Galen asked for a private meeting with Skervin on a Friday afternoon before the Monday vote and he shared his plans. Surely there would be opportunities for compromise going forward, he offered. But Skervin was enraged. Not overtly; he was too well schooled to yell or throw things. But Galen could see his face turning crimson and a look of pure hatred rising in his eyes. Galen was taken aback, and he quailed internally so much that he almost changed his mind, but it was too late by then. He left Skervin's office feeling battered and frightened for the future of his career.

How little he knew.

The next evening—Saturday, dark, raining—he and Joanna and Lillian were in an air taxi on their way home from a party. There was another air taxi, no one in it, autopilot gone haywire, traveling at top speed, smashed straight into them, no chance. And there was Lillian falling helplessly down into the dark abyss. And there was Joanna on the stretcher, dying with those pleas in her eyes.

And slowly, slowly, through the fog of sadness and tears and helplessness, Galen came to realize that autopilots don't just go haywire like that. It doesn't happen unless someone wants it to.

■　■　■

After several days he managed to find his way back into the office, where the other news was that the Our World Our Way policy had been approved by the committee and would be the new law of the land. Skervin had been promoted; he was a 90 now. And Galen's boss needed to see him right away.

So sorry about the accident, said the boss. But—and this isn't easy and I know the timing is terrible—there have been real concerns about your performance lately. Reports from all over. Not cooperative. Projects not going well. Not a team player. Afraid you just aren't suited to this kind of position. Wish I didn't have to tell you this, but no place for you here anymore . . .

■　■　■

Fuck it. Fuck it all to goddamn hell. Screw Skervin. Screw the Authority. Screw the whole goddamn system. Screw everybody. Get me out of here. Away. Just, far away. Far from everybody and everything.

Lake Peace

When Lana had finished telling Galen's story, Kessa and Marta sat quietly for a long moment, stunned and bewildered. At last Kessa said, "But I thought I knew Galen so well! Why didn't he ever tell me about this?"

Lana had a sad look. "It was hard on him, Kessa. Very hard. It's been twenty years and I think he's still trying to heal. He has buried it somewhere deep and he doesn't talk about it to anyone, not even me anymore, and I'm his sister. It doesn't really matter, anyway, it's in the past. . . . Except, what *does* matter, is the Authority and Galen don't really . . . mix. He has to keep his head low. If he were to break any rules, or do anything that caught their attention, they would be very, well, strict with him. Do you understand?"

The girls both nodded reluctantly. "So what do we do?" asked Kessa.

"Oh, nothing. Go. Have a good time. As I said, there's really no call for alarm. I don't think it will even come up. Just, well, just be careful. Don't draw attention to yourselves, or to Galen. It might be best if the Authority doesn't even know you're visiting with him. Maybe you're just visiting Earth for your Age Pilgrimage, touring all over. Just, don't get in trouble." She tried to lighten her tone and make a little laugh. "Don't get arrested!"

The girls laughed a little, too. They weren't going to get arrested.

4

Tuesday, August 2

Skervin's Conference Room, ORGA Headquarters

Skervin's personal conference room was luxurious, of course, featuring a stunning natural wood conference table inlaid with ORGA's leaf logo, and an artificial stream flowing over red stones and pebbles along one wall. The room was long and narrow, with a floor-to-ceiling window wall at one end and Skervin's seat at the other. This had the effect—which may or may not have been intentional on Skervin's part—of cramping ordinary attendees into their chairs while giving Skervin himself plenty of room and casting extra sunlight, spotlight-style, on his place.

"Thank you all very much for coming on short notice," Skervin began elaborately. He looked around the room at his audience: Green-eyed 91 Ettica, his trusted second-in-command. The shambling 78 Kapcheck, his chief food scientist. Old warhorse 77

Stasik, the no-nonsense, longtime head of Nutribase production and distribution. Blonde-haired, perfectly groomed 81 Sybil, the rising star in charge of propaganda. And at the far end of the table, as far from Skervin as he could arrange it, was his hated rival, the Minister of Citizen Welfare, 93 Perka Yang.

Skervin really hated 93 Perka Yang. There weren't many people he felt that way about: usually he neither liked nor disliked a person, but merely assessed them on their merits and treated them accordingly as either resources or obstacles, or sometimes both. But the Minister of Citizen Welfare just irked him. Her appearance, for one thing: the gray hair, the kindly face, the high quality but purposely humble wardrobe. And then there was her manner, always trying to come off as thoughtful and morally superior to the rest of us. He'd crush her, if she weren't so damn smart and effective, with rank and intellect rivaling his own. He earnestly wished she didn't have to be here, watching him wash all his dirty laundry, but given the circumstances he had no political choice. She sat there comfortably yet sternly, posture schoolmistress-perfect, just daring him, it seemed, to overstep the rightful bounds of his control.

Skervin stopped and looked seriously around the room. "I will remind you that these proceedings are strictly confidential and there will be no disclosures to anyone—*anyone*—not on the approval list without personal authorization from Ettica or me. Now, for those of you who have not yet been briefed, here is the problem." He touched a button and the glowscreen came to life with an image of a childcare center that had been holding a birthday party. There were balloons and decorations, and a table covered with plates of delicious-looking cake, decorations, and presents. But instead of happy children sitting around the table, there were two dozen corpses. The screen zoomed to show close-ups: children's bodies twisted and draped across their chairs and onto the floor. The faces were slack but the eyes, when they were still open, gazed with the echo of leftover agony. The mouths were open and tongues hung limply, and you could see brown gooey mouthfuls of half-eaten cake mixed with vomit.

The executives in the room looked on with mixtures of revulsion and sadness. Even those who had seen the images before were not unmoved. Small sounds emerged from the back of several throats, chairs shifted, and a deep silence descended.

Skervin looked severely around the room. "These children died from a toxin that was in their Nutribase. These particular deaths were an accident, probably an unforeseeable one. But they are not the only ones. We have reason to believe that more people have died, and are going to die, from the same cause. Our mission right now, very simply, is to stamp out this problem. Preferably, before too many more people die, and definitely, before too many people find out. Understood?" Skervin looked around the room and made eye contact with his attendees, one by one, as if pinning them to the wall.

"Okay now, 78 Kapcheck, Nutritional Products Lab, you start. What is your latest status?"

Kapcheck cleared his throat nervously and spoke from his chair, eager to improve on yesterday's disastrous briefing for Skervin at his lab in Atlanta. Why was it that the confidence with which he ran his lab so easily escaped him here at headquarters? He made a swipe at his sandy hair and tried to lower his voice and speak with authority. "We know for certain the problem is toxic Nutribase, but we still don't know exactly what the toxin is, or where it's coming from. Every assay we run on soybeans or finished Nutribase turns up empty. The *Glycine max*—soybean—plants show up as completely normal and healthy. We've analyzed everything we can think of. Hell, by now we've tested for just about everything we can test for. We've used every machine in my lab. It's like this thing is invisible."

Skervin fumed. "Well damn it, Kapcheck, what are you *doing* about it?"

"Just this morning we made the determination to recalibrate our tests to run at much higher sensitivity. It's going to take some time to reconfigure our equipment, and then the tests themselves will take longer, but we're, um, hoping that will make the difference."

"How much time? People are dying here, Kapcheck."

"I know, 96, I know. It's going to be . . . well, it's going to be several days at least."

Skervin turned reluctantly to his rival. "Perka, Citwel has labs, too. Can you—" he almost said "help us," but then he thought of stronger wording and said, "—contribute to this effort?"

Perka smiled helpfully. "Certainly. We at Citwel would be happy to help out in any way we can. You understand, our expertise is really on the medical side—the human side—and not so much on food supply and toxins. But yes, Kapcheck, just let us know what you need."

Kapcheck perked up at the offer of assistance—the first one he'd had from anyone since the crisis began—and started to respond, but Skervin cut him off again, wanting to maintain control. "Hang on, Kapcheck. Perka, what we're really going to need from Citwel is a medical response to this toxin. Something we can give to people who get poisoned—or preferably, something we can give to people *before* they get poisoned. You should start mobilizing for that effort."

Perka did not appreciate being given an order by her peer, but other than a slight lift of her chin her response was perfectly cool. "Of course, yes, an immunization drug will be our responsibility at Citwel . . . once we know what we're immunizing against." She looked Skervin straight in the eye. "Naturally we'll need ORGA to characterize the toxin before we start work."

Skervin sighed internally. "Naturally."

As if to rub it in, Perka added, "I do hope you'll have better luck once Kapcheck gets the help he needs from us."

Ettica, who had been watching her boss's skirmish with Perka with growing discomfort, quickly changed the subject. "Kapcheck," she prompted. "You said your second problem is determining where the toxic Nutribase is coming from. What do you have on that?"

Kapcheck frowned. "Nothing yet. Our lab has been coordinating with Stasik here, trying to track the problem back to particular Nutribase factories or pipelines or something. But there's no pattern. Outbreaks are popping up all over the place."

"But it can't be entirely random," pressed Ettica. "There must be other factors you're overlooking."

"No doubt," concurred Kapcheck. "But without having characterized the toxin it's hard to know even where to start looking."

Ettica shook her head. "*You* don't have to know where to look, Kapcheck. That's what data mining algorithms are for. Just give the computers all the data you can find, anything that could possibly be relevant. If there's a pattern in the poisonings, they'll find it."

There were nods of agreement around the room, and Perka jumped in to control the conversation before Skervin could. "What I want to know," she said, "is what you're doing on *prevention*."

"I was just coming to that," Skervin said, more peevishly than he meant to. "Just yesterday I instructed Kapcheck to coordinate with Stasik on a rat-based monitoring program. Tell us about your status, 77 Stasik."

77 Stasik Sakharov, ORGA's Chief of Nutribase Production and Distribution, was a self-possessed man late in his career, heavily built with thick shoulders and big hands and short white hair, who'd been doing his job since even before Skervin came along. He didn't seem particularly impressed with this latest monitoring program, but he explained it anyway. "Right. At 96 Skervin's suggestion, we're putting thousands of rats in the factories and feeding them production samples in real time to increase quality control."

Skervin was dissatisfied with Stasik's presentation of his new initiative and he restated it. "Exactly. We're going to have them living off the same Nutribase we are, sampling the flow out of every plant we have, every five minutes. If a rat dies, we'll know there's a problem with the Nutribase."

Stasik half-grumbled, "You realize the rats might not find anything. We don't know where the contamination is being introduced. It may be downstream from the plants."

"So then we'll know."

"And if the contamination *is* coming from the production plants, the quality control will still be imperfect. Quantities of toxic Nutribase could still leak out between samples."

"So be it."

Skervin glanced at Perka to see if she was sufficiently impressed with this plan, and he decided he needed a bit more. "Stasik," he added dramatically. "If a rat dies, or goes into convulsions, or anything dramatic, stop the line. Pull the whole day's supply, clean out the whole damn factory, and don't start again until the martyr's comrades are feeding happily and healthfully on the new supply."

No one laughed at the "martyr" line, and Stasik scowled. "Are you sure you want us to close whole plants? That seems extreme. It would wreak havoc on production targets if we closed an entire plant. Wouldn't it make more sense to just stop one line at a time?"

"No screwing around. We need to minimize risks. Shut down the whole plant. You'll still have plenty of backup production capacity at other plants."

Stasik still had a sour look. "Not a lot. We run supply and demand very close to each other to improve efficiency. That's your own policy, 96."

It was indeed Skervin's policy. He was unabashedly proud of his global Nutribase system's efficiency, and running with minimal reserve capacity was part of his secret. In a system as well tuned as his, additional reserves would be a waste, as he was happy to explain to anyone who asked. "You have enough spare, Stasik. If a plant is pumping out poison, shutting it down for a day or two so you can clean it out is the only reasonable course." Skervin noted with a touch of satisfaction that Perka finally seemed to be nodding.

Stasik shook his white-haired head and looked around the room for anyone willing to join him in objecting to Skervin's draconian measures, but heads were down all over. After several moments, he shrugged and said, "Okay, that's what we'll do."

5

Wednesday, August 3

Tappet's Office, ORGA Headquarters

It was late in the day. 68 Tappet was in his nondescript office deep in ORGA headquarters when his brainbox gave him an alert. One of the algorithms he had assigned to the problem of what Ettica Sim had called "incidental inferences" had a hit! The "field monitor" idea Skervin had mentioned had correlated with someone out there in the soybean fields making inquiries recently to the net and two other field monitors about starving coyotes, which the algorithm flagged as an unusual event. It was a thin lead, but since field monitors had been Skervin's suggestion, Tappet thought it was worth following up. He watched recordings of the guy's net inquiries and comm conversations, and then, deciding to err on the side of caution, he sent a signal to Maggi in Skervin's office.

Minutes later Tappet was telling Skervin about the inquisitive field monitor in Southwest Saskatchewan asking about coyotes.

"You have a name on him?" Skervin asked.

"Let's see. Here it is. 22 Galen Sjøfred."

Skervin paled. "What!?"

"22 Galen Sjøfred."

"My God. I thought he was dead."

"Sir?"

"Somebody I used to know years ago. He dropped out of society; sank into the depths. I never expected to hear of him again." Skervin turned his head and a hard look appeared in his eyes. "Tappet, 22 Galen Sjøfred is dangerous. We have to stop him immediately. I want a strike force on him. Now."

"A strike force? But this guy is just a field monitor, living alone in a ground-house—"

"*Now*, Tappet!"

"Yes, 96. We'll pick him up at first light tomorrow."

Skervin's Office

An hour later, though it was now well into the evening, Skervin called Ettica into his office for a serious conversation about improving information security. They were just beginning when Maggi buzzed in.

"It's 78 Kapcheck. He says he has some news."

Skervin nodded. "Send him in."

Kapcheck, sandy hair uncombed and still dressed too casually for headquarters, was all smiles as he breezed in and sat down on the edge of a chair. "I have great news, 96. Ettica, you were right, and we found something!" He stopped himself and touched his ear. "By the way, do we need to turn recordings off?"

Skervin sniffed and Ettica scowled and said, "Of course not, Kapcheck. 96 Skervin and I are both 90s. Our private conversations with others are never recorded."

"Oh, right, sorry. Well, so anyway, we've been mashing more and more data into the data mining algorithms as you suggested, and one of the things we added was our crop harvesting records. And guess what? Certain very specific geographic crop regions are highly correlated with Toxin-X contamination downstream."

Skervin restated. "Toxin-X is coming from particular soybean fields?"

"Right."

Ettica objected, "But that seems too simple. There's no geographic pattern to the poisonings, and you said there's no relationship to particular processing plants."

"Both true," Kapcheck confirmed on the comm screen. "But the fields we're talking about are just small patches, maybe 10 or 20 hectares each. They're tiny spots compared to the thousands of square kilometers of cropland that feed a typical processing plant. Say there's one poisonous field that gets harvested. Its beans go into the factory pretty much as a group, get processed, and come out as a sort of poisonous gob hidden in the middle of the Nutribase feed. But as that gob moves through the pipelines of the distribution tree, it is gradually broken up into smaller and smaller blobs at each branch point, until finally all these little poisonous pieces are delivered to individual fabs, which are in widely distributed locations. The poisonous bits arrive at about the same times, but not exactly. Result? It looks to us like intermittent outbreaks in random locations."

Skervin nodded with satisfaction. "At last, Kapcheck, you're making some sense. And the poisonous infection or whatever it is in the fields must be spreading. There's getting to be more of it, so we're seeing bigger poisonous gobs, more often."

"Right."

"Excellent. So now we know it's a blight of some kind. Weeds, or a plant disease, or something. An invisible blight, but still a blight. What are you going to do about it, Kapcheck?"

Kapcheck smiled, feeling strong and confident again. "We'll kill it, sir."

"Good. How?"

Soybean agronomy was a good part of his lab's responsibilities, and Kapcheck was back in his comfort zone. He stood up and walked over to a blank wall, pacing and gesturing like a professor. They had a pathogen elimination process, he explained, a six-step procedure, that always worked. It had an acronym. It had standards and procedures. It had machines. He confidently reeled off statistics on how many days each step took and how many hundred pathogens they detected and controlled each year. "Average time from detection to eradication, 106 days," he boasted. "Maximum, 232, but that was an outlier. Best time, 29 days."

Ettica asked, "What kind of disease do you think it is, Kapcheck?"

"We will pursue three possibilities. First, fungal, which I estimate is most likely. Second, viral. Plants are not normally susceptible to viruses without a vector like an insect or nematode, so we'll look for those, too. Third, a parasite."

"Have you considered bacteria?" Ettica asked.

Kapcheck gave an involuntary dismissive shrug. "Bacteria? No, it's not that."

"Because . . . ?"

"Because we conquered bacterial infections decades ago. *Vanquishin.* It's unbeatable."

"Remind me again," Ettica said, flashing those green eyes and managing to sound intelligent rather than uninformed.

"It's the way Vanquishin works. Before that, they had a lot of antibiotics, but the problem was that bacteria evolve. Every time you rolled out a new antibiotic, the bacteria would turn around and evolve a resistant strain. It was a never-ending battle. But then the Vanquishin guys realized that bacteria live in *colonies*, and that was their weakness. See, each individual bacterial cell produces beneficial molecules that float around outside the cell and are shared by everyone in the colony, kind of like—well, this is a very approximate analogy—kind of like honey in a beehive. All the bees make it, and all the bees use it. Vanquishin poisons the honey, which kills the bees. With me so far?" Ettica nodded.

"Now let's say one of the bees evolves a beneficial mutation that allows it to produce Vanquishin-proof honey molecules that don't turn poisonous. Fine, but the rest of the colony is still producing the old kind of honey molecule, so the community honey store is still 99% poisonous. All the bees still die, including the one that came up with the beneficial mutation. That anti-poison mutation isn't passed along to future generations, and the bacteria are back to square one. It's brilliant! And it works, too. Has for ages now. It's kind of interesting that in this case, working collaboratively as part of a community is a weakness for the bacteria."

"Okay, so not bacterial," coached Skervin. "Maybe fungal, maybe viral, maybe parasites."

"Correct."

"Very good, Kapcheck. Get to it. You have 29 days."

"But 96, 29 days is our best time ever! This outbreak is clearly more complicated—"

"29 days, Kapcheck."

6

Thursday, August 4

Galen's Farmhouse

It had been a week since he shot the third coyote, and Galen's investigation into starving coyotes was going nowhere. He had asked the med analyzer every question it could answer. He had asked his friends and the net all the questions he dared ask. Yet he had promised Kessa he would investigate the coyotes, and now she and Marta would be arriving this afternoon. He didn't want them to think he didn't know his business as a field monitor.

And so, just as the sun came up, Galen set out to break a rule.

Recreational use of their aircars by field monitors was against the rules, and in fact each aircar trip a field monitor took required its own authorization from above, which Galen, on this morning, didn't have. Nevertheless, with a feeling of calm deliberation, he climbed into his aircar's cabin and told it to start.

"Up to 100 meters," Galen instructed. "Spiral outward from the house in a search pattern." The aircar whined loudly into action and he was off.

The view from the air was little different from the view from the ground: rows and rows of soybeans, stretching to the horizon in every direction. Galen's practiced eye noted with a grower's satisfaction how the beans were growing nicely in the mid-summer heat, solidly green from proper irrigation, good height and spread, pods well set and plump. All seemed well. He soon gave up looking out the window and instead turned his attention to his viewscreen, which showed images from aircar cameras and sensors aimed at the ground. He set it to infrared and found the view more interesting, full of speckles and undulating shapes reflecting subtle variations in plant and soil temperatures due to myriad factors like moisture, subsoils, plant health, and—his favorite—small mammals, which showed up as little warm dots scurrying about their little lives. But as his aircar moved east, Galen watched with alarm as the small animal dots thinned out and then completely disappeared.

"Over there," he commanded the aircar, and they flew farther east, into the depths of the region of infrared-dark. Interestingly, it all looked normal out the window. "Land," he ordered.

Galen was feeling brave that morning, but he was also old enough not to be rash. Before he climbed out of the aircar, he tucked his pants into his tall boots and pulled on a good, heavy pair of gloves. He stepped to the ground and waded gingerly into the soybeans, thigh-high and still green and cool in the summer morning. At this time of year, the bushy soybeans in one row spread out and touched the next row over. He was just two rows in when he felt a squish under his foot. He looked down and started—he was stepping on a dead rabbit. He jumped away and set his boots carefully down on bare soil. He couldn't see the ground because of the bushes, so he squatted and, putting down one hand for balance, tilted his head down close to the ground and peered along the tunnel-like bower beneath the plants. He could see a long way in both directions down the agribot-straight rows exactly 75 centimeters apart, evenly furrowed on both sides and perfectly free of weeds.

And covered with dead animals. Every few meters for as far as he could see, little corpses lay flung up against the stems of the plants. They were little furry things, now lying splayed and flat, with mangy fur, decaying flesh, and tails flopped on the ground in all directions. Rabbits, rats, mice, voles, maybe even a coyote out there in the distance. Sometimes they were lying in pairs, as if two friends had died together. Galen gingerly poked at a mouse carcass with a gloved finger to look for a cause of death. There were no bite marks or cuts that he could see, but he did think the mouth looked oddly open. He could see the tiny little teeth.

Galen thought it was a plague. For a moment, he lifted an elbow up to cover his mouth and nose, but then he realized it was too late and he gave up. He'd just have to hope it wasn't airborne. He was no pathologist but he knew disaster when he saw it, and he had just discovered a major outbreak of something deadly. *This* was why something seemed amiss with the wildlife near his house. And this was why the coyotes were starving: they had a fatal disease!

He wondered if ORGA knew. The holocaust of dead bodies was hidden below the soybean leaves, so you had to be out here in the fields to see the physical evidence. And who from ORGA ever actually came out in person to the fields? Well, field monitors like him, Galen reminded himself. Technically, *he* was ORGA. But hell, he was just a 22-level outcast that no one would ever listen to. Though on the other hand, the infrared satellite imagery would show problems if anyone ever looked at it. Maybe they had noticed and just weren't telling anyone about it? Or, did they even care about the animals, or anything else for that matter that wasn't their precious *Glycine max*?

And yet, here it was, right beneath his feet. He frowned slowly and shook his head. This was bigger than he was.

Galen decided to collect evidence. He recorded a video, trying to capture everything he had just seen. Then, checking the fit of his gloves, he picked up a dead mouse and sealed it into a plastic bag from a box he found in the aircar. While he was at it, he broke off some pieces of soybean plants and sealed them up as well. Then, getting into the spirit of things, he dug up some soil samples, some root samples, and two more corpses. He wanted to show them to someone. He started to wonder if he was about to spread the plague by the gunk on this clothes and boots, and he resolved to wash off when he got back.

Suddenly he became aware of the time. It was bad enough that he was out in the aircar without permission; now his dawdling would invite even worse trouble. He climbed quickly back in and took off, heading for home. Someone would have been alerted about his trip by now and someone else, higher up, would not be happy. Who knew how they would respond?

Damn, and with Kessa and Marta arriving in a few hours. He should have waited on this. Stupid, Galen.

Galen flew straight back as fast as the lumbering aircar could go. Back home, he went hastily inside and straight to the same med analyzer machine he had used for his coyote blood the day before. It had nothing to say about his small animal corpses. "NO PATHOLOGY DETECTED," it said. For the plants and soil, the device needed a ground-up sample, so Galen used a pulverizer to mash some snippets from his plastic bag and hurriedly spooned the result into a test tube that went into the analyzer. The machine was consistent in its findings: "NO PATHOLOGY DETECTED."

Galen was hoping for more something helpful than that, but somehow, he wasn't surprised. He pushed the button and tried again, but still, "NO PATHOLOGY DETECTED."

Not sure what else to do, he decided to run all his samples through his 3D scanner. That way he'd at least have electronic versions of them; maybe he could send them to a lab somewhere. Though, come to think of it, an ORGA lab was out of the question. He decided to try a friendlier audience. Digging deeper into the controls, he found a way for the 3D scanner to send a data dump of all its technical information over to his messaging system. Then he walked quickly to his workstation and plugged in. "Message to Lana," he instructed, and started recording a message to his sister, the eminent plant scientist.

This looked like an animal affliction, but she could probably get him started, at least. He started recording.

"Lana, hi. I'm excited to be seeing Marta and Kessa this afternoon. But this is about something else. I'm sorry, but it's important. Please look at these 3D scanner files and tell me what you think. They're from a patch of the soybean field ten kilometers from here, covered with corpses of small animals. Hundreds of them, like an epidemic. I'm guessing that's what's wrong with the coyotes, if Kessa told you about the sick ones that have been showing up around here. I've never seen anything like it. Here, I'll include the video I took. I have some carcasses and the nearby soybean plants here in these bags—can you see them on camera as I'm holding them up?

"Lana, I'm . . . I'm concerned. The Authority surely knows about this, but they must be keeping a lid on it. Censoring until they can fix it, maybe. They probably don't want me to know about it either. I'm going to . . ."

Galen broke off. There was a whirring sound coming from outside. It sounded like aircars. There was no time to lose. He gave the "Send" command to his message and it was gone.

In the next minute, so was he.

ORGA Regional Enforcement Post, Calgary, Earth

ORGA was not, technically, Earth's police. Minister 96 Skervin Hough did, however, successfully argue that his responsibility included protecting Earth's organic resources, which meant preventing crimes against said resources, which meant acting against the criminal perpetrators of such crimes, at least until Authority Police were called in. Thus it followed, his argument went, that naturally and by any theory of law, ORGA needed its own armed agents dedicated to ORGA's particular needs. And that was why, in addition to the Authority's own Authority Police force for civilian purposes and Earth Force for on- and off-planet military purposes, there was also an armed organization called ORGA Enforcement that reported directly to its minister. (Naturally, ORGA's minister was dedicated to ensuring there was full and complete cooperation between his agents and the Authority Police. And also naturally, this never happened.)

As the sun rose that day, an ORGA heavy enforcement team, under the command of Senior ORGA Enforcement Officer 50 Smithson Jackson, departed Calgary in two P-17s. Their target was located at the edge of their territory, and it was not until 0735 that they thundered down around Galen's house, one P-17 in front and one in the rear, behind the chicken coops. Smithson and his nine men, clad in full uniform with ORGA's leaf logo on the sleeves, leapt out with guns raised and rushed the house. All exits were covered within seconds. Smithson's display showed Galen's tracking dot still inside—he wasn't going anywhere. "Open up, 22 Galen Sjøfred!" Smithson shouted. "You are under arrest!"

There was no reply.

Smithson gave a signal and one of his men blasted the front door open. With the grace of years of practice, they rushed in with perfect military movements, covering each turn, sweeping each room.

But somehow Smithson already knew: 22 Galen was gone. An illegal eardot was sitting there on a table, sending out a false signal.

∎ ∎ ∎

"Damn it!" shouted Tappet when Smithson called in. "How did he know we were coming? Where did he go?"

"I don't know, sir."

"Search the place he landed. And search his house top to bottom. Get into his computers. Find out if he's been talking to anyone or sending messages. Search for any signs of visitors. Post a 24-hour patrol around this place and shoot anything that comes near."

Tappet signed off and shook his head. "Damn it!" he thought. "What is this criminal up to? Where has he gone?"

Thirty Fit Bravo Gym, Denver

34 Jet Castilian kept his body perfectly still as he hovered, prone, three meters above the floor. Beneath his transparent facemask, his eyes—light brown, very clear, and exceptionally alert—darted all over the air polo court as his agile brain calculated his next move. Pressurized air shooting up through the floor kept him and the other players aloft, and it also allowed them to move in three dimensions using carefully calibrated body movements that adjusted the angles of their bat-like wingsuits. It was devilishly tricky to maintain control, particularly as other players moved around the court and set up swirls and eddies in the otherwise smooth flow of air. But Jet was good, and at any moment he could choose to flit suddenly to a new position and then stop still, like a dragonfly. Better yet, he had an intuition for the physics of the game: where the ball was, where the players were now and where they could get to, the dynamics of airflow, angles, speeds, probabilities. His mind was playing high-speed, real-time, 3D chess.

A pass came Jet's way and he shifted 10 centimeters right and down to catch it, compensating for the destabilizing grasping motion in his right hand with a tiny rudder motion in his left foot. His teammate Cab was breaking toward the goal and clearly hoping for a pass, but Jet saw an opponent crossing below on a path that would block Cab's air column and send him tumbling toward the floor in a few seconds, so instead Jet passed to Stoke, who was moving upward in what appeared to be the wrong direction.

Though this was not the reason for the pass, 31 Stoke Omroni was Jet's best friend off court. They were both 24 years old, and they worked together during the day. Stoke was a talented player too, but rather than doing physics, his brain was doing psychology. He had a way of reading the other players and guessing their next moves before they happened. He had foreseen Cab's problem just as Jet had, and he knew it would create a vertical hole in the air column right in front of the opposing goal. If he could get into position at the top in time, he would drop suddenly down to the goal when the goalkeeper was least expecting it. Jet's pass led him perfectly, Cab stalled and fell on schedule, and Stoke scored a beautiful goal that ended the game with a victory.

The air pressure was dialed down and the players settled to the ground and pulled off their helmets. Stoke's white, toothy smile lit up his dark-skinned face and he let out a whoop of triumph, shaking out his head of kinky black hair and reaching out an athletic arm to shake hands cheerfully with teammates and opponents alike. "That couldn't have worked better if you'd planned it," he smiled at Cab, and, "Awesome assist, there, Jet." Even the defeated team was grinning and laughing; it was a friendly group to begin with, and Stoke had that effect on people.

Jet was smiling as widely as Stoke was. "We read that one, didn't we?" Like Stoke and most people from Earth in that century, Jet had a mixed ethnic ancestry that in his case had produced a Spanish-style look with toasted tan skin, thick black hair, a straight nose, and a generally pleasant appearance that made others expect good things. He was a little taller than most people, including Stoke, and his sinewy muscles showed the effects of his self-imposed, strict schedule of daily workouts here at Thirty Fit Bravo, the 30-level gym for his sector.

Back in the locker room, Stoke immersed himself in the energy of the other players as they laughed and chatted away. Jet listened with half an ear, but part of his attention was drifting away. He popped his eardot back inside the right ear canal and his brainbox, Kimberly, launched her start-up sequence, scanning his person and his brainwaves, recalibrating herself after the game, checking on Jet's health and worldly status, and telepathically asking how the air polo went.

He ewaved his thoughts to her. "It was good, thanks, Kimberly. What did I miss?"

"The Denver Hawks won their game just now, 245 to 180. 62 Mnobo scored 95 points."

"95 points? Good for him."

"Spaceport statistics for July were just released, too . . ." Kimberly reeled off several sets of travel and business statistics and then switched to headlines from the worlds of science and technology, which Jet eagerly absorbed and often asked for more details about.

An outsider listening in might have thought Jet's interests were rather unusual for a 24-year-old single guy, but then, Jet was not usual. For some reason, the genetic and environmental lottery had granted him an intellect that was a tiger among kittens: bigger, faster, more maneuverable, and capable of making larger leaps than most others it encountered. Jet enjoyed his gift, and he lived a rich life full of interest and intellectual stimulation—it was just that most of it he generated for himself. Jet enjoyed playing with kittens as much as most people, but the tiger in his brain also needed plenty of time to run free on its own, at its own speed, twisting and leaping, just for exercise. And sometimes these days, without malice or misanthropy, he was finding other people . . . well, dull. Part of him knew it was a psychological symptom of something deeper, but the rest of him refused to engage. Just keep working, he told himself. You'll cheer up. Meanwhile, good thing Stoke's around. Without him you'd be dismal indeed.

As they walked out of the locker room, Stoke and Jet ran into a friend named 29 Ricker. "Stoke! Jet! Whatchya?" he greeted them breezily.

Jet gave a friendly nod and Stoke flashed his big white grin. "You're trying out that guest pass I got you?" As a 29-level, Ricker wouldn't be allowed here otherwise. Ricker's head was tilted down a fraction as if to help his dark bangs hide his eyes, and there was a shy smirk on his lips.

"Yeeah," sighed Ricker, gaping around at the respectable lobby. "This is sweet."

"All the joys of 30-hood," smiled Jet, and as he followed Ricker's gaze he added, "We even let in women, too."

"Whoa! I see what you *mean*," Ricker breathed, unabashedly gawking at a young woman in a skin-tight outfit walking nearby. "Us 20s aren't so lucky with the whole mixed-gender idea."

"Any day, my man," offered Stoke, laughing in a big-brotherly way. "Any day, you'll make 30-level too."

"Yeah, and I can't wait," Ricker murmured, swiveling his head to track someone else. "How do I meet that girl?" Another thought struck him. "Hey, when you get your 30, do they give you lessons on how to meet the girls?"

Stoke and Jet laughed. Jet went off to return his rented wingsuit, and Stoke mischievously tugged Ricker over to meet the young woman he had just been admiring. Stoke had a way with people, and before long "that girl" was turning out to be a pleasant person who shared some mutual friends, and the next thing Ricker knew they were all making plans together for later in the week. "Whoa, how *do* you do that, Stoke?" Ricker marveled after she had left.

"Do what?"

"Meet beautiful women!"

Stoke surprised Ricker with a suddenly serious look. "They're all beautiful, Ricker." And then he lightened up again just as quickly and joked, "That, plus the lessons they give you when you make 30."

■ ■ ■

Jet and Stoke walked back together toward their respective apartments through the indoor maze that was their home, the city of Denver. It was always crowded in the public spaces here in the 30-levels, with millions of people going about their lives. Jet and Stoke took a couple of slidewalks and, guided by Kimberley, they were about to catch a turbolift just in time when they got stuck behind a clog of people and missed it. Jet fumed in frustration while they waited for two minutes for the next one, but Stoke didn't mind the wait and sought to distract his friend with conversation. "So," Stoke said, "did I tell you about last night?"

Jet welcomed the distraction. "No, who was it this time?"

"Mm, her name was Alera. You should have seen her. Yummy."

"Where'd you meet her?"

"The Hot Cabin. It's a 20s place, I know, but who cares? We had a good time."

That was true, but Stoke didn't mention that when he woke up next to her the next morning, he couldn't even quite remember Alera's name.

Jet smiled appreciatively. "You going to see her again?"

"What? No. Of course not. She wasn't *that* kind of girl."

"Oh, too bad. I keep hoping for you. Girls like you so much, but I'm never sure you like them back."

Stoke was taken aback. "Of course I like them! Women are a gift to us all. I like every girl I go out with." But someday, Stoke thought to himself, someday I'm actually going to care in the morning. I'm going to wake up, I'm going to know her name, I'm going to like her, and by God, she's going to like me. Someday.

"You don't like them enough to see them again the next day," Jet was saying.

"All right, I'll admit that. But it's just because I haven't met the right person yet. Anyway, don't give me any crap. At least I see girls. Not like you, ever since you gave up on love."

"I have not given up on love."

"Yes you have. Ever since Caroline dumped you. What was that, six months ago?"

Jet's clear brown eyes crinkled a fraction, looking hurt. "It was five," he said quietly. Like all romantics, Jet had a heart that was slow to heal.

"Okay, sorry, five months. Come on, man, you have to get back out there."

"I'm not ready yet, Stoke. Not yet." Though as he said it, his heart gave an extra pump.

■ ■ ■

"Stoke! Where you been?" Jet called two hours later as his friend sauntered up a few minutes late. They were in the ready area of the hangar at Denver City Port 17, one of dozens nestled in among the skyscrapers and rooftops of the massive city. This one was on the eightieth floor in Sector B. Dozens of taxis were lined up and one took off or landed every minute or two in a frenetic bustle. Air taxis served city destinations only, flitting between buildings and stories, shuttling passengers who could afford it and who preferred a point-to-point taxi ride over threading their way through a maze of sliders and turbolifts.

Jet and Stoke, however, headed down to a separate section down on one end, reserved for another kind of craft: space orbiters. Here the pace was more deliberate, suitable to the careful attention appropriate to both their ambitious mission—all the way up to orbit and back—and to their elevated status as carriers of the elite. There was an extra checkpoint for entering the area, and as they approached the barrier a remote scanner recognized them, processed their data, and opened the gate. "Greetings, pilots," it said.

On days he allowed himself to think about it, Jet had to admit that the service he and Stoke provided for a living was a huge waste of resources. Certainly, people needed a way to get back and forth between the orbiting spaceports to the surface. And true, for whatever reasons—political, practical . . . something—Earth had given up on space elevators and committed to craft-based transport. But why in the world, why in the universe, couldn't his clients take the planet shuttle like everyone else?

The answer, of course, was rank. 70s and up simply did not ride mass transit like everyone else. 70-pluses could afford private orbiters, paid for private orbiters, and kept operations like Jet's employers in business. And, for that matter, they gave Jet and Stoke their jobs. So Jet could hardly complain.

And really, for a 24-year-old who was just getting started, Jet's was a plum assignment and a pretty sweet deal. He remembered how thrilled he'd been when he got the news he'd qualified for the private orbiter assignment twelve months ago. After five years of driving air taxis around the city it was like the clouds breaking after days of rain. Orbit! He was going to be flying in space!

Well, more or less. True, it was orbit, but his credentials limited him to low Earth orbit, less than 2000 km up. It was 32 still-thrilling minutes from surface to orbit, then a slow wait of minutes or hours matching orbits and docking. And what kind of driving was it?

Basically, back and forth. Same thing every day, sometimes twice a day.

Still, though! Space. His own spaceship, however humble. Vast emptiness just outside. Magnificent views of Earth below. Moving at 28,000 kilometers per hour. Even now it made a satisfied grin creep into his face. He only wished he could go farther and higher.

"It's been kind of quiet this week, don't you think?" Stoke asked Jet conversationally.

"Mm-hm," Jet nodded. "This is Thursday and I think we've only had six fares all week. Interplanetary travel is a shrinking sector here on Earth. Kimberly was telling me July was 3.2% lower than last year."

Stoke shook his head. "That's not good for us. The Authority keeps isolating us more and more from the other planets."

"We'll be all right. It's hitting the lower ranks more than our customers. We still get the moneybags. And anyway, we're not going to be doing this forever. Someday, Stoke, you and I are going to be spacers together."

Stoke smiled at that. Jet was always a good one for chasing the dream. "Absolutely right we are! And we're each going to meet the perfect woman, too."

Jet grinned. "I agree. All we have to do is keep working hard and making smart decisions."

"Or at least avoid screw-ups," laughed Stoke.

Jet laughed, too. What he did not know was that today, during the space of one fateful heartbeat, he would make the most idiotic, ill-considered, and downright stupidest decision—in other words, the most gigantic screw-up—of his entire life. But if he had known, he would not have been surprised it was for a girl.

■   ■   ■

"Now let's get going," Jet said. "*Chica* is waiting."

They walked reverently toward their orbiter, which was standing on the deck with hatchway deployed, awaiting their arrival. Her numeric markings designated her as LIVERY VEHICLE CC723, and she was sometimes generically called a CC orbiter, but to Jet she was just *Chica*.

His girl. *El Pato*, preferred Stoke. "Duck Beak." She was shaped like a giant but flattened bowling pin lying on its side, sculpted into the details of a spaceship . . . or perhaps, if you were Stoke, like a flying duck with its neck out. The thick body was the propulsion unit, and the outstretched neck and head were for passengers and crew. Her outer shell, made of dynamic material that constantly adjusted its surface to reduce drag, was shiny white, which was practical, and it was trimmed with gold highlights, which pleased the customers. The two pilots sat side-by-side on the forward flight deck or "beak," surrounded by a panoramic tinted canopy. Immediately behind them in the "neck" was the passenger compartment with room for nine, luxuriously furnished with comfortable, front-facing sofas and low tables nestling obsequiously in front of each. Passengers enjoyed gigantic views out the tinted polyglass top and sides, except when safety shields temporarily deployed during maneuvers.

Aft of *Chica*'s long neck was her bulbous propulsion module and the wings. Here in the hangar the wings were retracted into bumps on the side, but for atmospheric flight they morphed outward into agile wings that curved and stretched at the pilot's command. There were small conventional jets studded around the body for taxiing and maneuvers, but *Chica*'s belly housed the heart of the machine: her space engine and propellant tanks. She boasted a fusion-powered Class VI magnetoplasmadynamic thruster, capable of powering her all the way up from the thick atmosphere at the planet's surface to the airless vacuum of low earth orbit, with plenty of energy left for maneuvering in orbit and on the way back down. Its only exhaust product was environmentally friendly, neutrally-charged water vapor.

Chica was, thought Jet, a thing of many beauties.

Dispatch had no up-fare for them so Jet and Stoke would be traveling empty on the way up to their destination, Spaceport America, one of Earth's three orbiting space stations. After receiving final clearance, Jet, the senior pilot, formally transferred command to Stoke to help him accumulate flight hours. Using manual controls, Stoke taxied them to the hangar's launch area and then lit up *Chica*'s thrusters. They shot smoothly forward and out into the air outside

Port 17, already 80 stories above the ground as they turned quickly skyward and toward the stars. The G-forces of acceleration rapidly increased and pushed them firmly down into the cushioned backs of their chairs. The city fell away beneath them in a matter of seconds and they climbed rapidly through a thin cloud cover and up into the thinning air. Minutes later the blue sky began fading, to be replaced by the black of space and its brilliant field of stars. As they eased toward a stable orbit, gravity faded away and Jet and Stoke felt the familiar sense of weightlessness in their stomachs. Jet touched a button and gave *Chica* a quiet vocal command, "Match orbits and rendezvous, Spaceport America Sierra Alpha Zero Zero Four, craft discretion deviation alert."

If Jet had been feeling cynical (which was hard to do in this spectacular setting), he might have mused that not only was his orbiter service a huge waste of resources, but pilots—he and Stoke in this case—were too. *Chica* was easily intelligent enough to fly herself to the space station and back, and as it was, she was taking care of 95% of the necessary commands and controls. The official reasoning was that you still needed humans in the loop "to give direction," and "just in case," and platitudes of similar ilk. Jet knew the real reason, of course, which was that passengers were people, and people liked having other people working for them. Plus, someone had to carry the bags.

After 30 quiet minutes, Spaceport America came into view ahead. It consisted of a long spindle serving as the axis for a giant ring rotating gracefully to provide a pseudo-gravity environment for passengers and station operations.

Jet gave the necessary commands and *Chica* maneuvered to move inside the ring and match its rate of rotation, making it appear to slow and then stop "beneath" them. This didn't mean *Chica* could rest; she had to apply steady acceleration in several directions at once to mimic centrifugal force and maintain the illusion they were stationary. The combined forces restored a sense of gravity to the ship and Jet and Stoke felt themselves pressed down into their seats. Executing a complex ballet with her thrusters, *Chica* slid carefully in place over one of the several air locks that were waiting below them. At Stoke's command, she shot out four short mooring cables to points inside the lock. They self-attached and drew *Chica* neatly down inside.

Once *Chica* was safely ensconced, the lock cycled: large outer doors closed over the top and sealed out the vacuum of space, temporarily enclosing them in a miniature steel cave. The lock was pressurized with air, and then the inner doors beneath them retracted. Below was an immense, brightly lit hangar that served as the loading area for the passenger terminal. It was large enough for dozens of orbiters and mass transit ships to fly freely—albeit carefully—as they moved between the locks on the "ceiling" and the passenger loading and unloading stations on the "ground."

They could even queue up. Once upon a time, orbiters had been an on-request service like limousines, but at Spaceport America they worked just like taxis. High-status arriving passengers, after navigating the requisite layers of Spaceport security and clearance, finally emerged and headed for what was grandly called the Orbiter Lounge but that amounted to a taxi stand, where they waited impatiently as the next orbiter in line pulled up and whisked them away.

It was an age-old arrangement but Jet and Stoke did not like it at all. Spaceport America hosted thousands of space-faring travelers every day, which should have meant a steady flow of orbiter customers. But in practice the flow came in bursts, with peaks of activity broken up by long periods of quiet and, from the orbiter pilots' perspective, boring and frustrating waits in the pickup line of orbiters that strung itself out in front of the door to the Orbiter Lounge and looked exactly like a taxi rank from centuries before.

Once they steered into position, Stoke counted: "Twelve ahead of us. I hope you weren't in a hurry today." And then, wryly correcting himself: "I mean, I hope you weren't in more of a hurry *than usual* today." Jet was always in a hurry.

"Aargh," groaned Jet. "This is so inefficient! There *must* be a better way to run this thing."

"Got any better ideas?"

"As a matter of fact, yes," Jet fired back. "For one thing, why do we both have to wait here? Why don't you go inside and line up a fare while I wait out here?"

"Uh, that's not really how it works . . ."

"I know, but it should. The fares would like it, too. You could greet them, in person, with that killer smile of yours, and carry their bags out to the door. I could be waiting when you get here."

"That's called touting, and it's prohibited. Jet, there are rules."

"Well sure, but they're wrong."

"This is Earth. The rules come from the Authority. Right and wrong doesn't really pertain."

"I know. I know."

Stoke fell silent and the two young men sat quietly for a good five minutes, doing nothing. Jet tried to distract himself by redesigning the spaceport in his head, but he couldn't concentrate. So he gave up and did nothing.

Nothing.

"No motion in the line yet?" Jet finally asked, unable to contain himself any longer.

"Nope."

"Oh, come *on*." He squirmed and sighed and generally gave the impression of a person about to explode.

Finally Stoke couldn't take it anymore. "Okay, okay, I'll do it!" he burst out.

"You will?" said a very surprised Jet.

"Yeah, I'll do it. But just to shut you up."

"I hardly said anything!"

"Yeah well your body language is shouting at the top of its lungs."

Jet gave a nervous smile and his brown eyes lit up. He was not a habitual rule-breaker, but he was impatient, and today he was young and rash. His heart sped up. "This is awesome," he said aloud.

Stoke thought hard. "You'll have to get out of line," he pointed out. It wouldn't do if he escorted a passenger directly to the twelfth orbiter in line. Everyone would see it happening and no one would approve. "You know this is against the rules, right? We could get in trouble?"

"Sure, sure. It'll be fine. Tell me when you're ready and I'll go to the maintenance door. It's off in a corner and it's a normal place to be."

"Good idea. Any idea how to get to the maintenance door from inside?"

"You'll figure it out."

"Okay," said Stoke, taking a deep breath and checking the windows and his monitors for anyone watching. "Here I go."

Spaceport America, Earth Orbit

The interstellar spaceship ADS *Okafor*, bound for Spaceport America under the command of Captain Narisa Kunlabi, slowed out of warp speed and came shooting into normal space. Its trajectory took it carefully into the designated Sol-1 Deceleration Zone a little inside the orbit of Mars, where arriving interplanetary ships dumped their dangerous clouds of accumulated space talus before moving toward the protected orbit of Earth.

Okafor's crew began rousing the snooze cruise passengers, who had been sleeping, lightly anesthetized, in pod-like berths. After a few short medical procedures, they emerged and gathered into the ship's small viewing lounge. Among them were Marta—full of excitement and trepidation—and Kessa, still groggy from the anesthetic.

Kessa could hardly sort out her dreams from her real memories of the journey so far, all floating around in her mind like soap bubbles. She and Marta had left their house on New Gaia early in the morning three days ago. There had been the familiar air pod flight from Lake Peace over her beloved forests to the hyperloop station, and the short hyperloop ride to Fentral. The relatively unfamiliar and gut-wrenching planet tube ride shooting down into the depths of the planet and back up again at Zero West on the equator. The sights and sounds of Zero West, the little village that was closest thing New Gaia had to a city, and above all its beachfront access to the ocean. Kessa hadn't been able to help herself and impulsively waded all the way into the sea, fully clothed, exhilarating in the smell of saltwater and the gripping sensation of waves breaking over her shoulders. There had been the New Gaian-style informal boarding process with fellow interplanetary travelers, followed by a short, fast boat ride out to the floating base of the space elevator, whose braided cables reached impossibly up, up, and up into the sky. The long, other-worldly ride up the high-speed elevator car, looking out first on spectacular views of the ground and then on ever-thinning layers of atmosphere, until suddenly the sky turned black and starry and she was in outer space for the first time in her life. The unnerving jolts and bumps as their elevator car was seized bodily by a robotic space tender and accelerated out to a higher orbit, giving them the experience of weightlessness for the first time. The excitement of approaching *Okafor*, with its iconic Alçubierre form: a gigantic, matte-black ring with a small, cigar-shaped passenger pod aligned along its axis in the center. The fun of floating in zero-g through *Okafor*'s portal and into the cramped lounge, and then, at Marta's insistence but to Kessa's great disappointment, accepting the injection that put them to sleep for three days.

But now here they were at Earth, another planet! As the fog in Kessa's brain lifted, she began to focus on the viewscreens, which, in lieu of the spaceship's non-existent windows, presented spectacular views of the New Gaia-like planet Earth and her amazing, unique companion, the moon called Luna.

Captain Kunlabi stepped forward to address her passengers. "May I have your attention please, friends and travelers. We have arrived at Spaceport America, in orbit around the planet Earth!" There was a cheer and scattered applause. "Thank you for traveling with us here aboard *Okafor*, and we look forward to seeing you again soon. Now please pay attention to crewman Kai, who will help you with disembarkation. Peace be with you all."

The passengers were carefully shepherded out of *Okafor* and through a weightless tunnel in the space station that took them to an exotic elevator that started out in the weightless center and whooshed them outward to the pseudogravity of the outer ring. There, without ceremony or consideration, they were all herded bodily through xenophobic Earth's infamous "Dip," a giant pool of foul-smelling disinfecting liquid not unlike that used for cattle millennia before. Marta and Kessa emerged wet and bedraggled along with everyone else, but in their excitement, they accepted the ordeal with good humor and looked eagerly ahead for the next step.

But then they realized it was security screening. Suddenly their momentary girlish cockiness vanished, and nervousness overtook them as they approached an intimidating booth with a skeptical-looking security officer inside behind dark glass.

"Traveling together?" the officer said without introduction.

"Uh, yes," said Marta. "My name is Marta Dahlstrom and this is my sister, Kessa Dahlstrom. We're from New Gaia."

"Right hand in the scanner."

Marta dutifully placed her hand into a square hole in the wall, where it was quickly scanned.

"And hers, too."

Kessa obeyed. The twenty-ninth-century scanner had, in just a few moments, gathered gigabytes of information about the two bodies attached to the hands it had detected. Using analysis of the hairs, fingernails, vapor emissions, cells, blood, bones, and microbiota that it scanned, it quickly determined their physical characteristics, their DNA, their proteome, their microbiome . . . even details of where they had lived, childhood trauma and brain function. With scans like that, there was no need for something as primitive as "papers" or a "passport."

The still-unimpressed security official recited, "Purpose of visit?"

"Our Age Pilgrimage," Marta replied. The booth seemed satisfied. Age Pilgrimages were a normal custom in the Hundred Worlds—a chance for young people to take one big trip before settling into the domestic responsibilities of adulthood. "Where will you be staying?"

Marta was ready, yet careful not to rush her answer. She and Kessa had taken to heart their mother's warning about keeping Galen's name out of it, and they planned ahead of time what they would say: "Visitor Quarters 2, Calgary." It was a stretch. They were really heading for Galen's house in southwest Saskatchewan, *via* Calgary, but they thought that detail might raise flags. It was better to appear to flow in the middle of the stream.

"Length of visit?"

"14 days."

"What are your respective ranks?"

Marta wasn't quite ready for that one. "Uh, ranks?"

"Do you have a social rank previously determined by a recognized planetary authority," recited the voice in the booth, not even bothering to make it a question.

Marta looked over at an equally mystified Kessa. "Uh, I don't think so."

"Mm-hm," said the booth, making the first human-like sound yet. "Let me check your credit . . . It says here you two share an account with a balance in excess of 500 million credits, which is a, well, generous amount."

"We do?"

"You're not aware of this?"

"Well, I mean, the New Gaia citizen panel just told us to spend what we need . . ." Probably a New Gaian panel member, thinking practically, had figured a large limit would be helpful for emergencies. It would not have occurred to either Marta or Kessa to spend anything more than necessary. After all, they were traveling on communal funds.

"I am issuing you both the temporary rank of 75. Welcome to Earth. Now move ahead."

As soon as they were out of earshot of the booth, Kessa said to Marta, "That was the least welcoming welcome I could have imagined!"

"Terrible. But we've made it now, right? Do you think 75 is good?"

"No idea. I guess we'll find out."

It didn't take long. The next "stop" along the way was a series of what looked like storefronts, each with large numbers above their doors: "Under 20. 20s. 30s. 40s. 50s. 60s. 70s. 80s." The storefronts were all different, displaying a progression from cramped and cheap-looking to large and luxurious. There was no sign for 90s, Marta noted, but there were some unmarked doors that exuded a sense of privilege. The whole arrangement made the sisters vaguely uncomfortable, but everyone else was going in so they dutifully proceeded to the door marked "70s."

Inside, they found themselves in an attractive lobby with small glassed-in offices around the outside. "Welcome, 70s!" smiled an attractive receptionist as they entered. "Welcome to Spaceport America. May I offer you a beverage?" They were ushered to a plush booth and gushed over by a salesperson who was only too happy to equip them with what she assured them were the real necessities for a visit Earth.

An awkward forty-five minutes later that they emerged with new clothes and their own eardots. The clothes were simple jumpsuits— lavender for Marta, pale blue for Kessa—that were faintly perfumed and felt silky. They had tried to resist the peppercorn-sized eardots that you were bizarrely supposed to put into your ear, but the salesperson had insisted (correctly) that on Earth, the eardots' brainbox software was indispensable. Besides, purred the salesperson, the eardots came in lovely little cases.

Their funds account was, no doubt, charged some unfairly large amount for the visit, but neither of them had dared to ask how much. And anyway, though they didn't know it, the size of their funds account was soon to be the least of their worries.

■   ■   ■

The space station passageway opened out to a large, busy concourse dedicated to more shopping and personal services. Kessa found herself blinking and staring around the hall, feeling increasingly overwhelmed by the riot of new sights, sounds, people, and sensations. She felt as if she had been cast into a tossed salad of fictional objects, with nothing familiar and no anchor to stand on. Instinctively she reached out to Marta for a reassuring touch on the hand.

To Marta it was all new too, but for her it was more like a navigation challenge. Anxious to get down to the planet, she ignored as many distractions as possible and kept stopping and looking down at the floor and its blue-painted walking guidelines as she tried to get guidance from her brainbox, which she had named Millicent. Finally, Millicent understood Marta's questions and pointed her toward a promising sign: PLANET SHUTTLE.

"This way, Kessa," she said, pulling her sister's hand. "We take a shuttle down to the surface."

"Oh, that's right, they don't have a space elevator like New Gaia does. This will be interesting."

Marta led them in the direction of the sign, where a crowd was gathering near a large doorway. As they approached, Marta and Kessa began attracting looks. ". . . 70s . . . look at the blonde hair and blue eyes! . . ." Marta picked up. ". . . must be rich . . ."

Trying to ignore the unwanted attention, Marta pushed firmly forward toward what appeared to be the registration desk, towing Kessa behind her. But even before she could make it all the way to the desk, a prim young woman in the uniform of a Spaceport staffer intercepted them.

"May I help you, 70s?"

"Oh, hi," said Marta, smiling and pushing a loosened strand of blonde hair out of her face. "How are you? My name is Marta and this is my sister Kessa, and we'd like to take the next shuttle down to Calgary, please?"

The staffer wasn't having it. "I'm sorry, but I think there has been a mistake. I'm sure you would be more comfortable with a private orbiter. The orbiters are over there."

Marta held her nerve and persisted. "Oh, I'm sure the shuttle will be fine. When is the next one for Calgary?"

"I'm sorry, 75. I really do feel a private orbiter would be more appropriate for you. Let me signal for one . . ."

Even before the staffer could ewave a command to her brainbox, a handsome young man with dark skin and kinky hair, wearing blue and black orbiter livery, appeared. "Here I am," he smiled with a friendly air. "31 Stoke at your service, 70s. Our orbiter can take you straight to Calgary, no trouble. Do you have any bags? No? Okay, if you'll just follow me?" And Stoke cheerfully led a befuddled Marta and Kessa off toward the maintenance entrance.

It occurred to Marta to be angry, or to argue with this guy, but Stoke had a big toothy smile and a disarming way about him, and somehow she found herself talking cheerfully instead. "What exactly is an orbiter?" she asked.

"Mm, a private ship, I guess you'd say. Two pilots, and in this case two passengers. Your own personalized transportation."

"Sounds expensive."

"You can afford it," Stoke assured her.

"I can? How do you know?"

"That nice new 70-level jumpsuit you're wearing, for one thing. Plus, my brainbox told me."

"What, so your brainbox can tell how much money I have?"

"Roughly," smiled Stoke. "Jivey, my brainbox, asked your brainbox what your rank was, and your brainbox told Jivey, who told me. That's how things work here on Earth."

Something about this guy was making Marta feel unusually confident about herself, and she found herself replying with unexpected cheek. "Well maybe I should turn off the brainbox and go get us a ride on the shuttle?"

Stoke laughed good-naturedly. "I wouldn't do that if I were you. Rank is role, as we say here. Trust me."

"What a racket," mumbled Marta.

"What's a racket?"

"Never mind."

Kessa spoke up. "Why did we just pass the door that said ORBITER LOUNGE?"

"We have a private dock for you," said Stoke, smooth as ever. "Just a few more steps this way. My name is 31 Stoke, as I mentioned. And you are 75 Marta Dahlstrom and 75 Kessa Dahlstrom, I believe?"

Marta smiled. "That's correct! Brainbox, right?"

"You got it. Welcome to Earth, 70s. We are right outside this door."

Stoke led the way through the air-locking maintenance door and stepped as smoothly as possible onto the curb while hoping they didn't notice the MAINTENANCE sign and madly looking around for Jet to pull up in *Chica*.

■   ■   ■

Jet could hardly believe his eyes as he settled *Chica* in by the curb. There was Stoke waiting with the most perfect passengers he could imagine: two beautiful young women looking pleasant, eager, and rich—blonde and even blue-eyed—and they didn't have any luggage. What luck. One was tall, willowy, and slender and looked like she might be a dancer, wearing her hair loose and flowing; the other was not quite as tall, and curvier and relatively sober-looking, with her hair pulled back and a stiffer posture. Somehow, they both exuded a sense of optimism and openness that instantly appealed to him.

Jet deployed the hatchway and Stoke escorted Marta and Kessa up into the passenger compartment. Jet made a show of getting out of his pilot's chair and making arrangements for his guests. "Welcome to Earth," he said as charmingly as he could.

Marta, orienting herself to the new environment, gave Jet a slightly distracted look. "Oh, hello. Thank you."

As Kessa came aboard she went one way while Jet was going the other and they briefly bumped together. An unbidden shudder went up her spine. He felt strong and active. He looked almost like something from an Earth modeling poster—square-jawed and straight-nosed, several centimeters taller than even she was, with lovely brown skin and dark hair. His temples were a little too narrow to be perfect, but there was something about his quick brown eyes . . . how *aware* he seemed; how intelligent. She looked right up at him and couldn't help but smile. "Hello!" she felt herself saying in a slightly higher voice than normal.

Meanwhile, Jet's immediate instinct, barely suppressed, was to hug her. Her touch was soft and welcoming, and despite the Dip her hair smelled sweet, and her eyes: deep pools of the lightest clear blue water, full of depth and spirit.

Stoke made introductions. "75 Marta and 75 Kessa, this is your pilot, 34 Jet. Again, I am 31 Stoke, and welcome aboard the *Chica*. We'll be taking care of you on the short flight down to the surface. Now, are those seats comfortable? Is there anything I can get you? A sparkling water, perhaps . . . ?"

Jet's eyes caught Kessa's again, and for a fleeting, tingling moment he felt he had glimpsed someone from his own world. Not his planet; his *world*. The sequestered, private world inside his head. A person who was aware of more than usual. A person whose glimpse; whose eyes; whose even microscopic face muscle movements evoked something . . . well, he didn't know what.

Jet recovered himself quickly. Still cognizant that they were illegally parked in a maintenance zone, he moved back to his pilot's controls and began moving *Chica* away. "And where did you say your destination is today?" he asked over his shoulder.

"Calgary," Marta said positively.

"Okay, happy to. Which visitor quarters?"

"Oh, we're not staying there. We're going to visit our uncle out at a field station."

"Field station? I . . . I'm not sure I'm familiar with that destination."

"That's okay, I looked it up ahead of time. If you just drop us off at a port we can take aircars from there."

Jet cast a sidelong glance at Stoke. "That's not really how things work . . ." he stumbled.

Stoke came to Jet's rescue. "I think what Jet means, 75, is—"

"Please don't call me that. Marta is fine."

"Okay, thanks . . . Marta. Anyway, what I think Jet is trying to say is that we can take you to any port you want. That's one of the nice things about a private orbiter. What's your uncle's closest port?"

"My uncle doesn't live near a port."

"Well the sliders and lifts are very efficient here on Earth. It shouldn't take long."

"No, you don't understand. He doesn't live in the city."

It was Stoke's turn to look stumped. He looked back to Jet for help, but Jet just shrugged. He was trying to fly slowly to stall for time. "Then, where *does* he live?" Stoke finally managed.

"I told you. In the field. He's a field monitor."

"The ORGA Field Monitor for Southwest Saskatchewan," Kessa added in, trying to be helpful.

Stoke wasn't helped at all. "Can you tell me his name? My brainbox can find him for us."

"Galen Sjøfred," said Marta.

"Thanks. Ah, here he is. *22* Galen Sjøfred?" Both Stoke and Jet raised their eyebrows at the low rank number, but Stoke was tactful. "My brainbox says he's a field monitor, whatever that is."

"I've been telling you . . . !"

"Okay, and he lives out in the croplands. Here, I'll put it up on the map." A map appeared on *Chica*'s displays where everyone could see it. "It's . . . whoa, it's way out there. This is, like, 800 kilometers from Calgary. Is this right?"

"Yes!" sighed Marta. "Yes! That's where we're going!"

Stoke was still mystified. "But how does he live? That's in the middle of the soybean fields. Does he live on the ground? There's no city at all. Is there a settlement or something?"

"He lives in a house. By himself. It's okay. Look, can you take us there?"

"Uh, sure, we can take you there. No problem, right, Jet?"

Jet nodded. "No problem. Now can everyone check your retention nets, please? We're entering an airlock now and then we'll be going weightless."

Tappet's Office

68 Tappet was sitting at his desk when an assistant burst in.

"68, sir."

"What is it?"

"Per your instructions, we've been monitoring the net for mentions of 22 Galen Sjøfred. We got a hit, sir."

Tappet jumped out of his chair. "What is it?"

"It was a location query from a brainbox belonging to 31 Stoke Omroni. He's the co-pilot of a private CC orbiter. They're at Spaceport America."

"Spaceport? Galen is getting visitors? Excuse me. I have to go see Skervin."

Two minutes later Tappet was standing in Skervin's penthouse office, giving him the news. "What do you want to do?" Tappet asked.

Skervin didn't hesitate. "Stop the orbiter and arrest everybody on it. Lock them in a cell somewhere and don't let them out until this is over."

"Sir, the passengers are probably from off-planet. They might not know anything."

"Well they'll know quite a lot if they go visit his field station, won't they? They'll find out their friend is missing. They'll find something wrong in the fields. For all I know, he already sent them a message explaining the whole thing. And they're off-worlders, for God's sake. They're probably in on this. They could go broadcasting this to the whole universe. I'm telling you, I don't want any leaks. Get to them as soon as possible!"

"You realize they might be missed on their home planet?"

"Can't be helped. And Tappet, keep it quiet, ORGA only. Don't involve the Earth Force or Authority Police. We don't want any of the other agencies to hear anything about this."

"Yes, 96."

Chica, Spaceport America

Jet had maneuvered *Chica* into position beneath an outgoing lock on the "ceiling" of the loading area. Stoke gave a quick command and the mooring cables shot out and began reeling the ship up and inside the chamber. The cables pulled taut and the lower doors of the lock hissed shut, enclosing the ship once again in a temporary, airtight cocoon.

The lock began cycling, pumping precious air from inside the lock back down into the hangar below, evacuating the chamber to match the empty space waiting outside.

But suddenly the cycle stopped. There were several alarm bells, a flashing red light, and the unmistakable sensation of an automatic process suddenly halted in the middle.

Everyone aboard *Chica* jumped to attention. "What's happening?" demanded Marta.

"Looks like an emergency stop for some reason," Jet said, keeping his voice as even as possible. "Hang on . . . *Chica*, report status."

But before *Chica* could report, her speakers were overwhelmed by a disembodied, authoritarian voice. *"Livery Vehicle CC723: This is ORGA Enforcement. You are surrounded and being detained. Remain where you are."*

Video feeds piping into *Chica* from outside the lock confirmed it: there were two menacing, red ORGA ships—Raven 90 Patrol Craft—surrounding the lock now: one below in the hangar; another hovering above them in space.

Jet paled and looked over at Stoke, who was equally aghast. They'd been busted for their stunt picking up passengers at the maintenance door. This was not going to be good. Not good at all.

In the passenger compartment, Marta and Kessa were far beyond aghast. Marta looked nauseated. Kessa's head was spinning. She remembered her mother's warning from before they left, which sounded like a joke at the time: "Don't get arrested." But now that was about to happen. They were going to get arrested and shortly thereafter they would be connected to Galen. Galen would be in trouble. Galen, who couldn't afford any more trouble with the Authority. She pictured him in a prison cell. No! Kessa couldn't bear the thought of doing that to her uncle.

Every muscle in Kessa's gut tightened and every neuron in her brain sparked. She couldn't let it happen. She was going to fight. "Please!" she called out desperately. "Pilot—uh, Captain, Jet! Please, Jet! Don't stop. Get out of here! We *can't* be arrested!"

Jet hesitated. Everything had been going so well. He was on a roll. And now, suddenly, this? He was being arrested? It was unthinkable. It would be the end of everything. And this beautiful girl, 75 Kessa, was begging him not to obey? His mind was exploding. The situation was impossible. But it was not in his nature to give up on a challenge quickly. He needed a way out. His mind raced to think of angles and alternatives even as Kessa kept crying out, "Get us out of here!"

But there were the red lights, the cops on video, the insistent voice forcing its way through *Chica's* speakers: "*Shut down your power. Your vessel will be extracted back to the hanger.*" Jet had no choice. With huge reluctance, he reached for a special override button that had to be held down when he gave *Chica* the voice command: "*Chica,* power down."

Except, that's not how it happened.

Jet leaned forward and put his index finger on the override button, but when he went to speak, something else took over his brain. Looking back, he could never decide whether it was bravery, or cowardice, or taking pity on Kessa, or just blind adrenaline, but it overwhelmed and overpowered him. So instead of his words coming out "*Chica,* power down," they came out,

"*Chica, emergency escape! Blow the lock!*"

Instantly, there was a huge burst of power and then several explosions. *Chica* leapt to the command, ripping herself free of her mooring cables and hurtling toward the upper lock door. The door was closed, but *Chica's* violent motion caused automatic interlock safety circuits to trip. The door cracked open and instantly the air remaining in the lock rushed outward into space, blasting the door farther open just as *Chica*'s outer hull slammed into it, pushing with the full force of her engines. With a horrendous sensation of tearing and scraping noises, *Chica* crashed through the opening and ripped free into space.

The Raven 90 patrol craft hovering above the lock was blasted by shards of flying metal, and the shock of exploding outward forces blew it somersaulting backwards, spinning out of control.

Chica rocked uncertainly but then gained stability a few hundred meters out. In the pilot's seat, Jet was suddenly focused, pumping with adrenaline, and single-mindedly focused on his new mission: escape. "*Chica*," he commanded. "Immediate full thrust for the planet surface. Ride comfort override. Go now!" Once again *Chica* responded instantly, hurtling herself and her passengers fast and hard into a series of pitches and spins that shortly had her diving straight down to the nearest point on the planet, top speed.

Marta was screaming. Stoke was sucking in his breath, watching Jet and not sure what else to do.

And Kessa, if she had been paying attention, would have realized she was smiling. For a moment she wanted to climb forward and give Jet the pilot a kiss. But then she collected herself and started to cheer him on, instead. "Yes! Yes. Go! We can make it!"

Chica's speakers crackled with a weak signal. "*Livery Vehic... CC723, stop immediat... You are und... arres...*"

Stoke was on it with a command. "*Chica*, silence and ignore that transmission." *Chica* did.

Still, it was loud in the cabin as *Chica*'s engines screamed at maximum capacity. They were streaking through space at incredible speed, headed straight down toward the surface. The cabin, with dampeners turned off, was shaking and vibrating intensely. With the planet ahead and acceleration pushing them in the opposite direction, it was hard to tell which way was up.

Tappet's Office

Tappet was livid. "They did what?!"

"Escaped, sir," quailed the assistant. "The private orbiter they were in blew out a lock at the spaceport and disabled one of our cruisers. We're in pursuit now."

"They blew out a lock? This was supposed to be quiet, damn it!"

"Yes, 68."

"Does anyone know about this besides us?"

"Authority Police, sir. They patrol Spaceport America."

"Damn! Well quick, tell them it was an accident. And call off that pursuit. The last thing we need is a bunch of ORGA cruisers crashing into the atmosphere and attracting Authority Police and the Earth Force and who knows who else. Just track them. We'll catch up with them when they hit the ground."

"Yes, sir."

Chica

"Are they chasing us?" Jet called over to Stoke. His voice was tight with tension and his throat was dry. In the back, Kessa and Marta had quieted down and were sitting in frightened silence.

Stoke, who was still shaking but regaining a little of his native calm, checked two monitors and replied in an almost-regular voice. "I think the Raven 90 guy you blew over may be coming along now. Doesn't look like he's gaining very fast, though."

"Yeah, those space patrols don't like the atmosphere much," Jet observed, appearing to recover a little himself. "We're going to be swimming in air in a couple minutes now." He thought for a moment. "Then again, they're probably just lining up a welcoming party for us down on the planet."

"Oh, wonderful. A squadron of Authority cruisers waiting for us when we get to the surface?"

"That's what I'm guessing. Actually, that was ORGA Enforcement, not Authority Police," Jet observed in an ominously detached voice.

"Huh. I suppose they do a lot with immigration control," Stoke said, matching Jet's colorless tone.

Now both Jet and Stoke took on a sort of studied calm, trying not to shake, and barely containing the tumult inside both their hearts. They were in very bad trouble and they both knew it. And as the reality of their situation sunk in, there was utter silence from the passengers in the back.

"So they'll be waiting for us. Nice," said Stoke.

"Yep."

There was a long pause as they shot ahead, during which you could hear them both breathe. Finally Stoke said, almost carelessly, "So I guess you could back off the full-throttle descent then, Jet, if you wanted to."

"What? Oh, right. Sorry." Jet moved his body back from its hunched-forward position and took a breath before uttering a string of vocal commands to *Chica*. The ship, like its pilot, seemed to physically relax as she shifted out of emergency dive mode and slowed into a more careful pace and gentler descent path. "Nobody back there following us?" Jet asked.

"Not that I can see, anyway," confirmed Stoke.

"Yeah, okay." Jet raised his voice a little to make it clear he was speaking to everyone aboard now, passengers included. "So, we have a few minutes. Um, 27 minutes maybe, if I draw this out long enough. Time to do a little planning here."

"*Good!*" exploded Stoke, whose temper suddenly snapped and allowed him to start shouting furiously. "Good, because 27 minutes sounds like plenty of time for you to explain exactly what the freak you were thinking when you just threw my entire career away—and yours too—with that maneuver you just pulled! Jet, dammit! I mean sure, we were caught red-handed cutting the orbiter line. But that would have just been a fine or something, right? It would have been okay. But then all of a sudden you decide on *resisting arrest?* You listen to that pretty *fare* back there? You decide on blasting out of the space station and straight into an ORGA cruiser? Jet, you blessed moron, what the fuck were you thinking?!"

Jet reddened and went to shout back, but when he opened his mouth he didn't know what to say. He had always lived his life in complete control of himself and his environment, and somehow, for that one moment, he had lost control. The experience was beyond his comprehension. "Stoke, I was . . . I . . . I, I don't know what happened! She was begging, and I was worried about getting arrested. I don't know, I panicked! I was reaching for the button to power down and I . . . I don't know what." Blood was pounding in his temples, and bile was rising in his throat. "We are in so much trouble. We are so dead. Oh my god, what have I done?"

Leaning forward from her seat in the back, Kessa spoke. "It's not *your* fault," she said gently.

"Yes it is, I—"

"Damn right it is, Miss 75!" yelled Stoke. "What are you trying to do to us? This is serious, goddammit! Jet, tell her!"

Jet was shaking his head furiously but no words were coming out. "You— I—"

Kessa was staying calm. "You're right. I'm the one who begged you to do it. It's my fault. And anyway, *we're* the ones they're trying to arrest. Marta and me. We're the ones they're after."

Both Jet and Stoke were stunned. "What?" managed Jet.

"Look, I'm sorry! We had no idea it would be like this. We were hoping they wouldn't even notice we were here. You guys were just giving us an orbiter ride. It's not your fault."

For the next 30 seconds the cabin was filled exclamations and gapes, but no one could manage a coherent word.

Eventually, Kessa's sincerity sank its way in. Jet's pounding pulse slowed just a fraction and he tried to master his senses. "Let me get this straight, 75s. You're saying the Authority is trying to arrest you two? And my friend Stoke and I are just along for the ride? I think you better explain. And by the way, we now have less than 23 minutes."

Kessa's voice shook a little, but she managed to speak clearly and succinctly. "Our uncle Galen lives here on Earth. We're going to see him, only we were trying to keep it a secret. He doesn't—uh, he doesn't get along with the Authority, and we didn't want them to know we were here. But I guess they found out, so now they want to arrest us."

"But why?"

"I don't know! I just got here, I don't understand your rules. But why else would they be stopping our ship? I . . . I guess we should have let them. But I was afraid they'd find out about Galen and he would get in trouble."

Stoke snorted. "So you don't think they're going to find out now?"

Kessa said, "I know, I know. I guess they will. But I wasn't thinking. I just didn't want to get arrested. I'm . . . look, I'm sorry."

Jet could think of a million questions, but he consciously set them all aside and characteristically focused on actions. "Ah," he said. "Okay." After several seconds of mutual processing, Stoke and Jet found themselves trading a meaningful look. There might just be a way out of this fiasco after all.

Stoke was the first one to venture it aloud: "So, sorry about your uncle. But, listen, now that we're all about to be arrested anyway, I'm just wondering . . ."

"You want us to take the blame for running away?" Kessa offered. "Say we made you do it?"

Stoke simply grimaced, realizing the impertinence of his suggestion even in these dire circumstances.

"Seems only fair," Kessa breathed.

"What?" Marta objected.

"Honestly," Kessa said, "It does seem fair. These guys don't deserve all the trouble they're about to get. And we're foreigners. They'll have to treat us, you know, fairly."

"But Kessa!" her sister objected. "We're not the ones who blasted out of the space dock and sent that cruiser spinning."

"We're the ones they're after," Kessa said with a tone finality. "You guys, go ahead and give up when we get down to the planet. Marta and I will turn ourselves in. We'll tell the police it was all our fault."

Jet turned around and looked Kessa right in the eye, his brown eyes and her blue, both exceptionally clear and aware. He should be yelling at her right now, blaming her and scolding her and telling her how much trouble she had caused. But looking into those glistening eyes, all he could think about was how beautiful she seemed. Right then, the last thing in the world he wanted to do was turn her in to the Authority. "Tell you what," he said. "Let's just get away from the cops, and then we won't have to decide who gets blamed for what."

"What?" objected Stoke. "She just said—!"

Jet spun back to him. "She doesn't know what she's talking about, Stoke. The Authority's not just going to let us off the hook like that. If they get arrested, we do, too, for aiding and abetting if nothing else. We're in this together with them now. If we get caught right now, we're all done for."

"But Jet, what are we going to do? Where are we going to go?"

"I don't know! I don't know yet. But right now, we have to get away from these cops. We'll figure out the rest later."

Stoke emitted a loud, reluctant sigh. "I guess you're right. Damn this. Damn. But okay, let's do it."

In the back, Marta made a worried sound and Kessa took a deep breath as well. "Do you have a plan, Jet . . . er, Captain . . . er, what do I call you?"

"Jet," said Jet. "And no, I don't have a plan. All I know is we now have 19 minutes before we come into tracking range near the surface. Who's got ideas?"

"Well here's one," said Stoke, absently sticking his tongue between his teeth and poking a small tool into the instrument panel in front of him.

"Oh, poor *Chica!*" said Jet. He could tell where Stoke was going, which was the ship's tracking and navigation electronics module. *Chica* would still fly without being able to know where she was or where she was going, but, Jet imagined, she wouldn't enjoy it. Meanwhile, the Authority had just lost the ability to track and control them remotely. There was a popping sound and then a few sadly foreshortened chirps as Stoke snapped out the matchbox-shaped module and turned it off.

The distraction had given Jet a moment to think, and suddenly his lightning mind produced a plan. "Here it is," he announced. "We're going to hide."

"Hide *El Pico de Pato?*" scowled Stoke skeptically.

"Right. I'm going to pull up right now"—and as he said it, *Chica* began to slow her straight-down dive— "and skim along horizontally at 14 kilometers altitude, just above the tropopause. It's too low for space-based sensors and too high for ground-based ones. They'll have trouble tracking us. Stoke already took care of *Chica*'s tracking module. Now if we take care of ours . . . Sorry about this, Kimberly." Jet reached his right hand up to his ear and plucked out his eardot.

Stoke, looking uncomfortable, did the same. "How'm I going to get along without Jivey?"

"You'll manage."

"We take them out?" confirmed Marta, already tilting her head to one side. "How do you get it to let go?"

"Just tell it 'Release.' It has microscopic grippers that will let go."

"'Release.' Okay. Oh, all right, that works. Here it is."

Kessa had managed hers as well. "Do they turn off when you take them out?" she asked. "Will this turn off the tracking?"

"Oh, I hadn't thought about that . . ." Jet began.

"No, it won't," Stoke interrupted. "The tracking is always on."

Kessa asked, "So how do we stop it? Crush them?"

"No!" cried Jet and Stoke at once. Kimberly and Jivey were their friends. Jet knew what to do. "Anyone have a metal box?" he asked.

Marta perked up. "We do! They gave us these nice cases for ours. I think they're metal." She passed hers forward for Stoke's inspection.

"Yep, these are perfect," Stoke confirmed. Good thick steel with a tight seal. It makes a good shield. "Mind if I tuck Jivey in here along with yours?"

Marta smiled. "Sure, no problem. I named mine Millicent, by the way."

"Okay, and I guess that means Kimberly's in with Kessa's, if that's okay. What's yours called, Kessa?"

"Sven."

Stoke grinned mischievously, started to relax a fraction. "Great. Sven, you get to sleep with Kimberly."

"Hey, watch it!" chuckled Jet, despite himself. "Anyway, this is good. Now they can't find us through our eardots and they can't find *Chica* from her tracking module. As long as I stay at about this altitude, they'll have trouble with radar."

Stoke said, "Jet, there are plenty of other ways to find an orbiter."

"True, but as far as I know they'll all take a while. They'll have to bring a satellite online or send up a high-altitude aircraft. We should have a little more time, anyway."

"Okay, so now what?"

"Now we evade. As far as the Authority knows, we're headed for— what's his name?—Galen's field station in the croplands. We have to go a new direction where they won't be looking for us right away. Ideas?

"North Pole?"

"Fun idea, but we need a city. *Chica*'s going to be thirsty."

"Where are we now? Now that I killed the tracking and navigation and tracking module . . ."

"Approaching Paris, I'd say," said Jet.

"How'd you know that?" Stoke asked.

"I looked out the window."

"And you can tell just by looking?"

"I'm studying for my spacer license, remember? They make us learn stuff like this."

"Show-off."

"Think we should go to Paris?"

"Not really. I don't know anyone there."

"Me either. As a matter of fact, I don't know anyone anywhere, except for home."

"Denver? Yeah, me too. But you know they'll be looking for us there. They probably have our apartments staked out by now."

"Right, but we don't have to go to our own apartments. We'll stay with friends. Just for a little while, while we figure out what to do next."

Stoke turned back to Marta and Kessa. "70s? Is that okay with you? Denver?"

"It's your planet," shrugged Marta.

"Just as long as we don't get arrested," mumbled Kessa.

"Yep," said Jet. "That's the general idea right now."

Skervin's Office

Skervin responded to Tappet's briefing with the studied calm of an eagle being harassed by an ineffectual sparrow. He strolled slowly back and forth in front of the windows of his magnificent view, not letting his emotions interfere. Tappet stood erect, as always, in the middle of the room.

"Let me review the situation," Skervin said. "My former, er, 'colleague' Galen Sjøfred, who is now a 22 Field Monitor in Saskatchewan, starts asking too many questions about dead animals in the fields. We don't trust him to keep it quiet, so we fly a team out to take him in. But before we get there, he takes an unauthorized aircar out to the middle of what we discover is a small-animal death zone—probably a patch of soybeans infected with Toxin-X that kills animals just like it kills people. Then he disappears just before we arrive—as if he knew we were coming. Two hours later, someone at Spaceport America hires a private orbiter and asks for directions to Galen's field station. Do we know who that was yet?"

"Yes, we tracked it down. It's two young women arriving from New Gaia. Sisters, it seems. Temporary ranks 75 Marta Dahlstrom and 75 Kessa Dahlstrom. I have images here." Tappet brought up pictures on a glowscreen on the office wall.

Skervin flicked his active eyes at the images. "Mm, they're pretty. And you say they're Galen's nieces?

"That's what the DNA scans indicate."

"OK, so probably co-conspirators. We go to pick *them* up, but they commandeer the orbiter and blast their way out of there. Why, Tappet?"

"They didn't want to get arrested."

"Yes, but why? Why such a violent reaction? Most people sitting in an orbiter getting flashed down by two Raven 90s would put their hands up and go quietly."

"Don't know, sir."

"They must be desperate to connect with him. Rescue him, maybe. Maybe they're part of an entire terrorist organization. Did you get into his comms? Was he talking to anyone? Sending messages?"

"We're just sorting through them now. There were a number of p-caps."

"P-caps? To where?"

"New Gaia."

"Of course! He *was* plotting with them ahead of time. Have you listened to them yet?"

"No sir, they were being decrypted. I think they might be available by now, though. Shall I bring them up?"

"Yes. Show me the last p-cap he sent."

Tappet fumbled a bit, and soon an image of 22 Galen Sjøfred appeared on the screen. He looked concerned.

"Lana, hi. I'm excited to be seeing Marta and Kessa this afternoon. But this is about something else. I'm sorry, but it's important. Please look at these 3D scanner files and tell me what you think. They're from a patch of the soybean field ten kilometers from here, covered with corpses of small animals . . ."

By this time both Tappet and Skervin were turning pale.

". . . Here, I'll include the video I took. I have some carcasses and the nearby soybean plants here in these bags—can you see them on camera as I'm holding them up?"

Skervin, with a deathly look on his face, stopped the playback. "When was this sent?"

"Let me check. . . . Today, sir. About six hours ago."

"Can we stop it?"

"Stop a p-cap?"

"Yes."

"Sir, p-caps travel on interstellar vessels. Once one's gone, it's gone. All Alçubierres travel at the same speed, sir—you can't overtake one. Not to mention that we have no jurisdiction outside Earth orbit."

"I know, I know," Skervin snapped impatiently. "What I mean is, has it gone yet? Is the ship carrying the capsule still in Earth orbit?

"Let me check," said Tappet. His eyes rolled up slightly as he engaged in a long internal dialogue with his brainbox. P-caps were the domain of an independent organization called the Interplanetary Messaging Service, which had been established by an interplanetary treaty ratified by all Hundred Worlds on the principle that free and uncensored communication among the Worlds was a fundamental condition of a successful federation. There was no way to "beam" or "radio" a message across the vast distances between the Hundred Worlds. Electromagnetic waves traveling at merely the speed of light would take centuries to make the journey. P-caps, however, took just days. A message like Galen's to Lana traveled first along Earth's usual telecommunications network to an IMS service node, a highly secure building considered outside the jurisdiction of any host planet. Inside, carefully guarded machines transcribed the message in the form of a three-dimensional hologram onto a physical capsule, which was actually a tiny crystal less than a millimeter across known as a 'planetary capsule,' or 'p-cap.' Each message got its own capsule, and collections of them quickly accumulated like piles of salt, sorted by destination. Every time a spaceship certified as an IMS carrier departed for a distant planet, it took a canister of p-caps as cargo. At the destination, the crystals were read and decoded at another secure IMS facility and sent on their way.

IMS's operations were supposed to be private, but this was Earth. Tappet and his brainbox hacked into IMS systems quickly and without compunction. "I think I found it, sir. Sender is 22 Galen Sjøfred . . . receiver is Lana Sjøfred on . . . New Gaia, right? Don't hear about that planet very often. Sent this morning . . . Transcribed immediately thereafter . . . p-cap loaded onto ADS *Okafor* this afternoon . . . Looks like it's en route, scheduled to arrive New Gaia in . . . 73 hours."

Skervin pursed his thin lips and scowled. "Can we stop it?"

Tappet shook his head slowly. "Interfering with p-caps is highly illegal, not just on Earth but across the Hundred Worlds. There is no legal way to stop it."

Skervin looked down for a moment, thinking through actions and consequences. "And what is the illegal way?"

Tappet, contented to follow the lead of his superiors as always, answered evenly. "We may be able to intercept it before it arrives at New Gaia."

"How?"

"We can't overtake it, but the ship it's on is going to make a stop at the planet Hestia before it travels on to New Gaia. They call those routes to low-population worlds 'milk runs.' The ship just circulates all the time between the three planets."

"Excellent! So it stops at Hestia. For how long?"

"Hard to tell from the systems I can see, sir. A few hours, I'd expect."

"Very good, Tappet. We send a ship directly to New Gaia and it arrives before the p-cap does. We grab the p-cap before it's decoded and transmitted on their local network."

"Yes, sir. The timing will be close, but it's possible."

"What are you waiting for?"

"96, there is one more thing. In addition to violating interplanetary treaties."

"What?"

"There is no way to grab a single p-cap. They're all carried together in a canister. The only way to determine which one is ours is to decode them all. And that would require access to the IMS service node."

Skervin shook his head. "No, we can't invade an IMS service node. That would attract way too much attention. You'll have to destroy the canister before it gets to the service node on New Gaia."

"How, sir?"

"Grab the canister when it's being transferred from the ship to the surface."

"I see. Very good. 'Grab,' sir?"

"Okay, destroy."

"Yes sir. Sir, this is interplanetary. I'm going to need to get an Earth Force Intelligence agent involved."

"Absolutely not! Don't even think about it, Tappet. This stays completely within ORGA, you understand? If you don't have the people to do it yourself, use private contractors. Earth Force can't know about this. Ever."

"Yes, 96."

"Get on it."

"Yes, 96."

"And Tappet. Let me know as soon as your tracking data tells us where the Dahlstrom sisters are heading."

"Yes, 96."

Galen's Farmhouse

Galen heard the low rumble of an approaching agribot and decided it was time to move. He had been lying still in his body-width getaway tunnel for hours now. His aging bones ached all over, his left arm had fallen asleep, and the air was getting ominously stale.

He could still hardly believe the ORGA Enforcement raiding party hadn't looked for him in this escape tunnel leading away from the house. Maybe it was their modern city-rise culture: it was strange enough that his farmhouse was built directly on the ground, and practically inconceivable to them that someone would dig *into* the ground for a place to hide. Or maybe it was their habit of relying so absolutely on tracking brainboxes, which everyone always wore. Didn't Enforcement know there were ways to tamper with eardots? Galen's electronics workshop was well equipped, and over the years he had had many long nights alone to tinker. So when the P-17s were thundering in for landings in his yard this morning, it had been a quick task for Galen to deactivate his own tracker and turn on a fake one in the spare eardot he left on the table. Enforcement's entire reaction to his ruse was dumbfoundment, it seemed. They didn't have much imagination.

Still, they were undoubtedly continuing patrols, and he had to move. Slowly and carefully, suppressing a grunt, he squirmed another two meters along the tunnel until he was just below a trap door that led outside. Years ago, he had placed this door, covered with a layer of soil, in the middle of a well-used dirt road leading to the agribot pens. He just had to wait for one of the giant robotic tractors to roll by on its way to the vehicle barn, as one was doing now.

When the rumbling above reached a crescendo, Galen pushed up on the trapdoor, showering himself with dirt and revealing the hulking bottom of the agribot moving past just above. As fast as his stiff muscles would allow it, he clambered out of the tunnel and, still crouching, let the trapdoor swing back shut and hastily tossed a little dirt back over it. Before the agribot finished passing his spot, he grabbed onto the undercarriage, found holds for his hands and both feet, and pulled himself up. He clung on like a limpet to the bottom of the agribot as it trundled away toward its pen. Neither the patrolling guards nor the all-seeing satellite eyes far above were the wiser, and Galen enjoyed a free ride to a new hiding place.

Several minutes later the tractor parked itself at its usual station inside the cavernous vehicle barn a few hundred meters away from Galen's house and powered down. Galen gratefully loosened his grip and lowered himself to the ground. Very carefully, he moved enough to peer around the building from his odd vantage point on the floor, looking for threats.

None so far.

Any signal might give him away: heat the infrared satellites might see. Motion that could be detected by a tremble detector if they had one nearby. Sounds at any frequency that their scanners might detect. Luckily for Galen, dogs had been banished by the Authority long ago, because they would have found him in a minute. But Galen had to take some risks if he was going to get anywhere. Something awful was happening—he didn't know just what—and he had to do something about it. Though he didn't know that, either.

He rolled out from under his agribot and dug into his getaway pack for a calorie bar and his traveling clothes: a trench coat and a cowboy hat, chosen for their ability to hide him, at least a little, from prying satellite eyes. He still had a plastic bag containing his samples of dead animals and rotting soybean plants. The stuff inside looked horrible. He wondered if he still needed it, now that he had a 3D scan, which was recorded on a chip that was also in his bag.

He had to think. There was a plague out here that was killing all the animals in the fields. If it was going to infect humans, he had to warn people. Even if it wasn't going to infect humans, he still had to warn people. The soybeans were part of an ecosystem—diminished though it was in these agribot times—and without animals the system would rapidly crash. The soybeans would die, too, and the world absolutely depended on its soybeans. So, whom to warn? How?

Galen thought about ORGA. Shouldn't they have detected this outbreak by now? Well of course they had—that's why they were trying to arrest him. Even *they* wouldn't send a heavy enforcement team all the way from Calgary to raid his house just because of one unauthorized aircar trip. It had to be something really bad. They were covering it up, weren't they? Why else react so strongly? Yes, Skervin was in charge these days. A cover-up would be just his style.

Once he realized Skervin was behind whatever was happening, Galen suddenly realized what he had to do. Skervin was a madman. He had killed Galen's wife and daughter, he had set Earth back by decades with his Our World Our Way policy, and now, Galen was sure, he was in the middle of trying to cover up the outbreak of a deadly plague.

Galen could feel an old, long-smoldering fighting instinct deep inside begin to rekindle. He had been hiding out here in the croplands long enough. It was time to get back to Capital City and go on the offensive.

Chica, Near Denver

When thinking hard, Jet had an unconscious habit of tilting his head to one side and reaching up a hand to rub the back of his neck. Possibilities filled his mind and he sorted through potential threats and options at lightning speed. He was accustomed to doing most of his thinking for himself, because, as far as he could tell, his brain worked so much faster than everyone else's. But there were exceptions, like Stoke, who thought of angles Jet never would have, and occasional new acquaintances like, he was starting to suspect, the new fares sitting in the back. They might actually have some ideas.

"So the trick," Jet said aloud to his passengers, "is not attracting attention."

"And we do that how?" asked Stoke.

"Blend in. We'll stay at this altitude until we intersect the route of other orbiters descending from Spaceport America, then we tag along near one of them until we get down to Denver."

"Someone's going to notice that our tracker is off."

"Maybe if we stay near another ship it will be just enough distraction."

"Hope so."

"Stoke, is there some part of the computer you didn't kill that can calculate the trajectory for orbiters en route from Spaceport America to Denver right around now?"

"That would normally be the navigation system that I just zapped, but I still have some local systems working. Let me see . . . Here we go. I have waypoints and coordinates."

"Nice, but seeing as we don't have a navigation system, it's going to be kind of difficult to fly to particular coordinates."

"Sorry, that's all I've got."

"Alright, I'll use my nose."

Jet continued piloting *Chica* ahead, watching his displays intently and looking frequently around at the ground, the clouds, and the sky above. Stoke privately marveled at how Jet could make any sense of where they were now that *Chica*'s tracking and nav systems were disabled. All Jet had left were basic bits of information like speed, altitude, and direction. Stoke, who was accustomed to the detailed and sophisticated information provided by the ship's computers, felt completely lost in the endless expanse of the high atmosphere. But Jet seemed confident, so Stoke just sat back and trusted him. That was usually a good bet with Jet.

"Okay, somewhere around in here," Jet muttered, looking skyward. "Everyone look around, and let me know if you see another orbiter. It will probably look like a little white speck dropping really fast through the sky."

Stoke, Marta, and Kessa all leaned forward eagerly in their chairs and craned their necks to search the sky. A minute passed with no sightings. Jet mumbled a frustrated sound and started arcing *Chica* into a long, slow turn to begin circling.

"Still sure this is the place?" Stoke asked for reassurance.

"Pretty sure."

Just then Kessa sucked in her breath. "There! On my side. Down low."

"Right! I saw it too," Stoke agreed. "Moving fast. Four o'clock low."

Jet responded immediately, tilting *Chica*'s nose down hard and to the right. Everyone was thrown against their restraining nets. There was a long moment of disorientation, and then Stoke, looking out ahead, said, "Yep, that's it. Ten kilometers out, right in front us."

Jet gave a satisfied nod. "Okay, now to blend in."

For some reason, everyone took that as a command to hold their breath. They stared tensely forward at the ship they were now following, waiting for anything to happen. Nothing did, and gradually the tension eased and they began to breathe again.

"You know where you're headed on the ground?" Stoke asked Jet.

"I was thinking the maintenance hangar—"

But then their comm light blinked on and a pleasant female face appeared on the viewscreen. "This is Livery Vehicle CC27-Niner to the unidentified spacecraft approaching our stern. Please identify yourself."

Jet and Stoke shared a look. "Blend in," Jet told Stoke.

Reluctantly, Stoke touched a button and spoke back to the screen. "Good day, CC27-Niner. This is Livery Vehicle" —he grimaced, making up a quick lie— "CC873. How can we help you?"

"CC873? Where's 36 Vasquez?"

Damn. Wouldn't you know it. "Um, no, 36 Vasquez is off rotation today. I'm filling in."

"Oh. Is 38 Malinkatu still piloting?"

"Er, no. He . . . she . . . is off rotation too."

The woman on the display looked confused, but willing to be tolerant. Maybe it was Stoke's good looks. "Oh. Well anyway, your AIS is down."

"Oh, really?"

"Affirmative. We're getting no readings over here."

"That's strange. Our diagnostics show green. We'll have a look when we land."

"Roger that. Better be careful on approach. Earth Force is likely to blow you out of the sky and ask questions later if they don't recognize you."

"We'll be careful."

"Roger that. Have a good flight. CC27-Niner out."

"Thanks. CC373 out."

"CC373? I thought you said 873."

"Oh, right, sorry. CC873 out."

"Roger. Out."

The viewscreen went blank and Stoke shook his head. "That was smooth of me."

"Don't worry. It'll work."

"Hope so."

■ ■ ■

As Denver came into focus far below, at least one part of Stoke's brain finally began to relax: he knew where they were. *Chica*'s navigation screens were still blank, but Stoke could finally find his way just by looking out the window, the way Jet had been doing it since

Paris. The familiar form of the Rocky Mountains' Front Range was hard to miss, a north-south line of mountains jutting up at the edge of the flat plains to the east and setting the stage for the snow-capped Continental Divide not far to the west.

"There it is, 70s," Stoke announced to his passengers, "Denver, the Mile-High City."

"What does 'mile-high' mean?" asked Marta.

Stoke said, "It's the historic altitude. A mile was something like a kilometer, I think."

"1.61 kilometers," muttered Jet. Jet knew stuff like that.

They were already gazing out their windows. To Kessa, the city looked as if an immense machine made of black metal and glass had fallen out of the sky and landed in a heap of broken, harshly glinting pieces on the ground. It was almost hard to look at.

But Marta was fascinated by the alien city—its immensity, its geometry, and the mind-boggling idea of millions of people all living together indoors. She wanted to learn more. "How many cities like this does Earth have?" she asked.

"About a thousand," Jet answered.

"I guess that's a lot. But weren't there more cities in the past?"

"Centuries ago there were. Smaller cities, towns, villages, spread out all over the place. It was incredibly inefficient. People spent half their time just driving groundcars to get places. But over time the small places died out or were shut down by the Authority. Now we just have the big cities, and the rest of the land is used for growing food. It seems to work."

"So *everyone* lives in a city?"

"Just about. Except your uncle, I guess."

■ ■ ■

Tappet was feeling much better. Surveillance had finally gotten a fix on the fugitive orbiter over Denver. Their nav tracking signal was off, but radar picked them up and they were easy to identify from the mere fact they weren't broadcasting an ID. Tappet quietly dispatched two ORGA Enforcement T-2s to intercept, telling the pilots there was no need to involve local Authority Police at this time. It was . . . it was plant smugglers. Trying to smuggle in exotic food plants. Happens all the time. Definitely ORGA's jurisdiction.

■　■　■

With no warning an aircar flashed over Chica's canopy, just meters away. "Air cops!" Stoke shouted. "T-2s!" Before they knew it, another craft appeared on the other side as well, boxing them in. T-2s carried light armament—projectile guns and laser pulse cannons. They were short-range weapons, but they could do serious damage in a direct hit.

"That didn't take long," said Jet evenly. Looks like ORGA ships again. I can see the leaf logo."

"Not Authority Police?" asked Stoke. "That's weird."

"I think they're trying to crash into us!" Marta said urgently.

"Nah, just force us down," Stoke told her. "They don't want to cause a scene. We killed our comms so they can't yell at us over the speakers, so it's this instead."

"Pretty clear message," Kessa observed wryly.

Jet wasted no time at all. He seized manual control from *Chica* and banked hard and fast to the left, looping tightly around a building at its 65th floor. Despite its morphable wings, the orbiter didn't corner well and it took every ounce of Jet's skill to keep it simultaneously turning and in flight. All fibers of his attention focused on flying and cornering as fast and nimbly as he possibly could. Before the T-2s could react he was already heading in the opposite direction, dropping fast toward the ground and weaving expertly through Denver's forest of building towers and branches.

The T-2s tried to follow Jet closely for a minute or two, but they weren't crazy enough to keep it up as he dove and wove wildly through the three-dimensional city grid. With a short command, they pulled up and contented themselves with flying along above the rooftops, pinning him down and waiting for him to make a mistake.

Everyone aboard seemed to be holding their breath except Jet. "Got an idea," he said quickly, not moving his eyes off where he was going and making a sudden turn to the right. "Everyone get ready to bail."

"Bail?" Stoke asked.

"Yep. Don't worry, I'm going to stop first." Jet was talking as tersely as possible while he maintained his hellbent pace.

"Stop?"

"Yeah. We get to a hidden spot. We all jump out. *Chica* flies away on autopilot." A building materialized directly ahead and he shot up over it and then immediately back down again.

"Uh, okay," Stoke said, gathering himself up. "70s, you up for that?"

Marta wanted to be brave, and she sat up straight in her chair and reached out to give Kessa a reassuring touch. "Uh, ready. Right, Kessa?"

Stoke was already fiddling with *Chica*'s nav box, wiring it back up so she could fly on her own.

The T-2s were getting impatient and starting to worry about the rogue orbiter crashing into a building and doing serious damage. "We have to flush him out," said the mission commander to his partner. "You go down under him and I'll be waiting when he comes up high."

The city was a honeycomb of buildings. It was not just a collection of the old-time vertical spires that had dominated urban architecture in the days of one-dimensional up/down elevators and the constricting pull of ground-based transportation. Now horizontals were as common as verticals, and in an aircraft you were nearly as likely to find yourself *below* a long building wall as above or beside one. All Jet's plan required was a nice large plaza deep in the maze, with a horizontal building above it.

"Archibald Plaza?" Stoke asked Jet.

"Think so," Jet said, not even nodding. He turned slightly left, then down, then harder left and into a straightaway.

Archibald Plaza was just what they needed. Perched on the roof of a building 30 stories up, the plaza itself was a semi-outdoor urban park with fountains, sculptures, and a collection of small café tables. Walled on two sides and covered by another building above, it was open on the east and west ends, like a large, short tunnel.

At that moment a half-dozen people were scattered peacefully around the tables, enjoying some raw outdoor air and cups of late-morning coffee. They were totally unprepared for what happened next. *Chica* came screaming into Archibald Plaza from the east side, a space orbiter exploding into a space where it wasn't supposed to be. With roaring engines and an overpowering wash of air, it strained to a fast stop, hovering just off the ground and crushing a fountain and some sculpture-work below it. People at the tables were nearly knocked over and all turned to stare in amazement. The noise was deafening. Seconds later, the ship's hatchway deployed and first one, then three more young people tumbled out and landed in disarray on the pavement. One of them seemed to give a signal to the ship and it was immediately moving again, shooting out the other side of the plaza and disappearing into the maze of buildings to the west, leaving its recent passengers crouching in a huddle on the ground.

"Everyone okay?" Jet panted as he got his feet under him and looked around at his passengers, reaching out a helping hand to Kessa without thinking. "Good, let's go. Follow me. Run!"

The four of them raced across the plaza, dodging overturned tables and gaping onlookers, and made for a door on the south side. Thirty seconds after *Chica* had come screaming into Archibald Plaza, her four passengers had disappeared inside.

And seven seconds after that, a T-2 came roaring through the plaza, chasing *Chica*, who was already out of sight. The T-2 blew straight through, trying to gain on the fugitive orbiter.

"That worked!" reported the T-2 commander hovering high above to his companion. "You flushed him out. He's coming up high again, trying to make a run for it. I'm on him!" *Chica*, now on autopilot, came shooting up out of the urban gridwork, heading straight up. The T-2 pilot accelerated hard right at her, aiming to intercept. But the orbiter was finally doing what she was meant to do—fly into orbit—and the T-2 just couldn't move that fast. *Chica* shot past her pursuer and rocketed into the sky on the full power of her magnetoplasmadynamic engines, blue flames shooting from her tail. The T-2 pilot tried to pursue, but he knew it was a lost cause.

"He got by me."

Tappet, monitoring the action from his office in far-away Capital City, cursed under his breath. "Not to worry, T-2. We got his nav signal back. He won't get far."

■　■　■

During the first few minutes they were inside, Jet could only think about leading them away from Archibald Plaza. They found themselves in a broad, high-ceiling corridor that bordered one side of the plaza, separated by a wall of windows. Shops and storefronts of every description lined the opposite wall: clothing stores, electronics stores, drug stores, food counters, coffee shops. In the corridor here on Level 30, people were everywhere, some wandering in and out of shops, others hurrying through on their way to another destination. Neither Kessa nor Marta had ever seen so many people before in their lives.

With Jet running in front, they hopped on the first slider there was—a moving sidewalk with four parallel lanes in each direction. Kessa danced easily onto it without thinking, but her head was bowed as if to shut out the din and press of crowds. Marta stumbled slightly on the unfamiliar footing of the slidewalk and Stoke gave her a friendly hand.

Hearts racing, they pushed their way quickly through the crowds to the inside lane, which moved the fastest of the four parallel belts. Their pell-mell run slowed to an urgent jog and they shouldered their way past other passengers. They reached a junction and the slider came to an end, forcibly merging them by means of a diagonal railing to the slower lanes and finally off the slider altogether. Not hesitating, Jet led them dashing across to another slider. Once they were in the fast lane there, Stoke, still jogging and jostling his way along, found enough breath to speak.

"Jet, where are you taking us?"

"Away from the plaza."

"Yeah, but where *to*?"

"No idea. Without Kimberly, I'm completely lost."

"Me too."

"You're lost?" Marta worried as she jogged to keep up behind them.

"Uh, sort of," Stoke tried to reassure her. "I mean, not *generally*. Just, well, just specifically."

"Specifically?"

Jet ignored them both as he led them forward. "Watch it! Cops!" he called over his shoulder as he abruptly changed lanes. They slid past two official-looking women in red jumpsuits. Stoke looked purposely away but Marta and Kessa twisted their heads awkwardly, first having to look to see what a cop looked like and then trying to quickly avert their gaze.

Stoke tried manfully to reassure Marta. "We're fliers. We know the city from the air, but once you get inside all these buildings, it's kind of a maze.

"A maze? But you live here! It's your city. Don't you know your way around?"

"Uh . . ."

"Well aren't there signs or something?" It was just occurring to Marta that there *were* no signs. Everyone just seemed to know where to go. "Or, can't we just ask directions?"

Despite himself, Stoke almost chuckled at that. "We *would* be able to ask directions if we had our brainboxes on. That's the problem."

They were separated for a moment as they pushed through the crowds. "Well forget the brainboxes. Let's just *ask* someone!"

"No way! That would be a dead giveaway we're—" Stoke stopped himself. "You know what I mean." Fugitives, he meant. On the lam. Running away from the law. God, how had he gotten himself into this mess?

"Oh," said Marta abashedly, looking around to see if anyone was listening to them. "But surely one of these people would help us quietly?"

"Quietly?"

"You know, without telling the—" she lowered her voice to a whisper— "the police?"

"Nope. Even if we could find someone who was willing to break the law like that, it wouldn't matter. Everyone's brainbox is monitored and the whole conversation would go straight to Authority headquarters before you know it."

"Aargh! This whole place is insane!" Marta couldn't believe it. She wanted to go home.

Jet led them through a large set of sliding doors and into a turbolift full of other people. The inside of the turbolift was like a large elevator with windows on all sides. The lift car shot upward for a few moments and then slowed and smoothly switched to sideways motion, then shortly back to up again. When it stopped, the doors slid open and Jet led them back out onto a new level, this one in the 50s and notably more urbane. They found themselves, for once, in a quiet spot and stopped to catch their breath and talk, glancing around frequently to look for red-uniformed Authority Police. Kessa was looking relieved to be away from the crowds and noise, and for the first time she picked up her head and looked around at her companions, her eyes lingering longer than normal on Jet.

"Where are we now?" Marta asked Jet.

"Still no idea."

"But this is your city. Can't you find your way to, I don't know, your own house?"

"Apartment, you mean? Not from here. We're way over in Sector E now. It's a completely different part of the city. I have a good sense of general direction but no idea of the transport web. If we keep going randomly like this, it could take us hours to get anywhere." Jet paused for a moment, thinking. He hated to admit it—it was a weakness—but there was no alternative. He looked at Stoke reluctantly. "We need our brainboxes."

Marta asked the obvious question. "But didn't you say they could be tracked?"

Jet, keeping his eyes on Stoke, said, "Stoke may be able to help us there."

Stoke looked uncomfortable. "You realize that would be, you know, really illegal?"

"Like this isn't already?"

"Well, right, but . . ." He screwed up his face for a second. "Damn. Okay. But you're going to have to get me into a box shop."

"No problem."

"In the back, where the electronics workbenches are."

"On it. The 70s will help. Won't you, 70s?"

Marta's eyes got a little bigger, but Kessa nodded knowingly, starting to suspect there was a game afoot. "Okay. What do we do?"

■ ■ ■

All *Chica*'s autopilot system knew was it was supposed to go to altitude 14 km—the top of the troposphere at this latitude—and wait. This command came from *pilot_1* and therefore took precedence over the numerous other commands streaming in from the law enforcement systems of ORGA, Authority Police, and Earth Force. To carry out the command it had been necessary to deprioritize numerous other protocols including external hazard avoidance, collision detection, airspace management, and several others. She was shooting upwards on full thrust, passing 12 km, having left the T-2s in her figurative dust far below. The nav system, which had been unresponsive for some time, was now fully functional.

But now there was an alert at a priority level that could not be ignored: fuel load was critically low. She would barely achieve the commanded 14 km before fuel was entirely expended, and "waiting" there would be impossible.

Chica's artificially intelligent algorithms considered alternatives. Following the command from *pilot_1* took precedence over almost all else, but in this case adherence was physically impossible. Attempts were made to contact *pilot_1* for guidance, but all iterations failed due to as-yet-unresolved problems with the comm system. Pilot Intent Derivation subroutines returned ambiguous results except with respect to law enforcement commands, which were clearly meant to be set at low priority. This left *Chica*'s own self-preservation rules, whose precedence levels were set almost as high as pilot guidance, and there were numerous timings and weightings and likelihoods to be factored . . .

After several thousand nanoseconds of calculation, *Chica* made her decision. She slowed her vertical ascent, tilted over and downward, and headed for Denver Port 17.

■ ■ ■

"Good," Tappet said when the report came in that the fugitives were on descent. "I bet they're running out of fuel. 40 Alpha, 40 Bravo, when they get low enough, escort them to the ORGA Enforcement port."

A few minutes later, 40 Alpha reported picking them up. "But they're still not responding to comms and they won't deviate from their course."

"What is their course?"

"It looks like Denver Port 17."

Tappet frowned and thought about it a minute. He still didn't want to create a scene by shooting them out of the sky. "Okay, let them go to Port 17. We'll pick them up there." He made another call and directed an ORGA patrol unit to Port 17. "Arrest them quietly and get them to ORGA Enforcement as quickly as possible."

Section E, Level 70, Denver

31 Philip Soma, the well-dressed clerk at the baronial, rarely-visited, and currently-empty brainbox shop on Level 70 in Sector E, was mechanically polite when Kessa, Marta, and Jet walked in through his door. "May-I-help-you," he recited, and then gave a little start when he made eye contact with first Kessa and then Marta, admiring their blonde hair and sky-blue eyes. He gave Jet, who was wearing livery and looked like an assistant, a less friendly look. "I am 31 Philip. Your brainboxes aren't on, I notice."

"Well that's the problem," simpered Kessa, embracing her role as a fatuous tourist and starting to tug at her left ear. "We just got these at the spaceport when we arrived, and I don't think they're . . . well, gosh, you know, working right."

Philip gave one more quick look at Jet but then happily prioritized and turned his attention to the pretty young women. "Let's have a look."

He led them over to a velvety banquette and they all sat down at the table to discuss the troublesome brainboxes. Kessa sat first and took the seat facing the door, ensuring that Philip sat facing away. Philip offered chocolates and wine, but there were no takers. "Watching my figure," simpered Kessa. Jet was amazed at how easily Kessa slipped into character, all empty head and flirt and blonde hair-toss and accidental flash down the top of her jumpsuit now and then. She seemed to be having a ball. Philip had no chance.

Half a minute later, Stoke walked stealthily in the front door and slipped unnoticed through the curtains in the back, making his way to the electronics benches. Finding, to his relief, that no one else was there, he sat down at a station and pulled Kessa and Marta's ornate brainbox cases from his pocket. The station was well equipped with specialty computers, micromanipulators, magnifiers, tiny parts, and a Faraday cage workbox that blocked signals going in and out. This was all familiar to him; he worked at a bench just like this in the early days before his piloting career. It was a boring way to spend your days and it made your neck ache by the end of the shift, but, if you had a mischievous streak, and you were curious, and you happened to have a gift for electronics, you did learn a thing or two. Like how the Authority's tracking mechanism worked, for example. And how to disable it in a subtle way that would go undetected for a long time.

It wasn't simple—there were redundancies and encrypted command codes, and you needed to do the firmware update three times in a certain order to cover your tracks . . . But he got them. All four eardots. He actually smiled as he slipped Jivey back into his ear and felt the start-up sequence begin. "Hi there, Jivey!" he ewaved.

Stoke's procedures had taken maybe two minutes each. He carefully checked his station to make sure everything was back in place and stole quickly back to the curtains at the back of the main shop, peeking out to check on his friends. Kessa, with a little help from Marta, was still at it, laughing and flirting and telling improvised stories. They weren't even letting the clerk look in their ears yet, which of course was the whole point. Kessa was doing an amazing job, as if she had become a completely different person, but Stoke thought the clerk, whose back was to him, was starting to show some impatient body language. Stoke gave Jet a quick nod as he disappeared out the door.

Jet interrupted the conversation. "You know what, Kessa? I just realized—we have to go! Your mother is going to be waiting for us."

Philip was taken aback. "But your eardots . . . ?"

Kessa gave him a wonderful look suited perfectly to the moment. "Oh dear. I guess we'll just have to come back and get them fixed later!" To seal the sale, Kessa leaned out and gave Philip a kiss on the cheek. "You've been *so* helpful," she cooed. "Thank you *so* much for everything." That was all it took to distract Philip's attention from their sudden departure, and moments later Marta, Kessa, and Jet were all on their way out the door, leaving Philip behind, touching a happy finger to his cheek.

■ ■ ■

After they left, Philip decided he deserved a treat for his good service, and he nipped one of the chocolates he had offered to the girls. It was a filled dark chocolate raspberry truffle, freshly made by the fab. In a fit of self-indulgence, he popped the whole thing into his mouth at once. It tasted . . .

But he never found out how it tasted. The toxin in the food was immediately absorbed through the skin in his lips, tongue, and throat, where it invaded his peripheral nervous system, attacking nerves and glia and setting off a catastrophic cascade of signals that spread rapidly to his brain, causing immediate, massive tissue damage. There was an accompanying complete breakdown in the immense yet delicate pattern of chemical and electrical brain signals that seconds earlier had been the personage of 31 Philip Soma, including but certainly not limited to his ability to appreciate the flavor of dark chocolate raspberry. His eyelids sagged, his face muscles went slack, and then his entire body seemed to melt from the top down. He collapsed in a heap on the floor, never to move again.

Tappet's Office

68 Tappet was waiting for the call and he looked expectantly at the ORGA patrol squad leader on his viewscreen. "Got them?"

"Livery Vehicle CC723 is in our custody, 68. But there's no one aboard."

"What?!"

"No one aboard, sir."

Tappet threw a fist in the air in frustration. Damn! Damn it! There was a slack feeling in his belly. What an idiot he had been. Of course! They had bailed out at Archibald Plaza! He'd been chasing an autopilot for the last 15 minutes.

He turned to his assistant. "Do we have their tracker signals yet?"

"Nothing, 68."

"Damn it!"

Tappet sighed and faced up to an uncomfortable necessity. He pinged Maggi at Skervin's office and requested five minutes as soon as possible.

"Good news or bad news?" Maggi asked.

"Not good."

"You better come up right now," Maggi replied.

A minute later 68 Tappet was standing in front of 96 Skervin's desk, giving his report as factually as possible. Skervin scowled and felt a rising anger in the back of his throat, but he contained it with one deep breath. "Tappet, you have to do better than this! We can't afford this kind of blunder, and you know it."

"Yes, 96."

Skervin sighed. "We have to involve the Authority Police now. Tell them we have smugglers on the loose."

"They'll need more to go on than that."

"Yeah, I suppose. Put their names and ranks and face scans out on the net. Might as well admit we can't find their trackers. Don't give anyone any more detail than that. It's an ORGA matter."

"Yes, 96."

Sector E, Level 70, Denver

"Kessa, you were brilliant!" complimented Jet.

"Yeah, Kessa. I didn't know you had that in you!" said Marta, sounding genuinely surprised.

Kessa smiled a little shyly and snuck a look at Jet. "It was actually kind of fun."

"Thank God, I feel whole now that Jivey's back," Stoke sighed when he rendezvoused with the others a short distance away from the box shop and the others were putting their eardots back in their ears. "I can talk to people again." Unlike his friend Jet, Stoke didn't spend a lot of time having conversations inside his own head. He preferred the company of other people and the energy and stimulation they provided. When friends weren't around in person, it was Jivey who put him in touch via individual messages, group posts, and endless chats full of news and gossip and jokes. Jivey was also his trusted source whenever he needed to look up a fact or analyze a problem— well, either Jivey or Jet. It would be fun to run a contest between Jivey and Jet someday and see who was quicker. Stoke's money would probably be on Jivey for facts and Jet for analysis. Jet was crazy smart, and even though he was humble about it, it tended to show. Whether that made him arrogant or intriguing was in the eye of the beholder, but Stoke liked it. Jet was always full of interesting ideas, which Stoke enjoyed. It helped, too, that Jet always had a plan. His drive and focus were, Stoke had to admit to himself, just what Stoke needed. If not for Jet, Stoke would probably still be having a grand time living a directionless life as a 27-rank and working in the back of an electronics store, not really getting anywhere, and spending all his energy on girls and booze. I'm better than that, Stoke thought, and I'm going places now ... Assuming, that is, we can get out of this mess without losing our jobs and landing in prison.

Jet smiled about Stoke's brainbox making him whole. "Me, too. And now that we know where to go, let's get moving." Turning quickly away from a red-uniformed cop across the corridor, he led the way for the four of them once again, moving quickly but not running, this time with a confident step and no hesitation at intersections.

Kessa was fussing with her ear. "Do I really have to wear this thing?" she asked Stoke.

"It will help avoid suspicion. I turned off tracking, but it's still giving out a fake name and rank and such. People here expect that."

Kessa scowled. "Okay. But I'm not going to talk to it. It's too creepy."

Stoke cracked his white smile and said, "Fair enough."

"Where are you taking us?" Marta asked Jet.

"The New Gaian Consulate here in Denver. I'm sure they can take you in and find your uncle Galen. Kimberly says it's in the Diplomatic Quarter—Sector C, Level 40."

Now that they had a specific destination their progress was fast, and Marta remarked on how efficiently the city's three-dimensional transport network really was. They took slidewalks for short links and high-traffic areas, and turbolifts for longer links and vertical transitions. Their route was calculated and constantly updated by Jet's seemingly omniscient brainbox Kimberly, who knew not just which turns to take, but exactly when a turbolift would arrive and even, it seemed, where crowds would part. Thus the experience of rushing to the consulate across kilometers of a crowded, honeycombed, 160-layer city was one of walking quickly along fast-moving sliders, transferring smoothly to turbolifts just as they opened their doors, and being whisked easily toward the destination.

At least, that's what Marta was thinking. Kessa, on the other hand, had a vicious, throbbing headache. The city was assaulting every sense she had; harsh, loud, bright, pushy, smelly, unrelenting. People were everywhere. Jet was rushing them too fast. The ubiquitous artificial lighting glared and intruded. There were too many noises, especially the metallic and screechy ones. Her eyes ached and she wanted to cover her ears. She longed to curl up in a ball on the moss under a tree in the woods somewhere.

"Diplomatic District," Jet announced as they stepped off their last turbolift. They found themselves in a huge atrium with sunlight penetrating down from skylights 20 levels above. The atrium was overlooked by ranks of balconies that led to office suites housing the Denver consulates of the 99 other worlds.

But as Jet, Stoke, Marta, and Kessa stepped away from the turbolift and began taking in the sights and sounds of the breathtaking space, it took all of eight seconds for the first Authority Police officer to get a good look at the little cadre. As Officer 35 Hyung focused her gaze, her electronic contact lens automatically processed the images of their faces and, within milliseconds, identified them as fugitives. "Alert!" Hyung's brainbox told her. "Active fugitives. Disable and detain immediately. They are interplanetary smugglers."

"Halt!" Hyung yelled, reaching for the weapon at her belt.

But Jet was a second ahead of her. He was already throwing out his hand and yanking his friends backwards. "Run! Turbolift!"

Together they half ran, half dived back toward the turbolift doors, pushing and falling over the last few passengers who were still disembarking. They tumbled into the turbolift and into a jumble on the floor just as there was a *pfftt* from Hyung's electropulse gun. Marta screamed in pain. The turbolift doors whisked shut and the car began moving.

"Marta!" Kessa cried. "What is it?"

"My legs! They shot my legs! Arrgh! It hurts!" She was doubled over, grabbing her thighs. Tears were streaming from her eyes. The two turbolift passengers who had gotten trapped in the middle of the chaos had flattened themselves against the wall and looked on silently, utterly horrified.

Kessa bent over Marta's legs, looking and feeling for damage. She felt devastated. It had been her job to keep Marta from harm, and now this. She wrapped her arms around Marta's shoulders and said, "I don't see any blood, though?"

Stoke looked on. "It's electropulse," he said gently. "An e-gun. No blood, but it hurts like hell and you can't move. Is it just your legs, Marta? Both of them?"

Marta nodded slightly through a pained grimace.

"That's actually good," Stoke said comfortingly. "It could have been your whole body. You must have dodged part of the beam."

Jet gave Marta a sympathetic look, but he stayed all business. "We have to get her someplace safe. And fast! The cops are going to find this turbolift and reroute us any second." With that he smashed a glass plate in the wall with his elbow and pounded the emergency stop button with his fist. The turbolift, which had been moving horizontally, braked hard to a stop and the doors quickly retracted. They were out of alignment with the nearest gate, but there was a thin vertical opening, just barely large enough to squeeze through, leading into the building.

"I'll go first and check outside," Jet said. He crammed his trim body through the opening, disappeared for a second, and then poked his head back and reported all clear. "Let's get Marta out next."

Marta's legs were useless. Kessa and Stoke lifted her upright anyway and hefted her over to the opening. They turned her sideways, and she reached her arm through and stretched it as far as she could around Jet's waiting shoulders. Then, painfully and awkwardly, she struggled the rest of her torso through the narrow opening. Outside, Jet held her as best he could and dragged her hips and legs through, and then he laid her gently on the floor outside. Kessa and Stoke squirmed through after them. They all crouched over slightly, panting from exertion and stress.

Stoke looked anxiously up and down the near-empty corridor and then at Jet. "Now what?"

Jet pursed his lips and spoke directly to Stoke. "You think Ricker would take us in for a while?"

"Probably."

"Yeah, I think so too. Of course, he might give us away by accident."

Stoke gave a wry smile. "I'll comm him." With that he rolled his eyes up the way people do when they're contacting someone via brainbox, and a minute later he was nodding at Jet. "Okay, I told him we're coming."

Jet tilted his head. "Did you tell him to keep it quiet?"

"Yeah, I told him it was for a birthday surprise."

"Whose birthday is it?"

"No one's."

"Ah. Good idea."

"Now what about Marta?" Stoke asked.

Marta broke in from her place on the floor. "I'm so sorry about this. Do you all want to just go on without me?"

"Don't be ridiculous," Stoke chided.

Crouching next to her pain-wracked sister, Kessa couldn't help but ask, "Is she going to be all right?"

Jet responded. "Absolutely. It wears off after a few hours. No long-term effects. We'll find Galen, but we just have to get to someplace safe for now. 29 Ricker's a friend of ours; he's going to let us stay at his place. The only question now is how we get there."

"Should we rent a roly?" Stoke wondered aloud. They had seen one on their way here: a sleek, self-balancing wheelchair navigating its way along the edges of a crowded corridor.

Jet shook his head. "I don't think so. Ricker's place is kilometers from here. Rolies are great but they're slow through crowds. I think we have to risk an air taxi. And we better get moving, fast."

Stoke and Jet carried Marta—one on each side, with her arms around their shoulders—in a half-jog down the corridor and out to a slider. They had only a short way to go before arriving at an air taxi pier. The pier was little more than a large, outdoor, covered balcony accessed by sliding glass doors. They stepped out onto it and found themselves 40 stories above ground, looking out into the city's forest of buildings. There was a bench and Jet and Stoke gently lowered Marta down onto it.

"So it's a flying taxi?" Kessa queried.

"Kind of," Jet confirmed.

"Jet used to be an air taxi driver," Stoke added.

"Uh-huh," Kessa nodded. "So why do you look so worried, Jet?"

"The Authority monitors taxis very closely. They'll get facials on us the moment we climb aboard." He paused for a moment. "Everybody keep your heads down when it comes. I think I know where the cameras are. Let me go in first and I'll cover the lenses or something."

Having been summoned by Stoke's brainbox, an air taxi came swooping up to the pier from the airspace below. Per plan, Jet slid into the passenger seat at an odd, camera-avoiding angle, made a couple of quick motions, and then reemerged all smiles to help load Marta aboard.

The taxi driver, whose mind was dulled from years of tedious routine, seemed none the wiser, and after a short, sedate flight through the three-dimensional air lanes of the city, they alit on a pier near Ricker's apartment. The driver mumbled his usual question: "Whose account shall I use?"

"Oh, this is a medical," Jet said off-handedly. "Didn't you see my friend is hurt? Just code in 4562."

"You know the codes?"

"Yeah, I used to drive a hack myself."

"Hmph. So it's a 4562 on her account?" said the driver, nodding his head in Marta's direction.

"No, 4562, but not her account. She's my passenger so actually it has to be on my employer's account." He spoke both quickly and cheerfully, as if there were a lot of details that were nothing to worry about.

The driver was looking addled. "Your employer?"

"Yeah," Jet continued blithely. "America Direct Orbiters. ADO. I think it's Alpha Foxtrot 617728."

"I don't need that. The box will tell me."

"Yeah, well it's something like that. Maybe Alpha Charlie, though. 617528."

"So you're saying it's supposed to be coming up with an Alpha Foxtrot something?" The driver was looking at his screen with a scowl.

"Yeah, or Charlie. 617028."

"Didn't you just say 528?" The driver was trying to key something in, but Jet kept interrupting.

"Oh, right, 538, with the Alpha Charlie, probably. And don't forget the medical code, the 4652."

"Ain't medical 4562?"

"No, no, 4652. But that's not the same as the 671138."

By this time the rapid string of confusing numbers had made the driver lose all focus and his simpler instincts kicked in. "Space it! I'll just make it a 9000."

That was the code for "Customer Satisfaction – Other." In other words, the fare is so pissed off I'm just going to take off and not charge him. Air taxi drivers got crap from dispatch for using 9000, but they did it anyway. No big deal.

"You sure?" Jet said, feigning surprise.

"Yeah, get out of here."

A few moments later they found themselves standing on the pier, still holding up Marta and watching the driver fly off, shaking his head.

"Nice one, Jet," said Stoke.

Near Galen's Farmhouse

Galen had fired his spirit to go to Capital City and do battle, but then his mind intervened with practical realities. He was still pinned down in a vehicle barn, probably surrounded by ORGA Enforcement patrols, 800 kilometers from the nearest city, 3200 kilometers from Skervin's office, lacking any form of transportation, and being spied upon day and night by satellites high above.

Okay, he told himself. Stay calm. One step at time.

Stealing away in an aircar was his first idea. He'd sneak into one of Enforcement's P-17s, or maybe even his own sluggish aircar, and get away before they caught him. No, too risky. Very low probability of even getting off the ground, not to mention making it to a city.

Hitching more rides on the bottom of agribots? No, too slow and painful to make it 800 kilometers.

Then he had it: supplies. In addition to all their other functions, the agribots fed the soybeans with a steady diet of fertilizers, pesticides, and weed-killing herbicides. These were imported in bulk from distant factories, sometimes by pipeline, but often by transport tractors that trundled along across the vast fields with long trains of supply cars towed behind them. They moved pretty fast. There was a delivery and storage depot a few kilometers north of Galen's house. If he could get to that safely, then he could stow away on the next transport tractor that came along and be in Calgary or Lethbridge—he wasn't quite sure where the things came from—in a day or two. It would have to do.

Galen looked at the hulking agribot that had brought him here to the vehicle barn. It had brought him this far safely; it could probably take him a few more kilometers in the same way, with him clinging unseen to its belly. The problem was that it had a mind of its own, following routes and procedures that came from ORGA computers in the sky and its own primitive artificial intelligence. He couldn't just tell it to drive to the storage depot; it wouldn't take orders like that from him. No, he would have to trick it into deciding to make the trip itself.

Cautiously, Galen approached the beast and climbed up its side to the station where a person could look at its simple diagnostic display. Its pesticide fluid tank was getting low. Perfect.

Breaking the tank open wouldn't do; the agribot would detect the major damage and call for help (which, ironically, would normally come from its human field monitor, Galen). Instead, Galen hunted furtively around the vehicle barn until he found a good old-fashioned screwdriver. He went back to the agribot and, thinking hard about exactly where to strike, drew back and stabbed a hole in the pesticide tank. A small stream of dangerous-looking green fluid came spurting out and started dripping down the side of the agribot, forming a puddle on the floor. It was a small leak that, Galen hoped, would go undetected by the agribot's self-monitoring routines. But at some point, the agribot's little brain would decide it needed a refill and it would head for the storage depot up north. As Galen looked at his little stream and then up at the huge tank above it, he realized it was going to take hours. Just as well, he thought. Less chance of detection. He settled in for a long, tense wait, thinking alternately about stopping the plague and how much he hated 96 Skervin Hough.

Diplomatic Quarter, Denver

Officer 35 Hyung stood in front of a blank wall, looking at an image of 68 Tappet in her lensie. "I got a shot off," she reported. "I couldn't see if it was a hit before the turbolift door closed."

"Did you follow them?" Tappet demanded.

"Their trackers are off. No way to know which way they went."

Tappet threw his hands in the air in frustration. "Damn it!" Cops were so dependent on trackers they had no idea how to think for themselves. "Where was the turbolift headed?"

"Uh, not sure, 68, sir."

"Well, were there any disturbances in your vicinity in the next few minutes?"

"Other disturbances, 68? I guess I'd have to check . . ."

"So check then! Damn it!" And Tappet abruptly signed off.

His assistant looked on with concern. "What do you want to do, 68?"

"We just have to stay on them. They can't stay this lucky forever."

Skervin's Conference Room

Skervin had reconvened his Toxin-X task force. Kapcheck was looking dejected again. He had no new developments to report on funguses, viruses, or parasites, and he knew full well his 29-day clock was ticking. Eyeing Perka, Skervin said as little as possible and moved quickly to the next item on his agenda.

77 Stasik, the white-headed chief of Production and Distribution, stood up and walked sturdily to the display screen as Skervin, Ettica, Perka, Kapcheck, and Sybil looked on. "It wasn't easy to do it this fast, but we now have rats sampling the Nutribase feed in most of the production plants. We can detect anything toxic and shut off the feed before it flows out into distribution. Remember, though, the system is imperfect. There are still going to be small bits of product that we miss; nothing we can do about it.

"But the bad news is, we have some dead rats. And what that means is, we've had our first plant shutdowns." Stasik gestured toward a map on the glowscreen. "The first one was here at the Zimbabwe installation, which serves a large portion of the African distribution system including Harare and Pretoria. The second was Brasilia, which serves São Paulo and Rio de Janeiro, among others. Now fortunately, the system is a self-healing network with many alternate routes, so we've been able to make up the shortfalls from the closures with supplies routed in from Botswana and Argentina, respectively."

"See, Stasik?" said Skervin with satisfaction, "Rerouting from other factories makes up for the temporary closure, just as we designed it. You didn't have to worry."

Stasik frowned. "But I have to say, it puts a lot of stress on the system."

"What do you mean by stress?" Perka asked.

"Stress on our ability to deliver product to end users. The system is highly efficient—finely tuned, you could say—but that means there is very little excess capacity. Taking those plants offline reduces total supply and brings us close to the point where we don't have enough Nutribase to go around."

"Better than sending out toxic Nutribase, though," observed Ettica.

Skervin said, "You better clean those plants and get them back on line fast, Stasik."

"Of course."

Apartment B-14-2911A, Denver

It was not far from Landing Pier B-14-29 to Ricker's apartment. Jet and Stoke carried Marta along between them again with Kessa tailing closely behind. Here on Level 29, the halls were a little smaller and less well-lit than the public spaces in the 40s they had just left. There were just as many people.

They found their way to into a residential section and toward a nondescript door, which opened for them as they arrived. 29 Ricker was waiting inside, sloppily dressed and apparently still not worried about the bangs in his eyes.

"Whose birthd— Whoa! Is she okay?"

"Heya Ricker," Stoke said as the door slid closed behind them and they made their way into the one-room apartment. He tapped his ear twice in the universal gesture that meant 'please turn off eardot recordings,' and Ricker complied. "This is 75 Marta Dahlstrom, and this is her sister 75 Kessa. They're from the planet of New Gaia. Can we uh . . ." he hesitated, nodding his head in the direction of Ricker's junk-covered sofa.

"Oh, right, sorry." Ricker grabbed an armful of stuff and moved it unceremoniously to the floor. "Here you go. What happened?"

Stoke and Jet lowered Marta onto the sofa and then stood up, massaging their shoulders. With a warning look from Jet, Stoke was careful in his reply. "It was an accident. She was just, uh, we were just walking along and the cops, they, uh, they were chasing somebody. Yeah. And they missed the guy and they hit Marta instead." Marta and Kessa kept their faces impressively expressionless through this blatant lie.

"E-pulsed! Whoa. That hurts like hell. I been a couple times. My drinking buds, too. It gets better, though."

Kessa said, "Is there anything we could give her? Do you have any analgesic herbs or tea?"

"I got vodka," Ricker offered. He seemed to be taking notice of how pretty and blonde his new visitors were.

"Vodka?"

"It's alcohol," Stoke translated. "Regular painkillers don't help with electropulse because of the way it works, but vodka might take the edge off."

Marta shook her head, and Kessa said, "Oh, no thanks." She was feeling too delicate for drinking. She ran her fingers through her hair as a way of relaxing and said, "How about hot chocolate?"

Ricker wasn't familiar with hot chocolate, but his brainbox was. His eyes rolled up for a second and then he said, "Okay, hot cho-co-let. Coming up. Anybody else want some?" He walked the few steps to the kitchen corner of his one-room apartment, where a slightly dingy fab filled most of the space. He pulled cups from a cupboard and slid them into the machine, then recited "two hot cho-co-let." The machine made a few rumbling and hissing sounds and then dinged, and Ricker reached in and pulled out two brimming cups of delicious-smelling brew.

"That's amazing!" said Kessa as she accepted hers. "How does it work?"

Ricker gave a little shrug and looked in Jet's direction. Jet casually obliged. "It's molecular recipes. If you think about it, most food is a combination of water, carbohydrates, proteins, fats, and the five flavors our taste buds can detect. The food fabricator—fab, everyone says—takes in raw ingredients—mostly water and something we call Nutribase—rearranges them at the molecular level according to the recipe, heats them or cools them or whatever, and outputs food that looks and tastes a lot like the primitive version did."

"'Primitive'?" Kessa raised a suspicious eyebrow.

"Okay, like the version made from naturally grown materials," said Jet more carefully.

"What's this Nutribase made out of? Unnatural materials?"

"Hah, no. It's mostly soybeans. They're natural, I'd guess you'd say. It's just that we don't use them in their primitive form."

"There you go with 'primitive' again!" Kessa seemed to be getting slightly angry.

Stoke was laughing at the exchange and Marta, playing the peacemaker, broke in. "Well wherever this comes from, it tastes delicious. Thank you, Ricker."

Kessa took a sip and, though she was privately suspicious, nodded politely in agreement. "Does it make alcohol, too?"

Stoke grinned slyly. "That would be illegal. Technically it's easy, but they lock it out in the control circuitry."

Ricker nodded in conspiratorial agreement. "Too many problems with abuse. Of course, Stoke knows how to override it. But me, I get my vodka from a separate source."

Kessa figured he meant some kind of black market, but she didn't pursue it. Her head was already overfull of information about this strange world.

"Hey Ricker," said Jet, helping his friend with manners. "Think we could get your fab to do some more work? I don't know about the girls, but I'm starving."

"What? Oh, sure, yeah. No problem. What does everyone want?"

Several minutes later the five of them were sitting around Ricker's apartment, perched wherever they could find a seat or clear piece of floor, feasting on the traditional Earth delicacy called pizza and drinking what Stoke and Ricker swore was non-alcoholic beer. Ricker gave an enthusiastic account of the flash-pick-up power-disc game he had participated in that afternoon, in which he and 21 other people who had just happened to feel like playing right then had found each other in the vastness of the city and self-convened for a game 20 minutes later. Marta was particularly impressed, thinking of how events like that were one of the many advantages of living in an immense, well-organized, well-connected city.

Kessa was finally feeling more relaxed. "Now somebody has to explain to me this whole thing with numbers in front of your names."

Stoke laughed. "Jet's the explainer."

Jet gave a modest shrug, but when he made eye contact with Kessa he couldn't help smiling, too. He was still trying to make sense of her. His brain knew he should be suspicious of her after she got them into this whole mess by begging for escape from the spaceport, but his heart kept feeling differently. For the moment, he pushed the thought to the back of his mind and answered the question. "Rank, we call it. It's just a way of telling people's position in society. 1's the bottom, 100's the top."

"Position in society? What does that even mean? How is it determined?"

"Combination of things, I guess. Professional occupation and position in the hierarchy, reputation, wealth, age, family. Maybe some other minor factors. There's an algorithm."

"An algorithm?! You mean it's calculated by a computer?"

"Uh-huh."

"And whatever the computer says, that's it? That's your position in society? Can it ever change?"

"Definitely. It's continually updated. Ricker here is going to get his 30 any time now, aren't you Rick?"

"Hope so."

"How? What for?"

"In Ricker's case, it'll be a promotion at work. Income is a big factor. The rule of thumb is income doubles with every decade of rank. But it could be educational certifications, or fame, or influence, or making more money, or who you marry, or a lot of other things."

"Who you're married to matters?"

"Sure it does. Also who your parents are, and your whole family."

Kessa was taking this all very skeptically, and Jet was starting to feel defensive. Stoke tried to insert himself and spoke too quickly. "Yeah, ask Jet about that one." He regretted it as soon as he said it, but Kessa was already looking at Jet inquiringly. Seeing the look on his face, her tone quickly changed to something more sympathetic.

"What, Jet?"

Jet shifted uncomfortably. "I'd rather not say."

There was an awkward silence and both Kessa and Marta turned back to look at Stoke. "Sorry, Jet," he said.

But Jet didn't like to look weak. He forced himself to buck up and sound nonchalant. "Okay," he said. "I guess it's a good example. My mother was an 81—"

Marta interrupted. "81? Wow, that's high, right?"

"Yeah. Her family was well-to-do. But anyway, when she married my dad, he was a 55. An engineer. Really smart, but otherwise just a regular guy, right? So when they got married they both ended up in the high 60s."

"I get it," Marta nodded. "About halfway in between. So then when you were born, was your rank . . . ?"

"Kids don't have formal ranks until they turn 18, and then it's usually about 20 points below their parents. So, 48. I was supposed to be a 48." It was suddenly uncomfortable in the room. Jet looked at the floor. "And now I'm a 34."

Kessa looked at Jet kindly. "What happened?"

"First my dad died. It was a brain aneurism, just one of those things even modern medicine can't predict. Then my mom—she was distraught. She really, really loved him. And I was almost old enough to move out and start living on my own, anyway. She . . . she left. Emigrated off-planet. She just picked up one day and rocketed off to the Trappist system. She took her money with her, and she started a new life."

"My god. Are you, are you still in touch?"

Jet nodded ruefully. "Sure. We talk by p-cap sometimes. It's fine. I'm an adult."

There was another long pause before Marta finally got the nerve to ask, "So your rank . . . ?"

"No parents, not much money, just getting my first job. I went all the way down to 27."

"Which is not so bad!" Stoke said, trying to improve the mood. "I was born a 25, and I'm okay. And anyway, it didn't last long for Jet. He's moved up super-fast. He was the hardest-working kid when we were in school together. He saved money, went to school, qualified for orbiters, and look at him now. 34 already, and it's only been six years. I'm only up to 31. Plus, Jet's studying for spacer qualification."

"Yeah," Jet said as positively as he could. "It's all good."

Kessa was still filled with disapproval. "Rank is stupid. No one is better than anyone else."

Jet looked back at her. Where he came from that would be like saying 'gravity is stupid,' but he was wise enough to entertain the hypothesis. "Maybe so," he said. "Maybe so."

Ricker finally got around to stating the obvious. "You guys aren't here for a birthday surprise, are you?"

Stoke shook his head. "Uh, no."

"So why are you here? What's going on?"

The four visitors all looked around at each other. "Great question," Jet finally said. "Let's recap and see if even *we* know what the hell is going on."

Stoke again swore Ricker to secrecy, and they ran through it together. Kessa and Marta coming to Earth to visit Galen. Jet and Stoke picking them up at the spaceport. The attempted arrest at the spaceport, probably triggered, they decided, by looking up Galen's location. Their wild chase down here to Denver, first aboard *Chica* and then on foot, with ORGA and Authority cops on their tails the whole way. The way they conned the brainbox shop clerk and how their trackers were now turned off. And the way they conned the air taxi driver to give them an untraceable, transaction-free ride here to Ricker's.

All Ricker could respond with, repeatedly, was, "Holy crap!"

After they had all finished telling themselves their own story, Stoke turned to Jet. "What do we do now, Jet? You gotta know they haven't given up looking for us."

Jet looked around to invite suggestions. "The consulate isn't going to work. We lasted there like, what, eight seconds?"

"And Marta got shot," Kessa added.

"Can't we just go back home?" Marta asked. "There must be a return spacer." And then, in an uncharacteristic flash she added, "You guys could come with us!"

"Sorry," Stoke said. "Spaceports are the most closely controlled places we have. It would be worse than the Diplomatic Quarter."

Ricker took a slug of his beer and offered, "Hate to say it, but prob'ly you guys should just give yourselves in. They'll go easier on you that way."

There was a collective snort around the room, but then a long pause. Finally Kessa broke the silence. "I think we should try to find Galen. He'll know what to do."

Jet looked at her seriously. "Don't you think they've arrested him by now?"

"Well they've probably tried, but maybe he got away. Maybe he knew they were coming and went into hiding."

"That's kind of a big maybe."

"Okay, but what else can we hope for?" Kessa said.

Jet tossed his head. "I guess you're right. But if he's in hiding, how do we contact him?"

"It depends where he's hiding, I suppose. This is your planet. Any idea where he'd hide?"

Jet and Stoke looked at each other, trying to think. Stoke said, "He's starting out in the middle of nowhere at that field station of his. Does he have an aircar?"

Kessa knew the answer from years of being in touch. "There is one, but he's only allowed to use it on official business."

Jet nodded knowingly. "Makes sense. And of course they track it all the time. Think he could disable the tracking, like Stoke did for *Chica*?" Everyone shrugged, so Jet continued. "Well let's say he did. Then, where would he go?"

Stoke shook his head. "Could be anywhere. Starting way out there in the soy fields he could just stay really low and avoid radar. If he was lucky, the satellites wouldn't see him for a while. I bet he could get pretty far."

"Okay, good. But still, where would he go? Kessa, Marta, did he ever mention any special place? Any friends or anything?"

"No, not really. He never goes far from his house," Kessa replied.

Jet frowned. "Damn. Well, why don't we start there? Maybe he left us a message or something. If he thinks we're looking for him, that would be the smart thing to do."

Stoke raised his eyebrows. "So, fly to Galen's house and look for clues, basically?"

"Yup," said Jet.

"And assume he hasn't been arrested already?"

"Yup."

"And assume ORGA's not just sitting there waiting for us to show up so they can arrest us, too?"

"Um, yup. Though I suppose we may want to be a little careful on our approach."

"Oh, and, how did you say we were going to get there, again? Last I knew *Chica* was headed off to 14 clicks on autopilot with 5% fuel load."

"Ah, that," said Jet. "Hmm. Where do you think she is now?"

Stoke thought about it. "Assuming she didn't get shot down, they probably impounded her."

"So, Denver Main Impound, then?"

"Either that, or she may have found her own way home to Port 17, in which case she would be in the impound area there."

Jet nodded. He knew Port 17 well. "Let's try both," he said. "Maybe Port 17 first, because that would be easier."

"What do you have in mind?" asked Stoke.

"Well if we could just . . ."

■ ■ ■

Not long after, the exhausted Marta and Kessa were asleep next to each other in Ricker's bed-pod in one corner of the one-room apartment. From the outside, the bed looked like a giant clam shell with a retractable cover. Inside, there was a cozy environment isolated from the noise and lights of apartment and city. To dispel any feelings of claustrophobia, the inner roof of the shell was covered with a high-resolution display that could mimic a tall ceiling or far-away night sky, the effect enhanced by clever manipulation of micro air currents within. Meanwhile, the Earth friends sprawled themselves out on the sofa and floor. Jet told Kimberly to wake him up in two hours. That wasn't much sleep, but it would have to do.

But Kimberly didn't wait two hours. They had only closed their eyes for what felt like moments when Kimberly woke Jet up with a gentle but persistent tone. "Is that two hours already, Kimberly?" Jet ewaved.

"No, but there is danger."

"Danger? What is it?" Jet asked, rolling over and forcing himself further awake. As he did he heard the same noises Kimberly had: someone banging on doors down the hall. His heart leapt. It was a search party!

"Wake up, everybody, *wake up!*" Jet ran around the room shaking his friends out of their groggy slumbers. "They're searching apartments down the hall. Come on, fast, we have to get out of here. Marta, how are your legs?"

Marta, still waking up, flexed her legs experimentally. "I think I can manage."

"Good. Come on, we have to be ready to move at just the right moment."

Everyone listened intently as the police pounded their guns on the door of the apartment two doors down. "Authority Police! Open up!" There was groaning and commotion on the other side of the apartment wall, and Jet, his ear to Ricker's door, could tell the two cops had gone inside to search the neighbors, leaving the corridor outside temporarily clear.

"Now!" he said. "Quietly!" He led the way as Kessa, Marta, and finally Stoke followed him out the door, trying to hold their breath and move fast and quietly, all at the same time.

"Thanks, Ricker! Remember, you're sworn to secrecy," Stoke said as the door closed behind him.

Jet dashed down the hall in the opposite direction of the cops and leapt around a corner out of sight, closely followed by the other three. They'd made it without being seen. Jet and Stoke looked at each other silently, hearts beating and brains churning.

"Where to?" Stoke breathed.

"Ground level?" Jet ventured.

"Level 0? That's nervy."

Jet nodded slowly and seemed to firm up his decision. "I'm thinking outside."

Stoke wrinkled his nose. "Level 0 outside? On the ground? Fut. Is that safe?"

"Safer than up here with the cops around the corner."

"Space."

Marta and Kessa had been anxiously listening to this whole exchange. "What's wrong with outside on the ground?" Marta whispered.

Jet answered, "Nothing, really. It's not a location they're likely to look."

"Why not?"

"It's just not a place we usually go." Jet nodded slightly, his mind made up. "But it will be good. Come on, let's go down." Jet furtively led the way through the mostly-deserted nighttime corridors to the nearest turbolift stop. During the day, turbolifts operated on fixed routes and it was up to travelers' brainboxes to find the routes that would take them to their destination. But at night the turbolifts were near-empty and would accept custom destinations. Once everyone was in, Jet took a breath and commanded, "Level 0."

The turbolift made a buzzing sound to indicate an error. Marta and Kessa were confused, but Jet and Stoke both rolled their eyes up slightly to listen to the error message being transmitted into their brainboxes by the turbolift. Marta, looking startled, realized she was hearing it, too.

"Oh, it doesn't go that low," Jet interpreted. "Fine, take us as low as you go," he told the turbolift. It obediently hummed into motion. "That'll be Level 10," Jet said. He and Stoke shared a nervous glance.

Kessa noticed the look. "What's wrong?"

Stoke answered. "Things get a little rough below Level 10."

A minute later the turbolift rumbled to a stop and the doors slid open to reveal an entirely new, dark world. An unpleasant, acrid odor wafted into the car as they stepped forward. The corridor outside was unevenly lit, with unadorned concrete walls and a low ceiling. The nearby slidewalk was making a loud mechanical grinding sound that made Kessa cringe. There was little motion, but there were five or six people arrayed up and down the hallway, lying on the floor or sitting up against the wall, dressed in rags and looking ill. One of them turned to the four newcomers emerging from the turbolift and stared malevolently. "Hey," he called throatily, sounding drunk. "You kids new here?"

Jet ignored him and led them off briskly in the other direction while the drunk kept calling after them from the background. "Girls! Baby! You two are hot!"

They skipped the decrepit slidewalk. In addition to the grinding sound it was making, it only had one lane in each direction and that was moving slower than they were. The concrete floor felt cold and rough beneath their feet. Without thinking about it, Kessa moved forward to walk next to Jet, and Stoke fell back to escort Marta, who unconsciously grasped his hand for comfort. They walked as fast as they could without running.

The corridor led out onto a large plaza that felt claustrophobic despite its size. At its center, a cluster of ill-kept store kiosks stood mutely, locked for the night behind rusty metal gates and door cages. More people were strewn here as if spending the night, and a few looked up dully at the passersby. The whole place smelled like stale urine. A woman's voice in the distance was spitting out a steady, unending stream of profanities.

Just as they reached the far side of the plaza they heard a disturbance behind them. It was a group of cops, moving in a cluster for safety. Their weapons were drawn and they stopped at every sleeping or huddled person they passed, shining bright lights in their faces and then moving on, as if searching for someone. "Searching for us," Kessa realized.

Moving quickly along the wall, Jet found another turbolift that turned out to be just an old-time, windowless elevator that only went up and down, controlled by mechanical buttons on the wall numbered 3 through 10. Jet pushed 3 and they lurched downward.

They came out on another plaza at Level 3, this one even darker and colder with lower ceilings. A heavy, throbbing noise pulsed through the entire space. In the distance a red light was blinking on and off, and a rat scurried for cover. They couldn't see anyone here, but Marta, for one, was happy not to look too hard.

Muttering something under his breath about not even his brainbox knowing where things were down here, Jet had to search around a few moments before he found a plain metal door that led into a conventional stairwell. He dashed downward, taking the steps two at a time with everyone else following as best they could, the four of them making a racket on the groaning metal. They reached the ground level and, with an effort, pushed open a heavy metal door that swung off kilter on its hinges. It led onto a street outside.

They all looked around, and then up and into the tangle of buildings looming above them and disappearing into the night sky. It was raining, and Jet and Stoke both threw their arms over their faces in surprise, trying to ward off the droplets. Marta and Kessa just turned their hands up to feel its strength. "I guess we get wet," Kessa said, pulling her hair back with incongruous cheerfulness.

"Yeah," said Stoke, sounding annoyed.

Marta was feeling tremendously relieved to be out of the nightmarish buildings. "Oh, come on, Stoke, it's good for you!" she said playfully. "It makes you grow!"

"Maybe you," Stoke grumbled. "It's going to make me dissolve."

Marta laughed. Stoke was funny.

It was the dead of night, but the always-on lights from the buildings gave the atmosphere a gray glow that grew brighter and brighter the farther up you looked. The street itself was lit only by navigation lights from the regular flow of ground vehicles rolling mutely by in both directions. Looking closely at them, Marta realized the vehicles were all robotic, windowless machines.

"No passengers?" Marta asked Stoke.

"No. Those are all ground-mechs. Garbage and maintenance, mostly. Why would anyone want to be a passenger on a ground vehicle?"

"So," Jet announced, "now all we need is someplace out of the rain. Kimberly says she has no idea where to look, and neither do I."

"No problem," said Kessa cheerfully, taking Jet's hand and turning her face upwards to catch the rain. "Now that we're outside, it's my turn to lead." Jet, noticing that Kessa had apparently forgiven him now for being party to Earth's rank system, was happy to follow.

The streets were like nothing any of them had experienced before. For Kessa and Marta they were a confusion of moving vehicles, odd noises, uneven pavement, strange lighting, and the maze of towering buildings on all sides. There were no trees or grass or plants of any kind. For Jet and Stoke the streets were cold, rainy, windy, dark, and unnervingly unfamiliar. They walked along the edge of the streets, trying to stay out of the flow of mechanized traffic and dodging puddles that were forming everywhere from the rain. Their clothes were soon soaked through and water dripped down their faces and into their eyes. Kessa, spirits seemingly high, led them in short, purposeful bursts from one landmark to another: "let's try over by that light," or "just up to the next corner."

"I think you actually like this rain, Kessa," Jet said ruefully.

"Sure I do," Kessa chirped. "What's not to like?"

"It's cold, and wet, and it gets in your eyes, and it runs down your back."

"Oh, don't be such a mollycoddle. You and Stoke. You're supposed to be big, tough guys!"

"Hey, if you want to fight, bring it on," laughed Jet.

"Hah! I'll just jump in a puddle and splash you to death."

"Unfair tactics. If you do that I'll fight back with loud, metallic noises."

Kessa did a double-take. "You know that about me?"

Jet smiled kindly. "It's kind of hard to miss."

Kessa smiled inwardly. Jet was paying attention to her.

After 15 minutes they finally reached a bridge-like structure close to the ground, spanning between two buildings and creating a dry, traffic-free urban cave. It was unlit, but as they ventured a few tentative steps in, their eyes adjusted to the darkness and they found they could see well enough from the ambient lights of the city outside. The floor was concrete and cold, but it didn't smell too bad and it looked empty and uninhabited. Kessa turned to look at the others. "You think?"

They all nodded. It would work. It suddenly occurred to Jet, like an apple dropping on his head, that he would not have found this place on his own. It was Kessa with her spunky initiative that had led them here from the moment they stepped outside, not he. And she had been so good in the brainbox shop, too. He cast a secret, appreciative look in her direction. Then he realized he should be appreciating Stoke, too, for all the brilliance he'd contributed to their escapes today. Jet gave himself a mental kick in the butt for his habit of assuming he had to do all the thinking himself.

Kessa picked a spot up against one wall and walked around it in a small circle, as if staking out a nest. "Come on," she said, settling down to sit on the ground with her back against the wall and inviting the others to join her. "Right here. Space, am I exhausted. Now if only we can figure out what to do about these wet clothes." She gave a sideways look at Jet, who was sitting next to her. "Mind if we take them off?"

Jet's heart jumped a beat but he kept his cool. "Might be a good idea, actually. But Stoke and I have to get going."

"We do?" Stoke said, tearing his eyes off Kessa, who seemed to be making motions in the direction of unfastening her jumpsuit.

"Yes," Jet said insistently, grabbing Stoke's shoulder.

"Now?"

"Now. Come on. We're going to get *Chica* back . . ."

■　■　■

After Jet and Stoke had left, Marta and Kessa huddled together in the concrete cave. It was the middle of the night and they tried to settle down, but their heads were spinning.

"This wasn't exactly what we expected to be doing here on Earth, was it?" Marta observed.

Kessa laughed. "Ha! Not hardly."

"You think we'll get out of this?"

"One way or another, I'l know we will."

They were quiet for a minute, and then Marta spoke again. "What do you think of these guys?"

"Jet and Stoke?"

"Mm-hm."

Kessa's mouth curved into a quick, accidental grin, but then she controlled it and feigned nonchalance. "They seem nice enough."

"Nice enough looking, too," Marta said with a little smile. "And Jet seems really smart."

"I think they're both smart, in different ways."

"Unless I'm missing something, I think you kind of like Jet."

Kessa flushed lightly. "Maybe I do."

"I like him, too, but he's not exactly the warmest personality I've even met."

Kessa nodded. "Yeah, he's closed off a little, isn't he? But, somehow, I think we sort of understand each other. It's not what he says, so much, or what I say. It's just when we look at each other . . . Well. I can't explain it."

"Sounds, I don't know, sexy?"

Kessa shrugged cheerfully. "Ma-ay-be. As I said, I can't explain it. Anyway, I think he just needs some love."

Marta smiled and teased her sister. "Hah, and wouldn't *you* like to be the one to help him with that?"

"Well what about you and Stoke?" Kessa said, defending herself. "I thought I saw a few sparks pop off there a couple times?"

Marta shrugged girlishly. "Maybe. He acts kind of happy-go-lucky, and he seems like a girl-chaser, but I think he pays attention to people. I get the sense he, you know, *gets* me."

"Ah! So maybe you want to *get* him?"

"Oh, be quiet."

Apartment A-3-3203B, Rio de Janeiro, Earth

"We're home, Banji," 32 Caphaletta Maiz said to her son as she lifted him off her shoulder and deposited him gently on the sofa. He had been asleep, but the movement woke him and he looked up groggily at his mother, rubbing his eyes. He had a three-year-old's cherubic round face ringed by a shock of wispy, unruly dark hair and a little birthmark on his pudgy cheek that she kept telling herself she'd get fixed one day. "Long day, wasn't it?" she said, allowing herself to collapse down next to him. She shared her son's wispy dark hair, but her cheeks were the opposite of pudgy, looking almost gaunt beneath high cheek bones that propped up tired-looking eyes.

They were just now back from the medical lab way over in Rio de Janeiro's Sector B, where Caphaletta had taken Banji for specialized tests recommended by the medical program in his brainbox. Low weight, they were saying. No one could figure out why. Before that she had picked him up from crèche, where the teacher reported he had a tough day. To tell the truth, Caphaletta had had a tough day, too. Her co-workers seemed uniformly grumpy and her boss had yelled at her. She had a headache. But with a glance at Banji her maternal instincts kicked in and she perked herself up. "Ready for some supper?"

With a toddler's magical ability to switch moods in no time at all, Banji was suddenly alert and enthusiastic. "Yeah!"

"What sounds good?"

"Um . . ." Banji said, mushing his face into a child's version of a scowl of concentration. "Um . . . I know! Mac-em-cheese!"

"Okay! Great choice. Mac and cheese it is." Caphaletta headed to their small eating area and touched a control on the fab. "Mac and cheese for Banji and me," she ordered.

But the fab emitted a short *bzzt* that Caphaletta had never heard before. "Error," said the display. "Check Nutribase feed."

"What? What are you talking about?" She reentered her order. But the fab buzzed again and gave the same error message. "Check Nutribase feed."

Caphaletta rolled her eyes and asked her brainbox what was going on. It recommended checking the hose in the back of the fab that fed in Nutribase, the substance from which, together with water, the fab created all its outputs. Caphaletta shoved the appliance around until she could peer into the back, found the hose, and wiggled it around a bit. It seemed fine. Caphaletta didn't know what else to do.

"What's wrong, Mommy?" Banji was asking. "I want mac-em-cheese."

"I know you do, sweetie. But something's wrong with the fab right now. Come on, let's go over to Rosa and Yuliana's and get some mac and cheese there. How would that be? Maybe you can have supper with Yuliana."

Caphaletta gathered up Banji and carried him three doors down to her friend Rosa's apartment. But Rosa, full of her usual nervous energy, greeted them at the door in a bit of a huff. "Something's wrong with my fab," she announced.

"Yours, too?"

A few minutes later Caphaletta and Rosa found themselves, toddlers in tow, in the atrium nearest their apartments, trading stories and complaints with dozens of other residents, all of whom were finding themselves without supper for the night. Social messages on their brainboxes were telling them there were Nutribase outages in spots all over the city. Some kind of breakdown in the network, they all figured. Strange, that had never happened before. The hungry children tugging at their knees were increasingly loud and short-tempered.

The gathering attracted the attention of a red-uniformed Authority Police officer, who walked firmly into the center of the group and looked sternly around at all of them. The crowd quieted. It was unwise to draw attention from the Authority. "No loitering," the officer said, and Caphaletta and the others gradually turned around and returned to their apartments. Rosa caught up with Caphaletta in the hall.

"What are we going to do?" Rosa asked.

Caphaletta sighed. "Sounds like the cafés up on Level 41 are open. Want to splurge?"

"I'm not sure I *want* to pay Level 41 prices, but I guess I will. Come on, Yuliana! We're going to have supper with Banji and Caphaletta."

"Mac-em-cheese!" chirped Banji.

■ ■ ■

In a world where perfect-tasting food was available in every apartment at the touch a food fabricator's button, restaurants on Earth had evolved to offer far more than a merely gustatory experience. A meal at a good restaurant was intended to be a symphony for senses. Banji's macaroni and cheese, for example, would have come in a lump on a standard plate had it emerged from Caphaletta's food fabricator. But at the restaurant on Level 41, it was interpreted by the restaurant's food artist as a whimsical spiral galaxy, with individual macaroni noodles all lined up in a three-armed spiral formation, and the cheese sauce dyed black and layered in the background to represent the void of outer space. A tiny accent spotlight attached to the side of the plate projected a pattern of sparkling white and blue stars down onto the dish to add to the galactic effect. The flat stone serving plate was tuned to vibrate like a bell at 65.4 Hertz each time Banji touched it with his fork, a deep C note the food artist felt best represented the comforting feel of the dish and the elemental, childlike character of the cosmic scene. (Banji paid no attention, though, and made a mash of it within 20 seconds. He should have gotten the animal-shaped noodles; they were more fun, but he couldn't remember the name of the dish.) Meanwhile, Caphaletta's seafood stew appeared as an aquarium containing a coral reef with a circus of ornately decorated "fish" swimming around, suspended in the transparent stew broth "water" by some trick of the chef's art. Each fish was served at its own unique temperature, and the entire dish emitted sounds of the reef, including gentle surf, the occasional call of a distant humpback whale, and the static-like sound of parrotfish nibbling coral.

Caphaletta's friend Rosa sat across the table and spent a moment admiring her own meal—a creation of spinach and tiny eggs constructed into a dogwood tree—before looking around conspiratorially and then whispering, "Have you heard what they're saying?"

"About what?"

"The fabs. What's wrong with them."

"No, what?"

"Well I don't know if this is true or not, but there's a guy named Piers in my office who commed me about it when we were coming up here, and just before we sat down my friend Jazza messaged the same thing."

"What?"

Rosa leaned even the table and whispered even more quietly. "They're running out of Nutribase!"

"That's not news," Caphaletta said at almost normal volume. "That was the message on my fab when it went on the blink. It said, 'Check Nutribase feed.'"

"I know, but Piers told me it's because there's not enough! Like, worldwide supply!"

"That's crazy, Rosa. That could never happen."

"But what if it did?"

"It didn't. It couldn't have. The whole world lives on Nutribase. We have been for practically ever. They must have reserves, and back-ups, and, I don't know, all kinds of things. They would never let that happen."

"I'm just telling you what I heard."

"Anyway," said Caphaletta, changing the subject. "I'm glad you're around. At times like this I wonder if people had it better in the old days, when they had big extended families that all lived together in one house. That way they could all take care of each other."

Rosa smiled maternally. "Are you saying you want your mommy right now?"

"Ha! Sort of. I mean, nothing against you, Rosa, and our other friends, too. In a way, our city is like a really giant house where everyone lives together. There are millions of potential friends living minutes away from each of us. But we're not a family. We're not locked into that unconditional pact for love and mutual support that families used to have in the past."

"You may have a rosy-colored view of what families were like in the past."

"I suppose. Anyway, thank you for being my friend."

The conversation moved onto happier topics and both mothers and children felt much refreshed by their pleasant dinner. They went home feeling better than they had in several days and everyone slept the satisfied way you sleep when your belly is full.

7

Friday, August 5

Tappet's Office

68 Tappet's brainbox woke him up at 0600 after a few hours' sleep on his office sofa and he checked his reports.

The fugitives were still on the loose. He had lost them after they showed up in the Diplomatic Quarter of Denver. They had somehow disabled their trackers, and so far they had been smart enough to avoid any traceable electronic transactions. In fact, Tappet even wondered if they were using their brainboxes at all. Was that possible? And they had somehow evaded facial recognition cameras so far, too.

But things were looking good this morning. His criminal tracking algorithms had been combing through crime data from Denver in the last 24 hours and they had some leads. First, there was a report from an air taxi near the Diplomatic Quarter that had its camera broken and showed a 9000 fare right after. When questioned, the driver said the fare was four young people who acted suspicious. The lead had come in overnight, and the Authority Police had already starting searching apartments in the area they had been dropped off.

Second, there had been an overnight disturbance at the temporary impound at Port 17 where they were keeping the fugitive's space orbiter. The guards had chased away an intruder. The guy didn't have a tracking signal, but they'd found some blood where he'd cut himself on a sharp edge of equipment. It was 34 Jet Castilian, one of the fugitive pilots, probably trying to get his ship back. Not that he'd be a 34 much longer. Anyway, no harm done, but Tappet ordered the orbiter transferred to Denver Main Impound as soon as possible. It would be safer there.

Port 17, Denver

The morning shift was just starting at Port 17 in Denver when two officers from ORGA Enforcement arrived, looking sharp. They had orders direct from headquarters in Capital City to transfer the CC orbiter to Main Impound, stat. They scared up the local guard for the fenced-in impound area, pulled rank, and sent her scurrying to release the ship. She raised a gate, and under the watchful eye of the ORGA Enforcement officers, a robotic tractor moved in and towed *Chica* over to a fueling station. Fueling took a few minutes, and then the tractor maneuvered the ship through the crowded hangar and out to the staging area, ready for the ORGA pilots to climb aboard and fly it over to Main Impound.

Then something crazy happened.

The orbiter, apparently of its own volition, powered up and began taxiing toward the portal. The shocked officers gave chase on foot, but the orbiter had a mind of its own. Its hatches swung shut, it gained speed, and in seconds it was flying out the portal and disappearing into the morning sky.

One of the ORGA officers ran to the nearby console yelling, "Stop it!" and trying to punch buttons on the screen, but nothing worked. "I can't control it!" he called.

"At least track it, then," called the other officer. "I'll call for backup."

"I can't track it either!"

"You can't? Let me try . . ." The second officer arrived at the console and started trying to give it commands of his own, but it was no use. The CC orbiter had just flown itself away. He looked at his partner and said, "What the hell just happened?"

Winfred Plaza, Denver

Stoke was sitting at a small café table on an outdoor courtyard close to Ricker's apartment. Though he was sleep-deprived, in danger, and on the run, he couldn't help but crack his white-toothed grin. The caper he and Jet had pulled in the wee hours last night had worked perfectly. They had snuck into Port 17, and Jet distracted the guard with a fake break-in attempt followed by hide-and-seek around the vast hangar. Meanwhile, Stoke had slipped aboard poor, impounded *Chica* and quickly installed a secure, private comm link in a hiding place inside her instrument panel. This morning it was working perfectly, and *Chica* was responding to commands he was sending her remotely as *pilot_2*, her second-highest priority command set. She was ignoring other lower priority commands from ORGA Enforcement and others—along the lines of "Stop it!"—and flying her way straight to Stoke instead.

Jet, though on the lookout for police and not relaxed enough to grin, ran his fingers through his thick black hair and looked pretty satisfied, too. His work as a decoy last night in the hangar had gone quite well, except for a nasty slice in his hand. Even that wasn't so bad: Kessa had patched it up for him using a stolen napkin, and even if the cut hurt, her hands around his had felt just fine.

"It's working?" asked Marta, who, though shaggier than usual this morning, was looking much healthier and walking normally. She was going to be glad to be moving forward again; it made her uncomfortable when there was nothing for her to do.

"Yup, it's working," nodded Stoke happily. "Get ready for a loud noise." Kessa, always sensitive to noise, bent over and covered her ears, and moments later *Chica* swept into the plaza and hovered just off the ground, deploying her access hatch. Jet, Stoke, Marta, and Kessa all ran in, and the four of them were on their way.

Chica, Denver Airspace

Jet flew with urgency but not like quite such a bat out of hell this time, keeping *Chica* as low as possible while threading his way through the bottom of the Denver honeycomb. He headed west to begin with, making his way up and over the Front Range before turning north to parallel the snowy peaks of the Continental Divide for as long as he could before they tapered down and faded off to the west. He stayed on a northerly course, heading out over Wyoming on the way to Saskatchewan.

Stoke decided it was okay to retract the safety shields and de-tint the canopy, which gave Kessa and Marta good views out the top and sides. Everywhere they looked was the flat expanse of the southern Wyoming plains, covered with soybeans as far as the eye could see. Besides the crops, the only visible features were regularly spaced irrigation ditches and the occasional enormous agribot trundling slowly across the hectares.

Kessa said, "Hey Stoke, would it be okay if you and I traded places for a while? I'm wondering what the view is like up there in front."

"Sure! No problem." Stoke gave Jet a surreptitious wink as he climbed toward the back. Jet smiled.

Kessa settled lightly into Stoke's chair next to Jet and gazed around, taking in the view—Jet included. She allowed herself a fleeting extra glimpse to admire his tan skin, brown eyes, and pleasant looks.

"Soybeans, right?" Kessa asked him.

"Right," Jet answered.

"What else do they grow around here?"

"Nothing that I know of. It's all soybeans."

"All of it? That's crazy!"

"Why?"

"Well you can't have much of an ecosystem with only one species, can you?"

"Guess not."

"I mean, it's monoculture. The risks are terrible! If anything goes wrong with that one plant, you're totally screwed, right?"

"Um, I guess so. Haven't really thought enough about it . . ."

"Not to mention the complete destruction of the natural food webs and interspecies checks and balances. Every heard of the Great Famine in Ireland? That's what happens with monoculture. Nobody in their right mind does monoculture at this scale, regardless of modern technology. My God, Jet, how do they even pollinate all those?"

"I think they're self-pollinating. Your brainbox could tell you if you ask it."

But Kessa was too disgusted to do research. She just said "Hmph," crossed her arms, and tossed her shoulders back against her chair.

Jet, struggling not to be defensive, gave her a minute before saying, "You don't really approve of Earth, do you?"

Kessa was a little startled by the directness of the question. "I wouldn't say that. It's just so . . . *different* here compared to back home."

"Like how?"

"Back home we have a lot more species diversity, for one thing! And not as many people, and . . . well, you'll just have to see for yourself someday."

"See New Gaia? That would be interesting."

Kessa turned her head and decided to be as direct as Jet was being. She smiled a little and there was a twinkle in her blue eyes. "You say that word a lot: 'Interesting.' You're interested in a lot of things, aren't you?"

"I am! I think being curious or interested is one of my favorite emotions."

"'Interested' isn't an emotion!"

"It's not? What is it, then?"

"I don't know . . . a state. A brain status. It's not like happiness, or despair, or fear, or lust."

Jet shrugged. "For me, I think it kind of is."

Kessa chuckled. "So for you, interest is comparable to lust?!"

Jet smiled. "Okay, I have to admit I don't have a *lust* for seeing your planet. It's only interest."

"Whew, glad to hear it. I was going to start worrying about what you lust after."

"Or who?" Jet said playfully.

Kessa laughed. "Hah! I'm not sure I'm ready to hear about that yet."

There was a cheerful pause, and then Jet changed the subject. "Do you have any more family back there on New Gaia, besides Marta?"

"Lots! I mean, depending on what you call family, I suppose. In our house, we have Marta and me, my grandmother, my mother, my uncle, aunt, and three cousins."

"All in one house? Wow, that *is* different. Most of us here on Earth live in ones or twos in our own apartments. Does everyone in your house get along okay?"

"Heh, mostly."

"But, uh, your father?"

"He died a long time ago, when I was little."

"I'm sorry."

Kessa spoke more slowly. "It was okay. I had Uncle Kjell. And Uncle Galen, too, even if he was all the way out here on Earth. I got over it. Just like you will."

Jet was taken aback. "Whoa. You think I'm not over my father yet?"

"Honestly? Maybe not. Why should you be? Him, and your mother taking off that way. That was a lot."

"I guess."

"Probably anyone would feel, um . . . never mind."

"Come on. Feel what?"

"It just seems like maybe you'd feel like . . . like no one loved you."

Jet gave a rueful nod. "That's an arrow to the heart. Maybe you're right."

"I'm sorry. I talk too much sometimes."

■ ■ ■

Back in Chica's passenger compartment, Stoke and Marta were talking about eardots.

"I understand about looking up directions and sending messages," Marta was saying, "which is handy I suppose, but what else do they do?"

"All kinds of things," Stoke answered. "They can answer any factual question. They can carry out any command involving themselves or other computers, robots, or other connected devices anywhere on the planet. They record everything you hear, and sometimes even what you see."

"Everything you *see*? How do they do that?"

"Not that well, actually. They read signals from your visual cortex, just like they read your brainwaves when you communicate with them. But the resolution isn't that great. That's one reason some people wear lensies."

"Lensies?"

"Contact lenses that pair with the eardot. Those are handy because they let the eardot see what you're seeing, and they can also project images back on your eye to display visual information."

"That sounds useful. It can show you pictures and videos and such?"

"Yep. Also a virtual overlay on the real world, like what a piece of furniture *would* look like if you put it in your apartment, or arrows pointing directions; things like that. It's called augmented reality."

"That sounds pretty useful. Why doesn't everyone use them?"

"Lensies? I don't really know. Kids use them all the time for playing games, and police use them on patrol, but I guess most people get kind of tired of them once they become adults. Maybe it's too much information."

"Too much information?" Marta said. "The way things are here on Earth I wouldn't have expected anyone would worry about that."

Stoke laughed. "Nope, even Earth people like a little mystery in their lives."

Marta nodded thoughtfully. "That's good to know. I was starting to think you people were totally different from us Newgies."

"*Newgies?*" Stoke asked, looking amused.

"New Gaians! Don't laugh, that's what we call ourselves. It's no worse than 'Earthlings.'"

Stoke laughed anyway. "Earthlings? We don't call ourselves that. It sounds like babies."

"Well what then? Earthans? Earthers? Earthites? What's the word?"

Stoke shook his head. "Come to think of it, I don't think there *is* a word. That's weird, isn't it? We just call ourselves people from Earth."

"Too many syllables," Marta joked. "You have to pick one that's three syllables or less. I suggest 'Earthies.'"

"That means something else. How about Olympians?"

"That's four syllables," Marta said quickly. "Come on, hurry up. I'll give you 20 seconds. What's going to be?"

"Olympans?" Stoke tried in mock desperation.

"You don't live on Olympa. It has to use the base word Earth. Faster."

"No fair! Earthmen, then."

"That's sexist! Time's running out."

"Earthpeople. Earthfolk. Earth . . . things!"

"Earth*ings*? That's your final choice?" Marta guffawed. "You are Er-things?"

Stoke was laughing, too. "That's my final choice and I'm sticking with it."

"Okay," Marta said with faux solemnity. "I'll notify the Earth Authority. I'm sure they'll want to broadcast this important news out to everyone's brainboxes right away. Stoke has decided. You are all *things.*"

"Er-things," corrected Stoke. "There's a difference."

Tappet's Office

The satellite imagery monitoring algorithm pinged. It had found something.

Tappet rushed to the display and brought up the image, which was real-time, visible-wavelength imagery of eastern Wyoming. And there, conveniently circled in red by the tracking software, was a little white dot, moving north, fast. Tappet zoomed in and there, sure enough, was the unmistakable teardrop-with-wings shape of an orbiter in low-altitude flight.

"Gotchya."

Tappet commed Senior Enforcement Officer 50 Smithson in Calgary. "22 Galen's friends are in an orbiter headed directly for his farmhouse."

"Good news, 68. Our patrol is still deployed out there. They'll be ready. What's the ETA?"

"The ETA is 72 minutes. But Smithson, proceed with caution. There's a chance they're in touch with 22 Galen and they know where he's hiding. Give them a little space and with any luck they'll flush him out. That way we get two for one."

"Sounds good, sir. I'll tell the patrol to move out and conceal themselves five or six kilometers away from the site."

"Well done, Smithson."

Chica, Southwestern Saskatchewan

As they crossed into Saskatchewan, Jet raised his voice so Stoke and Marta could hear and brought up a new topic. As he started to speak, he realized that for the first time in a long time, he was honestly looking forward to not doing all his thinking by himself. His friends were going to have good ideas, too; he knew it. "So, any ideas on how to locate 22 Galen when we get there? Without letting the Authority locate us, of course?"

Kessa shook her head. "It's just 'Galen.' Don't make him have a stupid rank. He's not really from here, anyway."

"He's not?"

"No, he's from New Gaia, like us."

"What's he doing on Earth?"

"He immigrated here when he was young."

"Oh."

Marta spoke up from the back. "If Galen hasn't been arrested by now, he would have to have had a really good place to hide out."

Stoke agreed. "Yeah, lying on the ground under a row of soybeans doesn't seem like a good long-term plan."

"A secret place in his house somewhere?" Marta suggested.

"If there is, there's no way we're going to get to him," Jet said, grimacing slightly and rubbing the back of his neck pensively.

"I suppose you're right," Marta conceded. "Maybe outbuildings? A barn or chicken coop or something?"

"What are those?" Jet asked.

"Whoa, you don't know what a barn or chicken coop is? You guys really are city slickers."

"What's a city slicker?" asked Stoke.

Marta chuckled. "Doesn't matter. Anyway, Galen might be camped in a separate building near his house."

"Not connected?" asked Jet.

"Not connected. He'd have to go outside to get from one building to the next."

"Weird," said Jet. "But okay, let's look for something like that when we get close."

Stoke shook his head. "They're going to have the place guarded. We can't get close enough for them to see us."

Jet nodded in agreement. "Can you get us some imagery, then?"

"Probably. Hang on a second . . . Here we go." Stoke displayed a satellite photo on *Chica*'s screens where everyone could see it.

"Not much around, is there?" Jet said. The photo showed a vast field with Galen's small farmhouse and chicken coops in the middle and the agribot pens nearby.

"Where do you think the ORGA cops are going to be?" Stoke asked.

"In the house, I suppose," Jet answered. "Just waiting for someone like us to show up. They've probably searched the house and those other buildings already."

Stoke tried zooming out to show a larger area. "Hey, look at this, a few kilometers to the north. Is that another house?"

Kessa was finally tuning in again. "Not a house, but maybe a materials storage depot. Look at the long, low sheds. Those round things are probably storage tanks. And those piles of material could be fertilizer and pesticides."

"Think he could have made it out to there to hide?" Jet asked.

"Probably worth a look," Stoke said.

Jet adjusted course to swing past the farmhouse to the east and then vector around and approach the storage depot from the north. Stoke and Kessa traded seats again, putting Stoke back at the co-pilot's controls. When they started getting close, Jet slowed down as much as he could without stalling and flew down close to the ground; an orbiter's equivalent of slinking in. With apologies to Kessa and Marta, Stoke also raised the safety shields, blocking their view. At the same time, though, he turned on the display screens and switched on *Chica*'s close-range passive sensors, which in addition to visible light also sensed infrared and a broad range of electromagnetic frequencies including radar wavelengths. He was careful not to switch on any active sensors; the last thing he wanted to do was emit signals that someone else could detect.

"See anyone?" Jet asked as they approached the storage depot.

Stoke scanned his images for anyone or anything that looked like ORGA or the Authority—police, vehicles, anything. "Looks clear," he said, tensely. Everyone was leaning forward, scanning the monitors for threats and holding their breath.

"I'm going to set us down." Jet found a relatively empty space between the long metal storage sheds and brought *Chica* to a rest in a cloud of dust.

Moments later a figure appeared at the door of one of the sheds, running toward them. "Watch it!" Stoke called. The figure was wearing a long trench coat and running with one hand on his head, holding down a dark cowboy hat that was tilted over his face.

Every muscle in the orbiter was tight as the four of them stared at the rapidly approaching threat. "Who is it?" Jet asked aloud.

No one had an answer until the running man came to a stop outside, standing right where the entry hatch would deploy if it were open. Keeping his hand on his hat, he appeared to look left, right, and behind himself before looking up at them and then, in one quick motion, pulling the hat up to reveal his face.

Kessa and Marta both cried out at the same time. "Galen!!"

"Are you sure?" Jet said.

"Yes! Yes! It's him. Let him in, fast!"

With one more quick scan of the area in his monitors, Stoke deployed the entry hatch. Moments later the dusty trench coat and hat came bursting into the passenger compartment. "Go, go!" he called to the pilots, and then he threw off his hat and tumbled into the waiting arms of Kessa and Marta. Stoke retracted the hatch as Jet turned to his controls and lifted *Chica* back into the air, slinking back again in the direction they had come.

There were a few minutes of joyful chaos in the passenger compartment as Kessa and Marta greeted their beloved uncle. He was bigger and rougher in person than Kessa had expected from years of p-cap communications, with brighter eyes. His trench coat was heavy and the weathered browned skin of his face was half-hidden by bristly gray whiskers. His voice was deep and more nuanced than she had ever heard it. He smelled like soil and plants and dust.

For his part Galen was overwhelmed to see his nieces Kessa and Marta in person for the first time ever. Marta was just as he expected, but Kessa seemed somehow younger in person. Her slender frame and thin arms were more girlish than the mature personality he knew from the p-caps. But regardless it was wonderful to see her in the flesh, to hug her close, to run a fatherly hand through her hair and look into her sky-blue eyes. What a treasure she was.

"How did you know it was us?" Marta asked Galen.

"Didn't figure the ORGA Enforcement guys would be flying around in one of these things," he smiled, gesturing at *Chica*'s luxurious interior. "And how did you know where to find me?"

Marta chuckled. "Didn't figure you'd be hanging around where the Authority would be waiting for us," she mimicked. The three of them were so bubbling over with questions and stories and explanations that they barely introduced Jet and Stoke to Galen as they flew. But there was a lot of catching up to do on both sides.

Finally Galen recovered enough perspective to ask, "By the way, where are you taking us?"

"Over to Calgary at the moment," Jet said. "We're going to hide and try to figure out our next move. Unless you have any other ideas?"

"Calgary's good for now," said Galen. "I know some people there. But then I need to get to Capital City. I can fill you in when—"

There was a sudden *boom* and *Chica* was blasted sideways. The passengers were thrown from their seats and Stoke looked up to see a jagged crack splitting the windshield in front of him. "That was a cop blaster!"

"Evade, *Chica*, evade!" Jet called out. *Chica*'s engines screamed and she tilted almost straight up, headed high. In the back, Galen and the girls struggled to regain their seats as more explosions sounded around them.

Another *boom* and they were thrown part way over backward, pushing everyone halfway upside down and dangling by the safety nets that had automatically deployed. A deep, thudding vibration started coming from the engines in the rear.

Chica's artificial intelligence algorithms were assessing damage and searching for solutions. The main engine was in critical status and power was dropping rapidly toward zero. Diagnostics were unavailable. Air stability had also been lost and no solutions were available. Very little iteration was required to resolve into an action determination: divert all remaining resources to passenger preservation.

The orbiter, still half inverted and dangerously close to the ground, began careening wildly and thick black smoke erupted from cracks around the main engine. More noises began, including the high-pitched scream of something spinning too fast. Inside, the passengers were being helplessly tossed and jerked in all directions, able to do nothing more than grunt and scream.

Chica's processors worked as fast as possible; billions of operations a second, updating real-world status and readjusting actions millions of times a second. The strategy with highest success probability was a roll. Reorient so the passenger compartment would be facing up. This could be achieved with two hard wing twists and one last burst of the maneuvering thrusters . . . now!

There was as sudden twist and *Chica* rolled 180 degrees so she was, for a moment, 40 meters up and oriented as if climbing a steep hill. It didn't last long but it was enough: there was a controlled explosion and the passenger pod ejected, quickly shooting away from the fuselage and then falling fast toward the ground. The pod was designed to fall from outer space, so its circuits took several moments to deploy the landing chute. It was only half billowed outward when the pod landed in the soybean field with a huge, jarring thud.

Jet and Stoke, stunned but conscious, could only lift their heads at first. "Everybody okay?" Jet asked the passengers in back.

"Not sure," Kessa replied. "I think Galen might be hurt."

Jet moved to unstrap himself and offer assistance. But as he did his eye was caught by what he saw out the window 50 meters away.

Chica herself, now stripped of the passenger pod and completely out of power, slowed helplessly to a stop in midair. She seemed to hang there for a moment, as if suspended by the force of will. Then she fell like a stone and crashed in a heap on the ground. Jet's hand went up involuntarily, as if to reach out and help. Her screaming, crippled engine kept spinning for four more seconds until there was a bright flash and horrific explosion.

When the smoke cleared, there was nothing left.

"No! *Chica!* No!" Jet felt his throat tense and his eyes tear over. Time stopped for a long moment and he stared and stared at the spot where she had just been. He couldn't believe it. *Chica* was gone.

Next to him, Stoke was letting out a high-pitched moan and pushing his hands up against the window in the direction of the crash. *"Chica!"*

But then Jet came to his senses and remembered Kessa and Marta and Galen. He twisted himself out of his chair and moved to the passenger compartment. Kessa was leaning over Galen, who was sitting motionless in his chair, eyes closed, head turned to one side, with a huge, bloody wound on his forehead. Kessa placed two fingers at his neck.

"A pulse," she breathed. "He's alive."

Galen stirred. "Barely alive," he said, turning his head toward Kessa. "No thanks to your boyfriend, here."

"What? He's not my boyfriend."

"Could've fooled me." Galen moved some more and stirred his limbs, checking for damage. He seemed okay. Finally he dryly turned to Jet. "And not a very good pilot, either."

Despite his grief, Jet gave a quick, slight smile. "How about you, Marta?" he called back to her.

"I'm okay," she reported. "What's going to happen?"

Jet was on the verge of replying when there was a loud noise and the entry hatch hissed open. A uniformed, military-style ORGA Enforcement officer stood there, weapon drawn.

"Criminals!" he said, "You are all under arrest."

Skervin's Conference Room

Skervin stormed into the task force meeting in high dudgeon. "*Outages* in the Nutribase supply? Why didn't anyone tell me this was going to happen?! Half the city of Rio reporting nothing coming out of their supply lines? Do you know how bad this looks? What the hell happened, Stasik??" Skervin was so angry he hadn't even bothered to think about how this looked to Perka, who looked as concerned as everyone else when Skervin shouted out the news.

The normally self-assured Stasik was visibly shaken. There were beads of sweat on his forehead beneath his short white hair, and he sat looking at his big hands, finding it difficult to meet anyone else's eyes. Nutribase distribution was his responsibility and there had been a breakdown. It didn't matter that it wouldn't have happened if Skervin hadn't forced him to shut down entire plants against his better judgment. It was squarely his fault and Skervin was likely to fire him on the spot.

But Stasik gathered himself and looked up at Skervin's angry face glowering at him from the end of the conference table. "We ran out, 96. We just ran out."

"How? Why?"

Now Stasik spoke tensely and very carefully. "As we've, uh, discussed, the system has very little excess capacity."

Perka said, "You can't blame your man for that Skervin. You're always telling us how efficient your system is, but you know the price is lack of emergency capacity."

Skervin just squinted and kept his eyes on Stasik. "Keep going, Stasik."

"Our Brasilia plant was already off-line, and last night toxins were also discovered at the Argentina plant. We shut down Argentina, and the self-healing routing algorithms were simply unable to compensate."

"So what happened? What did the routing algorithms do?"

"May I show you a map?"

"Fine."

Stasik stood up and moved to the glow screen. Standing helped him gain confidence and he spoke more firmly. "Here is the pipeline network for South America. It pumps raw Nutribase from the manufacturing nodes to cities, then to buildings, then to fabs located in businesses and residences. As the network branches out, first the number of pipes and then their diameter gradually decreases, just like the network of blood vessels in your body.

"You can see it all on this animated map. This is what it looked like a few days ago. Now here it is after we took Brasilia offline. See how the flows compensated, with all this product coming up from Argentina especially? But then here goes Argentina and as you can see, the network had to radically reconfigure itself. Suddenly there's product flowing in all kinds of unexpected directions. It makes sense; it's mathematically optimized. But the only problem is, it can't quite fill all the demand down here in Rio."

"Why Rio?" Skervin asked.

Stasik zoomed the map to show the region around Rio de Janeiro. "Only the computer knows for sure, but I suspect the main reason is that it's off on the edge of the network, topologically speaking. See? Only one route in. In terms of the pipeline network, the city is a stub."

"Was it the whole city?"

"No, the algorithm prioritized. It starting cutting off supplies to the lowest levels and went up as high as it had to, which I believe was Level 33."

"My god," said Perka, simultaneously alarmed and disgusted. "Skervin, you're starving our people."

Skervin ignored her and said blithely to Stasik, "Makes sense, what else could it do? Is it going to happen again?"

"Not in Rio. We'll adjust the routing algorithms to give it a little more priority from now on. But there are dozens of other cities that will probably get hit instead. As I said, when supplies dip to these levels there's not much we're going to be able to do."

Skervin was now in full control of the room, Perka included. "Listen to me, everyone. That is *not* acceptable! There *must* be something we can do. Now I want ideas. Someone tell me how you are going to *prevent* these outages!"

There was a pause and then Ettica spoke. "What about switching away from soybeans? We have other protein sources: fish, kelp, algae?"

Stasik shook his head. "Those are all boutique operations these days. They're nowhere near the scale we need. At, uh, 96 Skervin's direction we've shifted to almost total dependence on soybeans over the last 10 years."

"It's more efficient," Skervin said pointedly, unintentionally addressing Perka. "We've demonstrated that our genetically optimized soybeans are the most productive source of nutritional materials."

Perka simply looked back at Skervin. She didn't have to say a thing.

Skervin hastily refocused. "Come on, everyone. *Solutions!*"

A long, uncomfortable silence ensued. Skervin refused to break it, instead staring around at individual executives as if daring them to give up.

Stasik himself finally broke the silence. "There is something we do for testing and research. It's called *bulking*. Like, adding bulk."

All eyes were on him. "Say more," Skervin ordered.

"We came up with it a few years ago when we were testing a new, larger pipeline design. We needed a lot of product to fill up the new pipes, and we didn't have enough. At first we tried using watered-down Nutribase, but the entire system is designed for a paste with very specific properties, and the thinner paste wreaked havoc with pumps, valves, sensors, and so on. We realized what we needed was an additive that was also a paste, but cheap and readily available in large quantities near Nutribase factories around the world."

"So what did you do?"

Stasik glanced around. "Everyone know what stover is? In the soybean fields, it's the rest of the plant that is normally abandoned after the beans have been harvested. Stems, leaves, all that. The material can be ground up and lightly processed into a paste that is similar in consistency to real Nutribase. We just mixed it into the supply. It worked okay, and now we use it at all the plants for tests and maintenance."

"But no nutritional content?" clarified Ettica.

"No, not really. It's only for bulk. But—" Stasik stole a glance at Perka, but then he decided to ignore her and looked back at Skervin and Ettica. "If we mix it into the production supply, it could make it look like we have full supplies of Nutribase, even when we don't."

"Oh, good heavens," snorted Perka. "You can't be serious."

Ettica looked skeptical, but Skervin wasn't rejecting the idea just yet. "We need *something*, Perka. This would at least stave off mass panic."

Perka scowled, but she didn't reply. Skervin had a point.

Kapcheck was shaking his head, though. "I can see how that might fool someone looking at the pipelines, Stasik, but what about the food fabricators themselves? They work at a molecular level, picking out the molecules they need to make specific foods. They wouldn't be fooled by this at all."

"So reprogram them," said Skervin.

"What?" said Kapcheck.

"Reprogram them. Broadcast out a software update. Tell the fabs to mix some of this stover paste into everything they make."

"Can we do that?"

Skervin snorted. "We are ORGA, Kapcheck. The fabs belong to us. They do whatever we tell them to do."

Kapcheck tried to recover. "Uh, yes, of course. I suppose we could. The food would still look and taste mostly like the real thing, I suppose, but it would contain a larger proportion of non-nutritive fiber filler."

"Cooks have been doing this kind of thing for centuries," Skervin said. "Just think of meatloaf."

Perka made a frustrated noise, but again, there was nothing more she could say.

"Public Relations, now," Skervin said. "81 Sybil, you've been quiet. Tell us, what are you doing about information containment?"

Sybil picked up her chin a little and tucked a lock of blonde hair away behind her ear. Even more concerned with appearances than most people in the group, she had invested in treatment that gave her permanently blue eyes that matched the light-colored hair. She sat upright in her chair but she didn't stand, and she spoke with confidence in her own expertise. "We're covered for now. We put out a cover story about a pipeline break near Rio and it's holding up. But Stasik's forecast of more outages to come is concerning."

"What are you going to do about it?"

Sybil paused and gave a quick, deferential look across the table at Ettica, who was sometimes good for a political hint but was now keeping her face impassive. Sybil turned to look at Skervin. "96, I'd like to make a suggestion. Rather than *protecting* Rio from the next outage, do the opposite. Make sure it *happens* in Rio. Cut off Rio if we have to, and divert supplies everywhere else."

"What? Why?" asked Stasik.

"Because then we only have one problem, and we know where it is. We can contain negative news from one city. We can't contain negative news from cities all over the world."

There were uncomfortable murmurs all around. Stasik was struggling to get Sybil's suggestion to sink in. "You mean, make things even worse in Rio de Janeiro?"

"Yes."

"But that . . . won't be good. Food shortages. Lines at food outlets. Kids going to bed hungry, crap like that."

Sybil shrugged. "If we start seeing outages all over the world, people are going to start making up stories that sound like that anyway. Perception is reality. As I said, we can contain news from a single city."

Stasik was about to say the whole idea was ridiculous when Skervin gave a small nod. "I see your point, Sybil."

Stasik's head kept spinning. "If this gets any worse, Rio won't be enough," he pointed out. "It's only, what, 6% of demand in the South American distribution system? If we start losing more plants, in South

America or anywhere else in the world, we're going to have to shut off a lot more cities than just Rio."

"So, how many would you guess?" Sybil asked. "A dozen cities? 50? Still easier to contain than *all* cities worldwide."

Perka looked shocked. "But that's purposely starving millions of people! You can't! *We* can't!"

Skervin stood up and everyone went quiet. He looked at around at the faces in the room, lingering longest on Perka. Then he spoke seriously. "Tough problems make for tough decisions. You all have guts or you wouldn't be here." He paused. "We are going with this approach. Think of it like a tourniquet if you want. We're going to cut off supply to part of the body to save the rest. Stasik, in the next two hours I want a prioritized list of other cities to be rationed if necessary. Perka, you'll want to redeploy some medical staff. Sybil, a complete communication plan by the end of the day. Keep it as contained as you can."

Skervin turned toward Kapcheck with the intention of giving him one last prod, but Kapcheck already knew full well that this all rested on him. He rushed out of the room looking ill.

Custody Level, ORGA Headquarters

Skervin's legal logic argued that just as ORGA needed its own armed agents in ORGA Enforcement, it also followed, again naturally and by any theory of law, that ORGA had a need, from time to time, to detain criminals. Which was why ORGA headquarters in Capital City had an entire level that looked and acted just like a jail.

The new prisoners arrived under the personal escort of ORGA Senior Enforcement Officer 50 Smithson Jackson, who had flown with them here all the way from Saskatchewan. Smithson was rightly proud of finally bringing in these bandits, who over the last 48 hours had been leaving a trail of havoc that extended from outer space, to Denver, to the middle of the western croplands. He paraded them through the entry way of the Custody Level to scattered applause from the gathered staff.

There were five of them. They had been stripped of their old clothes and issued coarse, navy blue coveralls. Their few belongings, including brainboxes and Galen's organic samples and data chip, had been confiscated. They were handcuffed.

The apparent ringleader was 22 Galen, a fair-skinned but weather-beaten older man with a bandage on his forehead who looked like something out of storybook about the Old West. He was followed by two 30-rank young men who looked innocent enough and healthy, but exhausted and dejected. They were the Earth pilots, it was said. Some onlookers, judging only from their downtrodden looks, wondered if they might have been dupes in the whole affair. Last came two tall, beautiful young women with blonde hair and sky-blue eyes. These were the aliens from an exotic planet, pure-enough looking but obviously capable of any kind of criminal subterfuge, given their foreign origin.

Smithson marched the handcuffed prisoners into a small office to be confronted by the lead officer in charge of the case, 68 Tappet Holson. Galen started demanding to speak with the prime minister, but Smithson slapped his face hard. "No talking!" Then he turned to

Tappet and said, "We've kept them separated ever since the arrest per your orders, 68."

Tappet looked them over one by one. He was in full police officer vein, standing straight and looking intimidating. "I am very pleased to see all of you. In custody, that is. You gave us quite a chase." He paused and paced along the line. "We are just going to have two questions for you: What the hell are you plotting? And who else is involved?"

This time three different people tried to answer at once, but Smithson yelled "Silence!"

"That's right," Tappet said. "Don't answer here. You will each be interrogated separately. I will be very interested to see if your answers agree. Take them, Smithson. Wait, not 22 Galen. He comes with me. There is someone who wants to talk with him."

Skervin's Office

It was a long ride straight up on the turbolift, and by the end Galen, closely escorted by Tappet, was not at all surprised to be stepping out into the lobby of an opulent executive suite on Level 160. He felt his face flushing and bile rising in this throat. He was going to see Skervin. Skervin on whose committee he had once served, long ago and in another life. Skervin whose "Our World Our Way" foolishness he had tried to oppose. Skervin who had tried to kill him for it, Galen was certain.

Skervin who had killed his wife and daughter instead.

Blood was pulsing through Galen's temples and breathless grunts were erupting spontaneously from the back of his throat. The moment they were admitted to Skervin's office Galen tore free of Tappet and rushed at Skervin in an uncontrollable rage. Skervin was standing in front of his desk, looking astonished. Galen's wrists were handcuffed together in front but that didn't stop him from raising them over his head, clenching his fists, and aiming a vicious blow at Skervin's neck.

Skervin turned and ducked, throwing up his arms to protect his head. Galen's blow sent Skervin stumbling forward and down with a short, involuntary yell. Galen raised his hands for another strike just as Tappet, with a policeman's trained movements, seized him from behind and threw him sideways to the floor. With arms encumbered by the handcuffs, Galen landed hard and awkwardly, and his face mashed into the expensive carpet. Moments later Tappet's knee was pressing into Galen's back and his electropulse gun was pressed against Galen's skull.

"Should I pulse him, 96?"

Skervin gradually returned himself to an erect posture and a more composed state of mind. "No, don't pulse this idiot. He's obviously cracked. Get some more security in here and put him in a chair."

Two security officers came rushing in and dragged Galen to a chair while Tappet kept a weapon aimed at his face. When Galen calmed down they stepped back just far enough to let him look openly at Skervin.

Skervin carefully wiped his heavy brows with a folded handkerchief and massaged his throbbing shoulder before giving Galen a long look. "I thought you were dead."

"No, only broken. It's Joanna and Lillian that you killed."

"Oh yes, that terrible accident. Your wife and daughter, right? Such a shame. It was an accident, you know."

"It was absolutely not. That air taxi was programmed to hit us. To hit me. But it ended up killing my family instead. You are a murderer!"

"Galen, Galen. Calm yourself. I had nothing to do with it."

"Maybe you didn't do it yourself, but you ordered it. Their blood is on your hands."

Skervin made a show of looking at his hands. "Oh really? 'Out, damned spot,' as Lady Macbeth would say? My hands are clean, Galen. I think you just feel guilty for letting it affect you so. You gave up, missed the crucial meeting on Our World Our Way, and forfeited your vote. My side won and your side lost. That must bother you still."

"To hell with your goddamned egotistical, ethnocentric, isolationist, misdirected policy, Skervin. I don't care. I haven't cared for twenty years."

"Ah, yes. That's why you went and hid yourself away in the dirt out west. Lost your rank. Crawled into a hole. You don't care about anything anymore, do you?"

"I was trying, but now this little question of animals dying by the hundreds in the fields has caught my attention. Is that what made you drag me all the way out here to Capital City?"

"Ah, yes. You've discovered our current crisis."

Galen shifted position in his chair, prompting his guards to lean forward. But he wasn't going to lunge. "What is it, Skervin? A plague?"

Skervin walked to the window and stared out thoughtfully. "It's a toxic plant pathogen. Toxin-X, we call it. It makes soybeans poisonous. It's not only killing animals; it's killing people, too. Worst thing I've ever seen."

"People too? My god! What are you doing about it?"

"We're working on it."

"Which immunization process step are you on?"

"Doesn't matter. We'll get it. But meanwhile, the real problem is information containment."

"You mean, keeping it a secret. Why? Afraid you'll look bad for letting it happen?"

"I'm not afraid of anything. I'm *aware* that if this gets out, we risk worldwide panic."

"Panic? Why? They'll know you're going to find a cure . . ." Galen's expression transformed from cynical anger to terrible concern. "Aren't you? Damn, Skervin. Aren't you? You must have a solution in the works."

Skervin squinted. "We will, we will. But meanwhile—"

"Damn, Skervin! You don't have a treatment for it, do you? You have a toxic plague on your hands, and you haven't figured out how to stop it, and you're trying to cover it up!"

"I keep telling you—"

"No! Don't bullshit me. Don't bullshit yourself! You have to do something. Get help! Use the prime minister. Bring in the scientific community. For the love of God, ask the Hundred Worlds! Skervin, those soybeans are the food supply for this entire planet. I've seen the dead animals. Are you saying infected soybeans are doing the same thing to people? Killing them? Stop screwing around, Skervin! Act! Fast!"

Skervin's eyes narrowed and his nostrils flared. He had had enough of being lectured by this, damn, 22, field monitor. "Out!" he spit. "Out! Get him out of here."

The guards wrestled Galen out of his chair and strong-armed him toward the door.

As he watched Galen taken away, Skervin wondered to himself whether his old enemy really was like Lady Macbeth's damned spot.

■　■　■

Outside in the lobby, Ettica watched Galen being marched out and wondered much the same thing. As Skervin's second-in-command, she was constantly navigating a spider web of political opportunities and imperatives, volatile personalities, technical topics more directly related to ORGA's nominal mission, and yes, ethical dilemmas. She had worked hard to reach her 91 level and her current prestigious assignment, moving all the way up from where she started her career 20 years ago as a 77. She was gifted with intelligence and poise, but in the world of the Authority the real key to success was reading the ever-shifting political landscape and moving in the right direction at the right time, and that was the greatest of her gifts. But she had a curse, too, which was her conscience. She had buried it deeply, down under many layers of ambition, but still it insisted on sending out muffled cries from time to time as the imperatives of her position led her down some of the darker paths of executive leadership. She would argue with it sometimes, and bury it deeper, but somehow it could never be crushed. And she thought she was starting to hear its voice again now.

"What are you going to do with 22 Galen?" Ettica asked Skervin.

"Lock him away. He's trouble. Always has been."

"And the kids?"

"Guilt by association. They'll be safer locked away, too. At least for now. You disagree?"

"No, you're probably right. It's just the diplomatic angle with New Gaia. They might want their citizens back."

"So, let them take us to Hundred Worlds Court. We'll tie it up there long enough that this will all be over before they ever see the light of day."

Ettica had worked with Skervin for two years, so she thought carefully before phrasing her next question. "Skervin, are we putting too much faith in Kapcheck? I think he might be over his head."

Skervin fought down the temptation to get defensive. "He, and his lab, are the best we've got. Anyway, what we're really putting faith in are the automated diagnostic algorithms. They're a lot smarter than Kapcheck. They'll crack it."

Ettica was watching him closely. Like all 90s, she was highly skilled at reading people, and she could tell that at this moment he was just on the edge of being receptive. "You know, we could put out an inquiry in strictly academic circles. Position it as a theoretical exercise—"

"No, Ettica! We're not taking this out to academics or anyone else. The risk of a leak is too great."

It didn't take refined people-reading skills to see where that came out. Ettica nodded quietly and left.

■ ■ ■

When Ettica returned to her office, she closed the door and poured herself a careful glass of her own fine cognac. On her viewscreen, she brought up Skervin's visuals from their last briefing and flipped through the photos of dead children at the birthday party. Then she switched to 77 Stasik's briefing on the supply problems in Rio and elsewhere. There were no pictures of hungry and desperate citizens in Rio, but Ettica had no trouble imagining them in her mind. And then she turned to studying profiles of Galen and the four prisoners Skervin had brought in. She was a quick study, and she absorbed the details of their life stories quickly.

ORGA's second-in-command stared into her glass with her green eyes, swirling the amber liquor and thinking about currents and whirlpools and children. After a long time, she took a large sip and commed her assistant. "Michael, tell custody level I need to see the Galen prisoners. Yes, all of them; there are five. Not here, make it a conference room down on one of the administrative levels. And Michael, no need to mention this to Maggi or anyone else."

Conference Room 63-200, ORGA Headquarters

When two guards escorted the prisoners into the conference room, Ettica was sitting at the far end of the long table like a queen at a banquet. "Wait outside the door," she told the guards. "They're handcuffed. I'll call if I need you."

Then she addressed herself to prisoners, eyes sharp, dark brown hair perfect, posture straight and tall in a dark green dress. "Don't sit down. This won't take long."

Galen, bloody bandage still on his head, stood at one end of the line of them, with Marta, Kessa, Stoke, and Jet all standing there in their navy-blue prisoner coveralls and studying her with expressions that ranged from frightened (Marta) to curious (Jet). "Who are you?" asked Galen. "They took my brainbox."

"91 Ettica Sim. I work with Skervin."

Galen tensed. "What do you want?"

Ettica ignored the question. "New Gaia is an interesting place. You're from there originally?" She was speaking carefully and slowly, with a sort of forced casualness in her pleasant voice.

"Yes."

"And you two girls, too? I love your sky-blue eyes. I hope you won't be offended if I say we hardly ever hear of your planet."

"Small population," Galen said.

"Yes. And a very unusual society, too. But I understand some of your science is quite advanced. Botany, in particular. Must be all that terraforming work over the last few generations. Ever seen this paper before?" She glanced down at her own viewscreen but didn't bother to show it to the others. "It's not my field but apparently it's referenced often. It's called 'Characterization of toxicity domains and methods of virulence screening in *Fusarium oxysporum*.' No? Well maybe you've heard of the author. Apparently she's a leading scientist in the field of phytochemistry and toxicology, especially poisonous mushrooms. Name of Lana Sjøfred?"

Galen, Marta, and Kessa all brightened, though cautiously. "My sister," Galen confirmed. "The mother of Marta and Kessa here."

Ettica smiled. "I thought so." She stood up and moved behind her chair, setting her hands on the back and leaning forward. "Do you know why you're being held here?"

Jet shrugged. "Blasting out of Spaceport America, for one."

"Resisting arrest," Stoke added. "Possibly something about tampering with Authority electronics . . ."

"True, true," Ettica interrupted. "But wrong. It's this toxic pathogen in the soy that's poisoning our entire planet's food supply. Galen discovered our terrible secret, and I'm sure he's told you all about it now, too."

"Just a few words. And you're locking us up for that?" Marta burst out. "Why?"

"Actually it's 96 Skervin that is locking you up. And maybe me too, depending on a decision that will be entirely up to you. And the reason is, the secret. This can't get out."

Marta, surprising herself, stuck to her guns. "Why not? This is a worldwide crisis. You should be telling everybody! Getting help!"

"Think a moment. There are billions of people on this planet, and that disease is on the verge of poisoning our entire food supply. Soybeans are our dominant crop and we can't switch to another source in any reasonable amount of time. It is physically impossible to import enough from other planets to feed us. If this plague is not stopped, we will be facing planetwide starvation. *Imagine* what would happen if that news got out and were not refuted immediately. There would be a worldwide panic. Everyone would start hoarding food, making the problem even worse. It would be the worst disaster in the history of the Hundred Worlds. Do you see this? Do you see what I'm saying?"

There was a stunned sense of understanding from the group. Marta nodded slowly and spoke for them all. "I get it. You have to keep this from the public until you have a solution."

After a few moments of processing Kessa spoke up. "But you only need to find a cure, right? Once you start curing it, it won't matter so much if people know."

"Probably."

"I see where you're going," Jet said, skipping to the end of Ettica's carefully unspooling thread. "You want us to enlist their mother's help, but keep it secret."

Ettica smiled appreciatively and nodded. "That's it."

"Makes sense to me," Jet said. "What's the catch?"

"Hah, you don't miss much, do you, young man? The 'catch,' as you say, is that my boss, 96 Skervin Hough, the Minister of Organic Resources, would not be in favor of this plan. He doesn't think we need outsiders to find a cure, and he doesn't trust any of you not to leak the secret."

"Ah."

Galen was following closely. "So why do you have us here, Ettica?"

Ettica left her guarded position behind the chair and walked down to their end of the room. She was almost as tall as Galen and she looked him straight in the eye. "I am going to take a very, very large risk right now. I am doing this because the future of my planet is at stake, and I am trusting that the five of you take that as seriously as I do. And that maybe, just maybe, you will be able to help."

"We understand," Galen said.

"You have to know Skervin will try to stop you, even beyond Earth orbit."

"You're going to send us to New Gaia to find Lana?"

"That's the idea. 34 Jet here is a space pilot, right?"

"Well, I'm studying—"

"Close enough. Now, on this chip are the complete transcripts of all the executive meetings we've had on this, so you'll know as much as I do. I'm sorry I don't have any detailed technical information; you'll be on your own for that. But I think I can help you with, shall we say, transportation. I have some temporary eardots here for you all; you're going to need them. And here's what you'll need to do . . ."

ADS *Gregor Mendel,* Outbound from Spaceport America

"This. Is. Swank!" Stoke sighed as he threw himself against the buttery leather cushions on the wall of the lounge of ADS *Gregor Mendel.* There was a huge grin on his face. 91 Ettica's clandestine arrangements had landed the five of them in a luxurious ORGA executive space yacht, posing as members of Skervin's executive team on their way to a security conference.

Why anyone with even a passing interest in security would be headed anywhere near the backwater of New Gaia was another question that was, thankfully, never asked. Ettica had managed to get them more suitable clothes and cleverly routed them here with a minimum of interference from guards and checkpoints.

Yet they knew time was short. Skervin or Tappet could discover them at any moment, and then the game would be up.

Now they found themselves aboard their own Alçubierre Drive spaceship, rushing to launch into an almost three-day trip to New Gaia. *Gregor Mendel* was designed to transport up to six passengers and two crew across vast interstellar distances with a minimum of discomfort and a maximum of luxury. Given the harsh physics realities of ADS technology the spaces were still small, but the craft's makers had gone to great lengths to make them otherwise as comfortable as possible. Natural, ORGA-grown leather and rare woods were everywhere. Gentle, indirect lighting automatically adapted to the position of the passengers and their particular needs at any time. Air was circulated, cleaned, and carefully conditioned at twice the normal rate. Useful appliances, including powerful computers, a 3D printer, and a cleaning bot, were tucked away in discrete compartments. The automated galley presented meals in weightless-ready fine china servers. And on it went.

"Stoke!" Jet called. "Forget that. Get up here and help me figure this thing out. Fast!" Stoke sheepishly pulled himself together and swooped through the weightless cabin up to the flight deck to help his friend. Jet had been studying for his spacer qualifiers for almost a

year now—one hour every morning after the gym and before work—
and he was an excellent student, so in theory he knew what he was
doing. On the other hand, hurtling one ship and five people across
423 light years of space at far above the speed of light was no trifle,
and he had never actually done it before.

"You know how to fly this, right Jet?" Marta asked a little
querulously as she floated weightlessly at the door of the flight deck.

"Sure, yes."

"It's not that different from an orbiter like *Chica*, right?"

"Right, pretty much the same," Jet lied.

"Okay, good. Just checking."

Once Marta was gone, Stoke gave a little laugh. "Yeah, right, Jet,"
he smiled.

Finally, after many feverish minutes of preparation, Jet had *Gregor
Mendel* ready to warp. He looked over for confirmation at Stoke, who
had been sitting beside him at the controls, providing moral support.

"You think?" Jet asked.

"Good as far as I can tell."

"Alright, here goes!"

Jet grimaced, closed his eyes for one last run through his mental
checklist, and then touched a control. There was a silent surge of
acceleration and then suddenly the stars on his screen were moving.
They were on their way.

It was an odd thing about ADS travel. You could be as rushed and
frantic as could be before and after, but once you were at warp there
was absolutely nothing else to be done. You were traveling at a speed
fixed by the laws of physics, and no amount of anything would get
you to your destination one second sooner or later. Communication
of any kind was pointless; you were traveling far faster than any
electromagnetic signal could. You were on hiatus. In limbo. All you
could do was wait, and maybe plan your strategy for after you
reentered regular space.

And the exact same was true for anyone who was chasing you.

They had 68 hours in warp. As soon as they were under way and started to relax, exhaustion caught up with them. They ate quickly and found their way gratefully to the berths for a long, lovely sleep.

8

Saturday, August 6

Skervin's Office

It was Saturday morning and a weekend, but Tappet and Skervin were both working as usual. "What is it, Tappet?" Skervin asked. "Why did you need to see me in person?"

This was hard for Tappet. He *never* questioned his superiors. It was not in his nature. "Permission to speak freely, 96? I would like to ask a question."

"Yes?"

"What was the, uh, thinking in releasing the Galen prisoners?"

"What are you talking about?"

"I just learned this morning that Galen and the other prisoners were released last night on your orders."

"My orders??"

"That's what I was told."

By now Skervin was rising out of his chair, looking genuinely alarmed. "I didn't give any such order."

"Sir? I just confirmed this with the custody watch commander—"

Skervin ignored him and commed the watch commander himself, practically shouting into the viewscreen. "Where are the Galen prisoners?"

"As I was just telling 68 Tappet, sir, they were released last night at 18:30 hours."

"By whom?!"

"I wasn't here, but the log says it was you, 96—"

Skervin threw down a fist and cut the connection. "Maggi! Security alert! Prisoner escape. Get me Enforcement. I want a search on *now!*"

■   ■   ■

It took very little time for Skervin, Ettica, and Tappet to determine the Galen prisoners had disappeared into space aboard one of Skervin's own executive yachts, but Skervin didn't care about the ship. He just wanted to know about his secret.

"Did they leak it, Tappet?" Skervin demanded.

"We haven't seen anything yet. There's nothing on the nets. But it's entirely possible they passed information on to a third party who is going to release it at a later time."

Skervin nodded. "Or maybe blackmail us. What kind of information did they have in their possession?"

"Actually not that much, 96. It would only be what they saw or remembered. We confiscated all their electronic devices and Galen's biological samples and they left those behind, so they don't have technical data that we know of."

"That's good. So they'll just be telling stories. I'll put 81 Sybil on it, she can crush them with her propaganda machine."

"So we're out of the woods, then?"

Ettica scoffed and spoke—it seemed—angrily. "You mean besides the diplomatic outcry with New Gaia and the stolen spacecraft and other mayhem these lunatics have caused? Maybe. How did this happen, Tappet? How did they pull off this escape?"

"We can't tell yet, Ettica. But the way they seemed to know where to go and who to talk to, we have to suspect an insider."

"That's what I think, too. But who? Perka? Kapcheck, you think?"

"I have no evidence against anyone at this time, 91."

Skervin shook his head moodily and looked at Ettica. "It had to be Kapcheck. Who else would do something so stupid? I'll interrogate him myself."

Ettica nodded her head. "That makes sense, he's been looking desperate. But don't be too hard on him yet. He may not understand security, but he's still our best chance at beating Toxin-X."

Skervin said, "I suppose you're right. But meanwhile, the escapees are still out there. Where do you think they went?"

Ettica shrugged. "As far away as possible, I would suppose."

"Right, one of the Hundred Worlds. If we ever find them we'll have to extradite, and that's never easy. I'm not even sure it would be worth it for us. But you know what I think? I think they just went back to New Gaia."

"That would be simplest."

Skervin turned back to Tappet. "That leads me to one question you haven't answered yet, Tappet. Did you successfully destroy the p-cap Galen sent to his sister Thursday morning?"

"Can't be sure yet. I sent a contractor to New Gaia, but he won't even be arriving yet."

"Someone you can trust?"

Tappet shifted uncomfortably. "It was, uh, hard to find someone on short notice."

"Tappet, that p-cap has hard evidence about Toxin-X. If they get their hands on that, then even 81 Sybil won't be able to plug the leak. Let me ask you again: is your man going to get the job done?"

Tappet looked down for moment, then back at Skervin. "I can't be certain, 96."

"Well then, 68 Tappet, you are going on a trip."

"But sir, there is so much for me to do here—"

"Ettica is here, and you have staff. They can run things while you're gone."

"But I'm not qualified for covert operations like—"

"You're as qualified as anyone. Besides, I trust you, and there aren't many people I trust. Just get out there, make sure that p-cap is destroyed, and get back here. Easy. And important."

"Understood, 96. I'll just pack a bag."

ADS *Gregor Mendel*

Once the space travelers awoke, they set about luxuriating in the free time and their sumptuous quarters. They used the 3D printer to make new, lounge-worthy clothes. They had long talks in pairs and groups. During one quiet hour Galen told them all his own version of his previous life, and how his wife and daughter had died, and how he had come to be a lowly field monitor living apart from society. Though she had heard it before, Kessa cried as Galen told his story, and afterwards all she could do was give him a long, loving hug.

The "kids" played with various games found in *Gregor Mendel*'s supplies, especially their favorite, weightless dodgeball. Galen had the onboard maker create a paper book for him; he didn't like reading from screens.

From time to time, Jet and Stoke made their way to the flight deck together for mid-flight checks and routines. It was relatively mindless work for both of them, and they tended to talk as they worked.

"So, Kessa, huh?" Stoke said with a sly smirk at Jet.

Jet couldn't help grinning at the mere mention of her name. The best verbal reply he could manage was a tilted-back head with a happy, throaty sigh.

"I thought so," laughed Stoke. "You're gone for her."

"Why wouldn't I be? She's so . . . beautiful."

"I know what you mean. Blonde hair, blue eyes, pale skin, almost as tall as I am, and she has that whole willowy long-legged thing going on—"

"I meant on the inside."

"Oh! Yeah, that, too. She's kind of off-beat, you might say. Lives in a world of her own, right? And I'm still not sure whether I forgive her for getting us into this mess to begin with. But she seems really perceptive and nice."

"I forgive her. I mean, look at this toxin thing. If the Authority can't fix it, we may be Earth's only hope, and it's because of her."

Stoke just nodded in sober agreement.

Jet allowed himself to return to dreamier thoughts. "And mm, she is nice. And she's playful . . . and sensitive . . . and intuitive, and passionate about things . . . There's so much *to* her. I feel like every other girl I've ever met was a single planet, and Kessa is a whole galaxy."

"Whoa, you really are gone."

Jet tossed his head apologetically and turned attention back to Stoke. "Why, are you getting a thing for Marta?"

"Marta? Why would you say that?"

"Hah, don't play coy with me. She's a hottie, too, isn't she, in a neat-and-tidy sort of way?"

"Hey, she has a lot more curves that Kessa. They're just harder to see because of the way she wears her clothes and fixes her hair."

"Aha, you're defending her! You do like her!"

"Maybe. I like a lot of people."

"Yeah, like you liked Alera a few nights ago, and I don't even remember who it was before her and before that one, too. You do like your women."

Stoke smiled self-indulgently. "Yes, I suppose I do."

Jet continued, "But if you ask me, Marta has it going on, too, in a different way from Kessa."

Stoke nodded. "I agree. I mean, Marta's smart and nice and everything, too, but she's also the responsible sister, isn't she? The one who takes care of everything that needs taking care of, people included."

Jet nodded. "Yeah, I like that about her. I think she pays attention to other people, kind of like you do. That's a good thing."

Stoke laughed. "You think *I* take care of people?"

Jet gave a little nod. "I don't know about that, but at least you pay attention. Now can you take care of that blinking light over there?"

■   ■   ■

Just outside the door to the flight deck, Marta had been accidentally eavesdropping on the conversation Jet and Stoke were having. She was watching a video that had its own soundtrack so she didn't catch every word they said, but she caught snippets here and there. " . . . Marta? Why would you say that? . . . Alera a few nights ago, and I don't even remember who it was before her and before that one, too. You do like your women. . . . Yes, I suppose I do. . . . Marta's smart and nice and everything, too, but . . ."

Marta reddened. She had suspected some time ago that Stoke was a skirt-chaser, and now the guys' conversation was confirming it. It made her feel twisted inside for some reason. She didn't know how to feel. She was finding him so easy to talk to and likeable, otherwise. But the idea of Stoke as a playboy rankled. And now what he said about her: "smart and nice and everything, too, *but* . . ." But what, she wondered? What was so wrong with her? She felt insulted, that was it.

Still, though . . .

■ ■ ■

At the end of the day, after a pleasant meal around a zero-g table full of cheerful conversation, Kessa absently ran a hand over her hair and said, "You know, I think there's something wrong with the light in my bed. Jet, do you know how to reset the control?"

Jet, not missing a thing, said, "Not sure. Why don't I come see?"

And that was the last they saw of Kessa and Jet for the next 18 hours.

Whoever said you can't have sex in zero-g had never encountered the combined creative and inventive genius of Kessa and Jet.

■ ■ ■

"Does your family love you?" Jet asked Kessa once as they lay side-by-side in her berth.

"Of course they do." Kessa paused. "They might not *understand* me, but they love me."

"What don't they understand?"

"I don't know. Why I'm so irresponsible, I suppose. Or why I'm so passionate about certain things. Remember when we were in the brainbox store, and I was acting a part?"

"Yeah, you were amazing."

"Thanks. But you know why? You know why I'm a pretty good actress? Because when I'm around other people, I'm almost always acting. I'm pretending to be a certain personality. I'm being polite, and I'm pretending that it's natural for me to behave in a certain way. I'm pretending to be interested in what the other people are talking and thinking about. Sometimes I am, but other times, I'm not at all! I'm sitting there talking with everyone about, I don't know, tiddlywinks, but in my head I'm running naked through the forest and singing aloud at the top of my lungs!"

Jet was nodding vigorously. "I know exactly what you mean! That feeling of being disconnected from everyone else sometimes—that's how it is for me, too. Well, not the part about running naked through the forest. But there's a world in my head that is way bigger, and way more interesting to me, than the mundane world everyone else seems to be living in. I don't know if I'm an actor, but I spend half my time kind of playing along with other people just to get along. I censor my thoughts. If I started talking about what I was really going on in my head, they'd lock me up."

"So what does go on in your head?"

Jet grinned. "Ah, wouldn't you like to know."

Kessa leaned over and took his head in her two hands and kissed his forehead. "Yes. I would!"

9

Sunday, August 7

ADS *Okafor*, In Orbit around New Gaia

ADS *Okafor* Captain Narisa Kunlabi watched her displays with satisfaction as the New Gaia space tender approached her ship. Although her bearing was as elegant as ever and no one would notice from the looks of her glowing dark skin and ready smile, she was tired. She had been in space aboard her ship for three weeks now and it was time for her three weeks off. She was going to spend this break on New Gaia, lounging by the sea and hiking in the woods. Much as she had great affection for *Okafor*, New Gaia's big, wild, unpopulated spaces and wonderfully fresh air—not to mention gravity—were just the thing after weeks inside a cramped and windowless craft.

The young man who was officer of the watch, standing next to Narisa on the cramped bridge, spoke up. "Captain, have a look at this."

"What is it?"

"Right here. This ship orbiting above us."

"So? Is there a problem?"

"Not exactly, Captain. It's just that I can't get a reading on it. The tracking system isn't picking up any Automatic Identification Signal."

"No AIS? Hmm, that is troubling. Hail them."

"No response."

"What is their status?"

"I detect no mechanical problems. No distress calls. Their orbit is stable."

"Range?"

"5000 clicks."

"Okay, that is outside our safety perimeter. I will ask STC about it." Narisa raised her friend Leilani at the Space Traffic Control Center down on the surface. "New Gaia STC, this is *Okafor*. Do you know who that is, Leilani?" she said. "I am getting no AIS."

"No, Narisa, I can't get a rise out those sons of bitches, either. But they're out of your way. You're clear to commence off-loading."

"Roger that. I am coming groundside today, so I will see you soon. It will just be me and Kai from the crew."

"Happy day. I'll see you in a few hours, then. Peace be!"

Captain Kunlabi turned her attention to the matters at hand, which included welcoming her own replacement. Someone else would be dealing with the mystery ship.

■ ■ ■

Ten minutes later, a new captain was at the helm of *Okafor*, and Narisa and her first officer, a tall, wiry man with raven-black hair named Kai Tong, had finished recording their logs and worked through their checklists down to the last item: p-cap transport.

Together, Narisa and Kai went to the safe containing the p-cap canisters. The safe was programmed to open only in the simultaneous presence of two certified couriers, such as Narisa and Kai, who were easily recognized by their brainboxes and verified by remote biosensors. Narisa reached into the safe and fished out two canisters destined for New Gaia: one from Earth and one they had taken possession of at Hestia. The canisters were each the size of her forearm, cylinders with rounded ends, designed to withstand every kind of shock short of a nuclear blast. She placed them carefully into a customized carrying pouch—the *mochila*, they called it, with reference to the pouches used by the Pony Express in ancient times—and closed the double seals. Kai took the mochila and strapped it onto the chest of his jumpsuit, with three extra clips for safety.

Narisa and Kai went through these motions mechanically, in the way that people do who have repeated the same procedure every few days for years on end. There was no good reason for it, really. Just procedure. Nobody ever stole p-caps.

Narisa mused, sometimes, about what was in all those p-caps. Business correspondence. Government correspondence. Personal messages between family and friends seeking to stay in touch across light years of space. Maybe one of them today was announcing a birth, or a death. Maybe one of them today, she thought, was the most important message in the world.

Amazingly, she was right.

Mochila successfully retrieved, Narisa and Kai boarded the waiting tender that would take them down to New Gaia's space elevator. Kai floated over to the nearest chair and strapped his wiry frame onto it, moving only a little awkwardly with the mochila strapped to his suit. Narisa moved directly to the simple nav control panel, where she exchanged messages with *Okafor* and then started the launch sequence. Then she headed for a chair of her own. The robots would take it from here to the space elevator.

Minutes later she watched *Okafor* disappear from sight in a dark field of stars as the tender sped them on their way, with the beautiful planet of New Gaia filling the field of view below.

But three seconds later, there was a sudden change. The straight, steady push of the tender's rocket was violently interrupted. Narisa and Kai were thrown up and sideways against their restraining straps. The whole ship began rotating.

Damage? Emergency maneuvering? Narisa gave a quick, concerned look at Kai, ripped off her restraining straps, and dove over to the nav control panel. "Report!" she called at it.

The simple display panel was making no sense. No damage, it said. No emergency. It simply showed the tender making radical changes in course and speed. There was no reason. There was also no way to stop it. Narisa hit the comm. "New Gaia STC, this is Narisa downlinking on the tender. Emergency contact!"

But there was no response. The comm channel was dead.

Narisa knew what she had to do. Quickly, she hooked herself into position in front of the nav panel and pulled open a small door that covered a retractable control wheel. It was slightly ridiculous to attempt to steer a spaceship rocketing through space by hand, but there was nothing else to do. She typed in a code to the control panel and touched the words EMERGENCY MANUAL CONTROL.

Nothing happened.

She touched the control again.

Still nothing.

She retyped the code.

Nothing.

"What the hell is going on?" she cried aloud.

Instrumentation and controls on this tender were primitive in the extreme and there was little else to do. Kai could only look on helplessly as they continued their hard turn. They were reducing speed, he realized, and heading in a new direction.

Then Narisa realized. "It's that no-AIS! The unidentified ship we saw before. They must be doing this."

"Why?" asked Kai.

"Well, either they want to capture us, or they want to kill us."

"Argh!"

"Don't worry, I am certain we'll find out which one it is very soon."

True to Narisa's prediction, another ship shortly appeared on the tender's proximity scope, and not long after they could see it with their naked eyes. They were headed straight for it. It was a relatively small Alçubierre spacer with no distinctive markings: it had to be private. It still wasn't broadcasting AIS. What was going on? Narisa had heard stories of space pirates, but she always figured they were urban myths. Space was far too big and dangerous for piracy to be practical . . . wasn't it?

As they approached the mystery ship it became certain that the tender was under remote control and being moved in for docking. It crossed Narisa's mind to try to destroy or disable her own controls or engines, but crippling oneself out here in space was suicidal. Better to take their chances with whomever this was.

The tender spun around in its familiar docking pirouette and there was a *thunk* when the docking port mated. Narisa and Kai maneuvered themselves into position, floating in the weightless car to face the portal. Kai became very aware of the mochila still strapped to his suit. Narisa pointed her electropulse gun.

The port opened and a muscular figure moved purposefully through the hatch. His face was stern and his eyes were cold and steady. There was something unmistakably military and belligerent in his bearing that told his story even more clearly than his short haircut and black battledress. When he looked up he was holding a gun. "I have a weapon, too," he said coolly. "And mine fires bullets." He came all the way into the room and braced himself against a wall.

Narisa didn't move her gun. "Who are you?"

"It doesn't matter. I won't be here long."

"You hacked the tender's nav computer?"

There was no reply.

"You know a projectile gun like that is a really bad idea in space. The recoil sends you flying and the bullets—"

There was an ear-shattering explosion as the man fired his gun at the wall. The bullet ricocheted once and then buried itself in a chair. Narisa and Kai both gasped, but the man stood there calmly, watching them as if nothing had happened. "Hands up, and drop your weapon."

Narisa quietly let go of her now feeble-seeming e-gun. In the microgravity it floated slowly away from her hand. She and Kai lifted their hands over their heads.

"What do you want?" Narisa asked.

The man tilted his chin in the direction of the mochila strapped to Kai's chest. "The p-caps."

Birth and death announcements, thought Narisa. Or maybe one of them today was the most important message in the world. "Those are being transported under the protection of an interplanetary treaty among all one hundred of the Hundred Worlds. You take those and you are a criminal on every planet there is."

The man moved closer and aimed his gun at Kai, who was now bracing his feet against the back of a chair for stability.

"Take it off slowly," he said. "No sudden moves."

Kai bent his head down to look at the fastenings of the mochila. The man watched closely. Just as he focused his attention to watch Kai undo the second clip, Narisa moved. With a fluid motion born of years in space, she arched out and grabbed her gun from where it was floating in midair. She turned it and fired.

That was a handy thing about electropulse guns: they weren't hard to aim, even when held casually at arm's length. She had hers set for a wide spread and all it took was a blast in the general direction of the man. He yelped and his body suddenly tensed and froze in place. Only his head and left arm still moved. The gun in his right hand remained clenched in his paralyzed fist, useless.

But she had hit Kai, too. "Oww!" he yelled. "My legs!"

"Sorry!" Narisa shouted. Come on! Get to the hatch!" The pirate cursed and flailed his still-working left arm, trying to grab at them, but the two seasoned spacers swooped easily past him in the weightless cabin and slipped through the portal, slamming the hatch closed behind them.

Narisa led Kai flying through the pirate's ship toward the flight deck. She propelled herself along with practiced hand-over-hand motions while Kai struggled to keep up despite the terrible pain in his useless legs. Once at the controls, Narisa pulled herself down into the chair and threw her hands at the instruments.

But they didn't respond. She was locked out. "Emergency override!" she tried. "Captain Narisa Kunlabi of ADS *Okafor*! Certified Planet Capsule Courier!" Nothing.

The man was no fool; he had programmed the controls to respond only to himself.

Narisa and Kai looked at each other, desperately thinking of options.

"Escape pod?" grimaced Kai.

It was a dangerous idea, but they were desperate. "Right. Let's try it. Go!"

ADS ships were all about the same, and Narisa and Kai knew right where to look for the small ship's emergency escape pod. There was a hidden panel in the "floor" of the main lounge. They yanked it open to find a hatch, unsealed it, and dove through. They found themselves in a cramped and dimly lit space that felt like the inside of an inverted canoe, all low ceilings and echoes but somehow long and large enough to hold what might have been the entire passenger complement of the man's small ship.

Kai worked to seal the hatch behind them while Narisa wormed her way forward to the control panel, whose display was glowing in emergency orange. Escape pod circuitry, she knew, was always independent of the rest of the ship to increase its chances of survival in the event of damage. Would the man have gone as far as locking these controls, too?

She pushed the LAUNCH button.

The escape pod lurched and they felt a sudden change in movement. They were away.

Space Traffic Control Center, Zero West, New Gaia

To be honest, New Gaia's Space Traffic Control Center was not impressive. It was housed in a single building on the outskirts of the village of Zero West, unremarkable except for a respectable-looking collection of antennas pointed up at the sky. Inside there were just three low-ceilinged rooms, all jammed with messy racks of aging technical equipment.

Presiding over the operation was a cherub-shaped, cheerful, middle-aged woman named Leilani. She was of Polynesian descent and therefore approximately as unusual-looking in this land of often-Nordic genotypes as a building full of electronics. But she'd been there for years, she knew her business, and everyone liked her, so she fit right in. Though she did swear like a sailor.

There was not a lot of space traffic around New Gaia. The only regular arrival was ADS *Okafor*, which came around on its cycle every six-and-a-fraction days, bearing New Gaian travelers and occasional tourists from other planets. The rest of the traffic consisted mostly of small craft that came and went only occasionally and at random. Leilani and her team—one regular named Kinga and two rotating citizen volunteers—monitored all the comings and goings, coordinated with Jaap over at the space elevator, and directed traffic if and when needed. It was important work and Leilani took it seriously, but it rarely departed from the routine.

Until today.

First there was the mysterious ADS ship that popped into New Gaian space and entered a high orbit without identifying itself. Leilani was still trying to raise it when *Okafor* arrived on schedule 20 minutes later, and her friend Captain Narisa commed her to ask about it. Leilani told Narisa not to worry, but that didn't solve the mystery.

Then, as Leilani was watching Narisa and Kai depart *Okafor* on the tender, things quickly went bad. First an alarm lit up saying the comm link to the tender had been lost. Then, much worse, she lost her link to the tender's nav system. The tender usually ran on autopilot, but if anything ever went wrong, Leilani could override it and steer remotely from the ground—if the link was working. When that went out, she was helpless. "What the hell are you doing, Narisa?" she thought.

The mystery ship suddenly broke out of its high orbit and began descending rapidly. Leilani's increasingly insistent hails and commands to break off were all ignored. At almost the same time, her screen blinked to indicate the tender was changing course and accelerating in a new direction: on course to intercept the other ship.

"Are you seeing this, *Okafor*?" Leilani commed urgently to the crew that had replaced Narisa.

"Affirmative, it looks like our tender is being commandeered by that no-AIS!"

"Can you stop it?"

"Nothing we can do from up here."

"Me either, dammit!" New Gaia had no space force. Leilani and *Okafor* were equally helpless to do anything but watch on their monitors as the unidentified ship docked with the tender. Leilani commed Karl over at satellite maintenance and told him to start an emergency launch of his service ship, but it would be almost an hour before he could reach orbit.

After that, Leilani punched furiously but fruitlessly at her equipment. What the spacing hell was the rogue ship doing?

Minutes later Leilani's monitor showed a new blip: the ship had ejected its escape pod! It was decelerating fast and heading for the surface. Was that the pirates getting away? Could it be Narisa and Kai escaping?

Leilani's emergency comm channel came to life. "Ahoy, New Gaia STC. This is the escape pod from an unidentified craft in orbit. Do you read me?"

"Escape pod, this is STC. I read you 5 by 5. Narisa? Is that you?"

"Affirmative, STC. Hi, Leilani, thank goodness. This is Narisa and I am here with Kai."

"What's your status?"

"That guy is a pirate! He had us at gunpoint, trying to steal the p-cap canisters. We are trying to escape. I pulsed him and last I knew he was locked in the tender. Kai got pulsed but we are okay. We still have the canisters in our possession. But this damn escape pod flies itself like a brick and I have no controls."

"Understood."

The escape pod was not simply falling in a straight line toward the planet. Escape pods were entirely automated, and in situations like this they were programmed to land on the nearest planet or moon, homing in on the signal of emergency beacons that were set up like lighthouses all over the Hundred Worlds. On Earth, for example, every port in every city had an emergency beacon that was active at all times. There were thousands of them. On New Gaia, there was one. Leilani had set it up herself, in the field out back, years ago. It had never been used.

When she realized what was happening with Narisa and Kai in their escape pod, Leilani checked the signal from her beacon. There wasn't one. It was dead.

"Crap! The beacon's not broadcasting! Shit! We have to fix it, fast! Kinga, run out there and check the base station! I'm looking here . . ." Leilani began desperately running diagnostics and checking screens, cursing a blue streak the whole time. She wasn't finding anything.

■ ■ ■

In the escape pod, Narisa and Kai were peering out the small viewports, trying to determine where they were going. They both knew the planet well from years of orbiting above it on *Okafor*. "This orbit is not right," Narisa commented edgily. "We should be equatorial, but we're inclined."

"The pirate must have tilted the orbit when he diverted the tender," Kai said, gritting his teeth from the pain in his electropulsed legs. "Maybe trying to make it harder to pursue?"

"Right, and it's going to make it difficult to get back to Zero West. In fact, shouldn't we be feeling some acceleration by now?"

"Yes, we should."

Narisa radioed Leilani. "Are you tracking us?"

"Most of the time. I lose you every time you go north or south of 15 degrees. We don't have coverage outside the equatorial band."

"I don't like the looks of this orbit. Does this autopilot know what it's doing?"

"Uh, Narisa? I guess I better let you know: our emergency beacon isn't transmitting. I'm really sorry. I think it's dead."

"That is not good. How is the autopilot going to know where to land?"

"Um, I'm not sure."

■ ■ ■

The escape pod's autopilot was (if computers could be called this) confused. It knew it needed to land on the planet, but it didn't know where, because there were no beacons. It examined the terrain and found no hard, flat surfaces resembling landing pads. Most of the land was covered in forests. The biggest settlement it could identify was on the equator, but it found itself in an unusual, awkward orbit that crossed above and below the equator and would never intersect the settlement without the expenditure of more delta-v than was available.

So, the autopilot (if computers could be said to do this, either) gave up. It chose a convenient clearing on one of the continents and headed for it.

■ ■ ■

Unlike the landing pads the autopilot was designed for, the clearing was neither perfectly clear nor flat. Confused by uneven terrain, the escape pod landed hard. One end hit a rock outcropping that tilted the whole pod over at a sharp angle, and Narisa and Kai were thrown violently sideways. Narisa's head slammed hard against a post and she was knocked unconscious.

When Narisa came to, her head was throbbing and blood was dripping down her forehead and into her eyes. She had trouble thinking straight. She looked over at Kai, and he looked unconscious or dead. Thinking she would rescue him, she unstrapped herself and

struggled over to release Kai's retention net as well. But his legs were
still paralyzed from the electropulse and he fell hard and awkwardly
against the side of the ship, emitting an involuntary grunt. One leg
was twisted underneath him at an unnatural angle.

"Oh, no," thought Narisa. The leg looked broken.

Narisa checked the controls and saw they had landed at 21 degrees
north latitude on the continent of Octavia. Everyone on New Gaia
lived on the continent of Sylvania.

She got the portal open, and with great struggle dragged first herself,
then Kai, outside and onto the ground. It was raining, the ground was
muddy, and a crow-like bird was cawing angrily. They were now
injured, in the middle of nowhere, and on the wrong damn continent.
Narisa allowed herself to cry.

10

Monday, August 8

Skervin's Office

"Kapcheck swears he didn't give aid to the escapees," Skervin was telling Ettica. "And all his tracking data checks out. I hate to say it, but I think I believe him."

"Are you sure?" said Ettica, acting as if she was still suspicious. "Because if it was Perka, she's doing a good job of hiding it. And I've been working my network, and no one seems to have credible suspects. Who else could it be?"

"I don't know," said Skervin. "When Tappet tracks the fugitives down, we'll just have to ask them ourselves. Whoever it was is going to pay dearly."

Ettica simply nodded. Slowly.

ADS *Gregor Mendel,* Approaching New Gaia

For an interstellar pilot, coming out of warp required as much attention as going in. Jet carefully decelerated *Gregor Mendel* and they came rocketing into normal space. He had appropriately set vectors for the New Gaia system's Deceleration Zone, but he made the rookie mistake of slowing too gently and found himself near the end of the zone, right where the concentration of accumulated space talus was thickest. Though it wasn't fatal, his displays started blinking orange and a warning buzzer went off briefly, worrying his passengers. He steered to safety quickly enough, but *Gregor Mendel*'s hull had gained some new scars.

As they flew toward New Gaia they came into comm range and, while Stoke signaled New Gaia STC, Marta eagerly contacted her mother, Lana. "Mom! It's so good to see you. We're back!"

"Good heavens! Already? But you only landed on Earth a few days ago!"

"I know, I know. We . . . we're in trouble."

"Oh no! Are you hurt?"

"We're okay. Kessa's here with me. And look, we brought Uncle Galen."

"Galen? Galen! You're here? You're on the ship with the girls?"

"Hello, Lana. It's nice to see you in real time! Yes, all three of us are out here in orbit somewhere high above you."

Marta broke in. "But Mom, did you get Galen's message? Do you know what's happening?"

"Message from Galen? No, nothing since you girls left. Apparently there was a problem with the last p-cap shipment. It's been all the gossip—"

"Oh no!"

"What? Was it something important?"

Stunned, Marta, Kessa, and Galen looked at each other with sinking hearts. "Important" was not a strong enough word. The p-cap Galen had sent included all his 3D scanner data from the dead animals and plants in the soybean fields. It would contain all the information Lana or anyone else would need to study the soybean disease and, they hoped, find a cure. Discounting Ettica's executive meeting transcripts, it was the only technical data they had on Toxin-X. And now it was missing.

Painfully and reluctantly, they filled Lana in on their story. Kessa felt they were like a rough storm on the coast, sending wave after wave of bad news crashing over their unfortunate mother. There was a planet-killing poisonous blight on Earth that the Authority couldn't stop and was trying to cover up. There was the embarrassing reality that they had been chased and arrested, and they were now fugitives in a stolen ship. They had hoped that Hundred Worlds science—and Lana's science in particular—might know how to cure the disease, but now their data was lost with the missing p-caps. By the time they were finished, the gravity of their predicament had sunk in for them as well, and their own tears were flowing freely.

As Lana listened, she grew increasingly pale and the habitual smile crinkles at the corner of her blue eyes turned down in sadness. When they had finally finished, she said what any mother would say. "Come home. It will be all right. I'll take care of you."

Kessa was most likely to act impulsively when stress was high. She floated up to the flight deck and said, "Oh, but Mom, there is some good news. We have some new friends! This is Stoke Omroni, and this" (with a kiss) "is Jet Castilian. They have numbers on Earth but I don't remember. Anyway, guys, this is my mother, Lana Sjøfred." There were smiles all around, but after the kiss Lana looked like her brain had just overflowed.

Orbiter *Theresia,* New Gaia

ADS *Gregor Mendel* carried its own small, gold-colored orbiter, dubbed *Theresia,* so its coddled 90-level passengers could be ferried back and forth directly to and from their planet-side destinations without the unpleasantness of navigating public spaceports or space elevators. It was mounted astern and accessed via a cherry wood-covered portal in the berthing compartment. Jet left *Gregor Mendel* in a parking orbit on autopilot and all five of them climbed into the *Chica*-like orbiter for a ride down to the planet. Marta had seen to it they all wore New Gaian-style clothes for arrival, featuring the planet's iconic multiple layers of semitransparent materials and sashes tied around the waist—bright colors for Marta and Kessa and more staid tones for Galen, Jet, and Stoke. After managing to pilot a spacer, Jet felt almost bored to find himself driving a humble orbiter again, but, being Jet, he quickly cautioned himself to stay disciplined and alert for the flight down.

Jet had suggested they go straight to Zero West to start an immediate search for the missing p-cap, but he was firmly overruled and they headed straight for Kessa and Marta's home on Lake Peace. It was just after noon there, and the heat of the August day was beginning to build. Jet flew in cautiously and settled the orbiter gently into the clearing next to the house. The high-tech luxury space yacht looked incongruous there, smelling like machinery and crowding up against the edges of the clearing, standing out from the forest as much as the house blended in.

The passengers tumbled out, led by a buoyant Kessa, and the family ran out into the clearing to greet them. Lana hugged each daughter tight, then hugged Stoke and Jet in welcome, and then turned to her brother Galen and gave him a long, long look as tears streamed down her face. "Galen!" was all she could manage to say. He reached out to her and they shared a long, loving embrace.

Grandmother Britta was no less welcoming when her son Galen turned to her. "I'm so joyful you're here in person," she said. "We have missed you all these years."

Aunt Mia and Uncle Kjell and the younger cousins all mixed in, and the joyous family reunion continued inside over bakies and chai, everyone talking almost at once and bubbling over with stories and questions and ideas. Jet and Stoke, though initially bewildered, were nevertheless swept up in the warmth and energy of the big family, and before long they found themselves laughing and telling stories of their own. Stoke knelt down to admire little Beatrix's new hair braid, triggering her to form an immediate crush and rush off, giggling, to spy on him from behind her mother's legs. It made Marta laugh. Not long after, the boys—Anders and Nils—persuaded Stoke to give them a tour of *Theresia*. Meanwhile Jet quickly fell into conversation with Kjell, who was only too happy to answer Jet's many questions about the construction and function of their earth-grown house.

In less than an hour, however, Jet's ever-present mental alarm clock went off and he broke in on Kessa's conversation by placing an affectionate hand on her shoulder. "Kessa. Toxin-X."

"Oh, swit, you're right! What are we doing? I got so carried away being home again! Swit. Come on, let's get organized. Marta? We need to plan."

In true New Gaian fashion, the whole family, children included, gathered around the table to review what they knew and plot strategy. Jet and Stoke had never seen anything like this form of decision-making, and they spent most of the time simply looking around and being amazed at how everyone had something to say, and everyone else listened. Jet gradually admitted to himself that he had a lot to learn about how people can work together.

Even though the travelers were currently safe and comfortable here at home, it remained that the entire planet of Earth was in grave danger and there was an earnest hope that they themselves—especially Lana the plant scientist—could do something to prevent it. Galen had the meeting transcripts that 91 Ettica Sim had given them, and he carefully handed over a chip to Lana. But the crucial 3D scanning technical data that Lana would need were lost on a p-cap somewhere, and they needed to find it as fast as possible. It seemed likely that this morning's pirate attack was related, and they wouldn't be the only ones looking for it.

Meanwhile, almost as an afterthought, teenage Anders pointed out they were here in a stolen ship and there was a good chance someone would be after them for that, too.

As the conversation drew to a close with a growing sense of urgency, they decided that Galen would stay here and work with Lana, making plans for what to do if and when the p-cap arrived. Kessa and Marta would go with Jet and Stoke to Zero West in search of the missing p-cap containing the crucial technical data.

Lana wouldn't let them leave without a quickly packed hamper of food, and Kessa went dashing back into the house for one last round of hugs, but then Jet fired up *Theresia*'s engines and the orbiter lifted noisily into the air and away.

Stoke watched out the window as they gained altitude and asked aloud, "So Marta, your house is the only one around here, then? No neighbors?"

"Oh, we have neighbors," Marta said. "Just not right in the same building like in your cities."

"Where are they then?"

"Oh, not far. Five or ten minutes by air pod."

"What's that in kilometers?"

"About 25 I guess, or 50."

"25 or 50 kilometers? And you call those neighbors?"

Kessa chuckled at Stoke's surprise and Marta shrugged. "It seems close to us. On our planet we have intentionally tried to spread out our dwellings so we don't disturb the land too much. We have excellent transportation, so the distances don't bother us."

Stoke just shook his head. For him, that would take some getting used to.

Zero West, New Gaia

Jet and Stoke took *Theresia* on a suborbital flight path that arced them up from Lake Peace almost to the edge of space before descending back down to Zero West at the equator. As they drew near, Stoke made contact with Leilani's Space Traffic Control Center, and after an almost casual exchange they were directed to a landing in an open field outside of town that served as New Gaia's groundside space-and-airport. There were a few other ships of various descriptions parked here and there, a fueling station, and a maintenance hangar. It was a sleepy little operation, though. Out of politeness to his New Gaian friends, Jet resisted the temptation to say, "Where is everybody?"

They climbed out and, ungreeted, struck off toward the building that, based on its antenna collection, looked most likely to be the STC. Jet had been leading the way, but when they reached the door there was a subtle, almost subconscious shift in roles. They were leaving the world of spacecraft now and entering New Gaian society. Jet stood aside, nominally holding the door, and Kessa came to a stop beside him. Marta glanced at Kessa as if for reassurance, took a little breath, picked up her chin, and led the way inside.

Things were busy here in Leilani's domain. Extra tables and chairs had been set up in the small front room and several people were working busily on comms and screens. There were quick smiles of greeting toward the newcomers. No one seemed to take notice of Stoke and Jet's dark, Earth-native looks. A large map of Octavia was displayed on a glowscreen that had been hung on one wall, and the room was filled with a sense of urgency and action, if not much organization. Leilani herself came swiftly out from the back room, looking busy but happy to see them. "New volunteers! Welcome, welcome! I'm Leilani."

"Hi," smiled Marta, already beginning to get caught up in the positive energy of the place. "I'm Marta, this is my sister Kessa, and that's Stoke and Jet. We're, uh ... yes, I guess we are here to volunteer. We just arrived here from Earth. You were probably talking to Stoke here on the comms for flight control. We heard there was an incident?"

Leilani chuckled. "'Incident' is a good word. Better than a freaking 'pirate attack,' I guess."

"All we know is what we've heard on the nets . . ."

"You're right. Who knows what kinds of fucked up rumors go around. The real story is some bastard attacked the elevator tender when it was ferrying Kai Tong and my good friend Captain Narisa Kunlabi down from ADS *Okafor*. That's Kai and Narisa's photos we posted on the wall. They got away in an escape pod, but then they crash landed butt-down somewhere half the frickin' way around the world in Octavia. We haven't heard from them since, and this team of awesome volunteers you're looking at is searching for them right now."

It seemed crass but Jet couldn't help but ask: "They were carrying a p-cap shipment, too, right?"

"I suppose so. I've heard some complaints. You'd have to ask IMS about that."

"IMS?"

"You know, Interplanetary Message Service. Their building's just out there to the left. Good luck with that, though. Those goddamn corporate drones don't talk to anybody."

Jet was eager to demonstrate his heart was in the right place and he turned his attention back to the people side of things. "Anyway, how can we help with the search for your friends?"

"Jet's a pilot," Marta offered. "And I guess you know, we have an orbiter." She felt no need to add that it was stolen.

"Yes, and that is bitchin' good news. We only have one other ship out searching right now, and the search area is huge. How soon can you start?"

"As soon as you want us. Right, guys?" said Marta.

Before he answered Marta, Jet, always one to think big picture, turned to Leilani. "Have they caught the pirate?"

"Hah, 'they' being 'us' in this case."

"You don't have a space force?"

Leilani grinned a big, impish Polynesian smile. "Welcome to the boonies, friend. It's just us chickens here. Us here in STC, our friend Agda over with the volunteer Security Patrol, and any other citizens who were kind enough to show up and help. Where did you say you were from?"

"Earth."

"Yeah, that explains it. Nope, no space force out here. Just you and me and our little team of heroes, doing what we can. Newgies aren't big on, you know, structure. And frankly I could care less where that bastard pirate disappeared to. I'm more worried about Narisa and Kai and getting the tender back working again."

"What's wrong with it?"

"The pirate hijacked the nav system and vectored it off to dock with his own ship. He's taken off, but he left the tender behind, and now it's in some weird-ass orbit and its nav system isn't responding. That's another thing we're trying to figure out. Until we do, space elevator operations are suspended and we'll have to rely on private orbiters for any links to the outside world. Which isn't good, of course."

Jet looked over at Stoke, whose eyebrows were raised in interest. "You know, Stoke here knows a few things about nav systems and how people might, uh, mess with them."

Leilani gave Stoke an evaluative look. "Really?"

Marta nodded enthusiastically. "Definitely. On one ship we were on he completely disabled the tracking—"

Kessa gave her sister a sharp elbow in the ribs.

"—well, anyway, I've seen him do things with nav systems. He's definitely an expert."

Leilani nodded and looked at Stoke. "Cool. So maybe you'd be interested in coming in the back here and sitting with my friend Kinga, who is working on this?"

The friends all looked at each other. Marta ran a hand down her ponytail and said, "I should stay with Stoke. I don't want to leave him alone here on a strange planet."

Stoke laughed. "Thanks, I'd appreciate that."

Kessa said, "So, I'll go with Jet on the search?"

Marta nodded. That agreed, Leilani led Stoke and Marta into the back room to meet Kinga, and Jet and Kessa sat down at a table with a volunteer to get a briefing on the search operation.

▪ ▪ ▪

After he and Kessa said their goodbyes and walked out the door of the STC, Jet turned to Kessa. "Before we leave, I think we should pay a visit to the IMS station."

"You think they'll talk to us?"

"Let's find out."

It was a short walk and Jet used the opportunity to talk. "That was *very* strange."

"Strange? How?"

"For one thing, I couldn't tell who was in charge."

"Leilani seemed to be organizing things, didn't she?"

"Kind of. But she wasn't actually telling anyone what to do. People kept coming up with their own ideas and not checking with her at all."

"Mm, you're right. But it seemed to be working okay."

"I guess. But it didn't seem very efficient. And I also have to get used to not knowing anyone's rank. I mean, I was talking to that older man who seemed so smart and experienced, and he kept treating me like I was the same rank as he was. Me! Who's like 24 years old and just landed here this morning."

"I keep telling you, everyone is equal here."

"I know, I know. It's just . . . hard to get used to. I think I might like it, but then again I think Earth's way of doing things might be more effective for something like this."

Kessa shrugged. "Just so long as we find Narisa and Kai, right?"

▪ ▪ ▪

The building housing the New Gaia service node for the Interplanetary Messaging Service looked nothing like the other buildings in Zero West. There could be no doubt it was a standardized design mandated by a corporate headquarters on a very distant planet.

The structure was a monolithic, windowless block, two stories high and covered with featureless, putty-brown walls. It sat apart from its neighbors on a gravel-covered square lot, surrounded by a tall wire fence topped with the biggest incongruity of all: rolls of barbed wire.

That said, it was staffed by local New Gaians and Kessa easily saw the people behind what she perceived as the scripted play-acting they were doing. "Hello, friend," she smiled at the first guard standing at the outer fence, and after a quick series of similar greetings Kessa and Jet found themselves talking to the man in charge.

"I am Osvald," said official, politely enough. He was round-faced and thick-bodied, and Nordic name notwithstanding, he had dark coloration that suggested normal pan-world ancestry. "What is your business with IMS?"

"I was just telling Sjurd at the front gate that we're joining Leilani's search; I'm sure you know about it. Are you in touch with Leilani? We heard the crashed escape pod might be holding some of your p-caps?"

"The IMS does not discuss details of its operations."

"Of course. I'm sure they don't let you say very much. It's just that *if* you were missing a shipment, they'd probably want you to recover it as soon as possible, right?"

"Of course, but—"

"Okay, and it so happens that Jet and I are going to be searching for the people who are, um, what do you call people who carry the p-caps?"

"Couriers, but—"

"Right, couriers. It's Narisa and Kai, right? I haven't met them yet, but you must know them?"

Osvald's stiff corporate visage turned more expressive. "Actually, Kai is a friend of mine."

"Oh! I'm, uh, sorry. Well, all the more reason to find them, then. Osvald, if Kai and Narisa are, you know, incapacitated, do you want us to bring back the package of p-caps?"

"IMS neither confirms nor denies reports that any p-caps are missing."

"But if they were?"

"If they were, IMS would conduct its own search for its own company property."

"Come on, Osvald. Out here? When? It will take days for your headquarters to even find out about this, much less send a search party all the way out here to New Gaia. If you want searchers, you're looking at us."

"We sent a message to Hestia."

"Nice, but they don't have any more resources than we do. They'll have to send to Earth. Osvald, come on. Let us help."

Osvald paused, thinking hard. Kessa could almost see the argument in his head, the forces of his common sense sparring with the forces of his obedience to rules created far beyond his purview. Osvald lowered his voice. "Okay, Kessa. But you have to keep this totally confidential, okay? I could lose my job."

"Of course."

"Okay. Here it is. Kai and Narisa *were* carrying p-caps when they were hijacked. Narisa told Leilani she still had them when they escaped in the pod. Leilani didn't tell you? I guess she's better at keeping our confidential information than I expected."

"Ah! So they'll still have them."

"I can't think why not."

"What do they look like?"

"They'll be in a special container called a mochila. It looks like a backpack. Inside there should be two canisters. The p-caps are inside those, but it doesn't matter. The canisters are securely locked and can't be opened except here at the service node."

Jet asked, "Do they emit a homing signal, or beacon, or anything we could scan for?"

"No, afraid not. You just have to find them. But anyway, it shouldn't be too hard. Kai carries the mochila strapped to his chest."

"Whoa, that's intense."

"Yeah, IMS takes p-caps seriously. So if you find them, and for some reason Kai and Narisa are—you know—you'll bring them straight back here, right?"

"Yes, definitely."

"And not tell anyone about it?"

"Okay."

"Thank you," said Osvald. But then he thought a little more. "Say, Kessa, why do you two care so much? I mean, it's only messages, right?"

Kessa was momentarily at a loss, but Jet replied for her. "Only trying to be helpful," he said, trying to sound as casual as possible.

"Well it'll save my ass, so I hope you find them. But more than that, I hope you find Kai."

"We'll do our best."

West Central Octavia, New Gaia

Kessa sat in the co-pilot's seat next to Jet on the flight to Octavia. Jet had taken them on another suborbital arc that shot up over eastern Sylvania, out over the vibrantly blue Vitalic Ocean, and then back down again toward Octavia, much of which was covered in thick, low clouds. As they approached ground level, Kessa made comm connections with the other search ship. It was one of New Gaia's few community-owned emergency vehicles, a large orbiter called *Frälsaren* that was painted white with red crosses on the sides. Its two crew members, Greta and Janna, were glad to have more searchers but had no results to report.

"The terrain here is all rock outcroppings and tight little valleys," explained Greta. Her flowing brown hair and intense brown eyes made an impression over the viewscreen. "And this heavy rain is not helping matters. Getting clear scans is turning out to be a real problem. We've been searching all day and all we've found are small animals."

"Anything from the pod's emergency beacon?" Kessa asked.

"Nothing."

"Okay. Well, Leilani's team gave us a search sector west of you two. We'll start in and see what we can find."

"Roger. But there's not much daylight left for today. You might want to consider finding a campsite before too long."

Their search instructions were relatively simple. The plan was to fly back and forth across their search zone from top to bottom, listening for comm signals and looking out the window for any signs of life . . .

. . . Or otherwise, thought Kessa. No one was talking about it, but everyone knew there was a chance Narisa and Kai were dead. She remembered the elegant, white-uniformed captain from her trip on *Okafor* a few days before, looking perfectly authoritative and secure. It was hard to think of her huddling in a crashed escape pod somewhere in the wilderness below.

After 45 minutes of fruitless searching, Kessa was ready to call it a day. This kind of focused, systematic work was a poor fit for her temperament. "I think Greta was right," she said. "We should find a campsite. It should be a clearer day tomorrow."

Jet was anxious about the search, but he had to admit to the circumstances and he reluctantly turned his attention to finding a place to land.

A little later he gingerly settled *Theresia* onto a flat piece of ground with a few scrubby trees nearby and powered down. His first reaction was to bed down within the small ship, but Kessa coaxed him outside. It had finally stopped raining and Kessa found a relatively dry, flat rock for them to set up a little camp furnished with a few cushions and blankets they pulled out of the ship. Kessa dug out her mother's hamper of food and they ate a makeshift supper as they watched the sun descend behind a nearby hill. Kessa soaked in the moment, but Jet's brain was still squirming. Finally, he willed himself to think about something besides their struggling mission. "Can I ask you something, Kessa?" he said.

"Of course."

"Does everyone on New Gaia have white skin and blonde hair like yours?"

Kessa laughed at first, but then she realized the dark-haired, brown-skinned Jet was serious. "Only some of us. It's usually about our great-grandparents, who were the founding generation. They all came from a small city in Scandinavia, which is why the place names and most of the family names are still Nordic, even though not all the people look like, well, me. But historically the founding city didn't interact much with outsiders, and a few of these recessive genetic traits have persisted for generations in some of the families, like my grandmother Britta's. There hasn't been much immigration to New Gaia so far, and we haven't had time to intermix the way people on Earth have. It's one of our weaknesses."

"*One* of your weaknesses? What are the others?"

Kessa was abashed. "Oh, I don't know. We're pretty good. But we are a young colony, and I think we still have some growing up to do as a society. We're too homogeneous, and we don't handle dissent and conflict very well, and we have trouble making big decisions. Marta talks about this a lot. She thinks our whole planet is naïve."

Jet grinned. "Well you're in luck then. Stoke and I are from crazy, mixed-up Earth, and we're here to show you the ways of the world."

Lake Peace

"Galen, we have to get more help!" Lana called out after reading through Ettica's meeting transcripts. "This Toxin-X thing is incredibly dangerous! I'm going to call in every scientist I know."

Galen shook his head. "No, Lana, that's the terrible thing. We can't call anybody. This has to stay locked down until someone finds a cure. Otherwise there will be total panic on Earth."

"But Galen!"

"I know, I know! It's crazy. But you see the logic, don't you?"

"So what, *I* have to find a cure for this thing? All by myself? That's absurd. At least let me get in touch with—"

"No, Lana, I'm sorry. It has to be completely secret."

"God, Galen! God!" Lana shook her head and looked slightly panicked.

The best Galen could do was give her a hug. Lana received it stiffly, feeling scared, inadequate, and angry—maybe at Galen.

Galen left the room awkwardly and headed out on a walk through the woods around the lake. He was glad to find some time alone to ponder whether this entire disaster was his fault from twenty years ago. And besides, though he was enjoying seeing his family in person, all the togetherness of the last few days was getting to be a bit much after 20 years living by himself. His head swam with thoughts of lost relationships, Skervin and the world of ORGA, dead animals, and dead children.

And oh my God, pursuers! His nephew Anders had pointed out earlier about the stolen spaceship, but it was worse than that: they had escaped Skervin, and Galen more than anyone knew how Skervin would react to that. He would chase them to the ends of the galaxy. Galen wasn't certain whether Skervin knew where they had gone, but chances were good they had been followed. The more he thought about it, the more concerned he became. He turned around and started running back to the house.

Space Traffic Control Center

Kinga, Leilani's friend-slash-tech wizard, was encamped in a back corner of the STC surrounded by viewscreens, controllers, and snacks, trying to get the space elevator's tender back under control. He was about Stoke's age and sported shaggy red hair atop a skinny face and frame. Leilani introduced Stoke and Marta and then disappeared, leaving them to their own devices. At first Kinga looked dubious about the intrusion, but Stoke's easy manner put him at ease, and the exchange of a burst of technical jargon sealed the deal. Within minutes Stoke was ensconced right there next to Kinga and they worked happily together as Marta looked on.

Marta understood none of it, but she enjoyed watching the exchange. Stoke, confident and outgoing, was such a contrast to the reserved Newgies like Kinga that she was used to. Stoke had a funny habit of twiddling his tongue against his teeth when he was thinking. And the way he tossed his head back when he laughed was impossibly infectious; she noticed herself laughing when he did, even when she had no idea what the joke was. At one point she starting thinking certain thoughts, but she stopped herself with a reminder of what a girl-chaser he was. . . . Wasn't he? At just that moment he happened to glance over and catch her eye, and for a brief second he looked as genuinely affectionate toward her as she could imagine, without the slightest trace of the insincerity or wolfishness a girl-chaser would have. Hmm. She left the techies to their work and made her way out front to the volunteer group, looking for something useful to do.

After a long time, Kinga said, "Hey! I think that's working! I'm getting something."

"Good," said Stoke. "Now if I just send this . . . ?"

"Yeah, yeah, I think that's it . . . Yes, we're in!" Kinga gave a few more commands and soon a standard nav control display appeared on his viewscreen. It was the tender, and he was in control. "Happy day! Let's get Leilani."

Leilani was even happier than Kinga about the breakthrough ("hot fuckin' damn!") and she immediately asked him to get the tender stabilized and back to the space elevator. Kinga looked uncomfortable. "I'm not really trained as a pilot—"

"I might be able to give it a try," Stoke offered gracefully. "If you can just give me some directions?"

Leilani smiled and turned to leave them to it.

■ ■ ■

By the end of the day Stoke and Kinga had the space elevator's tender back in normal operation and they were feeling rather pleased with themselves. When it was time to go home for the evening they walked out to the front laughing and clapping each other's backs like old cronies.

Working with the other volunteers, Marta had ended up taking it upon herself to set up a simple but effective centralized project information hub on the net to keep everyone organized and up-to-date. It was already getting good use and she, too, was feeling a little triumphant. She surprised even herself when she realized how excited she was to tell Stoke about it when he emerged from the back room with Kinga. Kinga said goodbye and headed home, and Marta fairly bubbled as she started to explain her work to Stoke.

Leilani smiled as she met them on the way out the door. "Where are you two staying tonight?"

Marta did a double-take. "Oh, I was so caught up, I guess I didn't really plan that far ahead. Back to my house, I suppose. Are we too late for the planet tube?"

Leilani stopped and shook her head. "Your house? Are you crazy? That's hours from here. Come on, you two are staying at my house tonight. It's not far."

■ ■ ■

Leilani's house was in a quiet spot in the woods near Zero West, reached by a wooded footpath that made its way out from the edge of town. It was a modest structure that consisted mostly of a wooden roof and low, half-height walls of sod. That left views in all directions out into the woods, and Marta thought it must be wonderfully light and airy during the day. Now that night was falling it might have felt exposed, but inside Leilani had set up "rooms" that were simply cozy collections of soft furniture and pools of low, warm light that provided the intimate feel of a campfire circle.

The three of them shared a simple supper of fish, fruit and nuts over a quiet conversation that was spiked with frequent reminders of Narisa and Kai crashed and lost somewhere on another continent, waiting to be found. Leilani turned in early, telling Marta and Stoke they would have to decide for themselves who got the sofa and who got the comfortable-looking pile of cushions.

Maybe it was Leilani's wine, but for some reason Marta was feeling spunky. She looked Stoke straight in the eye and said, "Can I ask you about something, Stoke? Without offending you?"

"Of course. What?"

"Are you a playboy?"

Stoke was taken aback. "Whoa. What makes you ask that?"

"I'm just wondering. You don't seem that way, but I've heard you talking to Jet about all your girlfriends."

Stoke's face suddenly softened and his usual cheerful outer layer faded away. Underneath was a sincerity and sensitivity that Marta had not seen showing in his expression before, though perhaps she had sensed it was within him. He smiled ever so slightly as he answered, as if he had thought privately about this subject often and was confident in his answer. "I tend to like people, and I make friends easily. Nothing wrong with that, right? But there are a lot of levels of friendship: acquaintance on one end, true love on the other. I've made a lot of friends with women at a level that's somewhere past acquaintance, so if you call that being a playboy, I guess I am. But to be honest, Marta, I've been kind of lonely at any level beyond that."

Marta's eyebrows went up. "You? Lonely?"

Stoke shrugged and flashed his white smile. "In ways."

Marta laughed and suddenly felt very relaxed. The wine must really be getting to her. But she still didn't feel tired, so she told Stoke he could have the sofa because she thought she might sit up for a while with a book and another glass of Leilani's local wine and try to think about other things for a while. Those cushions looked perfect for curling up with a good read.

Stoke surprised her with his response, which was "Actually, that sounds good to me, too. Mind if I join you?"

For some reason, Marta almost giggled. "Oh! Sure, of course!"

Stoke chuckled agreeably at Marta's enthusiasm. "You can have first dibs on the best cushion. I'll pour you some more wine."

Marta felt a warm sensation on her skin as she walked over to the cushions and knelt down to arrange them in a comfortable way, undoing her blonde ponytail while she was at it. She was just testing out a seating position when Stoke arrived with wine glasses, and she giggled again when he knelt next to her to help arrange. The lights were positioned in just such a way that he needed to sit down right next to her if he was going to be able to read as well. And when he did that, the cushions squished in a way that pressed him right up against her side, which felt quite nice. Very nice, actually. Though she did think it would be more comfortable if he could move his arm, maybe over here, behind her waist? Much better. And now his head was merely a handbreadth away from hers. She could sense the warmth in his cheek. He was turning toward her, looking in her eyes. She so wanted to . . . kiss him. And then in a rush she did, and he reached out another arm around her, and they dissolved down into the cushions. And it felt very, very good indeed.

Caphaletta's Apartment

Caphaletta had invited her friend Rosa over for the day. Banji was still too sick to go anywhere, and Rosa's Yuliana had the same bug. Or disease, or whatever it was. Low energy, stomach aches, and now diarrhea. It was the last thing a skinny little boy like Banji needed. Dozens of kids were getting it, and now there were reports of adults as well.

Banji lay at one end the couch, curled up under a blanket with his stuffed animal, looking pale and dull. Rosa brought Yuliana in and set her up at the other end, sucking her thumb and gazing dully at a video. "Do you want to show Yuliana your animal?" Caphaletta prompted her son.

He cheered up just a fraction, popping a big-eared, fuzzy rabbit up above his covers and pointing him in the direction of Yuliana, who looked over with mild interest. "What's his name?" Caphaletta prompted.

"Conay," Banji said in a voice that would have been cheerful and proud if it hadn't been feeble. "He's a space bunny."

Yuliana waved her little hand wanly at Conay and managed a "Hi." But then both children curled back into their cocoons to rest. The two mothers looked dolefully at the sad little scene. Caphaletta yearned to do more for the little ones, but she was out of ideas. Instead she shared a hug with Rosa and sat down to talk. It felt good to sit; she didn't feel too well herself.

Earth of 2816 was completely unaccustomed to mass illness like this, not to mention much illness at all. Everyone's body was constantly monitored by their brainboxes and any problems were immediately remedied through food supplements or medicines dispensed straight out of their food fabricators. Rio's few clinics had been overwhelmed in the last few days by increasingly worried parents, and most people were simply staying home and hoping to wait out the illness, feeding their children chicken soup and crackers from the fab.

What they didn't know was that the food from the fab was increasingly not food at all. It was bulk fill being secretly fed into the supply, consisting of leftover stems and stalks of soybean plants. It might as well have been sawdust.

Or, because toxin screening at production plants was imperfect, worse.

11

Tuesday, August 9

ADS *Paracelsus,* In Orbit Around New Gaia

Tappet didn't know what to expect when he arrived in orbit around
New Gaia. He had been incommunicado for three days and, much to
his dismay, Skervin's orders had not been particularly specific: he was
simply here to make sure the p-cap containing Galen's message to
Lana had been destroyed by a man named NA Speer, the disreputable
contractor he had hastily hired to carry out the felonious deed.
Because of his criminal past, Speer's rank had been cancelled
altogether, giving him the ignominious rank designation of "NA."
Tappet's plan, such as it was, was to find Speer, confirm the success
of the mission, and return to Earth as quickly as possible.

Tappet was not a pilot himself, so when he had requisitioned a
spaceship for his journey, he was assigned both this ship, *Paracelsus,*
and an accompanying space pilot. Her name was 40 Potet, she was

middle-aged and stocky, and she was quite possibly the most uninteresting person Tappet had ever met. She made no eye contact, spoke as little as possible, and maintained a facial expression that was equal parts ennui, torpor, and apathy. They hardly spoke for the entire trip and shared no meals, which for her, as far as he could tell, consisted entirely of beef jerky and potatoes. She spent all her waking hours on the flight deck, playing solo virtual reality games. Tappet strongly suspected that this assignment—escorting a 60-level ORGA policeman to a remote planet and back—was some kind of punishment Potet was receiving. Punishment for what, he couldn't imagine. Maybe boring a passenger to death.

Tappet did get as far as deciding that he should make his arrival as stealthy as possible. He instructed Potet to turn off the ship's Automated Identification Signal and to stay away from the "main routes," which Potet made a snorting sound about, but that was the full extent of Potet's articulation on the topic so Tappet ignored her.

They decelerated without apparent incident and Potet moved them into a distant orbit around New Gaia. Tappet couldn't help but admire the planet as it appeared on his viewscreen. With blue oceans, swirling white clouds, and hints of brown and green continents below, it could have been Earth without the big moon. No wonder they call it New Gaia, he thought.

But then he turned his attention to the problem at hand, which was finding Speer and confirming the outcome of his mission. Neither of which, he realized, he had any idea how to do. He went to the cockpit and had Potet display a scan of all ships in the area. He was surprised at how few there were, and only one caught his attention: one that seemed to be in a parking orbit. "This one," he said to Potet. "Can you tell anything about it?"

Potet swiped lazily at a couple of controls. "Not much. Looks like a small spacer, about our size."

"22 Galen's crew escaped in an ORGA executive spacer just like ours. It was called the *Gregor Mendel*. Could it be them?"

Potet touched a control and nodded at the screen, which now showed the craft's designation: ADS *Gregor Mendel*. They *were* here!

Skervin had been right. Now what was he supposed to do about it? Should he go recon the ship to be sure? Or should he spend more time getting the lay of the land before making any moves? Tappet had Potet tune into ground communications. His first reaction was to try to find the police and military channels, but either New Gaia didn't have any (which seemed unlikely), or they were well hidden. The civilian chatter didn't make any sense to him.

Tappet stood there, feeling lost, for several minutes. He wished Skervin were here to tell him what to do. But then Potet's control panel pinged and a new ship appeared in the deceleration zone. Tappet was almost relieved when Potet commented, "No AIS."

As soon as the new ship had moved out of the decel zone, a coded signal came in with an ORGA Enforcement encryption protocol. Potet turned the comms over to Tappet and they, recognizing Tappet's unique biosignature, decoded the signal and began displaying in the clear on the viewscreen. It was Speer.

"Speer! You're here. Situation report?"

Speer's muscular jaw tightened and he involuntarily glanced to the side. "Mission failed."

Tappet was stunned. He felt his stomach sinking. "What?! Failed? What do you mean? What happened?"

"As instructed, I attempted to intercept the p-cap canisters as they were being ferried down to the surface in the space elevator tender. I successfully took over the tender's nav systems by remote control, redirected it, and boarded. There were two couriers. They, uh, they overwhelmed me and got away in my escape pod. They locked me out of my own ship, but I managed to break back in. Last I knew they were headed for the surface."

"And they have the p-caps?"

Speer squinted and nodded very slightly. "Affirmative."

"Why didn't you follow them to the surface? It may not be too late!"

"I didn't have a way to get down. I disabled the tender and they stole my escape pod. I'm on a spacer; it doesn't land."

"Well get over here, then. We'll go down in my orbiter. Hurry! There's no time to lose."

Speer's face darkened with skepticism beneath its stony exterior, but he took in a breath through slightly flared nostrils and nodded. "Fine. Stand by. Tell your pilot I'm going to dock."

■ ■ ■

Tappet had never seen Speer in person before, but there were no surprises. He was just as soldierly as he had appeared in the comms, and his black military gear, heavy boots, and aggressive air only added to the impression. For his part, Speer was equally unsurprised by Tappet, who looked as sallow and weak in person as he did on the comms. Tappet instructed Potet to remain in this high parking orbit until they returned. She would have nothing to do for a day or two, he guessed, but from everything he had seen that would be no problem at all.

"How did you find me?" Tappet asked Speer.

"Wasn't too difficult. After the, er, incident with the tender, I needed to retreat to safety before the New Gaian forces came after me."

"Hmph, if there *are* any New Gaian forces. This planet is such a hinterland I'm not sure they have any."

"Just to be safe. But I figured you would send reinforcements sooner or later, so I decided to keep checking back on a regular schedule. I retreated to Hestia, which is only five hours from here—"

"Why all the way to Hestia?" interrupted Tappet. "Why not just somewhere in empty space, closer to here?"

Speer put a patronizing look on his face. "That's not how space travel works. If you're going to go faster than light, you have to scout and establish the route ahead of time. If you go jumping off to some random location, there's no telling what you may collide with on the way, or when you arrive. The only people who risk a blind jump like that are criminals on the run who would rather die than be caught."

"Oh," said Tappet. "I guess I knew that. So what did you do at Hestia?"

"I waited a couple hours, then came back to see if any friendlies had arrived. The first time no one was here, so I did it again and here you were. I was expecting a, hem, larger force."

"Well I'm it. Come on, let's get moving." And with that they prepared to descend to the surface using *Paracelsus'* piggyback orbiter, named *Jenner.*

Leilani's Residence, Near Zero West

Leilani, energetic as ever, woke Stoke and Marta while it was still dark. They were three hours behind Octavia and she wanted to be available as soon as the search resumed there at sunup. It took Leilani all of three seconds to realize what had happened between Marta and Stoke the night before. Seeing them nestled together in the cushions made her twinkle. They were a good couple.

Stoke was groggy and muzzy-headed when Leilani woke him, but as his brain ground into action it dawned on him that he felt very, very good. He looked over at Marta, who was lying comfortably in his arms. "*I know her name!*" he thought. "*And I like her. And by God, she likes me!*" His big white-toothed grin spread slowly, but increasingly surely over his face, and it lasted a long time.

The House on Lake Peace

Kjell gave Galen one last, disapproving look before finally winding up and smashing a sledgehammer into the outside wall of his house. Last night Galen had managed to convince his brother-in-law Kjell and everyone else that it was time the house had a second exit in case of invasion. It was difficult for the New Gaians to contemplate such violence, much less believe it could ever happen to them, but these were strange circumstances. Besides, a well-placed second door would make it easier for Grandmother to get out to the garden. The teenage boys quickly embraced the spirit of demolition, and soon Galen had a whole miniature construction crew banging and pounding away, working as fast as they could. The fact that the new entrance would be low and partially concealed between two flowering bushes fit well with the New Gaian style of blending into the environment, and Galen, late survivor of an escape tunnel of his own, thought it had tactical value. Besides, his fighting instincts had turned back on, and he needed the action. He picked up a sledgehammer and took a few swings himself.

Space Traffic Control Center

At the STC, Stoke and Marta made their way back to Kinga's station while Leilani busied herself around the center getting things started for the day. Kinga himself had not yet arrived.

Stoke powered up Kinga's systems—which had no security locks, Stoke noticed—and Marta looked idly at the displays. One of Kinga's viewscreens showed a little circle that was blinking on the screen. "Is that a new arrival?" she asked.

"Looks it," said Stoke in a croaky voice. "Actually, I think it's two! If I'm reading this right, an ADS popped out of warp over in the decel zone at, um, oh-five-hundred or so? Then another ADS popped in just a little while ago, and now they're docked together."

"I wonder if that's normal," Marta mused. She waved Leilani over. "Leilani, is this anything?"

Leilani gave the screen a puzzled look. "We don't have anyone on the schedule. Who is it, Stoke?"

"Um, I don't see an AIS for either one of them."

"What? More of these? I am getting so fucking fed up with all these damn UFO no-asses the last couple days. Can you tell what they are? Is our pirate back?"

Stoke settled into Kinga's station and studied the displays. "This one looks like a space yacht. Matter of fact, it's spectrum is a pretty close match with ours on the *Gregor Mendel*. And its decel track from earlier points to Earth."

Leilani turned to Marta. "Friend of yours from Earth?"

"What? No, I don't think so . . . at least, not a *friend*. Stoke, could that be, uh, someone we know?"

"Fut. Yes." Stoke muttered. "And the other one looks like it came from the direction of Hestia. Again, no AIS."

Leilani was nodding vigorously. "Yep, I think I recognize that one even without his AIS. That looks like the pirate's ship. And they've rendezvoused?"

Stoke and Marta gave each other a look of understanding. Marta turned to Leilani. "So whoever chased us here from Earth is in cahoots with your p-cap pirate."

"So which are they after: the p-caps, or you?"

Marta frowned. "Both."

Zero West

68 Tappet Holson felt uncomfortable the moment they landed in Zero West and *Jenner*'s engines whirred down to silence. They were directly on the ground, for one thing, and there was dust in the air and wild, alien trees all over the place, and the few buildings nearby looked like grass huts as far as he could tell. Also, it was hot, and windy. He almost decided to turn around and go back to the city right then.

But the most dangerous p-cap in the world was around here somewhere, he reminded himself, and he needed to find it fast. Speer joined him and they marched off quickly in the direction of the buildings.

That was another thing: there was no brainbox net on this planet so his brainbox didn't even know where to go. He'd have to ask someone. The first person he saw—Tappet couldn't tell her rank—smiled as they approached and gave a cheerful hello. Tappet was momentarily confused by this. "Have we met?"

"I don't think so, friend. My name is Katya." She extended a welcoming handshake.

Tappet took the hand distractedly and did not bother introducing himself or Speer. "Where is the IMS service node?"

Katya was a little taken aback by Tappet's abruptness but she quickly recovered. "Just over there. The one with the fence."

"Yeah, I see it."

Tappet and Speer hurried off, leaving Katya to look after them and mumble a quiet "You're welcome, peace be."

To Tappet, the IMS building looked like an outpost of civilization compared to the rest of the Zero West. True, there was a fence and the thing had no windows and wasn't very tall, but at least it had straight lines and looked in order. There was a guard at the outer gate, and Tappet addressed him without preamble. "I am here on behalf of 96 Skervin Hough, the Earth Authority Minister of Organic Resources. I need to speak to the person in charge."

The guard looked at him blankly. "So, does that mean you're from Earth?"

"Yes, of course. Earth."

"And what is your business here?"

"I need information about a p-cap that was sent here."

"I'm sorry, IMS does not discuss details of its operations."

"Damn it, this is an emergency. I need to see the person in charge!" After similar bluster and the next checkpoint, Tappet and Speer stormed through to the room where Osvald was waiting behind the high counter. "Hello—" he started to say, but Tappet interrupted.

"Where are the p-caps that came in on the last shipment from Earth?"

"I'm sorry, but IMS does not discuss details of its operations."

"Don't give me that crap. This is an emergency!"

"What kind of emergency?"

"A p-cap was sent that shouldn't have been. I need to stop it."

"I'm sorry, but that is not possible. Once a p-cap is transmitted, IMS is bound to deliver it, regardless of other circumstances."

"But this affects the entire planet of Earth!"

"Perhaps so, but how do I know that? IMS has no way of adjudicating the value or importance of particular messages we carry. We treat all messages with equal care."

"Damn it, you shithead! Just tell me where the shipment is!"

"I'm very sorry, but I can't do that."

Tappet shook his head in resignation and gave Speer a silent signal. In the blink of an eye, Speer had vaulted up onto the high counter and then down again next to Osvald. He seized Osvald from behind in one muscular arm that pinned Osvald's arms to his sides, and he threw his other arm around Osvald's neck in a choke hold.

Osvald was shocked and helpless. He gaped at Tappet and suddenly found it was hard to breathe. "Help! Arne!"

Arne, Osvald's guard at the door, came running forward, but he had no weapon and Speer simply glared him down.

"Where are the p-caps?" Tappet demanded.

"I—I can't breathe!"

Tappet nodded at Speer. "Let him breathe a little." Speer loosened his grip by a fraction.

"Okay, okay!" Osvald rasped. "I'll tell you. Let me go."

Speer shook Osvald free and he took a moment to catch his breath while staring at Tappet in disbelief. This had never, ever happened to him before, and he was shaking. "Look, I don't know exactly where the shipment is. Kai and Narisa—the couriers—had the p-caps when they crashed."

"Where did they crash?"

"I don't know exactly. Leilani over at the STC is organizing the search. Ask her. Or even easier, just look on the net."

"What are you talking about?"

"On the net. That's how they're organizing the search. They have all the communications and maps and everything."

"Good. What security credentials do I need?"

"Credentials?"

"Identity. Passwords. Security codes. Whatever it is you people use out here."

"Um, none. Why would it be secure? The whole planet's helping."

Tappet simply looked at Osvald. He could hardly believe it. Where he came from, a major problem like a spacecraft crash would certainly be kept secret. It would be taken care of by the Authority, not citizens, and even within the Authority it would be on a need-to-know basis. "Show me," he said.

Nervously, Osvald turned to a nearby viewscreen and said, "Crash survivor search." Immediately, the viewscreen lit up with a map of the search area on Octavia covered with annotations and data. There was a whole information hub that Marta had set up.

"Damn," breathed Tappet. "This place is nuts." Speer swung back over the counter and they both walked out of the building, heading quickly for their orbiter.

Osvald rubbed his neck and gave Arne an ironic look. "Some help you were."

■ ■ ■

Tappet was at a loss. Decades of instinct told him to check in with his superiors at this juncture, but he couldn't. Skervin was a three-day message away. Tappet was on his own. With Speer in tow he headed back to his ship, head down and thinking hard.

The dangerous p-cap with Galen's message and detailed data about Toxin-X was now sitting, unopened, in a crashed escape pod on a different continent on this planet. If he could get to it before anyone else did, that would be perfect. He would destroy it and that would be that . . . But destroy it how? Those carrying canisters for p-caps sounded nearly impregnable and indestructible. It was bomb-proof, but he could throw it over a cliff or something. Drop it in the ocean, that would work. Okay, good plan . . . But what if the New Gaians got to the escape pod before he did and found the canister first? Damn. They already had a search party going. He'd have to move fast.

Tappet picked up his pace, almost jogging toward *Jenner* and relieved to have a strong plan of action. Once they were aboard he told Speer to set a course for Octavia, following the search.

West Central Octavia

Not long after the sun rose on Octavia, Jet and Kessa were back in the air in *Theresia* to resume their search. They had barely taken off when Greta called from *Frälsaren*. "I think we have something!" Kessa touched a control and a dot appeared on her viewscreen showing Greta's location. After a pause, Greta said, "Yes, yes. It's them, I'm certain."

"We'll be right there," Kessa commed.

Minutes later, Kessa and Jet were over the crash site. It was a partial clearing at the foot of a rocky ravine. The escape pod had landed on rocks and was lying at an angle, looking damaged but mostly intact. *Frälsaren* had already found a spot to land right nearby, but Jet had to land a few hundred meters away to find enough clearance. He and Kessa jumped out and Kessa led the way slashing and running through low bushes to reach the site.

They found Greta and Janna kneeling over Narisa and Kai next to the escape pod. They were both alive. Narisa was sitting against a tree stump, barely conscious. She had a makeshift bandage around her head and looked exhausted and pale, as if she had lost a lot of blood. Kessa hardly recognized the woman she had last seen as the black, elegant captain of ADS *Okafor*. Skinny, raven-haired Kai was lying flat, his face pale and evincing the agony of his broken leg. Jet couldn't help but notice the satchel attached to his chest, though. It was the mochila.

Janna, young and eager-looking, appeared to have medical training and was already rushing to administer first aid. Kessa introduced herself and Jet by saying "Osvald sent us," and Kai spoke painfully. "Osvald? Great. He's my friend. Really glad to see you people. We've been here for a day-and-a-half now. The comms in the ship are useless. Listen to me: I need to get to IMS! I have a delivery."

"All in good time," Greta soothed. "Let's get you two patched up first. We have medical equipment in our ship."

"Right," agreed Janna. She looked at Kessa and Jet. "Can you help us with the stretchers?" Kessa and Jet pitched in somewhat inexpertly, and they managed to get Narisa and Kai safely onto beds in the ambulance-like interior of *Frälsaren.* "I need to get some more of your gear off," Janna told Kai, gesturing at the mochila strapped to his chest. "I'm going to run an IV."

"Okay, I guess. But keep that near me. That's the shipment. I can't lose it."

As Janna worked, Greta turned to Kessa and Jet. "Did Leilani reach you yet?"

"Not yet," said Kessa. "We've been too busy to check the comms."

"Uh-oh. I better tell you then. She told us this as we were landing."

"Told you what?"

Greta looked at the patients on their beds and hesitated before deciding to continue. "She said she got a message from the guy who runs the IMS service node."

"Osvald?" Kessa asked.

"I guess so. He said he was attacked by a couple of strangers from Earth."

"Attacked?" cried Kai from his stretcher. "Osvald?"

"Sorry. Leilani said he's okay, though. They're after the p-cap shipment. They made Osvald tell them about it."

There were murmured curses from around the group. Jet exchanged looks with Kai, who was lifting his head up from the bed and looking very worried. "It has to be the same pirate who boarded us," said Kai. "And now he has a partner?"

"When was this?" Jet asked Greta.

"It must have been less than twenty minutes ago."

Jet looked back at Kai. "That was in Zero West, so it will be awhile before they can get all the way over here. They'll have heard on the net that we found you. What do you think they'll do?"

"Come after us, I guess," Kai shrugged weakly. "Though come to think of it, they might be smarter to stay where they are. They must know we have to deliver the p-caps to the service node."

"But they can't assault you in the middle of the village in broad daylight," Jet pointed out.

"You're right. Do you know what they want to do with the p-caps? Just read them, you think? Or destroy them?"

"First one, I hope," said Jet.

Kai said, "Yeah, that's probably it. If they only wanted to destroy them, they could have done something up in space, like shooting us down, instead of the whole hijacking. Or maybe they would, I don't know, blow up the service node?"

Jet winced at the violence of Kai's suggestions. "I guess. But that would cause a huge interplanetary ruckus. If these guys are working for who I think they are, they'll still be trying to keep this a secret."

"Great. So they're going to come after us." Kai looked rueful.

"Mm, yeah."

Janna had been attending to Kai's IV and now it was finished. "Can you talk about this later?" she asked. "We have to get going."

"Hang on," said Jet. "I have an idea. We have two ships, right? How will they know which one has the p-caps?"

Kai said, "They'll probably guess I'm on the ambulance ship."

"Right. So why don't Kessa and I take the p-caps? We'll take a different flight path back. If the pirates go after you, they'll miss us."

Kai looked uncomfortable. He looked over at Narisa, but she was unconscious. "Uh, I don't know—"

"Better decide fast," said Janna anxiously. "We really have to go."

Kai looked at Jet. "Osvald sent you?"

"Yeah. We were just talking to him last night."

"You'll guard them with your life?"

"Of course."

"And get them to the service node for absolute certain?"

"Definitely."

Kai sighed. "Okay, let's do it."

"Great, now let's go," said Janna. She reached down and grabbed the mochila from its place on the floor, tossing it to Jet.

"Be careful!" called Kai.

Southeast Sylvania

Tappet and Speer, in the pilot's seat, were rocketing upwards in their suborbital arc toward Octavia when their comm lit up. Tappet had it monitoring the search operation, and his stomach sank when a female face appeared and he heard her excited voice announce, "I think we have something! . . . Yes, yes. It's them, I'm certain." He listened anxiously for more details, but the ground party was apparently too busy to provide real-time reports. He did notice two search ships converging on the spot.

"How far do we have to go?" he asked Speer.

"Almost one hour."

"Damn. No chance we'll get there in time."

"Should I turn back?"

"No, keep going for now. I'm thinking."

Again, Tappet missed having a superior to consult. What should he do? His head spun with possibilities. The main thing was, stop the p-cap. It wasn't too late. It was still on a different continent, so the New Gaians who found it still needed to transport it back to Zero West. Tappet knew exactly where they were headed. It would be easy to intercept them. In fact, this was perfect. He would intercept their ship and . . . what? This ship didn't have any weapons. What could he do? Force it down over the ocean, that was it. It might even look like an accident. True, the people on board would die. Unfortunate. But what else was there?

"Speer," Tappet said. "Track the returning ship. We're going to force it down over the ocean."

"There are two ships, and they're taking alternate routes. Which one should I track?"

"The official rescue ship. That's where the mochila courier will be. It's this one, *Fell In* or something. I can't pronounce it. Those others are just civilian volunteers . . . no, wait a second. Look at this! The other one is called ESS *Theresia*. It's the piggyback orbiter for ADS *Gregor Mendel*, the stolen ORGA spaceship! That's the escapees. 22 Galen's gang!"

Speer wasn't following. "68?"

"They're the ones who are leaking the secret of Toxin-X. Damn! They will have grabbed the p-cap for themselves, I'm sure of it. Now they'll have hard evidence. God, we have to stop them. Forget the rescue ship. Go after *Theresia!* Intercept them, fast!"

■ ■ ■

Speer had pulled up a course plot on the main viewscreen that showed *Theresia*'s projected path and their own with colored dots and two arcs that crossed twelve hundred kilometers north and east of Zero West, back above the continent of Sylvania.

"How are you going to force them down?" Tappet asked.

Speer squinted briefly as he considered how to explain. He was an experienced pilot but Tappet was not; he would need to keep it simple. "They'll be coming in hard and fast from the top of the atmosphere. We come in slowly from below, like a wolf ambushing a deer. We jump in front of him in the right place, and if their pilot's good, he'll be forced to dive. He'll either crash right then, or we'll finish him off with another dive from above." Tappet started to nod in satisfaction, but Speer stopped him. "Then again, if their pilot is an amateur, they might miss the turn and crash straight into us." That made Tappet squirm. "Do you know who's flying that thing?" Speer asked.

"Unfortunately, yes. The pilot is probably a professional pilot named 34 Jet Castilian. We chased him all over the planet a few days ago. I hate to say it, but he's good. He evaded us more than once."

"That's all right. For the maneuver we're about to use, a good pilot is just what we want."

Tappet shifted uncomfortably in his chair again, picturing another orbiter smashing through his polyglass roof at extremely high speed. "Right," he said weakly.

"Does he know we're trying to stop him?"

"I'm sure the others will have told him."

"Okay, so we're going to try to block his way, and he's going to try to dodge past. Grab your ass."

■ ■ ■

Tappet did not have to wait long in suspense. The colored dots on his 3-D viewscreen began to converge, and when he looked up high overhead he saw a vapor trail shooting downward. Speer switched to manual controls; no autopilot would allow him to fly as dangerously close to another craft as he was about to do. Tappet's heart accelerated as he pictured 34 Jet doing the exact same thing in the other ship.

Watching his screens closely, Speer climbed straight up, trying to position for a dive that would be faster and steeper than the dive that *Theresia* was already on. *Theresia* was streaking down like a meteor now, and Tappet could hear his own ship's engines straining at full power.

Speer picked his moment and tilted *Jenner* over and down. To Tappet it felt too early because *Theresia* was still above them, but Speer knew what he was doing. Seconds later *Theresia* shot past the horizon line and was suddenly below them and ahead. Speer's piloting had given *Jenner* extra speed and now, just as he had planned, they were diving down on *Theresia* from above like a hawk on a sparrow, gaining fast and looking as if they would collide with *Theresia*'s nose if she didn't break off and descend.

But *Theresia*'s pilot was good. At the exact last possible second before Speer got too close, *Theresia* juked fast to the right. It was a perfect dodge and Speer should have let it happen. But in the fury of the moment he was operating on instinct, and his instinct told him to turn right, too. The move brought him cutting across *Theresia*'s path straight ahead of her, irretrievably close.

Theresia's nose smashed through *Jenner*'s tail. The shock of the collision blew both ships spinning out of control. Speer fought for stability but couldn't get it. He quickly switched off manual and let the superhuman autopilot do its best, but with no tail it was hopeless. They went spiraling head first toward the ground.

■ ■ ■

Nearby, *Theresia*, with Kessa and Jet inside, was suffering a similar fate. The physical damage to her nose would not have stopped her flying, but her control electronics had been wrecked and were now on fire. She was pinwheeling uncontrollably.

Jet, despite the smoke streaming from the control panel in front of him, and Kessa shouting "Jet! Jet!," and his racing heart, and the crazy spins that *Theresia* was doing as she tumbled through the air, spent at least two or three seconds trying to think of other ways out. They just needed to get to Zero West . . . but no, there was no other way.

He took a breath, reached out, and touched the control marked EJECT.

It was almost familiar; this had all just happened a few days before in his beloved *Chica*. There was a quick explosion and *Theresia*'s passenger pod ejected, quickly shooting away from the fuselage and then falling heavily toward the ground. A landing chute deployed automatically and their descent slowed enough to give them a few moments to suck in huge, calming lungfuls of air before what would surely be a bumpy landing. There was nothing but the forest of Sylvania below them. No clearings.

Kessa turned her head away from the window to look at Jet. She felt a moment of mind connection again, as if they could intuit each other's thoughts. He was looking back at her, his clear brown eyes full of concern, frustration, and apologies. Kessa's first thought was for the protection of his fractured confidence. "It's wasn't your fault, Jet. That guy cut right into us."

"I cut it too close. I should have known he'd react badly."

"No, he was *doosa*. Anyway, they attacked us, remember?"

"I know. But we have to get these p-caps to Zero West. We don't have *time* for this."

Kessa half-laughed and half-yelled at him. "Jet! We are currently falling out of the sky onto a bunch of pointy trees! How can you think about time?!

"Botheration," grumbled Jet.

"*Botheration*? Is that a word?"

"Yes. It means this is an annoying, frustrating, vexing, impractical inconvenience."

Kessa merely shook her head and almost smiled, despite everything. And then the trees came rushing up at them.

The landing was a wrenching bump that jarred both their spines, but by luck, the falling escape pod missed any primary tree trunks and instead fell down through the side branches of a stand of New Gaian ash that had cushioned the impact. They quickly collected themselves and their gear—most especially the mochila and its p-cap canisters—and clambered out into a tangle of small branches and onto the ground. The communications gear was smashed and burned from the crash in the air, completely unusable.

"Whew," sighed Kessa, and reached out to Jet for a comforting hug

"Second orbiter crash in a week," Jet said. "Getting used to it?"

"Hah! No." For a moment it all became too much for Kessa and she felt tears welling up in her eyes. "Jet, this is all so crazy!"

"I know, Kessa, I know." Jet held her for a good long minute, letting her cry out the tension of their ongoing ordeal and feeling a few warm tears in his own eyes as well. Eventually they both calmed down, and their two lively brains started thinking forward again. Jet had been in the role of comforting Kessa, but as they both turned outward and began to take in their surroundings, the energy reversed.

"Hey! Is this your first time in a forest, Jet?"

"Doesn't last night in Octavia count?"

"No, not at all! That was a meadow with a few trees around it. This is a forest!"

"Oh. Well then assuming you don't count the arbor museum when I was a kid, yes."

"Wow! That's—I mean, I know it's normal where you come from, but that's, wow."

Jet laughed at his own predicament. "That's what I brought *you* for. Do you want to explain all about it, and then get us out of here?"

"How about I explain all about it *while* I get us out of here? Come on."

"Would it be better to wait here until we're rescued?"

"No. This is New Gaia. We're not really set up for, you know, rescues. Leilani and the others will probably know we went down, but not exactly where, and you saw how our searches work. It'll be a while. Meanwhile, this may not look it to you, but this is *home* to me. If we start walking we're bound to find some people sooner or later."

"Okay, then!" said Jet gamely. "Which way?"

"I didn't see anything on our way down, so it sort-of doesn't matter. Let's head toward Zero West just to have somewhere to aim. Not that we'll get there. It's still over a thousand kilometers away."

"A thousand kilometers? Space, Kessa."

"Don't *worry*, Jet. We'll find someone."

"Fine. Lead on, oh Forest Guide."

Kessa picked up her chin and turned her head slowly, looking all around, as if to sense the lay of the land. Then she put her head down and struck off through the trees. She went slowly at first so as not to lose Jet, who was having his first experiences with uneven ground, footing giving way, and branches slapping against his body. Kessa showed him how she held branches for him as she passed, and how it helped to lift his feet high, and how to choose where to step. After a while she started pointing out interesting things in the woods around them, gradually shifting to a running tutorial on the New Gaian forest.

Jet was a curious and appreciative student and the kilometers went by more and more easily. Birds sang, squirrels scolded. Kessa's keen senses, so attuned to nature, gave her an uncanny ability to detect the slightest sound or movement, so that she would sometimes point to a spot 50 meters away just a second or two before a small bird or rabbit emerged from that very location. Jet was amazed but accepting; he already knew about Kessa's special relationship with the physical world around her. At one point, to Jet's absolute astonishment, they even came upon a deer.

■　■　■

If Speer had been counting, he would have known that Tappet said "damn" 14 times during their parachute descent in *Jenner*'s passenger escape pod after the crash. Speer kept a sullen silence. His soldier's survival training was kicking in and he began scanning the ground below for landmarks and signs of civilization. Incredibly, there weren't any. He did, however, see a column of smoke rising off to the south—*Jenner*'s crash site.

They grounded safely enough and Speer deposited Tappet next to the escape pod while he himself inventoried supplies and considered strategies. The pod had an emergency radio but that was it; all the real comm gear was in *Jenner*. They were in enemy territory on an enemy planet: chance of a friendly rescue was nil. Travel on foot in this unfamiliar wilderness was ill-advised. Speer concluded there was nothing for it: they would have to camp and wait to be captured.

But Tappet was still overwrought. "They got out in an escape pod too, right? Did you see where they went down?"

"No, I didn't see them. They must have bailed after we did."

"Damn!" (That was 15.) "If they're alive they probably still have the p-caps. We have to get after them. Where do you think they went?"

"Could be anywhere. We'll never find them in thick woods like this."

"I suppose you're right. But there will be a rescue operation. That should lead us to the targets, right? Unless they send a combat team after us at the same time."

Speer shook his head dismissively. "Pretty sure these people don't have combat teams. And I'm not worried about rescuers. I have my weapons."

"Good. Whatever it takes to capture those p-caps before they reach the IMS service node in Zero West."

"Understood."

Near the Lindgren Residence, Southeast Sylvania

Kessa and Jet reached the top of a rise and Kessa paused. She tilted her head again, and then, sensing something, she stood a little longer, smelling, listening, feeling. "Jet, give me a boost." He did and she nimbly disappeared up a tall pine. He gazed up the trunk and watched her attractive rear end, clad in pants of that layered, shimmering New Gaian fabric, dancing away from him up into the highest branches. When she got as close as she dared to the top, Kessa balanced her toes on the base of two thin branches and hugged the narrow, flexible trunk close to her chest. Her hands gripped the soft bark, and sticky, aromatic pine pitch smeared against one wrist. Pine needles swept across her face, and a gentle breeze ruffled her hair and caused the trunk to sway gently, though giddily, back and forth. It felt wonderful.

She had an excellent view over the treetops. She was on a gentle ridge, and she could see the undulating landscape all around. And far in the distance, reading subtle changes in the pattern of the canopy, she saw what she was looking for. She let out a happy whoop and climbed quickly back down to Jet waiting on the ground. For her final swing from the lowest branch, she gave an extra kick and went flying happily through the air before landing. "Found a house!" she grinned.

■　■　■

Kessa and Jet emerged from the woods and into a clearing surrounding a house much like Kessa's, with that same grown-from-the-ground look and grassy roof. A healthy vegetable garden skirted the house, and a large work shed stood off to one side. The clearing was at the top of a gently sloping ravine, with a beautiful long view out the downhill side and a cheerful little stream flowing down the middle. The rest of the clearing was half-covered with a large collection of wooden tables at various stages of construction—or *creation*, thought Kessa. From a quick glance she could see they were ornately carved and beautifully crafted works of art.

"Halloo!" called Kessa toward the house.

"Halloo!" came a muffled reply from inside. Kessa smiled and took Jet's hand to lead him toward the door.

A warm-, comfortable-looking older woman with gray hair appeared at the entryway, smiling and waving. "Hello, hello! Welcome!"

Kessa and Jet walked casually forward. In the New Gaian way, Kessa spoke cheerfully yet cautiously, careful not to impolitely rush the conversation. "Hi! Good day to you. What beautiful tables these are!"

"Oh, thank you. I'm glad you like them. Gerd does them for a living. (Gerd! We have visitors! Come say hello!) He uses all the different kinds of wood that grow around here. Anyway! Come in! You are just in time for lunch. Tell us who you are and what brings you to our home."

Jet stole a look at Kessa that whispered, "Seriously? This is how you greet total strangers here?"

Kessa simply kept smiling as they were ushered inside and toward an intricate table. "Well, my name is Kessa Dahlstrom—"

"Dahlstrom? Hmm, no, I can't think of any Dahlstroms from around here. Do you live farther north?"

"Yes, up at 45. Near Aspen North. Lake Peace, we call it."

"Lake Peace? Isn't that where Britta Sjøfred settled?"

"Yes! She's my grandmother."

"Oh, wonderful! She's such an inspiration. Always has been."

"Thank you. Yes, we love her very much."

"And who is this dark and handsome young man?"

Kessa turned slightly and held her hands as if to present. "This is my friend Jet Castilian. He is from Earth."

"My word! Earth! Well *that* is a very long way away. How nice of you to come all this distance to see us, Jet. My name is Hedda Lindgren, and I am very pleased to meet you. May I pour you some tea? Oh, and there you are, Gerd! I'm just putting out lunch. These are some new friends, Kessa and Jet."

Gerd nodded and sat down, still wiping his hands on a cloth. He was an old man but strong, with bony fingers and the clear-eyed look of someone who had spent a lifetime finding truth in the work of his hands. "Good to meet you," he said.

"So tell us, Kessa, what brings you two out our way?"

Kessa said something quick and a little vague about crashing in the woods, and as soon as her most careful New Gaian manners allowed, she borrowed the Lindgrens' comms and called Leilani and Marta at the STC.

"Thank Gaia you're both okay," sighed Leilani. "Greta and Janna just landed with Narisa and Kai. They're both going to be all right. Kai was all concerned about the p-caps. You two still have them? Great. I'll ask Greta to fly up there and pick you up right away. Give her an hour or so."

"Will do."

Next, Kessa commed Lana, who was very glad to hear from her daughter after getting only scattered reports from Leilani and suffering through the New Gaian net's unreliable mix of facts and rumors about pirates, crashes, and rescues.

After overhearing Kessa's conversations on the comm, Hedda clucked, "Dear, dear. Those terrible pirates. I saw one or two reports but I didn't care to delve into the unsavory details. Did I hear you say they were with you recently?"

"With us? I, uh, I guess you could say that. They are the ones who made us crash."

"Oh, I see. Dear me."

While they waited for Greta to arrive, Hedda pressed Kessa and Jet to a hasty lunch of cheese, bread, crackers, and fruit, and before they could finish *Frälsaren* dipped down into the clearing.

■ ■ ■

"Listen!" Speer said to Tappet. His eyes widened and he cocked his head to one side. "Hear that?"

"An aircraft?"

"Yeah. Very faint and quiet though." They both scanned the small piece of sky they could see up through the trees. Speer had led them a few hundred meters away from where their escape pod had parachuted down, finding a small clearing in the woods that offered a better view in all directions, including up. As it happened, though they didn't know it yet, they were quite close to the Lindgrens.

"Can you tell which direction it's coming from?"

"No, but it's getting closer." Speer took out his gun and said "Come on, time to hide." He led Tappet to a thicket of underbrush and they crouched down, not quite sure which side to conceal themselves in. The whirring sound grew closer and louder, and then they saw it: the orbiter *Frälsaren* flying almost directly over their clearing. It had to be heading for the downed escapees, which was perfect. It would lead Speer and Tappet straight to them. Speer carefully tracked the flight path and then, the moment the ship disappeared from sight, dashed into the woods directly after it.

"Wait!" called Tappet weakly, but Speer had the scent of his prey and was not to be denied. Tappet struggled slowly after him, scratching and twisting his ankles on the tangled ground and holding his forearms in front of his face to ward off scraping tree branches.

Speer reached the clearing around the Lindgrens' house several minutes later, just in time to see *Frälsaren* lifting off from the far side. Two elderly people were standing on the ground, looking up and waving goodbye. Speer aimed his pistol and considered trying for a lucky shot, but he thought better of it. The noise would tell everyone where he was.

Instead, he watched the ship disappear into the distance and waited a full minute and a half for Tappet to come straggling up from behind.

"Where are they?" asked Tappet breathlessly.

"They got away."

"God fucking damn! How?"

"Not certain. They were just flying off when I got here. The people from the house were waving goodbye."

"Well come on! Let's get in the house. There has to be a way to stop them." He led the way running toward the house.

Inside they discovered a very startled Hedda and Gerd Lindgren, almost frozen in mid-motion. Hedda was standing at the sink and

Gerd was clearing lunch dishes from the table. They both gaped at the sudden intruders.

The Lindgrens' looks made Tappet catch himself in mid-charge and he heard himself saying, "Er, excuse us!" But then he recovered and burst ahead with, "Those kids who just left. We have to stop them!"

Hedda gave him a look that would wither a fresh blooming rose. "Good afternoon!" she said pointedly.

"Yes, good afternoon. Please, this is urgent!"

"Young man, I don't believe we've met."

"My name is 68 Tappet Holson and this is my colleague—"

But Speer had had enough. He stepped in front of Tappet and lifted his gun up to his shoulder, pointing at the ceiling. "Doesn't matter. Just shut up and tell us how to stop those kids."

Hedda looked scandalized. "Why, I should say! I'm sure that is no way to conduct a decent conversation—"

Speer pulled his trigger and a tremendous bang exploded through the small house. A hole appeared in the ceiling over his head. "Dammit! How do we stop them?"

Hedda was completely discombobulated and she looked to Gerd for support. He was squinting one eye and holding a hand up to one ear, as if the noise of the gun had annoyed him greatly. He gave no signs of planning to speak.

Tappet tried to intervene. "Speer, stop shooting. Listen to me, people," he said earnestly, "We are law enforcement officers from Earth. Those people who just left have stolen classified government information. We are trying to get it back before it falls into the wrong hands."

"Oh, is that so?" said Hedda, having regained some composure. "Well I am sorry to say that is not my understanding."

"Not mine, either," said Gerd.

Speer lowered his gun and aimed it straight at Gerd. "I don't care what your understanding is. We are in a hurry and we need action. If you don't raise them on the comm in the next 15 seconds I'm going to shoot, and this time it won't be the ceiling that gets a hole in it."

Gerd sighed, looking annoyed again, and said, "Fine, then." Finishing his table-clearing, he picked up two teacups and the teapot and headed toward the sink. "This way."

But as he passed Speer, Gerd suddenly swung the teapot and smashed it hard into Speer's outstretched wrist. The gun went flying and the ceramic pot broke into pieces, splashing sharp edges and scalding water all over Speer's lower arm. Speer yelped and involuntarily doubled over, clenching his hands to his stomach. Tappet rushed to his aid, looking down at the arm. While their attention was averted, Gerd, with what must have been a burst of adrenaline, seized the heavy kitchen table and tipped it over violently on top of them, pinning Tappet at the waist and Speer at the knees. They both yelled in pain and surprise. Speer immediately began wriggling free. Gerd watched in fear for several seconds before finally picking up a chair and swinging it like a baseball bat right at Speer's head. It landed with a thud and Speer collapsed, unconscious.

"Stop! Stop!" shouted Tappet from under the table. "I give up! This is crazy! We're law enforcement officers, for God's sake. Just let me explain!"

Gerd harrumphed. "We'll see about that. Hedda, dear, sorry about all this. Would it be too much trouble for you to fetch some good strong rope from my studio? I think there's some hanging on a hook on the wall over on the left-hand side."

"Oh, yes, I know where you mean." Hedda disappeared and Gerd leaned on the upturned edge of the table, ready to push down with all his weight if Tappet moved or Speer came to. Hedda returned shortly with the rope, and after quite a lot of fussing, Gerd and Hedda managed to get Tappet tied to a chair with his hands behind his back. They were only a little more efficient on their second try with Speer, who was still unconscious and heavy to lift, but eventually they managed.

Once her prisoners were safely settled, Hedda commed the Safety Patrol. "Hello, dear," she smiled at the no-nonsense, friendly-enough woman volunteer named Agda who answered the call. "This is Hedda Lindgren. How are you this fine day?"

"I am well, thank you, Friend Hedda. And how are you?"

"Well enough, I suppose. But I'm afraid I do need to report a difficulty."

"Oh dear, I'm sorry to hear that. What seems to be the trouble?"

"Well, Agda, I am hoping that this is all a misunderstanding, but these two men—here, can you see them if I hold the camera up?—these men came to our house just now, and well, I'm sorry to say they started behaving very impolitely."

"Oh really? How so?"

"Rather rude questions, to begin with. And then this one shot his gun and threatened to shoot again at my husband."

"Oh! Hedda, I am very sorry to hear that. Let me see if we can't send out a patrol craft right away to help you with that. Are you feeling perfectly safe now?"

"Yes, safe enough, I suppose. Gerd's been quite heroic. We tied them up. I suppose we'll be all right for a while."

"Good, I'm glad. Let's see here, the closest patrol is—well look at this. You know what? It looks like our friend Leilani from the Space Traffic Control Center already has the *Frälsaren* flying up your way to pick up the crash victims. Are they there yet?"

"Yes, yes. It was Greta and Janna on *Frälsaren*. They just left a little while ago. They picked up our new friends Kessa and Jet. Lovely young people. Kessa is Britta Sjøfred's granddaughter, did you know? And the young man is from Earth. I understand they're going back to Zero West. But you see, our new visitors arrived just a few minutes after *Frälsaren* left."

"I see. Well, Hedda, you are safe for now? I wonder if it would bother you too much if I just checked a couple of things and then commed you right back?"

"Very well, dear."

Agda checked in with both Leilani and Greta. Her first thought was that *Frälsaren* might turn around and go back to rescue the Lindgrens from the pirates, but, though apologetic, both Greta and Leilani made it clear that they had their own emergency and *Frälsaren* needed to get to Zero West as soon as possible. So Agda called in a pair of Security

Patrol volunteers based near Cedar, the hyperloop station closest to the Lindgrens. It would take them over an hour traveling by air pod to reach the Lindgren's house, but it was the best Agda could do.

Sitting tied up in a chair, Tappet was beyond frustration and beyond anger; he was deflated. He simply wanted to give up. The escapees had the p-cap, they were going to deliver it, and the irresponsible New Gaians were going to blab the whole story about Toxin-X to anyone who would listen. Which would be the entire population of the planet Earth. Never mind about Skervin's reputation or Tappet's orders, that was a worldwide crisis flying off in *Falls In* toward Zero West. He sat with head bent, saying nothing.

Zero West

Frälsaren had barely touched down in Zero West when Jet and Kessa came hurtling out the hatch and running full speed in the direction of the IMS service node. They arrived less than a minute later at the fenced-in compound and smiled at the guard. "Hi Sjurd it's us again," panted Kessa. "We have something for Osvald."

Inside, Osvald was waiting behind his high counter with an expectant look on his face. "Well?"

Kessa gestured at the mochila strapped to Jet's chest. "Does this belong to you?"

"Yes! I believe it does!" Osvald hurried out from behind his counter as Jet unstrapped the pouch and handed it over for inspection. Osvald looked eagerly inside and pulled out the two canisters, which looked unharmed through all their recent adventures. "These are the ones! You got them. Thank you, thank you so much!"

Kessa and Jet looked on, grinning wide. "How soon can you process them?" Kessa asked.

"I'll take them in the back and put them on the machine right now. With any luck we'll start transmitting e-messages within the hour."

"Fantastic."

"Now remember, you're sworn to secrecy, right? I could so easily lose my job over this. I'm just going to tell everyone that Kai and Narisa brought them here."

"Our secret."

Osvald gave Kessa a grateful hug and then, for good measure, gave Jet one too. He disappeared into the back and Kessa and Jet walked slowly out of the building, full of smiles.

They gave Sjurd a friendly goodbye wave and then sauntered over to the Space Traffic Control Center. When Kessa and Jet walked in the door of the STC someone called out "They're here!" and a whoop went up around the building. Marta, Stoke, and Leilani came hurrying out from the back and grinning and cheering, and there was a great, big, group hug.

"Are you both okay?" Marta asked, looking them up and down.

"Fine! We're just fine," Kessa beamed.

"Amazingly enough," nodded Jet.

Stoke scrunched his nose playfully and said, "Just don't look at yourselves in a mirror." And then he went on, "Did the, uh, 'package' make it to its destination?"

Jet smiled and nodded with satisfaction. "Yep. It's getting unwrapped right now."

Leilani was also happy to report that the Lindgrens had managed to capture the pirates on their own and a Security Patrol team was on their way to pick them up.

The friends all looked around at each other gleefully. Without warning, everyone in the room except for Jet and Stoke, who had no idea what was going on, jammed themselves into a tight, giggling huddle. They all reached a hand down toward the center then, as one, lifted it high while calling out a cheer that sounded like "whoop, whoop, oom-bah-bah!" and did it three times.

"Newgie tradition," Kessa explained to Jet, still laughing. He couldn't help but laugh and smile, too.

Lindgren Residence

When the Security Patrol volunteers arrived at the Lindgrens' to take Tappet and Speer into custody, Speer took one look and gave himself a secret smile. They were young, inexperienced, and from the way they were gingerly holding their e-guns it looked as if they had never fired them before.

All Speer had to do was wait for them to untie him . . .

Thirty seconds later, the security patrols were lying unconscious on the floor, battered by Speer's chair and fists. Five seconds after that, Hedda had been electropulsed where she stood in the kitchen, collapsing in a gentle heap.

Tappet, still tied to his chair, was yelling at Speer to stop, but adrenaline was raging through Speer's brain and he barely heard. Instead he turned his attention toward the door of the studio, where Gerd was reemerging. In one look, Gerd took in the collapsed forms of the security volunteers and his wife Hedda in a heap in front of the sink. His eyes bulged and his jaw set, and he riveted Speer with a look as hard as steel. "What have you done?!"

"It's only a damn stun gun," Speer said, pointing it nevertheless at Gerd. "Where's my real one?"

Gerd gazed steadily at Speer for several seconds before deciding how to reply. Much as every traumatized nerve in his gut wanted to lash out at the madman who had just shot his wife, there was no arguing with the gun leveled at his chest. "In here," he sighed. "On my workbench."

"Good." Speer snaked his way around the unconscious bodies and into the studio, keeping his electropulse steadily aimed at Gerd the whole time. Once there, he greedily retrieved his pistol with his right hand while holding the e-gun on Gerd with his left. He held his beloved weapon up to the light for a close inspection, spun the mechanism, and gave a self-satisfied sigh. Then he walked up to Gerd and leaned his face in close, pointing the pistol at his jaw. "This is what you get for knocking me out with a chair," he growled. With no more warning, he smashed the butt of the pistol against Gerd's skull. Gerd yelped and fell unconscious, his bony body slumping against the door frame before falling to the floor.

"God *damn* it, Speer!" yelled Tappet from the other. "What the hell are you doing? Stop attacking people for Christ sake!"

Speer strolled back out of the studio, finally beginning to calm down. "No one else to attack," he observed. But then he looked at the viewscreen and realized Agda had been speaking with Hedda and was still online, speechlessly and helplessly watching the melee unfold. "Except her," added Speer. He fired the electropulse gun at the viewscreen, but it had no effect. Instead he walked over right in front of it, looked Agda squarely in the eyes, and then lifted a boot and kicked hard, smashing the viewscreen to pieces.

"Are you done?" Tappet sighed. "Then untie me and let's get out of here."

"Where to?" said Speer as he began working on Tappet's knots.

"I don't know yet. Their air pods are a start, I suppose."

"How are we going to get back to your ship in orbit? We crashed the orbiter."

"We're not going back to orbit yet."

"What? Why not? They have the p-caps. Our mission has failed. Time to retreat."

"No! We can't fail. This is too important. There is still a way."

"What way?"

Speer finished with the ropes and Tappet stood up, gratefully rubbing his chafed wrists and thinking hard. "OK, so they deliver the p-caps to the IMS service node. What happens next? The p-caps get decoded and sent on the regular net as e-messages. The one message we care about is only addressed to one person. We get to that person before she can rebroadcast it back to Earth, and we're still okay, right? No one on Earth ever finds out."

"Seems like a long shot. She could send it to as many people as she wants on this planet, and anyone of them could send a p-cap back to Earth. Why don't we just torch the IMS service node? That's what we should have done to begin with."

"Taking out the service node wouldn't stop someone from carrying a message personally. We'd have to take out their whole ability to do space travel."

"Break their space elevator?"

"Not practical. No, I just want to get to Lana Sjøfred. She's the one the message was sent to. She's the one who's going to cause us trouble."

"Understood. Where is she?"

Tappet shook his head in frustration. "If we were on Earth I could tell you in a second. But I have no idea how to find people here on New Gaia. Let's get out of here before reinforcements arrive and we'll figure it out as we go." With that, he led the way out to the clearing, where the air pods that the security volunteers had arrived in awaited.

"What are we going to do when we find her?" Speer asked.

Tappet sighed deeply and sincerely. There was only one solution he could think of. "Kill her."

The House on Lake Peace

Lana's lab was tucked into the southeast corner of the house on the upper level, just off the spiral staircase that also served the hallway leading to the bedrooms. She was there alone, reading research papers on toxicology and trying to ignore the crashing construction noises coming from Kjell and Galen's door project downstairs, when the p-cap message came in. She jumped the moment she heard the ping. She turned to her largest viewscreen and said, "Play." Sure enough, there it was—Galen himself speaking urgently to her in the fateful message he had recorded five days before, when he was back on Earth.

"Please look at these 3D scanner files and tell me what you think . . ."

Attached to the message was a large data file from Galen's 3D scanner. It would give her a molecule-by-molecule profile of his samples. Not as good as the samples themselves, but it would have to do.

Lana's first move was to make several copies of the message and the data file and distribute them to various places for safekeeping. When that was complete, she went to the door of her lab and, to save her lame foot from another trip down the twisting stairs, called out excitedly to the whole house: "The kids did it! Galen's message just arrived! We have the data!"

Happy replies chorused from around the house and Galen himself came up to give her a celebratory hug. "Look, it's you!" Lana said, and played the message again.

Galen looked on grimly. They all knew now that the epidemic he was talking about in that video was much worse than he imagined back then. "The data file came through, too?"

"I have it right here."

"Good. Now the work really begins, doesn't it? Lana, I—I am feeling so many things right now. For one thing I'm grateful to you for attempting this. You know, if you don't figure out what's going on there and how to stop it, I genuinely fear that no one will." Lana started to reply, but Galen stopped her. "But I'm also—well, I feel like this is my fault in some way. I should have found it sooner. Or I should have stayed on at ORGA somehow and kept Skervin under control."

"Galen, that's absurd—"

"Or probably I should have just come back here, home again, a long time ago, and then this wouldn't be our problem."

Lana gave her brother a long look. "Galen, don't feel guilty or angry with yourself. I was angry with you for a while too, but now I've realized that if you hadn't discovered this outbreak when you did, we might never have found out about it. From everything we know so far, the people of Earth need all the help they can get, and if nothing else, we can *try* to do our part. It's the right thing. You did the right thing."

Galen responded only with a small look, full of worry, but also of relief.

Lana continued, "And now I'm going to do the right thing, too, which is to do as much research as I can on this thing and maybe make some progress. And you're going to help!"

Galen smiled and nodded, and they shared a long, warm, hug. This time it felt right.

Zero West

Agda was horrified. She had just witnessed the pirate batter and electropulse Security Patrol volunteers and an innocent older couple. Now that terrible man and his partner were on the loose. This was by far the worst and most blatant violence she had ever experienced. Her throat went dry and her head spun, and for a moment she felt on the edge of panic.

But somehow Agda controlled herself and considered what to do. There was no precedent for this situation. It wasn't like there was a higher authority she could call upon; the Security Patrol was all New Gaia had, and to be frank, it wasn't particularly experienced or effective. Right now, the response was up to her. First, she called Greta and Janna and asked them if they wouldn't mind going out on *Frälsaren* once again to tend to the wounded at the Lindgrens' house. Then Agda gathered her nerve and touched a control on her console that opened up an emergency comm channel to all patrols. As quickly as she could, she explained everything that had just happened at the Lindgren residence and attached a video recording of what she had just witnessed on the viewscreen. She instructed all patrols to find and arrest the pirates as soon as possible. "But if you see them," she added, "call for backup! These two are really dangerous."

■　■　■

A few hundred meters away at the Space Traffic Control Center, Agda's message came through and the mood suddenly transformed from victory to battle. Everyone cried out at once at the outrage, and when they saw the video, the four friends looked at Tappet in amazement. They had not realized until this moment that one of the pirates was the same police officer who had been chasing them back on Earth.

Leilani: "Those fucking bastards!"

Stoke: "Fut."

Kessa: "How could they do that to the Lindgrens?"

Marta: "Those poor Lindgrens! I hope they're okay! Let me go with Greta and Janna. I want to help."

Jet: "What were they thinking? We already delivered the p-cap message. Why don't they just give up and go home?"

After the consternated discussion, everyone agreed with Leilani: "This has gone too far. We have to arrest those *doosas* fast. Why don't you four go talk to Agda? I'm sure Security Patrol can use all the help they can get right now."

■ ■ ■

The four friends found Agda in a small office attached to the Government Center, close to the center of town. Like most things New Gaian, the Government Center was a humble building that seemed to embody the principles that locals called *schwoot*: well-made, practical, modestly attractive, and worthy of its purpose. The Security Patrol office, set off on one side, seemed to almost apologize for its existence, with reluctant pale gray lettering on its door sign, a small door, and compact windows as if to conceal itself from the light of day.

Agda, on the other hand, was forthcoming and, if not sure of herself, at least determined and energetic. "Yes, we would love your help! Patrol volunteers are so hard to come by around here."

"But after what happened to the Lindgrens and those two volunteers Johan and Claude, the whole planet must be ready to volunteer?" Stoke ventured.

Agda shook her head ruefully. "Maybe on Earth. Here I think it scared everyone off. We Newgies don't like to fight."

"Ah. Well, neither do we, but we will if we have to."

"Right. That's the attitude we need right now." Agda gave Stoke a long, appraising look, and then she opened a cabinet and pulled out an e-gun. "Ever used one of these before?"

Stoke swallowed. "Uh, no."

"Here, give it a heft. It's not difficult. Just point and shoot. Not at me! It takes four seconds to recharge between shots."

"Is there a power setting?"

"Not on this planet. New Gaian law only allows us to stun. It still hurts like hoo-ha, though."

Agda looked at the others. "Anyone else ready for one?"

"Me," said Kessa with an edge of her fierce streak in her voice.

Jet, slightly more reluctantly, said, "Sure, me too."

All eyes turned to Marta, but she shook her head emphatically. "Not me! I simply couldn't do it to someone. I've already been on the wrong end of one of those and I didn't like it at all."

Agda nodded. "No shame in that. Now then, where do you all plan to go?"

Jet and Stoke were taken aback. Stoke said, "Are we official now? Aren't we supposed to register, or sign, or swear in, or something?"

Agda looked mildly amused. "You're just volunteering to help the community. Do you want a parade or something?"

"No, but . . ."

"This is New Gaia," Agda said in a motherly tone. "We're a community here: a planet full of people all working together as well as we know how to make our world and our lives the best they can be. We expect and trust everyone to contribute as best they can. That's what you four are doing right now. Is there any reason to doubt that?"

"No, of course not . . ."

"Well then. Where do you plan to go?"

Stoke was at a momentary loss for words, so Jet answered. "Where do you need us?"

Agda shrugged. "I'm sorry, but I'm not really sure."

"The question is," Stoke said, "where do we find the bad guys?"

Jet thought aloud, focusing as usual on logic. "Where they go depends on what they want to do. If they want to escape back to Earth, they'll have to come back here to Zero West to take the space elevator or steal an orbiter."

Stoke, always good at reading others' intentions, looked uncomfortable. "I hate to say it, but they might not be trying to escape yet."

"Why not?" asked Marta.

"Because they haven't destroyed Galen's message yet. They might still be after the data file."

"But it's already gone out. Mom already has it. She's probably analyzing it right now."

Stoke's forehead wrinkled. "That's the problem. They might be thinking . . ."

Marta's face transformed into an expression of alarm. "You mean, they might be going after *Mom*?"

Stoke didn't need to say more. Marta, Kessa, and Jet all shifted uneasily. Agda scowled. "That's your mother, Lana Sjøfred, right? Who the p-cap message was sent to? And she's a scientist?"

Marta nodded. "Right. I guess they might try to, you know, attack her somehow. Get her to give back the file."

"But that's ridiculous," Kessa said. "It's not like you can put knowledge back in a bottle. If she's studying the data, then that's it. The only way to get rid of it would be to—" She stopped herself. "Oh."

"Look, it's only a possibility," said Jet. "We don't actually know what they're thinking. But just in case, how would they get to your house from where they are now?"

Marta answered right away. "Fastest way is the planet tube. They'd come right through here."

"Are there other ways?"

"Not really. I guess you could do it by air pods, but it would take forever."

"Okay, so either way—whether they're trying to escape back to Earth or whether they're going, um, after your mother—they'll have to come through here in Zero West? The hyperloop station?"

Marta looked at Agda and Kessa for confirmation. They all agreed. "Pretty sure."

Near the Lindgren Residence

Tappet and Speer each climbed into one the air pods that the Security Patrol volunteers had recently parked in the Lindgrens' clearing. They immediately discovered the always-on two-way comm channel between them, so they spoke as if they were in one ship together.

"Where should we go?" Speer asked.

"I'm thinking," replied Tappet, irritated. New Gaia technology was so backward. There was no brainbox network, so he had to come up with specific questions to ask a computer aloud. He had no superior to consult with, so he had to make all the decisions himself. And this whole damn planet seemed to be covered with trees, with not a building in sight. How was he supposed to operate?

He tried addressing the air pod's computer. "Take me to the location of Lana Sjøfred."

"That person is not shown in my directory," said the computer.

"What?" To someone from Earth, that statement was shocking. How could someone not be in the planetary database?

"Please specify a landmark or location."

"Kessa Dahlstrom. Take me to Kessa Dahlstrom's residence."

"That person is not shown in my directory. Please specify a landmark or location."

Tappet thought hard, trying to remember bits of conversation he had overhead inside the house when Hedda was chattering away or speaking with Agda on the viewscreen. If Speer hadn't knocked the whole damn house unconscious he could have asked someone. Then he had it: "There's another Sjøfred who's famous. The grandmother. B-something. B-something Sjøfred . . ."

"Britta Sjøfred is listed in my directory. Her residence is on Lake Peace, near Aspen North."

"Finally! Yes, take us there."

"Confirmed," said the computer as the air pod engines whirred into action and they took off. "Estimated flight duration is 22.8 hours. Replenishment of the fuel cells will be required en route."

"22.8 hours? You have to be kidding me."

"22.8 hours travel time is confirmed. The distance is 6400 kilometers."

"Crap. That's not going to work. Got any ideas, Speer?"

"Go back to Zero West and steal an orbiter?"

"Computer, what is the travel time to Zero West?"

"5.1 hours."

"Argh. We don't have this kind of time. How do people live here when it's so far to anywhere?" It was a naïve question that a reasonably responsible visitor would have researched before arriving, but Tappet, like anyone from Earth, was so accustomed to getting this kind of information effortlessly on demand from his brainbox that it had not occurred to him to study up beforehand. Finally he said, "Computer, what is the fastest way to reach Lake Peace?"

Those were the magic words and a map appeared on the viewscreen illustrating the optimal route: air pod to the hyperloop station at Cedar, 320 kilometers away; hyperloop to Zero West; planet tube to Forty-Five Central, another hyperloop to Aspen North, and another air pod to Lake Peace. Total travel time not counting connections: 3.8 hours. "Well that will have to work," sighed Tappet. His policeman's indefatigable temperament was on duty. He was going to complete this mission, and small setbacks were not going to stop him. "We can make it most of the way before dark," he said aloud to Speer. "Let's go! Computer, take me to Cedar."

Lana's Lab in the House on Lake Peace

Lana loved her work, but it had been a lifelong struggle to fit it in between family, community, and her yen to live outdoors with nature. She was a wonderfully talented and energetic person who was living life to its fullest, but the cost was something in her mien—a tiny droop in the shoulders, perhaps, or an extra darkness in the circles under her eyes—that gave the tiniest hint of a woman who had never in her life felt completely satisfied with her own accomplishments. Her lab was tight quarters jammed with stacks of instruments going up to ceiling, but Lana always kept the two small windows unobstructed so she'd have her view out through the trees to the lake. The only decoration was a small model of a DNA molecule with a little person climbing up the rungs of the double helix as if it were a twisted ladder. There were two work surfaces that waged a constant battle to stay clear, two stools, and a protean array of computers, scanners, analysis machines, and everything else that the planet's leading expert on poisonous plants might need.

In actuality, most of Lana's work happened inside one small but very powerful computer that was dedicated to simulating biochemical systems. It embodied the full corpus of twenty-ninth-century understanding of the field, and together with ingenious subroutines—many created by Lana herself—for conducting novel experiments, it made possible a practice called virtual research, in which the entire discovery process was conducted using simulated systems instead of natural ones. It was a relatively new and controversial approach that was not universally embraced, and scientists on Earth, who had effectively closed themselves off from the rest of the community 15 years earlier, were barely familiar with the concept. Purists still disapproved of virtual research, calling it circular reasoning and a dangerous departure from the scientific principal of separating theory from natural experiment. But Lana, who was an accidental leader in the field, found the method to be highly productive and she was as careful as possible to "ground truth" her virtual results with corroborating evidence from more conventional techniques. That's what all the other equipment was for. All this gear was expensive, but Lana had a well-earned reputation for making practical discoveries that could be sold to other planets, and the citizens on New Gaian volunteer Panels were very likely to grant any funding requests she made.

Galen was in the lab now, and Lana pointed him to one of the stools and pulled up the other for herself. She fixed her blue eyes on her brother, surprising even him with the intelligent intensity that seemed to be powering up within them. "I've reviewed the meeting transcripts that Ettica gave you," she said, "and I'm starting to get some ideas about this debacle. You've been telling me a little, but I need more background. So now, if you don't mind, I would like you to teach me everything you know about soybean agriculture as currently practiced on Earth."

Galen was emotionally ready for action now. He smiled at the extravagance of the question and tossed his own blond locks. "Hah! That's going to take some time, Lana! And probably not long enough, either, because I don't know nearly as much as I should. The whole operation is so thoroughly automated, I have very little to do with it. Mostly I watch the agribots every day."

"I'm sure you know a lot more than you think you do, big brother."

Galen walked over to the window and looked out, as if half expecting to spy the pirates attacking any minute. He was ready for some battle action, but his emergency door project wasn't what he was needed for. Strange as it seemed, this was. Sitting here, talking to his sister in a lab. He heaved a large sigh, gave Lana an affectionate look, and said, "Okay. Here goes . . ."

Galen talked and Lana asked questions—lots and lots of questions, only some of which Galen knew the answers to. But Galen really did know more than he thought he did, and after two hours Lana had 10 screens of technical notes and a firmer, more confident attitude in her nods, confirmations, and expansions. As they conversed, the comfortable patterns of their long-lost fraternal relationship began to reemerge, and Galen found himself enjoying just being with Lana again, the horrible topic notwithstanding. And he found himself starting to believe in himself again; in his own intellect and problem-solving abilities. It felt good.

They gave themselves a short break for afternoon tea and checking in with the rest of the household, and then they reconvened. "Time to talk about the toxin," Lana said.

"Ready."

"Let's start with what we know so far."

"All right," said Galen. "'We' meaning you and me. ORGA probably knows a lot of things I don't; I learned as much as you did from Ettica's meeting transcripts. I guess all we know for certain is that people on Earth keep dying from eating poisonous food. It's almost certainly toxic Nutribase, which means it's probably toxic soybeans, or at least a toxin in soybean plants. But it's not *all* soybean plants—otherwise every small animal on Earth would be dead right now. It must be just some of the plants that are infected."

"Right, good. So, my working hypothesis is that there's a pathogen spreading through the soybean crops and producing a toxin. Toxin-X, I guess ORGA has named it. When you were looking at the plants, you didn't see any signs of disease? Anything to distinguish sick plants from healthy ones?"

"I didn't notice any differences at all besides the dead animals."

"And obviously Toxin-X is not easy to detect in Nutribase, either, or else ORGA would have been screening for it by now."

"Right."

"So I guess that means we have two problems to solve." Lana pulled down a large, blank screen and wrote on it in large letters with her fingers:

Problem 1: Combat toxicosis in people.

Problem 2: Combat toxic pathogen in soybeans.

Galen scowled good naturedly. "Is 'toxicosis' really a word?"

"Sure. In our case it basically means food poisoning. And a toxic pathogen is a disease that creates toxins."

"I'll take your word for it. So in my language, it would go like this?" He wrote on the screen with his own fingers:

Problem 1: Food poisoning
Problem 2: Soybean disease

Lana smiled. "Okay, I'll let you get away with that. So obviously food poisoning is highest priority. We need to isolate the toxin—that is, figure out what the poison is—and then develop an antitoxin so that people who have been poisoned can be saved, and everyone else can be vaccinated against future exposure."

"Makes sense."

"And after that, cure the soybeans of whatever disease is making them poisonous to begin with."

"Right," nodded Galen. "Which will also allow my wild animal friends to survive. I don't fully understand the ecosystem out there, but I've got a pretty good hunch that it can't be good to be killing off entire populations of small animals."

"Good point."

"I notice the way you keep saying 'we,' by the way. You understand that we told Ettica we'd keep this secret, right? And you understand why?"

"I do, but it is certainly going to put a crimp in my style. I'm so used to working collaboratively with my colleagues from all over the Hundred Worlds on new problems like this. It's going to be odd to work alone. You'll have to be my lab assistant."

"Hah."

"Who else is there?"

Galen raised his eyebrows. "Kessa knows a lot of this stuff. She's going to be a scientist herself if she ever settles that restless soul of hers."

"She's not here right now. Come on, Friend Assistant. Your first job is a literature search . . ."

Hyperloop Station, Zero West

The hyperloop station at Zero West was, like most New Gaian operations, a casual affair. The stone-and-wood walls were not continuous and people strolled in and out from all directions. Hyperloops were completely automated, and free, of course. The small capsules ran on demand, so there were no lines to wait in or checks to go through, and except for arriving and departing passengers, the station was generally empty.

Pairs of transparent polyglass transport tubes, each one just two-and-a-half meters across, pointed off in several directions. Empty transport capsules, whose walls were also transparent, were queued up and ready to carry seated passengers shooting off through the evacuated tubes at 1100 km/h, giving them a sense of traveling on flying chairs.

As the four friends hurried into the station, Jet was immediately curious about how the whole operation worked, but he suppressed the urge to inspect as they dashed through the station and found a hiding place where they could look out on the arrival gate from Cedar, waiting for their quarry. Jet couldn't help but notice their role was suddenly transforming from being hunted to being hunters themselves. Or at least, he hoped it was.

They had made it just in time. It was only minutes later that a capsule arrived and Tappet and Speer stepped out. They were instantly conspicuous from their plain Earth-style dress, relatively dark hair and skin, and aggressive bearing. They both looked around warily, scanning first for enemies and second for directions to their next connection, the planet tube.

Kessa recoiled at the sight of Tappet and Speer. They had just terrorized the Lindgrens and now they were going after her own mother, and Kessa was overrun with fury. Her heart was racing and she could feel her face flushing. She had never been good at impulse control, and now her impulses took over her brain, blotting out all reason. Suddenly, foolishly, and irrationally, she ran out from hiding and straight at them as if she would tackle them herself. Jet gave a warning cry but then dashed after her, closely followed by Stoke, who was already anticipating what everyone was about to do.

Speer started firing his bullet gun and Tappet, Jet, and Stoke all sent electropulse beams flying. There was a series of leaps and dives, and there were three yells of pain. Kessa fell to the ground with a pulsed foot, and Jet doubled over with a bullet hole through this left hand. Speer cursed loudly at a stunned right hand, realizing he'd have to start shooting with his left. Tappet, surprised by the unexpected attack, ran for cover by diving back toward the capsule he had just left. It was a bad move, but Speer had no choice but to follow just as the capsule's door shut automatically behind him. Now the two were trapped back inside the transport tube, which, everyone soon discovered by shooting, was impervious to both e-pulses and bullets.

With Tappet and Speer trapped, there was a temporary stand-off. Marta braved the moment to run out from behind her pillar and help Kessa and Jet back to safety. Stoke was unhurt and stalked furiously around the tube, looking for weaknesses and practically daring Speer or Tappet to come out again. Then there was movement in the tube and the capsule started moving slowly into the turn-around loop, following its automatic maneuvering protocol as if nothing were wrong. It was going to the departure station, where the tube door was open and Speer and Tappet would be able to escape.

Stoke watched the operation helplessly. "Jet! Girls!" he called. "Look at this! What do we do?"

"Be right there!" Jet called. He nodded a thanks to Marta for bandaging his hand and told her, "Stay here with Kessa."

"Will you be okay, Jet?" said Marta, looking skeptically at the still-bloody hand.

Jet only hmphed as he jogged out toward Stoke, blood high. "Come on. We'll get them when they come out."

Stoke nodded. "Good. You take a position on the near side of the door and I'll take the far side."

The moment the capsule came in range of the door opening, everyone fired at once and immediately ducked back down for cover, to no effect. Stoke was focusing on Tappet, and he sidled a little farther into the open and took careful aim at the place he anticipated Tappet's head was about to appear. But just then there was a shout from behind him. "What's going on here?" It was a traveler who had just walked into the station.

Jet turned and yelled a warning at the newcomer. "Watch out! Get down! It's the pirates!"

The traveler was suitably shocked and immediately turned and ran, but Stoke had been distracted, and he had taken his eyes off his spot a moment too long. Tappet popped up, pointed his e-gun, and fired. Stoke yelled and fell backward, stunned in the midsection and unable to stand. Jet aimed a shot at Speer, but he was off balance from warning the newcomer and he missed again.

Moments later Speer and Tappet were at the capsule door with clear shots at both Jet and Stoke. Speer got a deadly look in his eye as he swung his pistol around to aim a bullet directly at Jet's chest.

But Tappet was doing the same thing, and before Speer could coordinate his clumsy left hand, Tappet fired his e-gun and Jet collapsed.

Speer's bloodlust was not stilled. Without pausing, he turned his aim downward at Jet's crumpled form and started to fire.

At just that moment an electropulse sizzled and Tappet fell sideways into Speer, who spun around and toppled over, his pistol firing wildly. Its bullet shot through the front of the capsule and slammed into the far door of the pressure lock that led to the transport tube. Tappet, yelling in pain and holding his side, had just enough time to look up and see where the shot that had hit him had come from: it was Kessa, leaning against Marta on her one good foot. The incredibly fierce look on her face said, "Never, ever, shoot at my Jet."

The moment lasted only a fraction of a second. The bullet that had hit the pressure lock door did not fully penetrate, but it made a crack that weakened the polyglass. Unlike the tube walls in the station, the door was under high stress from the pressure differential on its two sides. The crack gave way and a tremendous burst of air exploded out of the station and down into the evacuated tube. The capsule went shooting outward, carrying Tappet and Speer with it. The station was filled with a deafening *hoo-WOP* like a gigantic champagne cork popping, and those who could clapped their hands to their ears.

Downstream, emergency valves in the hyperloop tube slammed shut to contain the breach, and within seconds all was calm in the station and the tube. Marta and Kessa hobbled over to attend to Stoke—in agonizing pain but whole—and Jet, unconscious now and still covered with blood from his wounded left hand. The visitor called in cautiously from outside, "Are you all right? I'll go get help."

"Did they get away?" Stoke asked Marta through white teeth clenched in distress.

"I'm not sure. They disappeared down the tube—uh-oh." As she spoke, Speer and then Tappet came staggering through the lock. They had somehow survived the blast, crawled out of their capsule, and walked back down the tube. Speer was holding his pulsed right hand under his left armpit and Tappet was walking with a serious limp from the combined effects of pulsed toes and side, but they were mobile. Kessa gasped and reached for her gun, but Speer waved his bullet gun in her general direction and said grimly, "Don't even try." Kessa retracted and Speer and Tappet continued stoically past them and out toward the exit that led to the planet tube.

The mission, Tappet kept telling himself, the mission. He was *not* going to fail.

The moment they were out of sight Kessa yelled out, "Help! Someone! Stop those people! They're the pirates!" But there was no answer. After a while another traveler arrived and sat with them until more help arrived, but he didn't care to give chase to the fugitives. This was New Gaia. People didn't like to fight.

Leilani's Residence

After the four friends had briefed Agda, and the hospital had done what it could for them, the planet tube had stopped running for the night and there was nothing more they could do. Leilani had insisted they come home with her for the night. Despite its lack of outside walls, her house felt cozy and warm and out of the rain. The bullet wound in Jet's hand had been easily healed with wound-gel, which actually consisted of millions of healer nanobots applied to the wound and powered by ultrasound emitted by an external wand. But the medical people advised that the only treatment for electropulse injuries was time, and Jet, Kessa, and Stoke were all looking beaten and miserable. Leilani attempted to lighten the mood by declaring that bitchin' big servings of scrumptious food were the solution, and with dutiful help from Marta, who was unhurt, she turned out a table full of indulgent delights like creamy coconut-mango shrimp, chili-lime marinated white fish, feathery butter-puff rolls, and two variations on New Gaian double chocolate-strawberry cake.

But no one was in the mood for celebration. This had been an exhausting day and the pirates were still out there, probably stalking Lana. There was a dark cloud hovering, and they all slept fitfully at Leilani's house that night. Jet woke one time to find Kessa sitting up next to him, staring out a window to the north. "I know the Security Patrol and the whole planet is supposedly looking for them, but they're after my *mom*."

"They'll have to sleep too," Jet soothed. "We'll catch up with them tomorrow."

Near the Zero West Planet Tube Terminal

It was growing dark by the time Tappet and Speer limped their way away from the wrecked hyperloop station. Clouds had gathered and Tappet felt the unfamiliar sensation of a few drops of rain before they finished crossing the clearing and made their way inside the planet tube terminus. To Tappet's way of thinking, this was the most civilized building he had seen yet on this backwards planet. The ceiling was four stories high to accommodate the substantial machinery, there were rooms for what looked to be full-time staff, and there were large displays giving directions and schedules. Tappet almost sighed in relief.

But then he looked more closely at the schedule. Under the Departures column it said, "Next Launch: 10 August, 0600." That was the next morning.

Speer had noticed the same thing. They looked at each other, Tappet cursed and said he wanted his brainbox back, and then they trudged over to what looked like an information kiosk to talk to a clerk. The clerk, a skinny teenage boy with a protruding Adam's apple who looked very much like a volunteer, appeared to be packing up for the day. He looked up and did a double-take when he saw the dangerous-looking pair approaching, but he kept his nerve and said, "Yes, friends, may I help you?"

"When's the next launch?" Tappet demanded.

"Oh-six-hundred tomorrow morning. Or thereabouts, anyway. That first one in the morning tends to run a little late, you know?"

"No, we need to go tonight."

"I'm sorry, we only run during the day, six to six."

"But it's fifteen minutes before six right now!"

"Right, which means the inbound will be here any moment, and then we'll close for the evening."

"But the outbound? When does the outbound run?"

"Every hour on the hour, six to five. See, the last one leaves at five so it will arrive before six."

"Damn." Tappet looked over at Speer, who was scowling and putting his hand on the gun at his waist. But Tappet shook his head at him. They were already on the run. They didn't need to attract any more attention today. He turned back to the skinny teenager. "Where do we get some food and a place to spend the night?"

Because of where he worked, the clerk was more accustomed to hearing that question than most New Gaians, who would have simply asked a fellow citizen for shelter. "We have visitor quarters and a commissary for off-worlders right here in Zero West. It's just out the door and down to the right."

Tappet and Speer turned and left without saying thank you. There was something about how the clerk had given them directions, the way he had glanced sideways at his comm screen as he spoke. They had been recognized, Tappet realized ruefully. The moment they were out of sight the skinny little clerk was going to call their cops and there would be a greeting party waiting for them at the visitor quarters. And this time, if they had any brains at all, they'd bring a whole lot more force than those four amateur kids.

When they exited through the door, Tappet glanced at Speer, who had done the same mental calculation, and they both turned left, exactly the opposite of the clerk's directions.

It was full-on raining by then, dark, and chilly. Speer had experience with rain from his time on other planets, but Tappet had spent most of his life indoors and was not enjoying his first exposure to wet hair, wet clothes, and water dripping down the back of his neck. Plus, the places he had been zapped still hurt like hell.

"We still need food and shelter," Speer pointed out. They were frustrated by their first attempts to find any, though. The New Gaians apparently didn't believe in outdoor lighting so everything was dark, another new experience for Tappet. Apart from the tempting but dangerous commissary, they could find nothing resembling a café, restaurant, or even a public food fabricator. That's right, Speer reminded himself. Fabs were unique to Earth. What's wrong with these people? Don't they eat? The more Speer thought about food the hungrier he became. And next to him, Tappet seemed to be fading fast.

Finally losing patience, Speer pulled up at the door of the next building they passed, which happened to be the Government Center. They were closed for the night, but Speer had a gun that would very likely blow open any lock. He got it out and aimed at the edge of the door.

"Hang on," said Tappet. He reached out and tried the door. To Speer's astonishment, it was open. "I'm starting to get the idea," said Tappet, as he stepped gratefully inside and tried to shake off the rain, "that these people don't even know what security is."

Speer and Tappet found some soft sofas in an enclosed office in the Government Center, and they made themselves a reasonably comfortable camp for the night. A little later, Speer snuck over to the commissary after it had closed and everyone had gone home, including any security patrols who may or may not have been staking the place out based on a tip from the planet tube clerk. He broke— or rather walked—in and, working awkwardly with this left hand, rounded up as much portable food as he could carry in his pack, then took it back to Tappet in the Government Center, where they both ate greedily before falling off into a cautious sleep. But Tappet was a police officer and Speer was a soldier. They were on a mission and their blood was up. Tomorrow would be better hunting.

Caphaletta's Apartment, Rio de Janeiro

Caphaletta was fighting down a growing sense of desperation. Poor Banji was in bed now, too weak to get up. He was pale and so, so frail. Even his hair was lying flat now. She wanted to cry, but she wouldn't let herself. She sat next to him, cradling his head and shoulders in the crook of her left arm and trying to feed him soup with her right. It kept spilling.

"How about a cracker?" she asked. "Would that taste good? Here, I fabbed these two just now. They're cheese flavor, isn't that fun? You'll like them. Give this one a try."

Banji took a little bite, chewed, and took another. Then he even reached up a hand to hold the cracker himself and eat. Caphaletta felt a small smile creep across her sad face. "You like that? See? I thought you would. Cheese crackers. Want another?"

But something went wrong with Banji's left eye. The lid twitched several times and then drooped closed. "Something in your eye?" his mother asked. As she did, his whole left cheek began twitching as well, and then his whole face.

"Mama!" he whimpered. Involuntarily, she tightened her grip and hugged him close, watching aghast as his face muscles spasmed and his lips twisted in odd shapes, emitting tiny, quiet moans.

He curled his body into a ball and snuggled up to her, tense and jerking, and she squeezed him even harder, cooing "Baby, my baby! It will be okay, Little B. It will be all right." Then she commed the emergency line. "Help! My child is having a seizure! I need help!"

■　■　■

The holding room in the clinic was small and stark. Caphaletta had pulled her chair up right next to Banji's bed and sat there with one arm out holding his little hand, waiting for the next staff person to arrive. She didn't care who it was, she just wanted answers. Everything had been a blur so far: the ambulance aircar, the halls of the clinic, the medical people swarming all over. But Banji seemed stable now, with medical boxes attached to both arms and instruments nearby blinking steadily as if to say, "hold on."

Finally a young man appeared who had the uniform of a doctor. In this age of automated medicine, doctors were not revered quite the way they had been at other times in history, but their craft still called for putting patients at ease, and uniforms helped. "55 Luis Cabah, Medical 11," Caphaletta's brainbox told her. He was probably the highest medical rank a Level 32 like her would ever meet.

"How's he doing?" the doctor asked. He had a warm, friendly manner and Caphaletta liked him instantly.

"Oh, I don't know. He seems okay. He's just sleeping now."

"Mm-hm," said the doctor, putting his hands gently down on Banji's head and then proceeding to examine him all over.

Caphaletta stood up and looked on anxiously. She asked one small question, then another, and then finally burst forth with all the questions that had been simmering in her heart for the last week. "Is he going to be all right? What do you think is wrong with him? He's been low on weight, you know. Is this related? Was it a seizure? Is this normal? Will he get better?"

Luis just let her go. He nodded every now and then to let her know he was listening, but otherwise he proceeded with his examination, checked some instruments, took some notes. Finally, the distraught mother ran out of steam and deflated a little, ending with a sigh and a beseeching look into the doctor's eyes.

"Why don't you sit down," Luis said kindly, and he pulled up the only other chair in the room for himself. He paused thoughtfully, and then began. "Banji is okay for now. When he came in his blood glucose levels were low, he was dehydrated, and he was showing all the symptoms of this gastrointestinal condition that's been going around. Because he was on the small side to begin with, it might have hit him harder than most. For now, we have him on these machines that will get his levels back up to where they're supposed to be."

"'For now'?"

"That's right. I'm sorry to say we don't yet know enough to give a long-term prognosis. But the good news is you're not alone, because a lot of patients have this condition right now. The Authority has a lot of very smart people working on it in the labs and we just have to hope they'll find a treatment soon."

"Will he stay here, then?"

"Uh, no. There are so many people who need these machines . . ." Luis stopped and let Caphaletta reach the awkward conclusion: she would have to take Banji home again, because there was no room for him to stay in the clinic. She had just finished digesting this news when Luis caught her eye and said quickly, "And there is another thing you should know. It's, uh . . ." He stopped talking and glanced around the room to make sure they were alone. Then he held his hand up to his ear and tapped the lobe twice. The signal was an unorthodox request in a setting like this, but Caphaletta popped up her eyebrows in recognition, switched off her box, and nodded to indicate she was ready to talk confidentially.

"Sorry," smiled Luis. "It's just something I feel you should know about, as a mother. The Authority is trying to keep a lid on it, for good reasons certainly, but, well, I'm not sure they mean to keep it a secret from people who might be personally affected."

"What? What is it?"

"You see, little Banji's symptoms are not being caused solely by the GI condition. There's something else as well." He paused, choosing his words. "Over the past several days we've been getting scattered reports of a very dangerous toxin appearing in Nutribase. Food poisoning, you can call it. Reports are that it's a powerful, Category 1 nerve toxin."

"Banji has been poisoned?"

"Well, maybe. I can't be certain. If he was, it was a minute dose. Just a few molecules, maybe. But for a young child like him, with low body weight, that might be all it takes to cause some of the other symptoms I'm seeing."

"Is it bad? Will it get worse? Will it get better? What can I do?"

Luis smiled sadly. "You ask a lot of good questions, Caphaletta. I wish I had more answers for you. The main thing right now, relative to the toxicosis, is to keep him hydrated. Lots of liquids and electrolytes. I'm also prescribing antibiotics that may be of some help. And Caphaletta, it would be better if you didn't tell anyone else about this. As I said, the Authority has embargoed this information, and I'm violating a directive by telling you about it. I just feel . . . well, you know how I feel."

"Of course, 55 Medical 11. I understand, and I am very grateful to you. Even though it makes me want to cry."

■ ■ ■

Later that night, in their dim and quiet apartment, Caphaletta sat on the floor near Banji's bed, knees pulled up to her chest, rocking slowly back and forth and letting tears roll down her cheeks. She had not slept for days. She had commed the clinic so often they were blocking her comms now, even on the emergency channel. They had no room for Banji, and there was nothing more they could do.

Banji was still with her, but barely, it seemed. She had gotten some juice into him a few hours ago, but 20 minutes later it had come back up in pathetic little squirts of watery vomit that spilled down his chin and soaked his shirt. He bore the experience numbly, and she hardly had the strength to clean it up.

Now he was finally asleep and she was alone with her despair. How cruel this is, she thought. How grievous. What had she done to deserve it? What had Banji done? And why, oh why wasn't the Authority doing more? This was the twenty-ninth century, for God's sake, and they couldn't cure a disease? The Authority was in charge of everything here, and they had the power to do whatever they chose. Couldn't they put Little B back to rights, running gleefully around the apartment again, playing orbiter and breaking toys? Didn't they know about his impish smile and his wispy hair? Didn't they know how incredibly precious the little boy was?

Her stress-muddled mind grasped at that thought. Maybe they didn't! Maybe if only they knew who he was, what he was like, maybe then they would do more for him: find room for him in the clinic, maybe, or find a cure for this cursed disease. It was just that someone up there wasn't paying attention; had been distracted somehow; hadn't ever met the Little B.

Caphaletta's frayed spirit clung to idea and leapt to an inspiration: she would tell them! She would send a message upwards, into the heights of the Authority. It would reach someone who could do something, and someone who cared. It would alert them to Banji's particular predicament, and they would see what was happening and take action. She was sure of it.

Almost shaking with the urgency of her new mission, Caphaletta stood up unsteadily and walked to her work station. It turned on a light for her and she began feverishly sorting through her collection of stills and videos of Banji. She pulled his baby portrait, then a shot of his first steps, then finger-painting at the crèche, then that cute one of the two of them and Rosa and Yuliana all blowing bubbles at the camera. A few more too, and then, with sad resolve, she tiptoed back to the side of his bed and captured a still of him now: sick, sallow, and bedridden.

She collected them all into a file and then sat down to write her cover letter and plea. In her eagerness for closure she wrote quickly and without inhibition. She began, "To Someone I Hope Is Concerned:"

When her message was ready, she told her brainbox to send it to the highest ranking medical person she could think of: 55 Luis Cabah, Medical 11. The brainbox pinged a confirmation and Caphaletta closed her eyes in relief. Then she stumbled to her bed and fell gratefully asleep.

Skervin's Conference Room

The mood in the meeting room was tense. Across the agenda, the news was uniformly depressing, and people spoke in anxious voices edged with concern.

Citizen Welfare, 93 Perka Yang Reporting:
"Toxicosis deaths, suspected or confirmed, 5490. Nonlethal toxicosis cases, likely due to trace exposure, approximately 47,200. These are happening in all cities. Intestinal distress, or what we're internally calling Bulking Syndrome, is only manifesting in the targeted bulking cities. It's well over one million. We don't have a better number than that because clinics in the target cities are beyond capacity. From brainbox data, we suspect countless victims are not bothering to report."

Perka was practically shaking as she stepped through her numbers, and at the end she turned to Skervin almost in tears. "Look at this, Skervin! You have to do something!"

Skervin squinted dispassionately. "We know that, Perka. We all know that."

Infrastructure, 77 Stasik Sakharov Reporting:
"We are fully aware that the toxicosis cases that Perka is reporting are due to toxic material getting past our quality checks at the plants, but we're at the limit of statistical sampling. The only way to stop all leaks would be to stop production.

"With 96 Skervin's permission, we have changed our policy to shut down only one line at a time when toxin is discovered, instead of the entire plant. Nevertheless, we have so many lines and in some case entire plants shutdown now, I'm going to start reporting them as a percentage of worldwide capacity. As of one hour ago, it was 23 percent. For every one line we get up and running again, it seems like two close. Often, it's the same line again. We're still bulking to cover the shortfall, but we're even going to run out of bulking material soon."

"When exactly?" Skervin insisted.

"If no more lines close, we estimate eight to ten days. That gets shorter if we lose more lines."

Perka cut in. "Can't you reduce the bulking percentage? Bulking Syndrome is getting very bad, and those people are not going to survive on dried leaves and twigs forever."

Stasik raised his eyebrows. "We could. It's a tradeoff with how many people we're hitting. Right now we're only sending bulked Nutribase to Levels 35 and below in the target cities. If you want us to reduce the bulking percentages, we can either target more cities or raise the cut-off level."

Sybil from Propaganda said immediately, "I can't handle any more cities. You'll see when I give my report, I'm already in trouble."

Skervin nodded. "So, higher levels then, Stasik."

"Any guidelines?"

Skervin looked around. "We're all 70s and up in this room. Anybody have kids, relatives, whatever below 50? No? Okay Stasik, level 49 then."

Propaganda, 81 Sybil Messier Reporting:

"As you would expect from the numbers Perka is reporting, we just couldn't keep up with fully suppressing all tangible media and rumors containing negative reports on Nutribase. Yesterday we commenced seeding alternative reports and theories designed to confuse and distract the public as much as possible. For example, we have issued official Authority reports of polluted air, an intestinal virus, and faulty fabs. Even so, as you can see from this graph, negative traffic is rising at almost 5% a day. This is certainly the worst propaganda crisis ORGA has encountered in the past 20 years."

Research, 78 Kapcheck Wills Reporting:

"Unfortunately, we are still unable to characterize the toxin. Consequently, our efforts to detect a pathogen in the soybeans are also effectively at a standstill."

"Kapcheck," Skervin said sternly. "Seven days ago you told us you were going to run your assays at high sensitivity and find this damn toxin. What's happened?"

"It's taken more time than we expected. We started with sensitivity targets at 10 times our normal, but, uh, because of negative results we're now going for 100 times. You have to understand, this level of sensitivity is orders of magnitude more difficult to achieve. I'm happy to say we are really breaking some new ground on sensitivity and resolution in multispectral spectrometry—"

"I don't give a damned doughnut hole about breaking new ground on anything except finding this toxin, Kapcheck. Damn you! Focus on the problem, will you? Now have you characterized the toxin or not?"

Kapcheck was contrite. "Not yet, 96."

Skervin shook his head angrily. "That's what I thought you were saying." He stormed out and left the rest of the staff looking uncomfortably around at each other, demoralized and depressed, feeling time running out through their fingers.

Lana's Lab

The family was all turning in for the night when Galen knocked cautiously on the door of Lana's lab. She had been holed up in there all day, not even stopping for supper, which Galen had brought in on a plate. He saw now that she had hardly touched it. There were big dark circles under her eyes and she looked disheveled, but her spark of intensity was still there in her eyes.

"How's it going?" Galen asked as inoffensively as he could.

"One second . . ." she murmured distractedly. "Aha, yes! Look at this, Galen! My first breakthrough—I think. I think I've isolated the toxin!" For the first time in days, she was actually smiling and there were crinkles at the edges of her eyes. She gave a little girlish squirm of glee that reminded Galen briefly of Kessa.

"Really? That's progress, right?"

"Maybe! Let me try to explain and you stop me if I'm going too fast. This is so exciting!" She gave him a quick, spontaneous hug.

Galen smiled hopefully. "I am all yours!"

"Okay, look at this. Here in my containment field I have two samples of *Glycine max*—soybeans. Neither one of them is natural; I fabricated them both using an atomic-scale maker based on your 3D scans, but as far as I know they should be identical to ones that are growing on Earth. The one on the left is a normal, healthy one that I made from a standard library file. The one on the right is a contaminated one I made from the file you sent me in the p-cap. Clear so far?"

"Healthy on the left, diseased on the right. Keep going."

"Okay, as we know, the ORGA scientists have been running every test they have, trying to find differences between the left and right. But as of the time you left, anyway, they had found nothing. The two of these look the same, even under a microscope. They weigh the same. They even have the same chemical composition. So they should be the same, right? But they're not: one can feed an entire world, and the other contains a toxin that will drop you dead in sixty seconds. So what's going on?"

"That's the problem."

"Now I have to tell you about something called chirality. Heard of it?"

"Should I have?"

"It's also called handedness. Like, have you ever heard of a left-handed screw? It's just like a regular screw, but turning it clockwise loosens it instead of tightening."

"Oh, right, I know what you mean."

"So if you had a bag full of screws and one of them was left-handed, it would be hard to find, right? It would look almost the same, it would weigh the same, it would be made out of the same material."

"Makes sense."

"Well, a lot of biological molecules are kind of like screws. They have a specific physical shape that makes a difference in how they work. They're called *chiral*. Spearmint gets its flavor from a chemical called Carvone—the left-handed version. But the *right*-handed version of Carvone flavors caraway seeds! You and I can only tell the difference between spearmint and caraway because our noses detect chirality."

"You mean, our olfactory organs can tell the exact shape of individual molecules? That's amazing."

"Right! It is. But Galen, I'm guessing ORGA's tests *do not* detect chirality. They don't have an artificial nose. They could detect Carvone, but they wouldn't distinguish between spearmint and caraway. They'd think all screws were the same. They're only thinking about chemistry and ignoring biology."

"Okay, I think I get it."

"Now I've just discovered Toxin-X is a protein that is just like another protein that's found naturally in soybeans, except it's the chiral opposite. The technical term is enantiomer. It has a reverse twist in it, like a left-handed screw. It's not that hard once you think to look. In fact, their food fabricators know all about chirality; they have to, to make flavors like spearmint and caraway. But my guess is their toxin analytics are completely missing it."

"Lana, if you're right, this is amazing! You just found what ORGA has been missing . . . But are you sure? ORGA has been perfecting soybean cultivation for decades. I've seen the labs before; they're immense. How could they miss something so—no offense—easy?"

"You know what they say: If all you have is a hammer, everything looks like a nail. Those Earth people have fantastic tools for detecting incremental problems with their crops, and they've been working well for a really long time, so those are the tools they use. They've had no reason to think critically about a problem that's fundamentally, structurally different, even if that problem isn't that hard."

"I think I see what you mean. They're smart people, but they're caught in certain habits of thought. It seems—tragic."

"Right. If only Skervin weren't such an isolationist, the Earth group would have a lot more exposure to the rest of us on the Hundred Worlds and their entrenched assumptions would be challenged more. Their scientists have been completely cut off from the rest of us in the interstellar community for years."

"Don't remind me, Lana," Galen said, trying to suppress the painful memories from the Our World Our Way nightmare of his past life.

"Oh, I'm sorry Galen. I—I'm sorry." Lana moved quickly to change the subject. "Anyway, now that I know what the toxin is, I have a fighting chance at coming up with an antitoxin and solving Problem 1." She pointed at their big hand-written display from earlier:

Problem 1: Food poisoning
Problem 2: Soybean disease

"How?"

"I'll start with my immunosimulator program. It simulates the human immune system in a computer. I'll give it the toxin and, if all goes well, it will invent appropriate antibodies that I can synthesize and inject into real people."

"Invent?"

"Pretty much. That's exactly what a person's real immune system does when attacked by a new threat. In the old days, they made antitoxins by giving tiny, safe amounts to people or animals, waiting for their immune system to come up with a defense, and then extracting their blood and distilling out the antibodies. This is the same thing, only in a computer. Faster and safer. I mean, not that it's not going to take a long time to set it up."

"Does your immunosimulator program know about chirality?"

"Definitely."

"Glad to hear it. But Lana, shouldn't you get some sleep first? It's really late."

Lana took a long breath and gave Galen a serious look. Her temporary excitement at isolating the toxin was suddenly gone, but that keen look was still in her eyes. Her light hair was tousled and the skin over her strong cheekbones looked thin and tired. "I don't think I can sleep when people are dying," she said.

Galen could only nod. "I'll make you some fresh tea."

12

Wednesday, August 10

Zero West to Forty-Five Central

Kessa, Jet, Marta, and Stoke were all at the planet tube station 20 minutes early and they were among the first to board for the 0600 launch, eager to reach Lake Peace and Lana before the pirates did. Compared to the simple hyperloop capsules, planet tube carriages were more like spaceships: substantial, thick-walled, and windowless. Instead of seats there were "acceleration couches" with deep, contoured, active padding and restraint nets that a technician came around and checked for safety.

Marta gave the best layman's description of how planet tubes worked: "If you could slice the planet in half you'd see the tunnel shaped like an arc going down from here and then back up to the next station. It's a vacuum, of course, just like the hyperloop. We drop through it and then we're carried back up like the weight on a pendulum. Right now we're going from Zero West to Forty-Five Central—everyone calls it Fentral—6400 kilometers on the surface, and it's only going to take 42 minutes. A funny thing is, it always takes 42 minutes from station to station, no matter where the stations are located. Isn't that weird? Anyway, just like the hyperloop there are two tunnels—one in each direction—so we don't ever have to worry about getting stuck in the middle."

It struck Jet that getting stuck in the middle was very nearly the least of things to worry about with such heroically ambitious technology, but he kept mum. Dangerous or not, a planet tube was very, very cool.

The thirty or so passengers settled in to the near-full carriage, and everyone watched eagerly as the launch clock counted down to zero. In all the excitement, and because of the head-enclosing shape of the acceleration couches, no one quite noticed the two passengers who boarded last and slipped into couches close to the door.

The ride itself was not nearly as cool as the concept. Even Jet and Stoke, who juggled g-forces for a living, felt their insides twisting uncomfortably and their teeth rattling noisily as the carriage fell into the depths of the planet, reached speeds that were preposterous for any ground-based vehicle to reach, and then did the whole procedure basically upside and backwards on the way back out. But all passengers survived, and 42 minutes later the carriage door slid open in the station at Forty-Five Central. The technician came around again helping everyone out of their acceleration couches, and passengers left in ones and twos. By the time anyone else looked, the two late-boarding passengers near the door were already gone.

Forty-Five Central

It was market day in Fentral. The sun was out, people had come in from all over, and spirits were high. The tiny town's large central green was blooming with colorful stands and gaily dressed citizens trading goods, smiles, and gossip. A band was playing music and air pods were busily ferrying in more and more people and wares. Delicious smells of baking pastries wafted on the air and children chased gleefully through a maze of grown-up legs and trading booths.

Kessa and Marta were exulted by it all and happily led Jet and Stoke by their hands out into the festivities. "Breakfast!" Kessa sang.

"But Kessa," Jet objected. "There's no time!"

"Oh, come on, Jet. We have to eat. It will be quick, I promise." Blithely ignoring Jet's sense of urgency, Kessa led them all to the first food stand she found and ordered one of everything they had so her visitors could try them all: hot chocolate, fruit soup, almond coffee cake, fruit tarts, honeyed yogurt, and extravaganzas of freshly picked summer berries. On a normal day, she might have bartered for it all— perhaps with the mushrooms she so liked to collect, or maybe some of Grandmother's embroidery—but today she just gave the stand-keeper her name and he took a note to charge her community account later on.

Kessa wanted them to go find a place on the grass to sit down and enjoy it all, but at that Jet—backed up by Marta—drew the line, and they ate while walking rapidly back toward the hyperloop station. It was all delicious, Jet had to admit; especially the coffee cake.

■ ■ ■

Tappet allowed himself a cautious sigh of relief as he and Speer stepped out of the planet tube carriage, apparently unnoticed. Once again, he had reason to be thankful that New Gaians were so guileless. They walked quickly out of the planet tube station, looking for, but not finding, any police.

They were not at all prepared for the market day scene that greeted them. From Tappet's perspective, it seemed to be a large gathering of people in the middle of an empty field. He had assumed Forty-Five Central was another village, but everywhere he looked there were just disorganized crowds and ridiculous little vendor stands consisting of a table, some shelves, and a sign. No one in charge, no organization, and everything sitting directly on the muddy ground. It was like watching Neanderthals.

But Speer had something specific to look for, and he found it in a modest building sitting on a far corner of the green. "This way," he said.

The building had a sign that said "Scanners and Makers," and it had the feel of a service shop back on Earth. It had a real, regular door, for one thing. All along two walls and down the middle were neat rows of machines ranging in size from a compact 30-centimeter cube in the back to a room-height monster near the door. Scanners were on the left; makers on the right.

"Do you need any help?" asked the cheerful proprietor, who looked just old enough to be established but still young enough to be enthusiastic about his little enterprise. "Do you need a trade booth, too?" He gestured over at a couple standing in front of one of the larger machines, waiting as it made them a table for the market. "It will just be a short wait."

"No, I just need one of the smaller makers," said Speer, as innocently as he could manage.

"Oh, fine then. Help yourself. My name is Ulrich, by the way . . ." But rudely, neither visitor replied. So after an awkward pause Ulrich pressed on. "What are you making?"

"I'd rather not say."

"Ooh, okay. I see. A little something for the bedroom, ha-ha? Well, certainly, go right ahead."

Speer and Tappet went to one of the smaller makers and crowded shoulder-to-shoulder in front of it, doing their best to shield their work from Ulrich's prying eyes. Speer reached into a hidden pocket and fished out a small data card that he plugged into the maker. A contents menu appeared on the maker's screen and he scrolled through what struck Tappet as a disturbingly large collection of ordnance. But they had no choice, Tappet reminded himself. Right now, he and Tappet were the only thing standing in the way of a planet-wide panic on Earth. Force was necessary. He watched grimly as Speer picked out a plastic explosive grenade and touched the MAKE command.

Tappet half-expected the machine to object somehow: an alarm, or certification check, or something. A maker on Earth would never allow unauthorized making of weapons or explosives. But this was New Gaia, and they were just so damn *trusting* about everything. Either that, or clueless. The machine happily hummed into action and a few minutes later produced a menacing-looking device, black, the size of a grapefruit, and equipped with a rugged but simple timer. Speer quickly swept it out of sight in his rucksack, alongside what was left of his stolen food from last night.

Speer and Tappet turned to leave but Ulrich stopped them with a word. "Did you forget to leave your name?" he said, gesturing at the screen that was now asking for a name. "We'll just need that for adjusting your balance."

How dumb, thought Tappet. The machines should ask for name and payment first, otherwise people would rip them off all the time. But Speer replied smoothly— "Oh, of course, careless of me"—and stepped back to the machine and spoke the only valid New Gaian male name he could think of: "Gerd Lindgren."

The machine pinged with satisfaction, Ulrich smiled, and Speer and Tappet were on their way out the door.

■   ■   ■

The moment the pirates left his shop, Ulrich hurried to the back and commed the Security Patrol in Zero West. Agda, looking tired, answered right away. "Good morning, friend. I am Agda."

"Good morning, Agda. My name is Ulrich Johannsen. I run a scan-and-make shop here in Fentral."

"Oh, very nice. Are you there now?"

"Yes. Listen, I'm sorry to rush, but I think the pirates were here."

"Oh my! When?"

"Just now. They just left."

"Are you all right?"

"Yes, thank you. I'm fine."

"What makes you say it was the pirates?"

"They had terrible manners, for one thing. Also the way they looked and dressed. And then when I asked for a name, they told me Gerd Lindgren. Wasn't it the Lindgrens we heard about last night? Who were attacked by the pirates?"

"Yes, Gerd and Mina. You're right, it must have been the pirates. Who else would give a false name like that? I'll notify our Security Patrol volunteers up there right away. Maybe we can finally catch these people. Did you see where they went?"

"Unfortunately, I did not see where they went. But there is something else you should know. They made something on one of my makers."

"Oh? Do you know what it was?"

"Yes, I'm pulling up the log right now. It's, uh . . . Oh. Can you see this? I'm sorry to tell you, Agda. It's—"

"What?"

"It's a bomb."

■ ■ ■

At the hyperloop station, Marta pulled them over to a public viewscreen kiosk saying, "I just want to check in quickly with home before we leave."

As Marta initiated the comm, Stoke, who was admiring her from behind, stopped in his tracks and burst out, "Whoa! I just realized!"

"Realized what?" Kessa asked from his side.

"This public viewscreen. You don't have personal portable communications here, do you?"

"You mean like brainboxes? No, of course not. You're just noticing?"

"But I mean not even portable viewscreens or cellular comm units or anything."

Kessa shrugged. "Not really. Unless you count emergency radios and safety gear in air pods."

"But, but why not? It's such basic technology. Cell phones have been around for centuries."

"Hmm, I've never really thought about it. I guess we simply don't need them for our lifestyle. That, or we don't like having antenna towers all over. If we want to be in contact or look something up, we just ask a passerby or walk to a public viewscreen."

"But that's so slow," began Stoke, thinking about his own always-on brainbox life experience. "And it's inconvenient, and what if you're out in the middle of the wilderness . . . ?" He trailed off. Kessa was just looking at him with a mildly amused expression in her twinkly blue eyes.

"We manage," she finally smiled. Stoke shook his head and laughed.

When Marta activated the viewscreen she found an urgent message from Agda and commed her back. Marta stood close to the screen while the others listened in from behind.

"The pirates were spotted in Fentral," Agda told them.

"Where? When?" Marta asked, pursing her lips.

"Just a few minutes ago at a scan-and-make shop near the green."

"That's very near us. We're at the station right now. Do we know where they're going? Are they coming through here?"

"I don't know, but we need a search, fast," said Agda. "We have two other Security Patrol volunteers already on duty there in Fentral. I think they are there in the station. Can you find them? Their names are Tova and Svea."

Everyone craned their necks to look around the station. It was busy because of market day, and Security Patrols wore no particular uniform or badge, so no one knew what to look for. Kessa, ever impulsive, just raised her hands above her head and shouted out into the station. "*Hello*, Tova and Svea! Are you here somewhere?" Practically the entire station turned to look, and sure enough, two young women picked up their heads. They were both sturdy and blonde and looked like good friends.

"Here we are!" called one, and with a nervous laugh at Kessa's stunt. But as she and her partner began moving forward, Stoke noticed two people who had been walking toward the hyperloop loading area turn purposely away, trying to avoid his glance. He recognized them. "That's them!" he called out. The two figures broke and started running toward the entrance.

"The pirates!" cried Marta. "Catch them!"

The crowd erupted into screams and chaos as everyone tried to move at once. Tova and Svea spun around, trying to locate the criminals in the crowd. Stoke, Marta, Kessa, and Jet all started running at top speed in the direction they had seen movement. The people in the crowd all tried to move in the opposite direction as fast as they could.

Tappet had made a mistake by moving, and he knew it. He had instinctively reacted to suddenly seeing his pursuers across the room, and he had tried to move out of sight instead of staying calm. Now everyone in the station knew he and Speer were here, and they had to get out of sight, fast. The mob was slowing Tappet and Speer down through sheer numbers, so in predictable fashion Speer pulled out his bullet gun and shot at the ceiling, making a huge noise that instantly scattered everyone nearby. This gave him and Tappet a clear path to the entrance and they ran out of the building and onto the green. Tova, Svea, and the four friends fought their way through the crowds until finally emerging at the entrance themselves, panting and looking around desperately for any sign of the fleeing pirates among the booths and crowds on the green.

Jet, who was tallest, shook his head and said, "Nothing. We need a search plan." Then he gave a short smile to Tova and Svea and said, "Hi, by the way. I'm Jet."

"Tova. And she's Svea."

Marta made equally quick introductions. "Sorry, Jet, but now that those two are here, I have to get home and guard the family. I'm going to get them out of the house and off to someplace safe."

Kessa was nodding vigorously. "Right, Marta. I should come too. Mom's going to need my help. We'll take the hyperloop." She gave a quick look to Jet. "You guys catch them, okay? But be careful." With that, she and Marta dashed off to board a hyperloop capsule, leaving Jet and Stoke to huddle with Tova and Svea.

"Is there any way to shut down the hyperloop after Marta and Kessa leave?" Jet asked Tova. "We don't want the pirates to get any closer to Lana."

Tova and Svea looked at each other and shook their heads. "No idea," Tova said. "I guess I could ask Agda . . ."

Jet's face showed his frustration with New Gaia's recurring lack of control systems, but aloud he said, "Good, why doesn't one of you contact Agda and at least try? In the meantime, the other should stay here and guard the hyperloop in case they try to come back and board. Watch out, that one guy shoots real bullets."

Svea, the sturdier of the two volunteers, blinked a couple of times but then seemed to steel herself and said, "I'll do it."

"Great, Svea, thanks. And Tova, you'll get in touch with Agda and try to shut down the hyperloop? Stoke, that leaves you and me to try to flush them out, I guess?"

Stoke nodded. "Right, but I think we should stick together. Two of them, two of us."

Jet said, "Alright then, come on. Good luck, you two," and the four of them rushed off on their respective missions.

■ ■ ■

Tappet and Speer were trying to blend into the crowd and it wasn't going well. Their Earth clothing and drawn weapons made them easily recognized, and though the irenic New Gaians offered little physical resistance, they were very talkative and word of the pirates spread quickly. Jet and Stoke, standing at the edge of the green, started to see outbursts erupting from the crowd and following the pirates everywhere they went. As the crowd grew excited and more aggressive, tables of goods were being overturned, booths were collapsing, and shouts and cries came rolling across the green. Finally, someone managed to trip or tackle Tappet and he fell hard, bashing his head on the edge of a table on the way down. Speer had to run back to him, and as Speer knelt down, the crowd closed in around them. "Here they are!" everyone called out, and Jet and Stoke, looking official with their e-guns held high, went running in.

But before they could get there, Speer got out his bullet gun again and shot a hole in a nearby trade booth, frightening off the skittish crowd. Speer helped Tappet to his feet and the two of them turned to face Stoke and Jet, who were running in at a full sprint. Not taking time to aim a gun, Stoke simply dove bodily at Speer as if to tackle him. Jet followed suit on Tappet.

Speer was a professional fighter, and though Stoke was vigorous, Speer quickly leveled him with a karate chop to the neck. Jet and Tappet were struggling on the ground, but once Speer was free of Stoke, he turned and kicked Jet hard four times with a heavy boot. Jet released his grip and passed out. Speer grabbed up Tappet again and led him limping fast across the chaos-strewn green and back to the hyperloop station.

There, standing bravely at the center of the entrance, was Svea, e-gun aimed and face twisted up with determination. As the two pirates came running angrily toward her with their own guns raised, she aimed and fired.

It was too early. They were out of range, and they simply kept coming. Before she could collect herself for another shot, Speer fired a bullet and she instinctively ducked. The bullet missed, but Tappet fired his e-gun a moment later and connected perfectly. Svea yelped and then collapsed, unconscious.

Speer and Tappet, hardly breaking step, leapt over Svea and dashed breathlessly into a hyperloop car.

Nothing happened.

Tappet looked at Speer. "Why isn't it going?"

Rushed and confused, Speer looked around for signs or signals. Had their entrance failed to trigger some automatic launcher? What did they have to do? "Go!" he called out angrily to some imagined robotic controller. "Ready! Launch!" Nothing happened.

Then Tappet saw a small display screen above their heads and cursed. "Out of Service." Tova and Agda had come through after all.

Tappet refused to be put off. "We'll take air pods instead," he told Speer. "It will take longer, but we'll get there. Come on, they're back outside."

The House on Lake Peace

Kessa and Marta waited impatiently through the 20-minute ride as the hyperloop took them to Aspen North, where they grabbed air pods and flew as fast as possible for home, still another 50 minutes away. They landed and came hurrying into the house with strained smiles and short hugs all around. "Where's Mom?" Kessa asked right away.

"Upstairs in her lab," Galen replied. "She's been up all night."

Kessa dashed off to find Lana and left Marta looking anxiously around at the circle of gathered family. Little Beatrix reached up and hugged Marta around the waist. "What's happening, Marta?"

Marta took the cue to reach down and heft Beatrix into her arms. Time was short but she didn't want to worry her little cousin more than she had to. "You know what, Beatrix?" she said, affecting a cheerful, careless tone. "Today, I think you and the family are going to go visiting! Maybe you'll go to the Sorensens' house, if the Sorensens don't mind. You could get to play with your friend Vena. Would you like that?"

Kjell had no patience for Marta's game of cooing bad news to Beatrix. "We had a hurried message from the Security Patrol earlier, but it didn't make any sense. What are you saying, Marta? Are we in danger?"

Marta put Beatrix down and turned to her uncle. How much stronger she felt facing him now than she had just 10 days ago. "I'm sure it will be fine, Kjell. It's just that those pirates might be headed this way. It would be better not to be here when they arrive."

"Why here?" Kjell demanded.

Marta glanced down at Beatrix, who was now looking up with a worried brow. "It's because of Mom's research."

"But why?" Kjell demanded. "Lana's working on a cure for their disease. Why would they want to stop that?"

"Apparently they don't see it that way. They think she's trying to leak their secret. It's crazy, but they have guns, and they're—aggressive. Can we just get everyone out of here?"

Kjell shook his head in annoyance, but there were no more objections. "Can Anders and me go to the Jensens' instead?" asked Nils.

"Anders and *I*," corrected Kjell for the umpteenth time.

■   ■   ■

The whole house dove into action. Kjell and Mia rushed to pack hampers of food, Anders ordered air pods, and the whole household buzzed.

"What about you, Uncle Galen?" Marta asked him.

"I'm not going."

"What? Why not?"

"Lana needs me. I'm her lab assistant."

"But she has to go, too!"

"I'm not so sure about that. Every minute counts with her research right now, and she can't exactly take her lab over to the Sorensens'."

"But it's dangerous here!" Marta flashed.

"Let's go ask her."

They hurried up the stairs and crowded into the door of Lana's lab, where Kessa was already in deep conversation with her mother. They both looked up when Galen and Marta arrived.

"Hi, Mom," Marta said, trying to affect more calm than she felt.

"Morning, Marta," Lana said. She was trying to sound chipper, but her greeting came out weakly. She looked exhausted, with red eyelids and dark circles under her eyes. Her night's work had not gone well. She suppressed a yawn as she spoke.

Marta was alarmed at her mother's appearance. "Have you rested at all?"

Lana shrugged. "I may have dozed off a couple times. Hard to tell. I just keep telling myself the fate of a whole planet is resting on me."

Galen shook his head and tried to object, but Marta spoke first. "Whether it is or not, we have to get you out of here," she said urgently. "It's not safe!"

Kessa looked at her mother for confirmation and then turned back to Marta. "We know. We've just been talking about it. But not to Sorensens' or wherever. We have to go to Earth."

"Earth?!"

Galen looked shocked, too. "What are you talking about?"

Kessa nodded seriously. "Think about it. Time is everything on this, right? People are dying back there. If Mom finds a cure, we'll need to get it to Earth as immediately as humanly possible."

"Of course. But you don't have a cure yet, do you—er, do we—Mom?"

"No," said Lana, shaking her head tiredly. "I have managed to synthesize a sample of the toxin, but that's only the first step."

"It doesn't matter," said Kessa. "We start traveling now. We take Mom's equipment with us and she works on the way. It saves us three days in transit."

"Hah. You're kidding, right?"

"Not at all."

Galen said, "Lana, you can't just pick up this whole lab and put it on a spaceship, can you?"

Lana shrugged. "I've been talking it through with Kessa. Most of my work is in the computerized virtual simulations."

"I know, but you still have all this equipment for natural experiments . . . ?"

"No time for all that right now. We're going to have to trust my simulations." Lana looked reluctantly around the lab at her stacks of machines. "It's still going to be a lot of equipment . . ."

Kessa said, "We'll just take what you absolutely need. How much is that?"

"Hmm, let me think. Definitely my simulator, and then that one over there . . . I suppose I could get it down to five or six pieces if I had to . . . But girls, my foot. I can't travel—"

Galen guffawed. "Don't be ridiculous, Lana. You get around on that prosthetic foot as well as I do on mine."

"You'll be fine, Mom," encouraged Marta. "You guys are right. This is a good idea. With the pirates around we have to evacuate anyway, so it might as well be to a ship. Come on, let's get started. We have to move really fast. I'll get the boys helping with the equipment."

Lana was tired. She shook her head and closed her eyes. "I hope this works," she whispered to herself.

■　■　■

"I need to rest again," panted Tappet, slumping against a tree and mopping his forehead with a dirty sleeve. After the violence in Fentral, he ached all over and his head was throbbing. Speer turned around with a look of frustration. It was a cinch that their target, Lana Sjøfred, knew they were coming. She was sure to be guarded by now, even if it was with this planet's amateur security people. That's why he had landed their air pods a couple kilometers from her house and proceeded on foot through the woods. This way he would be able to get very close before attacking. Then it would just be a matter of his bullet gun. Or, if that didn't work, his bomb.

But speed was crucial and goddamn Tappet was turning out to be a real problem in these woods. Freakin' tenderfoot. "Keep it together, Tappet," he grouched. "We're getting close."

Tappet said nothing, but after several painful breaths he struggled to his feet and soldiered forward. 200 meters later, Speer made a sudden downward motion with his hand and whispered "Shh! I can see the house." Tappet froze and Speer gave a long look and listen. There was nothing. "Okay, perimeter search," he instructed Tappet. "Circle the clearing and look for guards or hostiles. You go left, I'll go right, and we'll meet on the other side. Be quiet and stay out of sight . . . if you can," he added ruefully.

When they met again, there was nothing to report except for what looked like recent construction on a half-hidden door in the back. It all seemed suspicious to Speer, but it was time to move in. He pulled out his weapon and told Tappet to do the same. "Okay, Tappet.

Follow my lead and stay close." Speer raised his gun to ready position, stepped quickly through the woods until he reached the clearing, and then ran full out for the house. There was no front door to burst through, but he leapt through the entry foyer and pointed his gun into the main room.

There was no one there. Tappet came running up behind him and took up a covering position, and Speer rushed into the one side room where Grandmother Britta slept, but it was empty as well. Next he crept to the spiral staircase and climbed cautiously up, listening intently. At the top he found a narrow hallway with doorways on both sides. "Tappet!" he whispered, and made room while Tappet came up behind him. One by one, they burst into each room, guns raised. But each time, the rooms were empty.

"We missed her," Speer said flatly. "She's gone into hiding already."

One of the rooms was clearly a lab, which Tappet peered around with particular anxiety. "This is probably where she's accumulating her case against us. God, I hope she hasn't started broadcasting yet. Look at this: it's messy, but can you see where the equipment has been moved around? Damn."

Speer reached into his bag and pulled out his bomb. He smiled grimly at it and said, "If they left anything dangerous behind, it won't be here much longer."

Aspen North

Kessa easily found her way to the small clinic in Aspen North, which was actually just a room with a separate entrance in the home of a civic-minded citizen. Jet, Stoke, and Svea were all sitting up in cots, attended by Tova and still very much recovering from being pulsed and pummeled earlier in the day by Speer and Tappet. Svea had that recently-zapped look, whose symptoms were a cross between a migraine headache and the aftereffects of a marathon run: dull eyes, painful motions, and a strong inclination to curl up into a ball. Stoke and Jet had bruises everywhere and it looked like they all hurt. The clinician had done what she could for them, and now it was just a matter of time.

They were all happy to see Kessa's friendly face, and she worked her way down the line of cots giving out gentle hugs, plus a kiss on the lips for Jet. "What's happening?" Jet asked dully. "Did somebody catch them yet?"

"Not yet. We moved the family out of the house, so they should be a little safer."

"Including Galen and your mom?"

"Um, working on it. Actually, they're just finishing packing. We decided . . ." she hesitated, realizing this was big news. "We decided to take them to Earth."

"Whoa!" Jet's head wobbled and he reached up his hands to his temples. "Earth? Now?"

"Yeah. It's the only way. We need the time."

Jet's lightning mind was slowed, but still working. "Mm, I see what you mean. Your mom's work is mostly virtual. She can keep working on the way, right? Makes sense . . . Yeah, smart . . . Okay, when? Now?"

"Yes, now. I'm going to help you to the hyperloop station and we're going to meet Mom, Galen, and Marta there. We have to keep moving fast."

Stoke groaned in such a way that Kessa couldn't quite tell if he was serious. "That means we have to move?"

"Afraid so."

"Uhnk. Okay. Let me see here . . ."

With appropriate coaxing from Kessa, Stoke and Jet managed to get to their feet, collect themselves, and head for the door. "It was nice, um, working with you both," Stoke grinned weakly to Tova and Svea.

"Peace be!" they chorused, and they waved them out the door.

Not long after, Lana, Galen, and Marta met them at the hyperloop station. Anders and Nils helped carry Lana's equipment from the air pods to the hyperloop, said goodbye, and watched the very full hyperloop capsule slide off into the distance. Then they headed back home.

The House on Lake Peace

Tappet was still looking dispiritedly at Lana's empty lab when Speer tapped him on the shoulder and said, "I set the bomb timer for two minutes. Time to get out of here." He led the way out of the house and off to the edge of the clearing, where he found cover for them behind a large boulder. "This should be fun to watch," he said. "90 seconds."

But then Tappet said, "Quiet! Hear that? It's air pods."

Speer looked skeptically at the approaching pods. "It's security. They're after us," he said. "Let's get out of here. The bomb will take care of them, too."

Tappet looked around urgently. He knew the clock was ticking. "But what if it's not security? What if it's just the people who live here? We can't blow them up!" The air pods were getting close now. If they were close to the house when it blew, they would surely go too.

Speer looked frustrated. The only way to prevent the bomb from going off would be to run back into the house and stop the timer. "Too late!" he glared at Tappet.

"No, it can't be. Look, Speer, look! It's just kids in those things!" He was right; it was 14-year-old Anders and his 12-year-old brother Nils, returning from the station. The boys climbed out of their airpods, conversing quietly and oblivious to their perilous situation.

Tappet squirmed inside and out, filled with turmoil. But looking at those kids, his better nature overcame him and he couldn't stay still. He leapt to his feet and dashed out toward them. Speer growled and stayed where he was.

Tappet's movement caught Anders' eye and he called out in surprise. Nils turned and saw Tappet too, and for a moment they both simply stared at this stranger sprinting toward them, waving his arms and yelling something unintelligible. But then a wave of fear swept over Nils and he called out, "Run, Anders! Inside, quick!"

Nils took off toward the house, but Anders hesitated, his eyes fixed on the rapidly approaching Tappet. The guy was shouting, "Stop! Stop! Don't go in there!" which didn't make any sense. Finally a cog in Anders' head clicked in and he recognized the stranger from all the images that had been going around. It was one of the pirates! Anders felt his teenage male hormones rising within, full of rage, and he steeled himself for a fight.

In the five or six heartbeats Anders had taken to process the situation, Tappet, charged by adrenaline and fairly flying across the ground, closed the gap and was two steps away. Anders braced himself for a collision, but Tappet shot straight past him, heading for Nils. Nils was just entering the door of the house when Tappet took a flying leap and tackled him around the knees. Nils yelled and fell forward, leaving both on them flat on their stomachs. Before either one could move, Anders came up from behind with a warrior's cry and jumped onto Tappet's back, trying to wrestle him off Nils.

"Get off me! Get off!" Tappet shouted, struggling to get free. "There's a bomb in there! The house is going to explode!"

Anders and Nils both ignored him at first, but Tappet managed to roll over, seize Anders by the shoulders, and put his face two inches from the boy's, finally locking into his gaze. "Listen to me!" he shouted as forcefully as he could. "There is a bomb in there! It's going to go off any second. We have to get out of here, *now!*"

The message finally penetrated. Anders stopped struggling for a moment, shared a panicked look with Nils, and then in a moment of mutual consent, all three of them stood up and started running pell-mell toward the woods.

They were barely ten meters away when the house exploded. The sound and force of a thunderbolt hit them all from behind and threw them forward through the air as the shockwave burst outward. Their bodies flew forward through the air and they landed hard, knocked senseless.

■   ■   ■

When Tappet regained consciousness he was lying on the ground, looking at Speer, who was standing over the horizontal form of one of the boys, prodding him with a black boot. "Who are you?" Speer was demanding.

"I'm Anders," the boy stuttered. "And this is my brother Nils."

Tappet struggled to his feet and interjected. "Are you kids okay?"

Speer did give them time to answer. "Where is Lana Sjøfred?"

Anders, still lying on the ground under Speer's boot, was thinking vaguely of protecting his aunt by keeping his mouth shut, and he hesitated. But Speer gave him a hard poke with the boot and that was enough to scare Nils, who was lying on the ground next to his brother.

"She's on the hyperloop at Aspen North!" cried Nils. "We were just there! We dropped her off."

Speer turned his gaze down toward the boy, looking hard to make sure he wasn't lying. "Where's she going?"

"Earth!"

"Dammit!" burst out Tappet. "I knew it! She's going to tell the whole damn planet. It's going to be bedlam!"

Speer bent down, grabbed Nils by the shoulders, and with one powerful motion pulled him to his feet. Not letting go, he glowered down and the frightened boy and said, "Alright, you contact her right now. You tell her that if she doesn't turn around and come back here this second, you two little boys are going to come to serious harm."

Nils looked back at Speer in confusion. "How?"

"What are you talking about?"

"How do we contact her?"

"I don't know! Ewave her. Message her. Whatever it is you do on this damn backwards planet."

Anders, who had climbed to his own feet by this time, shook his head. "I hate to tell you this, but our only viewscreen was in the house. And it just . . ." He stopped, looking weakly at the pile of ashy rubble where his house was supposed to be.

Speer and Tappet exchanged a sudden, shocked look.

"Don't you have a portable device?" Tappet demanded. A handheld unit or something?

Anders just shook his head.

"The air pods, then," Tappet insisted. "They must have communicators of some kind."

Anders kept shaking his head, a little teenage sense of mischief overtaking him. "Nope. Just pod-to-pod."

As he said it, Nils caught his eye and almost started to say something. They both knew that air pods had emergency radios. But Anders managed to keep a straight face and Nils caught on, keeping quiet.

"Damn it," muttered Tappet. "Come on, Speer, we'll just have to catch up with her. We'll take their air pods." He started running for the nearest one, but as he did he couldn't help calling out to the boys. "Your mother's crazy, you know!"

"She's our aunt, not our mother," Nils called after them. And at the same time Anders shouted, "She's not crazy. She's trying to help!"

"Yeah, right," snarled Tappet as he disappeared.

By this time, Tappet and Speer had air pods figured out and they knew what to do. "Aspen North hyperloop station!" commanded Tappet, and they lifted off and headed west. They never did discover the emergency radios.

Down on the ground, Anders and Nils watched the pirates go and then turned their gazes back to the smoking wreckage of the only home they had ever known.

Space Traffic Control Center

Lana, Galen, Kessa, Jet, Marta, and Stoke arrived in a bustle at the door of Leilani's operation and she rushed to greet them. Marta had commed from home to say they would be coming. "Are you all okay?" she had to know.

Marta answered, "More or less. Stoke's neck is stiff and Jet hurts everywhere. And we're lugging my mom's equipment."

Leilani gave everyone quick looks of appraisal and said, "Okay, good. Glad you're managing. And you're going back to Earth now? Is that safe?"

"We don't have a choice. Anyway, Mom has already started finding the cure. If it works, they should be glad to see us." At this Lana rolled her eyes, but she stayed mum.

Leilani said, "Well, it's your decision. But you better hurry. Did you hear what happened to Anders and Nils?"

Lana, Marta, and Kessa all squawked at once. "What?! No! What??"

"It's okay, it's okay! Don't panic. They're okay. Just scared, is all. You must not have stopped for messages along the way. There was a, um, incident back at your house. The neighbors heard it and went to investigate, then they called here to let us know. The pirates showed up at your house after you left. I guess they—well, I hate to tell you this. I guess they blew up your house."

It was momentous news, but compared to everything else, it hardly seemed to register. "Space!" gasped Marta. "The boys are okay?"

"Yes, as I said, they're fine. But the pirates made them tell where you were going. They chased after you in air pods."

"They're chasing us now? Still?" asked Marta.

"Probably," said Leilani. "Have you seen them behind you?"

"No, of course not. We wouldn't be standing here if we had."

"They probably missed the planet tube that we took," Kessa realized. "They'll be on the next one, an hour behind us."

"Okay, then!" Leilani said, cranking up her already-energetic pace. "Let's get you out of here fast. The space elevator is going to be too slow, and you crashed your landing craft—"

"Sorry," Jet said distractedly.

"I'm going to let you borrow Karl's orbiter. He's our maintenance guy, and he uses it a lot. It's not the slickest ship ever built, but it will get you back to your ADS. You'll take good care of it, won't you Jet?"

"I'll do my best."

"You better. It's out on the back field, fueled and ready to go. You best go right now." Marta gave Leilani a quick hug, whispering "Thank you for *everything*" with a sly nod toward Stoke, and then with hasty *peace be* s all around, they headed across the field toward the ship. They all moved as fast as they could between the heavy equipment cases, Lana's bad leg, Jet and Stoke's bruises, and Galen's knees. It wasn't elegant, but they got there and loaded themselves in, and shortly thereafter they were rocketing into orbit. Everyone's head was spinning, and the Dahlstroms were finally absorbing the news that on top of everything else, their home had just been destroyed. Lana had not been in space for years, and Jet, of all people, noticed her looking anxiously around the orbiter. To put her at ease, he asked her if she knew what a magnetoplasmadynamic drive was—he loved that term—and then, because she didn't, he told her all about it as they ascended above the clouds.

■ ■ ■

Slightly less than one hour later, Tappet and Speer darkened the door of the STC, waving their bullet guns and not taking shit from anyone. They were *not* going to let their mission fail. Leilani arrived on the scene and tried to speak reasonably, but Speer just fired his gun at the ceiling and said "Get us an orbiter, *now*."

Leilani had no choice but to turn over the only other orbiter she could still access, which was *Frälsaren*, the emergency vehicle that had rescued Narisa and Kai. Tappet and Speer pushed and bullied their way in and shot up toward orbit 45 minutes behind Lana and the others.

As soon as they were gone, Leilani commed Stoke and let him know the bad news. But there wasn't anything she could do from down on the ground. He and the others were on their own.

In Orbit Around New Gaia

Jet and Stoke steered their borrowed orbiter successfully back to the ADS *Gregor Mendel,* the ORGA executive starship they had arrived on just two days earlier. It was waiting obediently for them in its parking orbit, and with only a little navigational drama they docked and transferred passengers and gear. There were six of them now, plus equipment, but Stoke still sighed happily at the sight of the 90-level luxuries they would be enjoying for the next three days.

"Come on, hurry," Jet and Marta kept urging the rest of them. Jet was thinking about orbits. Just because they had a 45-minute lead on the pirates when they left the surface didn't mean they would keep it. It was just a matter of chance where *Gregor Mendel* had been in her orbit when they were able to catch up. If she had been on a different side of the planet it could have taken another 15 or 20 minutes to rendezvous. And the same went for the pirates: if their ship happened to be in an optimal position for docking when they reached orbit . . . It didn't matter. All they could do was move as fast as possible. "Let me help you with that, Galen," he said, reaching out a strong arm.

■　■　■

Tappet could have sworn that Potet had not moved an inch since he left her with instructions to wait in a parking orbit a day-and-a-half ago. There she was at the flight deck of *Paracelsus,* languorously poking at the controls, hardly looking up to say hello. "Potet!" cried Tappet. "Back to Earth! Move! Every minute counts!"

"It's a three-day trip, what does it matter?"

"It matters! Hurry!"

And so Potet did what she needed to do, talking to the ship and working the control panel until *Paracelsus'* ADS drive sprang into action and they leapt into warp drive, heading off at over 50,000 times the speed of light.

■　■　■

Aboard *Gregor Mendel*, Jet went through the same procedure as Potet had, albeit with more enthusiasm and, given this was his second time ever, less expertise. But he did it correctly and he and his passengers were also on their way to Earth at precisely the same speed. Compared to *Paracelsus* they would arrive exactly as many minutes earlier as they had left.

Or as many minutes later.

In all the excitement neither Jet nor Stoke had thought to check who was in front.

Skervin's Conference Room

Citizen Welfare, 93 Perka Reporting:
"It got about 10% worse in the last day. Toxicosis deaths, suspected or confirmed, 6039. Nonlethal toxicosis cases, likely due to trace exposure, approximately 51,900. Heaven help us."

Infrastructure, 77 Stasik Reporting:
"Production capacity shut down: 25 percent of total, which is two points higher than yesterday. Bulked product now routing as high as Level 47 in the hardest-hit cities."

Propaganda, 81 Sybil Reporting:
"Negative reports across platforms have doubled since yesterday. My team is working around the clock. We're doing what we can."

Research, 78 Kapcheck Reporting:
"We have initiated a program of sterilizing soybean fields suspected of harboring the pathogen that creates the toxin. Fields are identified by two methods: a.) back-tracing from problems found in production plants; and b.) fauna die-offs detected by infrared satellite imagery. This should reduce food poisoning cases, but it will also reduce our food supplies even further.

"Efforts in the Nutritional Products Lab to isolate and characterize the toxin by using extremely high-sensitivity automated assays are continuing. We think we're seeing some hints of unusual structures in the amino acids, which is good. I have given the researchers a deadline of 48 hours from now."

13

Thursday, August 11

ADS *Gregor Mendel,* Bound for Earth

Lana was finally feeling focused again. Yesterday after boarding everyone had worked on setting up shop in this starship's strange tunnel of an environment: weightless, serried, luxurious, artificial, hermetic. They had quickly dedicated the yacht's dining room to Lana's lab equipment, and she had given everyone aboard a strict and detailed lesson on lab safety, reminding them they were dealing with a deadly nerve toxin in a confined, dangerous space. With lots of help from Stoke especially, she had found sufficient power sources for her gear and strapped everything securely to the walls so it wouldn't float away in the microgravity.

The whole operation had taken hours, and by that time Lana, who had been up for a day-and-a-half, was utterly spent. She crawled into her sleeping berth and spent six precious, luxurious hours catching up on sleep. Now better rested, decently fed, and relatively fresh, she was at last ready to dive back into her work.

The first thing she did was pop open her immunosimulator program, which had been running on the problem of developing an antitoxin the whole time she slept. It should have a solution by now. But the screen showed an unpleasant surprise: "No solution found." Lana rubbed her temples and closed her eyes. Maybe she should have slept a little longer.

She noticed that someone—Marta, she figured—had decided to put up a display in a spot where everyone could see that showed a clock counting down the hours until their arrival at Earth. Altogether it was a 68-hour trip, and just as she looked the clock passed 50 hours and switched to 49:59:59, counting down. Wonderful, she thought ruefully. Just what I need. "Marta!" she called out, louder and more angrily than she meant to. "Do you mind turning off that silly clock? It's going to drive me to distraction!"

Marta floated herself in from the main lounge. "Hey Mom, how are you doing?"

"Not so well just yet. The immunosimulator isn't coming up with anything. I still don't have an antitoxin, and I've barely started on the pathogen." Lana paused for a moment and looked at her daughter's worried face. "I'm sorry Marta, it's just that it's a lot to do. Too much, I think. And that clock!"

By this time Kessa had drifted up next to Marta in a show of support. "Mom," Marta said, "Let us help. There are six of us on this ship. We're not scientists like you, but there must be things we can do. Think about it: Kessa knows a lot of biology, and Jet is super smart, and Stoke can do anything with machines. Galen was helping you at home, wasn't he? And I—I'm an organizer. I'll keep everybody on schedule. And feed everyone, too! Come on, give us jobs. We promise not to slow you down. It will be a team effort."

Lana's face twisted into a complex smile that came from being proud and grateful for her daughter while simultaneously thinking her idea was hopeless. Lana was accustomed to doing her lab work alone. But by this time everyone on the ship was listening in expectantly, and she could feel their eagerness and support. She looked over at the clock counting down and gave it a long thought. Finally, she said, "Oh, fine. It can't be worse than trying to do it all myself. If I'm going to fail spectacularly I might as well take you all with me. Come on, everyone, let's talk about what needs to be done."

A little cheer went up and everyone crowded around to get organized. Galen pulled up the image he and Lana had been using back in her lab and put it on a large display:

Problem 1: Food poisoning

Problem 2: Soybean disease

Lana said, "The good news is, I've isolated the toxin itself, Toxin-X. As I've told you, the small sample I made is right over there. It's in a weak solution, in a sealed container, inside a polyglass cabinet, inside a containment field. But don't go near it! Even the tiniest amount will kill you in 60 seconds. We're going to need it for our work, but please, no one touch it but me. Okay?"

She collected sober nods all around. "All right. And now the bad news, I'm afraid, is that I'm already stuck on Problem 1, preventing food poisoning by inoculating people against the toxin. I ran my program the whole time I was sleeping and it failed. This is going to be harder than I thought."

"If we're stuck on Problem 1, why not work Problem 2 awhile?" Galen offered gently. "Curing the plants?"

"It's not as urgent."

"But it's important, too. Besides, it might give us some new ways of thinking."

"Fair enough," Lana sighed, trying to muster some optimism. "Okay, Problem 2, the soybean pathogen. Well, you've all seen the two plant specimens. They look identical, but one is deadly poisonous because it contains a reverse-twisted protein called Toxin-X. The job here is figuring out how the toxin is getting there. Is it a bacterial infection? Virus? Fungus? Parasite? No surprise, all my preliminary scans have come up empty."

"If it were easy to find, ORGA would have found it a long time ago," Galen agreed.

Marta, deciding to take her self-appointed "organizer" label seriously, went to the display and started a list under the heading of "*Problem 2: Soybean disease.*" She wrote,

- Bacteria
- Virus
- Fungus
- Parasite

"What else?" she asked.

Kessa thought about the giant, endless fields of soybeans they had flown over on their way to Galen's, all tended by huge, tireless agribots. "Does it have to be one of those four things? They've automated their agriculture so much, could it be something artificial?"

Lana tried to follow her line of thought. "You mean something about the genetic modifications they do all the time? What do you think, Galen? Could something have gone haywire with their genetic engineering?"

"It seems possible. The production *Glycine max* cultivar genome is constantly being updated, just like software. Maybe there is a bug in their genetic engineering."

"Okay, good lead," nodded Lana. "Let's work on that one." Marta added

- Genetics

to her list while Lana continued, "Any other odd angles we should explore?"

Marta said, "When Kessa said 'artificial,' I thought she meant chemicals. It seems like the agribots are constantly pouring chemicals on the plants. Could those be doing something unexpected?"

Galen nodded. "You're right about the chemicals, too. There's a steady diet of fertilizers, pesticides, and so on. Also Vanquishin, which is the antibiotic they use."

Lana concurred. "I've already seen traces of all of those inputs in the scans. There are a lot of them, though I haven't noticed anything exotic so far. That seems like another good path to explore."

Marta wrote

- Chemicals

Suddenly it seemed like a really long list. Marta had written down six whole paths of inquiry to pursue for Problem 2, and any single one of them could easily take months. Lana sighed.

All this time Jet had been staring a little blankly into space, not seeming to pay much attention. But now he spoke up, addressing himself uncertainly toward Lana, or maybe Marta. "I was just thinking. We have to assume that if it's anything conventional, ORGA would have found it, or will soon. Right?"

Lana answered. "Mostly. I think they are missing the chirality, which is only a little bit unconventional."

"Okay, but we should be focusing on unconventional solutions, right?"

"I suppose . . ."

"So then we start by looking for the simplest solution that is also unconventional."

"Er, what would that be?"

"I'm not sure."

Lana was looking perplexed but Kessa was following Jet's thinking, feeling a touch of their mind-meld at work. Kessa said, "I get it, Jet. So the simplest solution would be whatever usually makes plants sick. The first four items on Marta's list, right? And the unconventional part would be reverse chirality. Mom, you did say the Toxin-X protein is right-handed, didn't you? Even though most proteins are left-handed?"

"Right. I'm guessing that's why ORGA is so confused," Lana said.

Jet nodded. "Is DNA right-handed or left-handed?

"Right-handed," Lana replied.

"Is there such a thing as left-handed DNA?"

Lana raised her eyebrows thoughtfully. "There actually is something called Z-DNA. It's rare. It's like regular DNA, except the double helix is twisted in the reverse direction, like a left-handed screw."

Galen joined in. "So, thinking unconventionally, could there be a pathogen—a bacterium or virus or parasite—that uses Z-DNA instead of regular DNA?"

Lana shrugged. "I suppose there could be, but I'm not sure it would matter. The direction of twist in the DNA doesn't matter, only the genes that it's encoding. She stopped for a moment and there was silence in the room. But then she started. "You know, here's an interesting idea: maybe we're dealing with a kind of DNA where the *nucleotides* are enantiomers!"

"The whats are what?" asked Galen.

"Hah, sorry," said Lana, with growing excitement. "The nucleotides. The rungs on the ladder of DNA's double helix. You know, A, G, C, and T? The letters in the genetic code? Each rung on the ladder is either A linked to T or C linked to G. What if the pathogen that is making Toxin-X uses a kind of DNA where those *rung* molecules are twisted the opposite direction? So it's not the DNA helix that's reverse-twisted, it's the rungs on the ladder?"

"Would that be possible?" Kessa asked. "Could that support life?"

"Well . . . I don't know, maybe. If there were such a thing, it would go completely undetected by ordinary scans, which would explain why ORGA can't figure it out. And who knows, in an organism where nucleotides are reverse-twisted, maybe proteins are reverse-twisted too and you get right-handed proteins like Toxin-X. All the usual rules would go out the window."

"What would you call that kind of DNA?" Kessa wondered.

Lana chuckled. "I suppose you think 'enantiomeric nucleotide DNA' is too long a name?"

Everyone laughed. "Way too long," Kessa said. "How about just 'reverse-twisted DNA'? Or better yet, DNA with a Gaia twist?"

• • •

It took Lana all morning and several outbursts of unmotherly swear words to reengineer her specialized programs around to make them scan her samples for something that wasn't quite DNA, but when it finally started working the results were swift. "Found some!" she called out. "There really is an organism with Gaia-twist DNA in the infected plants. My God!"

The next hours, ticking down on Marta's clock, were a blur for Lana as she immersed herself in her programs, computers, and equipment. This was deeply technical work now, and there was nothing the others could do to help. Marta spirited in some food and drink now and then, which Lana consumed without attention. At last Lana sighed in happy relief, pushed back from her displays, stretched, and floated her way into the main lounge to report.

"It's a bacterium!" she announced excitedly. "I've never seen anything like it. It really does use DNA with reverse-twisted nucleotides. As best as I can figure, it infects the soybeans but doesn't cause them any damage except for producing this innocent-looking protein, which turns out to be a reverse-twisted version of a protein that soybeans contain naturally. And that twist makes it fatally toxic to animals."

Galen said, "But if it's a bacterium, how can it survive ORGA's antibiotics? ORGA has been so confident in Vanquishin all these years."

"This is a bacterium that uses Gaia twist DNA instead of regular DNA. It's a new lifeform! I guess they didn't count on that. No wonder it doesn't respond to conventional antibiotics. I guess we should call it Bacterium-X."

Kessa asked, "Does this tell us anything more about how it's spreading?"

"As far as I can tell, Bacterium-X is getting directly into the plant's cells somehow, not through a parasite. I guess it could be coming from irrigation water, or contaminated agribots, or soil, or who knows what. ORGA is going to have to figure that part out."

There was a pause and Marta looked up hopefully. "Does that mean you're done with Problem 2?"

"Gosh, I— You should never ask a scientist if she's done. There's so much more to be understood."

"I know, but for now? Is this enough to take to ORGA, and will they be able to figure it out from here?"

Lana tossed her head uncomfortably and looked around the room for any guidance. All she saw were hopeful, expectant faces. "Okay, I'll say yes. If ORGA knows what to look for, their fancy agriculture systems should have no problem taking it from here. They should be able to eliminate the disease in their soybeans. So, yes! We're as finished as we're going to be with Problem 2."

Cautious cheers emerged around the room. "Cool, then! Way to go, Lana! Congratulations!"

"Team effort!" Lana corrected. "Hurray for us all!"

The high-fives were barely abating when the smile disappeared from Jet's face and his eyes found their way to the countdown clock. It said 31:00:00. One day, seven hours left.

But her own ticking countdown clock notwithstanding, Marta had insisted that everyone have an evening meal together and sleep for the night before returning to Problem 1. The food came from *Gregor Mendel*'s onboard fab, which everyone was looking at with more suspicion of late, thinking about toxins. Lana had never experienced a fab before this trip, and she almost laughed when it produced the most outrageous thing she could think of to ask it for: an edamame salad. In other words, soybeans put back together more or less the way they started. They tasted almost real.

Skervin's Conference Room

Citizen Welfare, 93 Perka Reporting:
"Toxicosis deaths, suspected or confirmed, 6653. Nonlethal toxicosis cases, likely due to trace exposure, approximately 55,400. This is becoming more than I can bear, Skervin."

Infrastructure, 77 Stasik Reporting:
"Production capacity shut down: 31 percent of total, up another 24%. Bulked product now routing as high as Level 49 in the hardest-hit cities."

Propaganda, 81 Sybil Reporting:
"There is still high growth in negative reports on all platforms, but our program of disinformation, confusion, and distraction appears to be having some effect."

Research, 78 Kapcheck Reporting:
"The pursuit of higher-sensitivity automated assays is continuing. The unusual structures we were seeing in the amino acids turned out to be due to anomalies in a property called chirality, but that led nowhere and we have concluded it was an unimportant distraction. The researchers now have 24 hours left on the deadline I have specified. Nothing else to report at this time."

14

Friday, August 12

Ettica's Office, Capital City

Something a little magical happened to the message sent to 55 Luis Cabah, Medical 11, by 32 Caphaletta Maiz of Rio de Janeiro. Luis read it, even though Caphaletta was 23 levels beneath him and supposedly blocked besides, and then he forwarded it to his boss, even though he probably shouldn't have. The boss read it, even though she likely shouldn't have taken the time, and then she sent it to a peer in another department. She read it too and, though it wasn't necessarily appropriate to do so, forwarded it again. In this way, the message somehow threaded itself all the way up to almost the top of the Organic Resources Administration, where it finally reached the address of the Head of Operations, whose name was 91 Ettica Sim.

And, though she shouldn't have, Ettica opened it. It was addressed "To Someone I Hope Is Concerned," which caught her attention.

Well of *course* there were going to be pleas like this, thought Ettica. 32 Caphaletta and her cute little three-year-old weren't the only ones affected by the toxin problem, thousands of people were. 62,053, at last report. That's why Ettica and her team were fighting it so hard. This was a touching reminder of what they were fighting for, but she couldn't allow herself to get emotionally involved. That could quickly become overwhelming, and then maybe lead to poor decisions. Ettica was a 90-level; it was important to maintain perspective.

Still, he was a cute little guy. What was his name, again? Banji? That was a funny name. She liked the still with the soap bubbles. She stared at it for a long time, thinking.

ADS *Gregor Mendel*

It was artificial "morning" aboard ship and time to get back to work. Lana said, "All right, geniuses. Let's see if you can do your same magic on Problem 1. I need some brilliant ideas on this one, too."

They all crowded back into her "lab" again and Marta went to the display board, where she made a great show of crossing out *"Problem 2: Soybean disease."* Then she circled *"Problem 1: Food poisoning."*

"Mom," she said, "Why don't you tell us where you are so far?"

Lana nodded. "Okay. I'm trying to come up with a way of inoculating people against Toxin-X. But my immunosimulator isn't producing a positive solution."

"And your immunosimulator is . . . ?"

"It's a computer program that simulates the human adaptive immune system."

Jet, who was paying attention this time, said, "There is such a thing? That's really impressive."

"Right, but maybe not impressive enough, because it's not working."

Kessa said, "Keep explaining, though, Mom. How does it simulate the immune system?"

Lana looked at her audience. "Maybe I should just remind everyone how it works in humans first?" There were nods all around. "It's remarkable, really. For a beginner's explanation, you can think of it like a battle for control of a castle, which is your body. Your attackers are called antigens, and your defenders are called antibodies. There are thousands of different antigens, and your body needs a different, specialized antibody to fight each kind. When an attacking antigen comes along—the toxin, in this case—the immune system first has to identify which antigen it is. If the system recognizes it, it calls in a squad of appropriate antibodies to kill it off. That's what we call immunity.

"But if the antigen is something that has never attacked the castle before, the system has to invent a new kind of antibody to defend against it. It's as if the castle already knew how to defend against archers and swordsmen, but then a fire-breathing dragon shows up. It needs to invent an anti-dragon defense. And it does!"

"Invent? But how?" asked Jet.

"It's a process called somatic hypermutation."

"Somatic hypermutation? That sounds almost as cool as magnetoplasmadynamic drive."

Lana grinned. "Fewer syllables, but yes, it is cool. Essentially, it randomly tries thousands or millions of defenses until it finds one that works. It's done by purposely mutating certain immune cells really fast."

"Crazy!"

"Right. It's invention by trial and error. It might not be elegant, but it's effective. My immunosimulator program tries to mimic the process, though with some artificial enhancements, of course. But look, it ran for all this time and couldn't create an appropriate antibody—also known as an antitoxin—for Toxin-X. If I were back in my lab I could try some other approaches, but this is the machine I have. I think I'm going to have to reprogram it to try a larger universe of variations. I'm afraid it's going to be complicated, and, unfortunately, time-consuming."

Stoke had been following the conversation and now he spoke up. "Should we look at the Gaia twist angle again? Would it be possible to reprogram your immunosimulator to look for Gaia twist DNA?"

Lana's first reaction was to explain gently how the type of DNA would not affect the antibodies the immune system could produce, and therefore Stoke's idea wouldn't make any difference, but in the spirit of cooperation she stopped herself. She said, "Interesting idea, Stoke. I wouldn't have thought of that. The Gaia twist DNA shouldn't make any difference . . . but now that you say that, I wonder if the immunosimulator doesn't have some programming shortcuts built in that assume a certain chirality in the nucleotides."

"Right, Mom," said Kessa, flashing some of her deeper understanding of biology. "Do you think its algorithms assume normal left-handed amino acids and right-handed alpha helixes in the proteins?"

"Good question, Kessa. Those would be very reasonable assumptions. Let me look. If it does, I could easily reprogram it . . ."

As it turned out, reprogramming the immunosimulator to use reverse-twisted biological components was much harder than Lana expected. After half an hour she was emitting confused *hm*s through pursed lips; after an hour she was starting to growl; and after two hours she was shaking her head and throwing up her hands in exasperation and starting to curse.

Galen was on the verge of intervening and suggesting it might be time for a new line of attack when Lana suddenly pulled her hands back and stared at her screen in surprise. She sat there motionless for several seconds, reading and re-reading the display.

"I . . . I think . . . I think I may have something!"

"What?" said Galen, who was closest. Everyone in the ship came floating in right behind him.

"Well I was having problems with the light chain of the Fab fragment, but then because of the reverse polarity of the ionic bonds I added an alternating purine-pyrimidine sequence—"

"Mom!" interrupted Marta. "Can you please speak in English?"

"Eh? Oh, sorry. I, uh, well, it's hard to explain, but I think this might work! I might have a formula for an antitoxin."

"Are you sure? You don't seem too positive," Marta said.

"Well again, it's so hard to tell. There are so many unanswered questions. And it's all just a simulation for now. I think . . . I think we'll need to actually synthesize a sample of this and test it out."

"Can we do that?"

"I honestly don't know. In my lab at home it would be no trouble. I brought the equipment, but now here we are in outer space, with no gravity. What's that going to do to my chemistry?"

Jet and Stoke gave each other a look. As experienced space travelers, they knew a little about it. Jet answered for them both. "Does your chemistry involve liquids?"

"Definitely."

"Then the short answer is, it's going to do a *lot* to your chemistry. The fluid physics is completely different. Mixing isn't the same, boiling isn't the same, measuring isn't the same. Just like we have to have our drinks here out of bags instead of cups, you won't be able to use test tubes, or beakers, or any container you're used to."

"Uh-oh."

Stoke stuck his tongue between his teeth, thinking. "I suppose we could rig up a mini-tumbler for you."

"What's that?"

"It's a way of mimicking gravity in space using the same centrifugal force concept that space stations use. There's a big spinning cylinder inside and everything gets pressed against the outside walls."

"Of course," nodded Lana. "Just like a centrifuge. We use those all the time at home. I should have brought one."

"Okay, then like that. How big would you need it . . . ?"

Lana and Stoke started exchanging design ideas, and then Stoke went to the ship's onboard 3D printer and started making parts. Like everything else aboard, the spaceship's 3D printer was small, so Stoke's design had a lot of piecemeal, interconnected parts to make a big, chest-high device. It was a mess, but it would work.

It had to work.

Skervin's Office

"Thank you for seeing me prior to the task force meeting, 96," said Kapcheck. He was moving and speaking with care, and Skervin already knew what he was going to say.

"Nothing?" Skervin said.

Kapcheck shook his head very slightly and spoke in a quiet voice. "They can't find it. They succeeded in increasing the automated scan sensitivity by a factor of 113, but still they found nothing."

Skervin moved very little himself and he, too, spoke quietly. "So. It's the wrong tests. They've gone too deep when they should have gone wide."

"Yes, that captures it."

Skervin sat silently for a long time, and Kapcheck couldn't tell what he was thinking. Finally Kapcheck said, "I'll give them new instructions this afternoon. Direct them to pursue a broader range of possible solutions. Does that seem right?"

Skervin now looked Kapcheck in the eye, heaved a mournful sigh, and then switched his gaze to the ceiling. "What you don't understand, Kapcheck, is that this afternoon is too late. The prime minister knows about all this now. I am to give a report tomorrow afternoon."

"Well, I'm sure you can tell him that we have a definite plan of attack—"

Skervin didn't want to talk to Kapcheck anymore. "Goodbye, Kapcheck. Thank you for the report. The task force meeting this afternoon is canceled."

Kapcheck mumbled something polite and left as inconspicuously as he could.

■   ■   ■

Skervin sat quietly for a long time after Kapcheck left. At first he told himself he was thinking, but then he admitted he was stewing, and that made him so angry with himself he stood up and threw a glass across the room. It shattered against the wall and left an ugly mark.

How had it come to this? What incredibly bad luck had befallen him, with this cursed toxin coming out of nowhere. It was going to be a scandal now, and he would need to explain himself to the prime minister. This wasn't going to be good for his career, not good at all. He'd been on such a good run for the last 18 years: always in control, always on top. He was born to this. He was probably the best executive the planet had ever seen. But this fluke; this mischance; this blackbird that had dropped out of the sky. It was like a Greek tragedy where the gods destroy a mortal, simply on a whim.

God, he was going to have to be good tomorrow. The prime minister was calling him to task and he was in a dangerous spot. But he *was* good, damn it. He was the best executive they had. He would pull it off. Somehow, he would get himself out of this and avoid blame. Hell, if he did it right, he'd come out looking like a hero. He just had to think awhile.

Think a lot. He poured himself a drink, walked over to the window, and gazed out at his magnificent view looking down on the rest of the city. He downed his drink in one and then walked back to his desk and commed Maggi. "Maggi, I'm taking the night off." Then he poured himself another drink; a tall one.

15

Saturday, August 13

ADS *Gregor Mendel*

Stoke's pseudo-gravity tumbler was far too large for Lana's already-cramped lab, so they made room in the main lounge and strapped it to a wall. Stoke clamped a reactant synthesizer in place inside, and after a short test Lana declared it would do. Using it for any kind of normal chemical mixing was immensely inconvenient, however. It wasn't like standing at a lab bench and pouring and mixing. You had to set up everything outside, in microgravity, using closed containers and tubes. Then you put your container in the tumbler and spun it up, waited for whatever chemical mixing or reaction, then took it out and moved to the next step. Lana kept Stoke busy at the 3D printer making odd, spill-proof containers, and before long most of the crew had been drafted into attempts to mix this or add that without spilling spherical droplets of liquid that floated randomly through the cabin.

It would almost have been fun, if not for the countdown clock on the wall. It now read 11:00:00. No one would be sleeping tonight.

■　■　■

Their first try didn't work. "Should have thought of that," Lana sighed, shaking her head. "We made what we were supposed to, and it's exactly the same compound that was working in the immunosimulator. But now that it's in tangible form, it's interacting with air in the room and changing its composition a little. It's going to reduce the effectiveness and it might even make it poisonous."

Jet shrugged and said, "It's a good thing we used the tumbler, then, because the problem might not have appeared in zero gravity. Better we found out about it when we did."

"So what now?" Galen asked.

Lana got a look of conviction and said, "I have to reformulate it to adjust for the air mixing. Then we have to do everything all over again."

The clock said 07:00:00.

The second time everyone was getting tired and something went wrong in the preparation process. Lana tests took all of five seconds to tell them it was wrong. 04:30:00, and they soldiered on.

Lana finally declared the third batch perfect. It was a clear liquid that sparkled, sapphire-blue, in a sealed glass vial. "Well done, all!" she smiled through tired eyes.

While everyone was congratulating everyone else with sleepiness-dampened enthusiasm, Lana casually transferred some of the compound to an injection gun. Then, still almost without looking, she touched the gun to her own arm and pulled the trigger.

Marta and Kessa rushed at her at once. "*Mom! Stop!* Watch out! What are you doing?"

Lana calmly put the stopper back in and shrugged saucily. "Someone has to test the antitoxin. I just gave myself an injection. Do I look okay?"

Everyone broke into expressions of consternation and debate about what Lana had just done, which Lana just ignored.

And then Galen realized what Lana was about to do next and he started moving toward her, crying, "*No, Lana! No! Don't!*"

But he was too late. Lana had touched the control and deactivated the containment field around her sample of the deadly toxin. She reached into the polyglass cabinet and seized the vial, pulled off the stopper, and drank.

Marta and Kessa, just armlengths away, were paralyzed in shock. Their mother had just drunk poison. They looked at her with mouths agape, not knowing what to do or say.

Galen reached his sister's side and pulled the deadly vial from her hand, quickly clapping the stopper back on and setting it carefully back inside the containment field.

Jet and Stoke, furthest away, simple stared at Lana, horrified and wondering what would happen to her.

And Lana, chin up, cheekbones strong, careless smile on her face, looked around wordlessly at each of them.

Seconds went by and everyone froze, not daring to breathe. They studied Lana's face for signs of distress, fervently hoping they would find none. They willed her to be well.

More seconds passed, and still she smiled carelessly. Still they stood frozen.

And then, finally, Lana gave a large sigh. "Tastes sweet!" she said.

Everyone still stood frozen, not quite daring to believe. But Lana tossed her head back and forth, swung an arm around Galen, and said airily, "Guys! I'm not dead. I feel fine. It works!"

"It works?" Marta said.

"Yes, it works! See? My eyelids are still open. My cheeks aren't drooping. I can move my limbs. I'm not vomiting. It works! It works!"

One by one, huge sighs emerged from everyone around the room and their tense bodies slowly relaxed. Unconsciously, they all gravitated in toward Lana and soon there was a very large, disorganized, and gravity-deprived group hug.

As the tension drained, little cheers started up, and soon everyone was laughing and bubbling and shouting all at once. "We did it! An antitoxin! Marta, cross off Problem 1! We have it! It's a cure!"

Jet couldn't help looking at the countdown clock, and as he did he caught Marta looking, too. They gave each other guilty smiles. It said 01:00:00.

"Better start packing up, everyone!" Jet called out lightly. "We decel in an hour."

Sol-1 Deceleration Zone

Tappet hovered anxiously over 40 Potet as she executed the delicate procedure of slowing out of warp speed and shooting into normal space near Earth in the Sol-1 Deceleration Zone. He had no idea that Lana and company had found a cure for Toxin-X, and he was still bent on completing his original mission of stopping the leak of the secret that Toxin-X even existed. For the entire trip back, picturing his own ship racing along somewhere near Galen's—maybe in front, maybe behind; it was impossible to know—he had been having nightmares about what would happen if Galen arrived first and started broadcasting his video to the entire population of Earth. Everyone would suddenly realize Nutribase could be poisonous. They would panic. Riots. Chaos. Tappet knew he had to destroy Galen the moment he came out of warp, before he had any chance to start broadcasting.

When his ship finally popped out of warp, its various communications and scanning systems, all of which had been dormant in warp, quickly powered up and initiated appropriate checks, connections, and surveys. Even the passengers' brainboxes came alive, plugging themselves into the net and updating on events since they had been gone.

Tappet leaned in close over Potet's fleshy shoulder and tried to scan all her displays. "Are they here yet?" he demanded, "Did we beat them?"

"*Gregor Mendel*, you mean? 22 Galen's people?"

"Of course that's who I mean! Do you see them on the scans? Any comm traffic?"

Potet, moving slowly as ever, gave a little grunt. "If you can give me a little space, here, 68 . . ."

"Hurry, come on."

"I don't see a ship of that name right now."

"Good. Good news."

"Want me to query Earth Space Control?"

"No. Move over. I need to talk to Skervin, fast."

"I hate to tell you, but I am still in the middle of arrival procedures here. I kind of need the comms. There's a comm panel for passengers in the main lounge—"

"Move!"

Tappet feverishly ordered the comm to contact Skervin. He wasn't looking forward to explaining how his mission had failed, but he was desperate for guidance. Operating on his own this past week had been a nightmare.

But the comm issued an error tone and said, "Unable to contact. Message?"

Tappet was stunned. Skervin was always available, for Tappet at least. "Retry!" he demanded. "Urgent."

"Unable to contact. Message?"

■ ■ ■

Down on Earth's surface, Skervin sat half-dressed in his private study, poring over his presentation for the afternoon. Stimulants were coursing through this system and he was fantastically focused, crafting what was about to be one of the most important presentations of his career. Later, his brainbox would alert him, he would clean up, and he would go off to face the prime minister and the assembled minister. But that wasn't until 1300 hours. For now, he was not taking calls. Any calls. He had made that very clear.

■ ■ ■

Tappet couldn't believe it. Skervin must have been incapacitated or killed while Tappet was away. Maybe it was something medical. Or a security black-out of some kind? Damn it! Now all the responsibility was back on Tappet again. Could he call in someone else? Skervin's second-in-command, perhaps: 91 Ettica Sim? No, she couldn't be trusted. Skervin had given Tappet his orders directly. Who knew whether she was in the loop. Damn! Too many uncertainties. He'd have to act on his own. If only his ship had weapons.

He pushed away from the viewscreen, pulled himself back, and then made a decision. "Connect to Earth Force, emergency contact."

Immediately, an alert woman in a military uniform appeared in Tappet's screen. She spoke with clipped precision. "We recognize 68 Tappet Holson aboard ADS *Paracelsus*. What is the emergency?"

"I am on a personal assignment from 96 Skervin Hough, Minister of Organic Resources. I am in pursuit of fugitives aboard ADS *Gregor Mendel*. If they aren't in orbit yet they will be soon, arriving from New Gaia. You must destroy them as soon as they arrive."

Earth Force was not moved. "We do not take orders from ORGA."

"Fine! Check your own records. You'll see that *Gregor Mendel* was stolen from ORGA eight days ago. It's a stolen ship!"

"If the craft is stolen, it will be detained, not destroyed."

"But the people on it are seditious! They are in possession of state secrets, and they're about to broadcast them in the open down to the whole planet."

"Do you have any proof of these accusations?"

"Not with me. It's, it's complicated. It's confidential."

Earth Force just looked at him.

"Fine, contact 96 Skervin. He'll tell you. But hurry! They could be arriving any minute!"

Earth Force, still stony-faced, said, "Stand by," and the screen switched to a standby message. Tappet waited very impatiently, feverishly pushing buttons and trying to make sense of Potet's other displays.

Finally, Earth Force reappeared. "96 Skervin cannot be contacted at this time."

Just then one of Potet's screens pinged and circled a new dot. It was *Gregor Mendel*! They had just flashed in out of warp. Tappet couldn't tell where they were but it had to be nearby. "There! That's them, isn't it? Shoot them! Quick! Before they can broadcast anything. You have to. It's a matter of planetary security!"

Earth Force turned her head and appeared to exchange words with another officer off screen. She had muted, so Tappet couldn't hear what they said, but he could tell from her body language that it was a relatively easy conversation, and at the end she nodded and turned back to Tappet.

"*Gregor Mendel* is a stolen ship and will be detained. In an abundance of caution, we will also disable their outbound communication until the passengers can be offloaded and questioned." Tappet sighed in relief and was about to say thank you, but Earth Force continued. "Meanwhile, 68 Tappet, you and your ship the *Paracelsus* are being detained. Your outbound communication will also be disabled. You are commanded to proceed immediately to Spaceport America, where you will be boarded and searched."

"What?! Me? Us? No, I'm a police officer. I'm—I'm on your side. I work for the Minister of Organic Resources!"

"We are not able to confirm your status at this time. Furthermore, we have detected another passenger identified as NA Speer who is listed as an illegal mercenary."

"But—"

"You will have the opportunity to explain yourselves during interrogation. End communication."

And if there was any doubt left in Tappet's mind, it was erased when he looked at an external viewscreen and saw an Earth Force military space cruiser sliding into position next to his ship, its laser cannons pointed straight at him.

Spaceport America

Tappet could barely contain himself. His ship was now docked at the spaceport and being held there by Earth Force. He wasn't being allowed out—he'd already tried the hatch three times—and outbound communications were blacked out. Potet had replanted herself at the flight controls, but it was like sitting in a parked car and there was nothing for her to do. Speer lolled in the main lounge, fiddling with his gun but as helpless as the rest of them.

Tappet took small comfort in knowing that Galen and crew were locked down and quarantined just as he was. At least they weren't leaking the secret of Toxin-X just yet. But if they did . . . !

Tappet performed the microgravity equivalent of pacing, floating himself back and forth through the cabin and uttering curses under his breath. "Hurry *up*," he kept saying to imaginary Earth Force officers on the other side of locked hatch. No one had come to see him yet, and he was practically dying of stress thinking about what would happen if the New Gaians got released before he did. He fervently prayed that Earth Force would talk to *him* before they talked to *them*.

But then it occurred to him that praying was not the right approach at all. This situation was far too risky to leave in the hands of fictional gods. He looked over at Speer and his gun. "Speer," he said, "Let's talk tactics."

Ettica's Office, ORGA Headquarters

Ettica's assistant 61 Michael simultaneously knocked once and pushed open her office door, bursting in on her meeting with two ORGA staffers. "I'm sorry! I'm sorry!" he said, rushing over to whisper in her ear. His face was flushed and he spoke in an urgently. "Galen's group is back! Their ship's been quarantined at the spaceport and outward communication has been blocked by Earth Force, but somehow, they have broken through on an improvised link. They sent an encrypted message to your private channel at my desk. They need to talk."

"Shit!" Ettica jumped up and almost shouted "Excuse us!" to her surprised visitors. They grabbed their things and disappeared as fast as possible while Michael dropped into Ettica's desk chair and starting tapping at her viewscreen, following directions he had just received. He spoke a series of numbers to set up a secure connection, and the viewscreen came alive. They were looking at Stoke, who had been doing set up on his end. "Oh, hi!" he said tensely, as if afraid of being overheard. "Let me get the others."

An anxious Galen appeared and centered himself in the view, with Lana right next to him and the younger people crowding behind. "91 Ettica, good. We're here. This is my sister, Lana Sjøfred. She's done it! She's found the cause of the disease and she has an antitoxin."

"Well, 90% there on the pathogen," Lana cautioned. "We have the bacterium, but we'll have to confirm its behavior in the field. But the antitoxin seems to work."

Ettica just gaped at first. She was shocked, relieved, and overwhelmed all at once. Maybe even frightened of what would happen next. "That's—that's amazing. How do you get it here? Or, how I do I get to you? Or . . . what? What form is it in?"

"I have formulated a small quantity of the antitoxin," Lana said, holding up a diminutive bottle containing her clear, sapphire-blue liquid. "And I have the complete technical specifications on the antitoxin and the bacterium in a data file, ready to send."

Ettica thought fast. "We have to get you talking to the prime minister, face-to-face. An electronic message will never get through. Skervin's going to be meeting with the PM and the whole executive team in less than an hour from now. They have to know about this before they make any really terrible decisions. I think they're about to declare a planet-wide emergency. Martial law, rationing, forced conscription, everything. There's about to be worldwide pandemonium."

Lana made a simple gesture. "Just tell them about this yourself. I don't mind."

"No way I could explain it even if they believed me. Besides, we have to get you out of there before Earth Force confiscates your samples and throws you in a jail cell somewhere." The last made Lana widen her eyes in alarm. "Don't worry, I've got you. Just move fast when you can. Now, let me talk with your pilot and your electronics mischief-maker again."

Spaceport America

An impressively short time after Ettica had swung into action on their behalf, Galen and company found themselves climbing along the weightless access tunnel in Spaceport America's spindle, transferring from their home and laboratory of the last three days, *Gregor Mendel*, to an Authority orbiter named *Earl Olsen* that had been allowed to dock out here with the interstellar ships. This time the clearance appeared to come from the office of the prime minister himself; Ettica truly had a gift for tricking the bureaucracy at its own game. Once inside the orbiter, Jet and Stoke rushed to the flight deck and began powering up. "Oh-for-two and they still let you drive these things?" Stoke joked to Jet.

"Third time's a charm."

■   ■   ■

Earth Forces officer M40 Nassar and a detachment of four guards arrived at the portal where Tappet and Speer's ship was being held. Nassar had been briefed on the strange case of this and the other ORGA executive space yacht that had just arrived from New Gaia, both surrounded by clouds of suspicion, confusion, and accusations. This 68 Tappet in particular seemed to be very excited about something or other. It sounded to Nassar like a royal mess involving way too many high-level executives in a civilian agency, and he was less than thrilled with the assignment of sorting it out. But he sighed and gestured for one of the guards to unlock the hatch.

The hatch came open, and before Nassar could even process what was happening, a man on the other side fired an e-gun straight at him. Nassar felt an explosion of pain and immediately blacked out, his paralyzed body floating right where it was in the weightless environment. Nassar's guards went for their own weapons, but they were unprepared and quickly fell, two on one side and then two on the other in rapid succession. Within five seconds, Speer and Tappet were out of the hatch and moving quickly along the spaceport's spindle, looking for a ship and a comm channel of their own.

They left Potet inside at the flight controls, playing a game with all the vivaciousness of a potato.

▪   ▪   ▪

Jet flew the orbiter *Earl Olsen* away from the space dock fast. Not as fast as the last time he dove to Earth in a mad escape in *Chica*, but fast. *Earl Olsen*'s prime minister-level credentials made for buttery-smooth movement through the spaceport's initial security checks. Stoke almost enjoyed trading authorization codes and traffic control messages with first Earth Force patrols, and then spaceport controllers, as Jet flew through the checkpoints. They kept saying things like "Right away, sir," and "Have a good flight" in particularly helpful tones of voice.

With all the traffic around the spaceport, neither Jet nor Stoke noticed the military orbiter that had identified them in the distance and was vectoring straight for them.

▪   ▪   ▪

Tappet and Speer had wisely moved fast, taking action before the Earth Force command and control structure could respond. They found a lightly guarded, Earth Force military-grade MK-88 orbiter in a parking dock near the end of the spindle and quickly commandeered it. Speer took the controls and Tappet dove for the comm panel, excited and relieved to finally have a communications link to the world he knew. His first call was to Skervin, but Skervin still wasn't taking calls. He tried 91 Ettica, but she was locked down, too.

Finally, Tappet reached an officer in ORGA Enforcement and got some long-missing respect. "I am operating under direct orders from ORGA Minister 96 Skervin. I am in pursuit of the criminals who escaped from ORGA custody last week. They are aboard one of the prime minister's orbiters, the *Earl Olsen*, down-bound from Spaceport America. They are extremely dangerous and must be destroyed!"

Tappet's rank was nowhere near high enough to justify an order like that, but the ORGA Enforcement officer was a hawk who relished the idea of a fight. "Roger that, 68. I'll order backup for you right away."

"Good. And notify Spaceport's Authority Police and traffic control as well."

■ ■ ■

Spaceport America's down-bound traffic controller that day was named 42 Lonzo. He had been doing this for quite a few years and thought he had seen just about everything: military, civilian, accidents, criminals, drunks, you name it. He was in the midst of handing off a downlinking orbiter, who was on business for the prime minister as a matter of fact, when his emergency comm light went on. He hated to give any trouble to the bigwigs, but emergency was emergency. "Hold up, *Earl Olsen*," he said apologetically. "Please stand by."

"What's the problem?" Stoke said on the other end, as casually as he could manage.

Lonzo muted Stoke and turned to the emergency comm. It was an ORGA Enforcement officer, which was no surprise given ORGA's heavy presence here at Earth's largest port. "The *Earl Olsen* is stolen and carrying escaped ORGA prisoners. We have orders to destroy it!" said the ORGA officer excitedly.

Lonzo was incredulous. "*Destroy* part of the prime minister's fleet? Are you crazy? What authorization do you have?"

"This is from 96 Skervin, the head of ORGA. We have to take out *Earl Olsen*, fast!"

Stalling for time, Lonzo switched back to Stoke. "*Earl Olsen*, please retransmit your authorization code."

"Here it is, Spaceport. We are authorized by the office of the prime minister, 100 Ari Ravo."

Lonzo looked at Stoke on one screen and the ORGA officer on another, trying to decide whom to believe.

■ ■ ■

It didn't long for an Earth Forces soldier to discover and report M40 Nassar and his four-man detachment floating unconscious in the spindle near where Tappet's ship was being quarantined, and very quickly thereafter a commandeered MK-88 orbiter was reported as well. The alarm was raised and every available Earth Forces fighting ship in the vicinity swung into pursuit of their stolen MK-88. The problem was reported to Spaceport's Authority Police and traffic control at the same time, with a request for armed support.

■ ■ ■

Next to Lonzo, another controller jumped from her seat and rushed over to see him. "I just had a message from Earth Force. Someone stole an MK-88 orbiter. They're requesting Spaceport Authority Police support."

"So we're supposed to shoot down the MK-88? Who stole it?"

"A couple of rogue agents from ORGA."

"Wait, I have ORGA on the comm and they're saying *Earl Olsen* is stolen and carrying escaped prisoners. They're going to shoot it down. They didn't say anything about rogue agents. What the hell is going on?"

■ ■ ■

Speer was not trained on MK-88s, but piloting was piloting, and the good thing about this ship was that it had an armament control panel. He almost smiled as he looked across the range of weaponry that included a laser cannon, explosive projectiles, and a large-caliber inertially-dampened bullet gun. Working quickly, he managed to get the targeting computer working and he gave it the most specific instructions he could think of, which were, "Target is *Earl Olsen*. Fire at will and destroy."

Earl Olsen was far away from the MK-88 and aiming would be only approximate, but the targeting computer obeyed orders and fired the laser cannon in the right general direction.

■ ■ ■

"Someone's firing at us!" Stoke exclaimed. "Sensors show a laser cannon!"

Jet made a battle noise in the back of his throat and swung *Earl Olsen* into a quick, hard turn. "Evasive maneuvers!" he shouted at the controls.

■ ■ ■

"That was a cannon shot!" cried Lonzo, looking at his displays. "But it wasn't ORGA shooting. It was the MK-88. They shot at *Earl Olsen*."

"*Earl Olsen?*" said Lonzo's colleague. "That's the prime minister's ship! Stop them!" She dove back to her own console and opened up an emergency channel to Spaceport Authority Police. "Shots fired! There is a rogue MK-88 firing at the prime minister! Destroy it immediately!"

Lonzo tried to correct her about it not actually being the prime minister, but it was too late: chaos had erupted and the fog of war descended. Shots exploded everywhere. An Earth Force ship had located Speer and Tappet in the MK-88 and was firing at them, and an ORGA ship had found *Earl Olsen* and added its own firepower to Speer's. Several different red Raven-90 Authority Police patrol craft entered the fray and, thoroughly confused by conflicting messages from Lonzo and the mayhem they were seeing on their own screens, starting shooting at more or less everyone.

■ ■ ■

Jet and Stoke had no weapons; they were the rabbit in a den of battling wolves. *Earl Olsen*'s automated evasive maneuvering was working for the moment, but Jet knew he had to get them away from the fracas. Just one laser cannon shot, and the ship and everyone on it would explode. Jet's heart raced. He resumed manual control and dove downward toward the planet, jinking left and right every few seconds and hoping against hope he would avoid deadly photon beams. Everyone else held on for dear life.

After many long, breath-holding minutes they reached the highest layers of the atmosphere, which meant better protection from laser weapons and a reduction in the types of craft that could pursue them. "It will be orbiters chasing us now, until we get close to the ground," Stoke explained to the passengers, trying to offer some comfort despite his own shortness of breath and perspiring brow. But as he spoke there was a flash of light outside the window as a laser cannon shot just missed them and vaporized atmosphere molecules instead.

"Who was that?" Jet asked.

Stoke tensely checked his displays. "It's that MK-88. They're still on our tail."

"Why is Earth Force after us?" Jet cried.

Stoke shook his head in frustration. "Ten get you one it's Tappet. That guy won't quit. He must not know we have the cure."

"Can't we tell him?" Marta asked form behind. "Send him a message or something? This is crazy!"

Stoke just shook his head. There was no time and no way.

The MK-88 was a military craft and consequently larger and heavier than *Earl Olsen*, which was a sleek executive orbiter. In theory the relative potency of the MK-88's engine made it almost as fast, but in practice piloting made a difference. Speer was competent, but Jet was expert, and he exploited every trick of orbital mechanics and fine aerodynamic control he knew. Gradually, *Earl Olsen* gained distance on the MK-88, and eventually she crept beyond the range of the military ship's deadly guns. By the time they entered Capital City's airspace, Stoke was beginning to think they'd lost him.

But more wolves were waiting. By this time Tappet, dropping Skervin's name in every breath, had harangued the ORGA Enforcement command structure into taking his orders. As soon as Jet dropped low enough, three of ORGA's ground-based T-2s were on him, joining Tappet's misguided cause and trying to shoot him down. Last time Jet had encountered T-2s they were purposely not shooting, but this time they very definitely were. Flashes erupted from the nearest one's gun ports and they heard the thudding reports seconds later.

Thinking fast, Jet flew straight at the first T-2. Shooting down from space, he was carrying tremendous speed and the T-2 had all it could do to dodge. The other two T-2s held their fire so as not to accidentally shoot their own, and in those few seconds Jet was past them all and diving toward his destination, the towering, red, 200-story Authority Tower, home of the prime minister's offices and the site, any moment now, of a dramatic presentation by 96 Skervin Hough, Minister of Organic Resources.

All three T-2s gave chase, diving flat-out down after *Earl Olsen*, guns blazing. Again, Jet tried to dodge and juke with sudden and unpredictable movements left and right. But under the full firepower of three armed pursuers, it was just a matter of time. Jet's passengers cringed helplessly as an overpowering barrage of gunfire sounded behind them and projectiles shot past on every side.

One of the T-2s, fractionally more patient than the others, stopped shooting long enough to fine tune his course and line up in perfect position to put *Earl Olsen* squarely in his sights. He aimed his gun carefully and was moments from touching the command to fire when there was a sudden explosion and his entire ship was blasted off course. He looked wildly at his screens and could hardly believe it: it was an Authority Police ship! As usual, Authority Police and ORGA Enforcement had no idea what the other was doing. "Stand down! Stand down!" the Authority Police officer was yelling into the emergency channel. "You are firing on Prime Minister 100 Ari Ravo!"

"No you're not!" came another shouted message. It was Tappet in the MK-88, still furiously chasing down from above. "That's wrong! Those are criminals in one of the prime minister's ships! Shoot them!"

All three ORGA T-2 pilots were suddenly confused enough to stop what they were doing. But Speer, next to Tappet at the controls of the MK-88, wasn't confused at all: he was back in range now and lining up his own explosive projectile weapon to fire at *Earl Olsen*. "Fire at will!" he shouted at his control.

At exactly the same time, the Authority Police ship, still thinking it was defending the prime minister of all Earth, fired at the MK-88. The shot just grazed its target, but it was enough: the MK-88 was knocked slightly sideways and its own shot at *Earl Olsen* was deflected just a fraction. It missed the crucial heart of *Earl Olsen*'s engine and impacted on one of the wings, blowing a ragged hole.

Earl Olsen jolted hard to one side and tipped sickeningly forward. Jet's finely-honed instincts reacted just fast enough to save the ship from flipping into a deadly spin, but suddenly they were pointing in one direction and moving in another in a way that a flying machine was not supposed to do. Jet broke into a sweat and fought to gain control as they dropped from the sky, spinning crazily like an autumn leaf in fast-motion. Stoke gaped out the front window, eyes huge, watching the ground and the clouds and the horizon all spinning wildly. In the passenger compartment, there were involuntary gasps and shouts as people were thrown randomly against their seats and their restraint nets, grasping out hands for support.

The ships above were caught up in their own chaos, trading shots between the Authority Police and ORGA Enforcement, completely losing track of the *Earl Olsen* as it skittered toward the ground.

Somehow, incredibly, Jet held on to just enough control of his damaged ship. They were falling fast toward Capital City's towering forest of buildings, half-wingless and spinning and torqueing unpredictably. But in it all Jet caught glimpses of a rooftop landing pad and steered for it as best he could, his intuition guiding him as much as anything. If they missed that landing pad there was no backup—they would crash painfully and fatally into random building roofs and walls as they fell the last 120 stories to the ground. There was the landing pad, closer and closer. He needed to get them farther north. Rudder hard left and just a spurt of power . . . now!

The ship lurched to one side. There was a hideous bang and then a horrendous screech. They barely made the landing pad and skidded across it to a precarious stop, lying on one side. Smoke started billowing into the cabin.

Moira Conference Room, Authority Headquarters, Capital City, Earth

The Moira conference room, though luxurious and well appointed, was by far the least spectacular of the venues on the prime minister's conference level. It lacked the throne-room feel of the Basileus, or the giddy and spectacular 270-degree, two hundredth-floor views from the Aerie, or the size and grandeur of the Forum. But Moira was the prime minister's favorite. He liked that it had no windows; no distractions. He liked that the metallic red table was relatively small, with only enough room for principals to sit elbow-to-elbow, face-to-face. He liked the acoustics, which muted background noises so that only intentional, articulate speaking could be heard.

Prime Minister 100 Ari Ravo was a man whose incorporeal *presence* overwhelmed any impression of his healthy but unremarkable physical form. His energy seemed to engulf the space around them, as if controlling and exciting even the molecules in the air through which he passed. His eyes were incredibly sharp and bright, capturing people's attention even from across a room, and almost overpowering anyone who looked directly into them from close by. His voice was sonorous and his articulation was so perfect that people tended to think he had an accent. And though the Earth Authority was anything but a democratic government, 100 Ari Ravo was—as he had to be— a brilliant politician.

This afternoon's meeting had been innocuously billed as a "status report" from the minister of Organic Resources on "nutritional products safety improvements," but every single attendee had worked their networks beforehand and knew the meeting was much more than that. It was on Saturday, for one thing. Weekend meetings were not uncommon, but they were never held just for "status reports." The buzz was that 96 Skervin was in some kind of deep trouble— though no one knew what for—and he was about to answer to the prime minister for it. Ari had invited all his top ministers. The ones who were lucky would just watch; the ones who were unlucky would be asked to help repair the damage from whatever Skervin had done.

They arrived, by careful political calculation, in reverse order of prestige, carefully choosing their positions at the table and tossing off refreshment orders to the waiting stewards. Their aides came in with them and took up positions standing behind their principals because the Moira room offered no extra chairs. Only two chairs were open when Skervin breezed in a separate door, which only he seemed to know about, and he glad-handed his way around the room before finally settling casually into the speaker's chair at one end of the table, still chatting. He had brought 91 Ettica Sim with him, partly because she knew things, but mostly for troop strength. Even she, a 91, was left to stand chairlessly to the side.

Ari appeared and the room suddenly became silent, intense, and focused. "Good afternoon," Ari said to a chorus of short and polite replies. "96 Skervin. You have a report for us."

"Yes, thank you, Prime Minister." Skervin stood and activated the glowscreen, all eyes upon him. This was the moment he had been preparing for all morning.

Skervin was an excellent speaker. He projected confidence and mastery of his subject; his explanations were clear; he provided just the right amount of information at just the right pace. If it had been in any other setting, or with any audience excluding the prime minister, he would have been the maestro of the room. But now, there was a tangy sense of doubt among the participants. The audience knew there was a weakness here; a vulnerability about to be exposed. They listened intently, hungry for the first drops of blood.

Earl Olsen

"Out!" shouted Jet from inside the crashed *Earl Olsen*. "Get out now!" He touched a control and, mercifully, the entry hatch deployed. It was facing the wrong way—straight down—but it was usable. Wasting no time, Marta dove into it first and then crawled out from under the crashed ship and away. Kessa followed. Galen stood by the hatch and motioned for Lana to go next, but she hesitated. She was holding her bag close to her stomach with one hand and a cane in the other hand, and she was looking back and forth worriedly between Galen and her own prosthetic foot.

"Here, let me take your bag." Galen said. "Don't think about it. Just go!"

The bag contained her vial of antitoxin, so Lana handed it cautiously to Galen. Then she took a breath, put on a brave face, and crawled through. Galen followed closely, and Stoke and lastly Jet clambered out behind them. "What was that you were saying about third times?" Stoke asked Jet wryly.

Jet looked quickly around to confirm that everyone was in one piece. Lana looked frightened, but the rest only looked anxious. And ready for action, Jet realized. He and his friends had hardened in the last few days. Smoke from the skidded ship and possibly burning engines was everywhere, but Jet could see the gate to the landing pad. "Over there, out of the smoke!" he called. They hurried over, limited in speed only by Lana's surprisingly fast cane-assisted gait.

"When's Skervin's meeting?" Jet asked.

Marta answered right away. "It already started!"

His own question had reminded Jet that he was back in civilization now, and his brainbox would work. He dug in a pocket and quickly pulled out his eardot case, gratefully popping the temporary eardot Ettica had given him back into his ear after a long absence. As it went through its start-up sequence, Jet looked around the group. "We have to get to that meeting," he said, half expecting objections. "Ettica said they're going to do something really dangerous if we don't show up with the antitoxin. 'Global pandemonium' I think she said."

"Of course we have to get there!" said Stoke, to vigorous nods all around. "But we landed on the wrong building. The meeting's over there." He pointed at the Authority Tower several hundred meters away, a pinnacle separated from their current location by a Grand Canyon in the city maze.

Jet was already a step ahead of him. "Air taxi! Come on." Their current landing pad was a crash site and a disaster zone; no air taxi would ever pick them up there. Instead, Jet, following directions from his now-functional brainbox, rushed them to a slider and then to a turbolift that took them several floors down and two hundred meters away, where he found a balcony taxi pier and hurried them out onto it. Lana was struggling by the end and arrived breathless, and Galen put his arm around her for reassurance.

An air taxi that Jet's brainbox had summoned arrived, and they all clambered in, the six of them filling the taxi's two bench seats to capacity. Galen helped Lana in first and the rest followed, with Kessa nimbly hopping in last.

The taxi driver was looking skeptically at the requested address appearing on this screen. "that's correct," Jet called to her earnestly from the back seat. "This is an emergency! We really do need to go to the rooftop pad of the Authority Tower."

The driver remained dubious and she made no motion to start moving. Jet looked urgently at Stoke. "Stoke! A little help?"

Stoke rolled his eyes up and ewaved Ettica's assistant, Michael. "Michael, it's us! No time to explain, but we're having, uh, a little trouble getting to the meeting. We're in this air taxi and the driver isn't cooperating. Can you . . . ?"

Twenty seconds later, a very official-looking Prime Minister's seal and some impressive-looking authorization codes appeared on the driver's screen. She gave a small startle, glanced back at her passengers with a new look of respect, and roared her heavy craft into the sky.

The taxi was 50 meters out, passing over a gap in buildings that went all the way to the ground 180 stories below, when there was a detonation in the air just outside. The taxi shuddered. Shocked, everyone snapped their gazes out the windows. *Bang!* There was another one. *Bang!* The taxi was being violently tossed like a ball.

"There it is!" cried out Kessa. She was seated closest to the door and was looking up and out. "It's the MK-88! They found us. They're firing explosive shells!" *Bang!*

They were all frightened, but for a moment no one knew what to do. They were in a slow, clumsy air taxi that had no chance of evading the fusillade. They were impossibly high in the air and too far from a pier to land. And there was no such thing as an escape pod in a taxi. There was only one thing left. "Driver!" shouted Jet urgently. "Raise them on your comm! I have to talk to them."

Another bang, and the door exploded into pieces.

Kessa, who was nearest, was knocked sideways into Galen by the blast. The taxi was thrown off balance and rocked first one way, and then suddenly the other.

The motion threw the passengers, too, and before she knew it Kessa was hurtled from her seat and outward through the now-missing door.

Her head and shoulders went first, then her hips. She screamed. She flailed her arms but caught only empty air. Instinctively, she bent her legs, and her left one just managed to hook a support rung at the base of the chair. For an instant she was dangling, desperately holding on with one calf while the rest of her was flung out into the rushing air, the ground far below.

Galen flung himself across the seat toward Kessa and grabbed her knee with both hands, holding on with everything he had.

It was happening again. The air taxi crash that had taken Joanna and little Lillian away from him, 20 years and a lifetime ago. Someone was screaming, just as Joanna had. And as Galen grabbed Kessa, he looked out and down, far down, into the city jungle below. *The jungle into which Lillian fell, reaching out helplessly and crying "Mommy" as she dropped into the abyss. Lillian who would have been Kessa's age by now.*

No! He couldn't bear it. He couldn't live through it again. A dark blackness crept over Galen's vision, and his muscles, like his will, began to go slack. His grip on Kessa's knee came loose . . .

But it would not end that way this time. In the moment Galen panicked, strong arms reached in from all around. Some reached out and held Kessa; others reached out and held Galen. Jet, with his heart pounding, flung himself down on the taxi's floor, stomach first, and as the others held his legs he wriggled out the door until he could stretch down, grab Kessa's waiting hands, and pull her firmly and surely back inside. She was safe.

Galen gazed blankly at her, still stunned. Kessa, sensing Galen's trauma, ignored her own pounding heart and whispered to him, "You're not alone, Galen. We're all together now. We have each other."

There was another *bang!* and Jet was jarred back into action. Somehow, the driver had managed to open a comm channel despite everything. "Tappet!" Jet called at the screen. "Stop shooting! We're not going to hurt anyone. We found an antidote for the toxin!"

Tappet found himself frozen. His mind was a blender. Adrenaline was pouring through his body, full of bloodlust, fear, desperation, triumph . . . but now, a horrible, nagging doubt that he couldn't crush. He touched Speer's shoulder as a signal to temporarily hold his fire. "Bullshit, Jet. You're bluffing!"

"I'm not! We have it! We synthesized it on the trip. We have some with us. Come on, Tappet, we're trying to save the whole planet, just like you. We're on the same side!"

Jet watched Tappet's face in the viewscreen as his eyes jumped wildly around. He seemed too confused to speak.

"Tappet, we're on the way to see the prime minister right now! Check our taxi's computer: we have the prime minister's explicit authorization. We are not going to leak the information. Why don't you come with us and make sure?"

Tappet's whirring brain settled down to an uneasy stop. He was looking at the prime minister's seal displayed on the taxi's credentials screen. He liked that. He liked knowing who was in charge. For whatever reason, the fugitives had the prime minister's authorization now, and that outranked everyone, even Skervin. Tappet was going to follow orders; that's what he was good at.

"Tell your driver to fly slowly," Tappet said. "You are my prisoners."

■ ■ ■

The moment they landed on the roof of the Authority Tower, the air taxi was immediately surrounded by six red-uniformed armed guards. Worried, Jet's group sat still inside the damaged taxi for 90 long seconds, trying to raise Michael on the comms, as Tappet and Speer emerged from their nearby MK-88 and began speaking with people on the ground. But then a senior-looking official came out and spoke to the guard captain, the guard relaxed, and the official walked up to the hatch. "91 Ettica says welcome," she said. "Please hurry this way." They filed rapidly out of the ship, Galen and Lana first, followed by Kessa, Marta, Jet, and Stoke.

Several meters away, Tappet and Speer watched with growing agitation as their prisoners were escorted away without permission. The official said a few more words to the guard captain, and suddenly four of the guards walked over to Tappet and Speer and, to their great surprise, levelled their weapons. One guard quickly frisked them, forcing Speer to part company, ever-so-reluctantly, with his beloved bullet gun.

Jet could hear Tappet's vociferous objections even from this distance: "What?! What are you doing? Those are my prisoners!" But apparently Tappet's guards weren't listening, because they closed ranks and hustled Tappet and Speer off in another direction, shouting all the way.

The last thing Jet heard Tappet say was, "Damn it!"

Jet's group was escorted, almost jogging, into a turbolift, across a plush lobby, through several well-guarded doors, and finally to a now-crowded waiting area outside the Moira room. Michael was there waiting for them. He briefly ewaved his brainbox to notify Ettica and then greeted them in a whisper. "I'm Michael."

Moira Conference Room

Despite his undisciplined binge last night, Skervin's brain stimulants this morning had worked as intended and his thoughts were now well prepared. He would begin with a short introduction reminding them of ORGA's many responsibilities and how efficiently he had run the operation for these many years. Next, he would segue to the specific topic of Nutribase production and distribution, emphasizing the complexity of the problem and how efficiently his organization was managing it. He would explain the numerous risks of food production and highlight ORGA's nearly unblemished safety record over the course of his tenure as its leader. In part three, he would relate that a completely random, unforeseeable event—probably statistically unavoidable given the size and complexity of Earth's food operations—had caused a problem—scratch that, an *anomaly*—that his organization had quickly detected and was moving purposefully to correct. Then he would present a list of assignments—rather, *requests*, he would call them—to other departments to assist ORGA in carrying out its plan of operations. . . . Alright, he had to keep reminding himself, they would need more details on the problem. He had some data on that ready: uncharacterized deadly toxin, undiagnosed soybean blight, rapidly shrinking worldwide supply of edible Nutribase, a certain number of accidental deaths, etc. He would move through that part quickly. Senior ministers didn't need those kinds of details.

But Skervin had barely started his introduction when Ari interrupted him, arresting the attention of every face in the room. "Skervin. Let us stipulate that ORGA is an important and well-run organization. Will you please proceed to describing your problem?"

Only a very perceptive person—of whom there were several in this room—would have caught Skervin's involuntary twitch of alarm at the immediate derailment. Anyone else would have seen him continue smoothly, barely taking a breath before starting his next sentence with "We have detected a statistically improbable anomaly . . ."

"Here we go," thought Ettica. "He's about to own up to it. Skervin's famously skillful spin versus 100 Ari and a roomful of hungry sharks. Expect blood everywhere. They're all going to panic about the food supply first, and then Ari's going to make Skervin admit he's been covering up and doesn't have a solution. Then Ari's going to fire his ass. Then *I'm* going to be in charge of this disaster. It'll probably ruin me but at least I'm going to save that little boy Banji."

Ettica felt a tickle in her ear and her brainbox ewaved a message from her assistant Michael. "They're here. We're right outside."

At that moment, 91 Ettica Sim made a decision to be evil. Or possibly good. Even years later she could never decide which it had been.

Skervin was breaking the news now and oxygen was disappearing from the room. When he said "fatal nerve toxin" there were gasps and shaking heads. He somehow managed to omit the death count. "Soybean crop 64% infected" brought looks of growing horror. "Nutribase reserves stand at 23%" elicited growing panic and throaty noises that might have turned into screams. Through it all Ettica stood still, saying absolutely nothing.

The room stood at the brink of chaos when the prime minister caught them in mid-air. He stood up slowly, emanating every ounce of poise and presence he possessed. He locked Skervin in his overpowering gaze and asked the only question that mattered: "Skervin. Do you have a solution?"

Ettica said . . . nothing.

Skervin held Ari's gaze for a long time, not speaking. Then, finally, fatally, he looked down and away. "Not at this time."

The room erupted. Everyone leapt to their feet, shouting and trying to move in all directions at once. "We're going to die! We have to get help! You fucking moron, Skervin! How the hell did you let it get this far? Fuck you, Skervin!"

For several seconds, Ettica stood with her head lowered, staring at the carpet in front of her. Unbidden, the corners of her mouth tugged into a tiny smile.

She stepped forward, put one foot on a chair, and climbed up onto the table. She placed two fingers in her mouth and blew an ear-piercing whistle. "Everyone! Listen to me! People!" Reluctantly, the room quieted and all eyes turned to look up at her. The group was still enraged and suspicious, seemingly holding themselves back for just a moment before they would shout her down.

"Everyone!" Ettica said fiercely, green eyes flashing. "Prime Minister. There *is* a solution. I have it. It is right outside that door."

"What the hell are you doing, Ettica?" shouted Skervin. "You don't have anything!"

"Actually, I do, Skervin. No thanks to you. I am following my own path on this one."

"You went behind my back?! Why you fucking traitor—"

The prime minister stopped him with a raised hand and turned to Ettica, barely containing himself. "I am sure we would all very much like to hear what you have behind that door, Ettica."

Ettica ewaved Michael and he pushed open the door, showing in Galen, then Lana carrying her bottle of sapphire blue liquid, and then Jet, Kessa, Marta, and Stoke. They stood in a ragged line, squeezed up against one wall.

Still standing on the table, Ettica addressed the room. "Yes, you will note these people do not have active brainboxes at this time. They have just arrived here from New Gaia, in violation, I will readily admit, of Skervin's explicit instructions not to call in outside help. Some of you may remember Galen Sjøfred from when he worked with us at ORGA headquarters some years ago, as a 68, I believe it was. And this is his sister, Lana Sjøfred, who is a well-known plant scientist from New Gaia. And if I am not mistaken, Lana, you are carrying the results of your recent work?"

Lana lifted her chin and looked at Ettica, and then carefully around the room. "Yes, she said. This data chip holds technical specifications for the *Glycine max* bacterial pathogen that is poisoning the plants. You should be able to use it to cure the soybean blight. And in this bottle is an antidote for human Toxin-X poisoning."

There was a stunned silence. "Just to be clear," Ettica said, "you're saying you have a cure?"

"Well . . . roughly, yes."

Once again the room exploded in turmoil, this time with sighs of relief followed by barrages of questions for Lana and Ettica. Lana was almost crushed by the crowd to the point that Galen and Jet stepped in front of her for physical protection. Even the prime minister was helpless to restore order for several minutes until adrenalin levels dropped sufficiently and the attendees gradually returned to their places around the table.

"This is good news," Ari finally managed to announce loudly enough that everyone paid attention and settled down. "But only in the context of the very bad news we have just heard. We have a global pandemic on our hands and I am quite certain that Lana Sjøfred's cures will not work while sitting in a bottle here in Capital City. We have an entire planet of people to be inoculated and food crops to be restored, and if I understand correctly we have very little time. We need a coordinated plan of action across the entire Authority, beginning with everyone in this room. *Would you agree*," he said, as if it were a command. "Good. Now, let's begin with ORGA. Where is 96 Skervin?"

Heads turned, but Skervin was no longer there. He had left in the confusion, disappearing out the same side door by which he had come. He had no wish to face a trial before his peers . . . at least not just now, with them in this mood.

Ettica, now back on the floor and looking fully in control, spoke up. "It appears that Skervin needed to leave, Prime Minister."

"So I see. In that case, 91 Ettica, perhaps you would be willing to describe to us your plans? —Oh, my apologies. I have an update from my brainbox. It seems congratulations are in order and I should address you as *94 Ettica*. So, 94, your plans?"

Epilogue

Galen's Farmhouse

A week after the fateful events in the Moira Room, Galen had invited his family and friends back to his farmhouse for a proper visit. "Last chance," he had told them, before he moved back to New Gaia. They were still adjusting to the terrible news about the destruction of their house on Lake Peace, but no one was hurt, and New Gaians were a little less attached to their material possessions than most people. There had been some grieving for their beloved home and the contents it had accumulated over a lifetime, but already they were making plans to rebuild. Lana assured Galen that the new floorplan would include a new room just for him. Galen would have to get used to living in a full house and the New Gaian community. After all that had happened, he didn't think he was going to mind at all. He was ready to join the world again.

Meanwhile, it was quiet out there on the Saskatchewan plains, and peaceful. After the five visitors plus Galen made quick work of Galen's chores, they found themselves lingering for long conversations around the meal table, holding epic 3D checkers tournaments, and taking long walks through the soybean fields. Jet and Stoke had been happily reunited with their trusty brainboxes Kimberley and Jivey, and Jet and especially Stoke spent a lot of time catching up with friends and introducing their New Gaian girlfriends all around the net.

Galen came out of his tech room one day looking thoughtful. Lana was sitting on a couch and she immediately set down her technical papers to look up expectantly at her brother. Galen couldn't help but notice how spry she looked now, as if the weight of the world had been recently lifted from her shoulders. "What is it?" she asked.

"I just spoke with Ettica on the comm," Galen reported.

"Come sit down. Tell me."

"She said there is a lot of talk about reforms now at ORGA, like better interplanetary cooperation and making the Nutribase system more robust. That, and she offered me a job."

"A job! Back in your old world at ORGA headquarters?"

Galen smiled wryly. "Yup. I told her not in a million years."

"Of course you did."

"Apparently she's in charge now at ORGA. Skervin still hasn't come out of hiding."

"That evil man. I hope he stays in hiding forever."

Galen looked meditative. "He really is evil, isn't he? I mean, even on top of what he did to Joanna and Lillian, he was responsible for the deaths of thousands of other people from toxin poisoning. And it would have been thousands more if not for you coming to the rescue."

Lana said, "*Us* coming to the rescue. It was a community effort."

"Okay, us. But Skervin was still committing mass murder."

Lana looked at Galen for a moment to confirm that he was ready for a detached analysis of his nemesis. She wasn't going to defend Skervin, but she was going to help Galen think him through. "I suppose you could argue that the toxicosis was accidental—sort of a natural disaster. You can't blame natural disasters on the person in charge of the recovery effort."

"First of all," replied Galen, "he wasn't only in charge of recovery: he was also in charge of preparation and readiness, or at least he should have been. He was so obsessed with efficiency that he built a system that was prone to disaster because it relied so heavily on a single crop and set aside so little in reserve. And besides that, he had such an overwhelming need for personal control that he cut his organization off from everyone else who might have helped—first the other planets with Our World Our Way, then even from other departments like Citizen Welfare."

"Right," agreed Lana. "In the scientific community, we've been disconnected with scientists from Earth for years."

"Good example, and it wasn't just scientists; it was all areas. And on top of all that, from everything Ettica has told us, it seems clear that he completely botched the response effort. He bullied and micromanaged his staff so much they spent all their effort working on the wrong things."

"Don't take this wrong, but just to think it through, do you think he really wanted to wreck everything up the way he did?"

Galen was in the right state of mind to be open. "No, I suppose not. I guess you could even say Skervin was trying to do the right thing. And you have to admit, he's extremely talented in a lot of ways. His intentions were selfish and narcissistic, but he didn't actually *want* to kill thousands of people. Yet by misusing his power, he did. That's a way of being evil, isn't it? We recognize it is a sin to intentionally use power to do harm, but I also think it is a sin to use power ineptly and arrogantly at the same time."

"Amen to that," said Lana.

"Oh, and another thing from Ettica. I'm not quite sure why, but she said she wanted me to look through some photos and videos she sent of a little boy from Rio de Janeiro. It seems he was one of the close calls. He got very sick from Bulking Syndrome and then he got a micro dose of Toxin-X, but then once they got your—uh, our—antitoxin, they were able to get it out to him and he was saved."

"Nice story," Lana said, looking through the images appreciatively. "Ah, this is a cute one with the bubbles. I suppose—I *hope*—there have been a lot of cases like this. It was nice of Ettica to send us an example. What did you say the little boy's name was?"

"It's a funny one. 'Banji,' I think."

■ ■ ■

Stoke's friends kept asking when he was coming back to Denver, and he always dodged the question. The truth was, he had a dilemma that he didn't know how to resolve. On one hand, he was eager to return to his friends and his old life, which he greatly enjoyed. There would be some changes, though. For one thing, he was going to bite the bullet and start studying for spacer qualification, just like Jet. He'd been avoiding it for too long, and now that he had a taste of interstellar travel he couldn't get his mind off the idea that there were 98 more worlds to explore. That, and he didn't want to be a 31 forever. For another thing, his nights of hooking up with girls from the Hot Cabin were over. His "someday" had come, and he had found out what it was like to wake up, know her name, like her, and by God, have her like him. There was no going back from that. But that led him back to the dilemma: What about Marta? She was from New Gaia, of all places. 423 long light years away. How was that going to work? Was she going to move? Was he? Would they have to give up on their relationship? That last option made him sad, and an unbidden image came to mind of her eyes filled with tears, and him trying to comfort her with soft touches on her cheek and strokes of her blonde ponytail. And in that scene, he was crying, too.

He was lost in just that contemplation when Marta breezed into the room and looked at him with sudden concern.

"Stoke! Are you okay? What's wrong?"

He started and his face quickly transformed to a happy smile. "Hi, Marta! I'm fine. Sorry, I was just thinking about, well . . . us."

"Uh-oh, you looked miserable. Are you miserable about us?"

Stoke laughed. "No, no! Not at all. I'm very happy about us—right now, anyway. But Marta, what are we going to do? I live in Denver and you live on Lake Peace. It's not exactly commuting distance."

Marta got a crafty look and sat down next to him. "Well, maybe it's time I told you about an idea I've been working on."

"Sounds intriguing. What is it?"

"Well, you know how I'm interested in government and law. I always thought it would just be New Gaian government and law, but these last couple of weeks have made me realize a lot of things."

"Like what?"

"For one thing, how much New Gaia has to learn about government and law. I mean, the way we as a planet dealt with that outside threat from the pirates, it was kind of pathetic, wasn't it? But on the other hand, I really believe in the cultural principles that our founders did, and just looking at Earth tells me we don't want to be anything like this, either."

"Thanks a lot," Stoke said with a smile.

"Sorry. But what I'm saying is, I think New Gaia might be too closed off when it comes to ideas about our society and our government. We were founded almost a century ago with some very specific ideas, and we really haven't reexamined them since. We're great at collaborating with the Hundred Worlds when it comes to science and art, so why not government?"

"Sounds good," said Stoke cautiously. "But are you going to tell me what that has to do with us?"

"I'm getting there. Here's my idea. And keep in mind, this is just an idea. I talked to Mom and Galen already, but Grandmother is the one who would really have to say. But here it is. I think it's going to take someone to take initiative on this. Someone to start some conversations about government with the New Gaian community, and maybe with other worlds as well. Maybe setting up interplanetary conferences, or professional exchange programs, or that kind of thing, where New Gaia could learn about other ways of running governments, and maybe get better at running our own? Couldn't you imagine the role of a New Gaian 'Civic Cooperation Ambassador' or something?"

Stoke was starting to smile. He knew exactly where this was going. "Ah-hah, I get it! So, would this Civic Cooperation Ambassador have to be a very good organizer? Who is good at paying attention to others, but has maybe recently gotten a bit braver about standing up for herself as well? And maybe doesn't mind the idea, any more, of a lot of interplanetary travel?" By this time, Marta was smiling and nodding at each question Stoke asked. "Especially Earth, which is, after all, the most convenient place for holding interplanetary conferences?"

"Yes!" Marta said. "Yes! Wouldn't that be wonderful?"

Stoke had to think about it, but soon he nodded. "You know, I think that might be about as wonderful as anyone could hope for."

Marta smiled a very big smile and pulled him over for a happy kiss.

■ ■ ■

One night after dinner, Kessa towed Jet mysteriously outside. "Follow me!" she whispered mischievously, and then proceeded to lead him to a corner of the house where it was just possible, and only slightly dangerous, to climb the wall and clamber up onto the roof. He just smiled and followed along; Kessa was Kessa and there was no point in trying to talk her out of it. The roof was slanted and covered with a slippery metallic substance that was designed to shed snow in the winter, so footing was tricky until they reached the top and could sit down on the ridge, dangling their legs down one side. Jet sat first and then Kessa positioned herself close on one side and pulled Jet's arm around her waist.

From this vantage point they had a clear view in all directions out over the vast plains and their perfect rows of soybeans. In the distance, a coyote trotted along an irrigation canal, on the hunt. The sun had recently set, and the sky above was a deep, textured dark blue, and a few stars were beginning to appear, promising a whole, wonderful field of them to come.

"So, I guess we saved the world, then," sighed Kessa a little dreamily.

"By which you mean, the six of us plus a whole lot of other people who helped along the way?"

"Mm-hm."

"Seems that way from here," nodded Jet. "It really was a community effort, wasn't it? I mean, it was your mom's science, but she couldn't have done it without you, and Marta, Stoke, Galen, Ettica, Leilani, Narisa and Kai, Agda, . . ."

". . . and you!" Kessa smiled. "It was actually rather beautiful, wasn't it? A demonstration of the power of community."

"Mm-hm," nodded Jet. It was a deep lesson he had learned from this adventure.

"So now what?" Kessa asked, breaking her gaze away from the peaceful view and turning her head to look deeply into his clear brown eyes. But there she saw turmoil.

"I don't know, Kessa, I don't know," murmured Jet, with small shakes of his head from side to side.

"Don't know what?"

"Don't know about us. I mean, how can it work? Look at us. I'm from the city on Earth. You're from the woods of New Gaia. I'm impatient, and introverted, and insensitive, and . . ."

". . . ridiculously brilliant, and curious, and ambitious, and handsome . . ." Kessa inserted.

"And you," Jet continued. "You're free-spirited, and creative, and fierce, and beautiful, and a lot more book-smart than you let on, and you have these sensory superpowers, and, and I just don't have the vocabulary . . ." he trailed off, feeling a description of Kessa as he perceived her was beyond words.

Kessa draped her hands loosely on his shoulders and gazed a long moment more, waiting for his spinning worries to settle down before she said: "And we're in love. And that wins over all the rest."

"Oh, hell," said Jet as his swirling thoughts suddenly resolved into perfect focus. "I know we are. Of all the impractical botherations."

They both laughed, and then they shared a long and loving kiss.

Jet finally pulled away. "So seriously, now what?"

"No fair, I asked you that first."

"Well how should I know?"

"You're the ridiculously brilliant one, remember?"

"True, but you're the creative genius. Create something."

The stars above grew brighter as they bantered on for several minutes, until gradually the banter turned more productive, and then

more deeply thoughtful, and then more exciting, as they plotted out
their plans for a future together.

Acknowledgements

As this book has so much to say about the power of groups of people working together, it seems fitting that I benefited from so much help writing that it often felt like a team effort. First on the list is my wife Mary, who has generously and lovingly supported this entire project in roles ranging from insightful reader and story advisor to sounding board and cheerleader. The DNA chirality angle was my idea originally, but Lisa and Jacob Witten—who unlike me actually know what they're talking about in this field—straightened out my mangled thinking and get most of the credit for the somewhat more plausible (though still very fictional) genetic science in the final story. Writer and producer Matthew Witten was kind enough to provide detailed notes and great advice, and literary agent Jonah Straus gave useful comments and helped me better understand the publishing world. Technical consultation on soybeans came from Ron Meyer of Colorado State University Extension, introduced to me by Jocelyn Hittle. Lawrence Walker, who has a long list of nonfiction books to his credit, gave me detailed and exceptionally helpful feedback. Many other trusted readers have also been generous with their excellent suggestions, perspectives, and advice, almost all of which has found its way into the finished work in one way or another. They include Rachel Cogbill, Douglas McRae, Sarah McRae, Margaret Sullivan, Eric Walker, James Walker, Margery Walker, and Priscilla Walker. Finally, thanks to Claire Branigin for helping me find my way around WordPress, the platform for my website at dougwalkerwrites.com. I am grateful to them all.

—*Doug Walker*
June, 2018

A Note to Readers

I hope you enjoyed *Gaia Twist*. I'm happy to field your questions and comments at **dougwalkerwrites.com**. There you will also find blog posts, written in character by Jet, Stoke, Kessa, and Marta, that provide more details on their worlds and answer some common questions.

As a writer, I want little more than to get my work out there so that readers like you can enjoy it. To that end, I appreciate any help you can provide in spreading the word about *Gaia Twist*. Tell your friends and your book club, share on social media, or post a review on Amazon. Or maybe all of the above! Future readers will be grateful to you, and so will I.

Thank you.

Doug Walker

CPSIA information can be obtained
at www.ICGtesting.com
Printed in the USA
LVHW041206070419
613259LV00002B/251

9 781719 187329